Lost Jade of the Maya

Also by Marjorie Bicknell Johnson:

Bird Watcher: A Novel

Jaguar Princess: The Last Maya Shaman
A Primer for the Fibonacci Numbers
(With V. E. Hoggatt, Jr.)

Lost Jade of the Maya

Marjorie Bicknell Johnson

Marjorie Johnson

INFINITY
PUBLISHING

ISBN 978-0-7414-6767-6

Published April 2016

INFINITY PUBLISHING
1094 New DeHaven Street, Suite 100
West Conshohocken, PA 19428-2713
Toll-free (877) BUY BOOK
Local Phone (610) 941-9999
Fax (610) 941-9959
Info@buybooksontheweb.com
www.buybooksontheweb.com

Acknowledgments

Many persons have helped me to produce *Lost Jade of the Maya*, and I wish to thank each one here. First and foremost, my husband, Frank Johnson, uncomplainingly gave up evenings and weekends while I worked at my computer; he read three complete drafts and helped me to rethink certain chapters. He accompanied me on all of my trips to Mexico and Central America, and his photographs of a Mayan funeral mask and of Maya girls appear on the cover. Chris Johnson and Tom Kirkpatrick refined the pictures, and Linda Judd designed the cover.

Members of my critique groups, Luanne Oleas, Edie Matthews, Carolyn Donnell, and Pat McAllister, heard my work one chapter at a time and read early drafts. They gave me advice and tore into my mistakes without tearing into me. Several friends also read parts of the book; Bertha Lewis corrected my Spanish, and Michael Shipp gave me a reality check. Pat McAllister proofread the final draft.

I am indebted to my Beta readers, ArLyne Diamond, Colin Paul Spears, Chess Desalls, Linda Judd, and Tom Kirkpatrick. After ArLyne Diamond pointed out that I had begun the book in the wrong place, I added a new first chapter. Chess Desalls, in addition to reading for story, made a careful proofreading. Colin Paul Spears not only made insightful comments about content but also sent me a vial of bromoform, a substance just as nasty as described in the *Lost Jade.* Linda Judd gave the manuscript a thorough edit with invaluable suggestions for changes in format and content and designed the cover. Tom Kirkpatrick helped me to improve several chapters.

When asked, these friends gave me the truth. As usual, the mistakes are all mine. I thank you all from my heart.

Also, I wish to express my gratitude to Wilderness Travel for organizing the December 2012 symposium, "World of the Maya: Cycles of Time," and the special tour program with Alfonso Morales, "Uxmal to Palenque."

To celebrate the monumental transition in the Mayan calendar, the symposium focused on Mayan timekeeping, astronomy, and archaeology. We heard from the following experts in the field:

Dr. Anthony Aveni, Professor of Astronomy at Colgate University, pioneer in Mesoamerican archaeoastronomy, and author of *The End of Time: The Maya Mysteries of 2012*;

Dr. Harvey Bricker and Dr. Victoria Bricker, Professors Emeritus of Anthropology at Tulane University, Research Associates at the Florida Museum of Natural History, and co-authors of *Astronomy in the Maya Codices*;

Dr. Susan Milbrath, Curator of Latin American Art and Archaeology at the Florida Museum of Natural History and author of *Star Gods of the Maya: Astronomy in Art, Folklore, and Calendars*;

Dr. Karl Taube, Professor of Anthropology at the University of California at Riverside and author of numerous publications on ancient writing and religions including *Gods and Symbols of Ancient Mexico and the Maya*;

Alfonso Morales, PhD candidate in the Institute of Latin American Studies at the University of Texas at Austin and Principal Investigator of the Cross Group Project, responsible for exciting recent excavations at Palenque.

This Wilderness Travel symposium took place at Uxmal, an authentic Mayan city well away from the more crowded sites of the Yucatán Peninsula, and gave us the opportunity to meet local Maya.

Characters in Lost Jade of the Maya

Pesh: Chanla Pesh, archaeologist and Maya shaman. Her Mayan name: Chanlajun Yaxk'in Pex Yaxuun B'alam. Kedar Herold's wife and Yash's mother.

Chiich: Pesh's dead grandmother.

Yash: Maryam Yaxuun B'alam. Pesh and Kedar's daughter.

Kedar: Kedar Herold, geologist and pilot. Pesh's husband.

Burt: Dr. Burtrand Wallace, chief archaeologist at B'alam Witz. Pesh's father-in-law.

Isolde: Isolde Herold Wallace. Burt's wife; Kedar's mother.

Steve: Burt's assistant at B'alam Witz

Paul and Vanna Anderson: Archaeologists who search for jade in Guatemala and live at Quetzal Centrale.

Zia: cook at Quetzal Centrale.

Alberto: foreman, jade workshop at Quetzal Centrale.

Ignacio: driver and bodyguard at Quetzal Centrale.

Arturo: bodyguard at Quetzal Centrale

Xmenoob Xiu: Shaman, famous within Guatemala.

Xmenoob Chel: Xiu's shaman friend from B'alam Ha.

Pedro: boy who befriends Yash.

Manu: Pedro's father, and **Maria:** Pedro's stepmother.

Cuxil: Pedro's uncle.

Rolana: Yash's friend who lives in Xiu's village.

B'alam: Mayan jaguar god, god of the hunt.

Cimil: Mayan god of the underworld.

Big-Beak Macaw, Five-Owl, Precious-Turtle: Neighbors at B'alam Witz.

The **Maya** are the "corn people," and Mayan is pronounced MY-ahn. Their word for corn is *maiz*, pronounced to rhyme with size. In Mayan, "X" has the "sh" sound; "Xiu" sounds like "shoe." Note that Maya can be used as an adjective, as in Maya king. A glossary appears at the end of the book.

1

Danilo's captors removed his blindfold but left his hands tied behind his back. Nearby, a man with a prominent black mole on his nose and ears too large for his head struck the branch of a tree with a long pole. He teased a snake, as long as the height of a man, poised over the head of a helpless Maya. The snake struck so fast Danilo couldn't see it and bit the victim's neck. The snake had the yellow chin of the most feared snake in Guatemala, *la barba amarilla.*

"*¡No! Muerto! Muerto!*" The Maya batted at the snake and screamed in agony. "I'm a dead man! *¡Muerto!*"

The snake dropped to the ground and slithered away.

Danilo's captors forced him to watch until the victim crumpled to the ground, groaned, and vomited.

"That is what happens to Maya who disobey." The man with the mole pushed Danilo along ahead of him. "And this is what he will look like tomorrow."

A corpse, smelling of death, lay on the ground. One leg was blackened. It looked like melted candle wax and smelled like rotted meat. The flesh on the thigh had liquefied into pus; the calf and foot were black and almost without flesh.

Danilo threw up on his shirt.

"Now you tell *El Cocodrilo*, where is the jade mine?" The man with the mole and the big ears was The Crocodile, one of the cruelest crime lords in Guatemala.

"I don't know, *Señor Cocodrilo*." Danilo shook with fear.

The other man punched Danilo in the solar plexus. Danilo bent over retching but refused to cry out.

"Find that snake, *El Zope*," *El Cocodrilo* said.

The Buzzard and The Crocodile: crazy *banditos* who could do whatever they wanted. Both were a head taller than Danilo and looked like Spaniards, not Maya.

"Please, sir, I really don't know." Danilo hung his head and tried to look small, meek, and harmless. "*Señor* Anderson tells no one where he gets his jade."

"The little *indio* doesn't know," *El Zope* said, flashing his gold teeth. "I have a better job for him in Antigua."

El Cocodrilo hit Danilo hard on the head with the butt of the gun, and *El Zope* beat him with a chain.

Danilo hurt too much to care about anything else.

"A one-way ride to Antigua," said *El Cocodrilo*.

Paul Anderson drove his wife Vanna to their retail jade shop in Antigua, Guatemala because their driver Danilo had disappeared along with the *Taller del Jade Maya* van. What had happened to Danilo? He was so responsible, so loyal.

Paul unlocked the shop and found a sheet of paper under the door. The same as before, printed in Spanish with poor grammar and misspellings, the note advised him to purchase insurance:

"To Whom It May Concern: Leave $10,000 in cash where we tell you. We will protect your business. If you don't give us $10,000, you will die."

Paul and the other business owners on the street had discussed similar messages and decided to ignore them. So far, that had seemed to work, but now, a second note?

"Vanna, look at this," Paul said. "Should we pay?"

"No way. Not one cent," Vanna said. "They're trying to scare us. They want our jade business."

"*Señor* Anderson!" Hai Wong, the Chinese owner of the business two doors down, burst through the door. "Come quickly! They left me a body!"

Paul followed Wong to his dry-goods store, half a block away. The Chinese entrepeneur had posted his "To Whom It May Concern" notice inside his front window. He had written "NO" across it in large red letters.

The body, covered by a towel, lay in front of the door.

"What should I do?" Wong asked. "The police never help. I think I lock up and leave the country, right now."

Paul pulled off the towel to see the facedown body. It wore no shirt. It had a bloody head and bruising across its shoulders. He turned it onto its back—*Danilo!*

"Oh, my God! It's my driver, Danilo!"

"Jade is sacred, and lucky, too." Chanla Pesh held out a cream-colored, lacy-looking four-inch ball and moved closer to the lectern. This was her first quarter as a lecturer in Mayan studies. At nineteen, younger than her students, she had worked with archaeologists at Mayan ruins for years.

"This ball came from China: three concentric spheres carved from one piece of white jade. Jade comes in many colors. There are two types: Chinese jade is nephrite, while Mayan jade is jadeite, a different chemical composition. Jadeite is harder and more difficult to carve. Both cultures revered jade." Pesh set the white ball on the table and turned on the computer.

"Jade was so sacred to the Maya that they threw it into a cenote, that's a kind of deep well, instead of surrendering it to their Spanish conquerors.

"It happened right there." Pesh pointed with a red laser beam to the painted murals of the ruins of Chichén Itzá that lined the classroom walls. "The Sacred Cenote is behind that building.

"Even today jade is sacred to the four million Maya who live in Yucatán." She didn't tell her students that she too believed in the old religion.

"The Maya often put jade into royal tombs." Pesh flashed several PowerPoint slides onto the screen. "This elaborately carved lid came from a stone sarcophagus, a splendid example of Mayan art.

"This jade funeral mask belonged to a Maya king who reigned a thousand years ago." She circled the face with her red pointer. "Note the rich color. The Maya kings preferred green stones, sometimes trimmed with red. Green jade: the most valuable stone in the Mayan empire."

After a pause, Pesh turned off the computer.

"I feel like a talking head, dwarfed by this tall lectern." She moved closer to her students. "Let's talk about other uses of jade.

"While green was reserved for royalty, everyone kept a small piece of jade for luck. In fact, a Maya warrior carried jade to keep him safe.

"The Maya were fierce fighters and clever strategists, but they had no horses, steel, or gunpowder to ward off well-armed Spanish invaders in the 16th century," she continued.

"But perhaps carrying jade was lucky. After the Aztec Empire fell in 1520, the Spaniards needed twenty-five more years to conquer Yucatán. The Aztecs surrendered their gold, but the Maya never told the Spaniards where to find jade."

"You mean—there are lost jade mines?" Robert, seated in the front, rocked forward as though ready to jump up and leave for Yucatán.

"Yes. An unsolved mystery for five hundred years." Pesh paused and referred to her notes. "Last time I showed you Mayan axes and hammers, chisels and spearheads. The Maya had no metal tools. Instead, they used obsidian and low-quality jade.

"Culturally, jade was sacred and more valuable than gold, especially the imperial green shade. The Maya shaman always carried jade in a deerskin satchel with other sacred pebbles. The shaman used jade in rituals to cure illness."

"Mayan witch doctors?" asked Alexander, an impudent young man who hid behind his red beard.

"No. Nothing like that." She wouldn't show her irritation toward him, and she wouldn't disclose that her grandmother had been such a healer.

"The healing shaman was a skilled herbalist." Pesh stood erect, her face devoid of emotion as her grandmother had taught. Alexander had refused to credit the Maya with their astronomical feats, even though she had shown a video of the snake-shaped shadow that slithered down the steps of the temple at Chichén Itzá on the day of the spring equinox.

"Some Mayan herbal cures are used in medicine today," she said. "I told you I grew up at a Mayan ruin. I always carry a jade talisman. This is *B'alam*, Mayan for jaguar. Have a look."

Pesh pushed aside her long black braid and pulled out the necklace she always wore beneath her shirt. A small reclining jaguar, carved from dark green jade and polished to the shine of a mirror, dangled from a cord. Moving about the room, she gave each student a close up view.

Amongst many oohs and aahs and beautifuls, Lupe Garcia, her only female student, asked where she got it.

"I'm a descendant of the Maya king, Yaxuun B'alam." Pesh drew herself up to her full four feet nine inches, thrust her chest out, and made eye contact with the red-bearded heckler. Her shaman's talisman—she wouldn't reveal that. *What would her students think?* "This piece of jade jewelry has been in my family for centuries."

"Where did the Maya get it? Jade, I mean," Lupe said. "From the Chinese?"

"Good question." Pesh liked her; Lupe wanted to become an archaeologist. But Lupe hadn't picked up on the two distinct kinds of jade: the Maya had jadeite, no nephrite. "While there's no record of Mayan trade with China, I read a book claiming the Chinese came to Central America in 1421. I'll give you the reference."

Lupe sat straighter and her face lit up.

"Back to the ancient Maya. They had ships as long as Columbus's galleon. In fact, Columbus wrote about them in his ship's log, but there is no record of the Maya sailing across the Pacific."

"But where did the Maya find jade?" Lupe clung to her question.

"The answer is, we don't know," Pesh said. "In recent years, jade has been reported in only one place in Central America—Guatemala—and only in loose rocks in a river."

"Where in Guatemala?" Lupe asked.

"The person who reported the find refused to give its exact location," she answered. "I'll email you the reference, but not for a while. Maybe you guessed that I am about to produce a new citizen for the great State of Texas." Pesh patted her round stomach, protruding like a basketball from her small frame, and the baby answered with a strong kick.

"Your Mayan name is Fourteen?" Lupe asked.

"Yes, Chanla is short for *Chanlajun Yaxk'in*, Fourteen Sun-Month in the Mayan language Yucatec." Pesh had told them about Mayan names.

"Will you name the baby, using the sacred calendar?"

"Thanks for asking," Pesh said. "We Maya don't name newborns for several months. During that time, the baby is referred to by birth date or terms of endearment, like Sweetie in English."

"I'll stay if there are more questions," Pesh said, glancing at the clock. "This is my last lecture for this year."

Several class members stayed to say that they'd miss her. Lupe said she had enjoyed the lecture on foods of the ancient Maya: no other archaeology professor had ever prepared tortillas in class. Pesh reassured her that she'd return next year.

After the students left, Pesh cleared out her mailbox and plopped into a recliner in the empty and quiet faculty lounge. Lupe's questions were on her mind.

She could find where her jade came from. As a shaman, her special gift was the ability to travel to the past in a vision. After such a dream in which she had visited B'alam Witz in 1562, she made detailed drawings of the buildings existing then. For such a vision-visit, she needed an object, a place, and a year. The ruin B'alam Witz had been easy: she held a bark-book written there in 1562. But to trace the jade talisman, she had only the object.

Pesh closed her eyes. Clutching her jade jaguar, she concentrated on its carving days. No metal tools. Bare fingers. Greasy sand. She felt a slight swirling as though swimming through air.

Smell the warm, cooked fat. Hold the cord with both hands, taut. Dip the cord in fat. Roll it through dark-red garnet grit. Pull it, scratch the jade. Over and over and over.

A faint picture formed. Two Maya men, dressed in loincloths, sat cross-legged working stone. She heard them:

"Spaniards ... jade," interrupted by static, "Never tell."

"Before ... tell," more static, "... crocodiles will fly."

The picture faded and she smelled stale coffee left from the faculty's morning meeting.

Pesh looked at the clock: gone fifteen minutes, but time had no meaning in a vision. No focus, but what had she expected, with no date, no place?

She could add a place, the caves beneath B'alam Witz, but she never wanted to go into a cave again, not even in a vision. Not after almost dying in one.

2

Chanla Pesh and her baby swung in a hammock where they had a good view of the Usumacinto River, the southeastern boundary between Yucatán and Guatemala. Steamy jungle air carried the scent of flowers and moist green plants and the squawking of scarlet macaws. The birds chased one another from tree to tree and crowded together on the small clay lick on the riverbank. In a frenzy to eat the clay, the birds flew about, painting the sky with flashes of red, yellow, green, and blue. She never tired of their company.

Adult macaws, symbols of power to her Maya ancestors, had wingspans of two meters—more than six feet, Kedar would say. Their powerful beaks could crack nuts and tear open unripe fruit, but they had trouble digesting it and suffered from diarrhea. The birds ate white clay this time of year, the very same type of clay her shaman grandmother fed her after she ate unripe fruit for the same digestive problem.

Pesh always felt as if she had come home when she made her annual visit here to the ruins of B'alam Witz, now in its third season of exploration. Three years ago, her husband Kedar had located this ruin from the air by tracing satellite images of ancient Mayan roads. Last year, she had married him here. Each season, she translated glyphs, drew enhanced images of ruined buildings, and catalogued finds with a team of archaeologists.

This year, she brought along her three-month-old daughter, too young for her first naming by Mayan custom. Her little *k'iin chaanpal*, sun-baby, was born in March on the day of the vernal equinox, a propitious date. The baby, half Maya, had her same skin tone, black hair, and almond eyes. She touched the baby's cheek and wiped away drops of breastmilk.

Ready to go back to work, she laid the sleeping infant on a mat in her tent. Pesh liked to sit by the fire circle, only a few steps away from the tent, and copy glyphs from this year's pottery finds into her notebook for later transcription. Tomorrow she would take the baby to work by a *stele*, a fallen monument stone. She stepped out into bright sunlight.

In the clearing, two Maya men stood by Dr. Burtrand Wallace, head archaeologist at this dig and also her father-in-law. In the sun too long again—his pale skin had pinkened. His students affectionately called him Dr. Burt; she had followed him around Mayan ruins for eleven years. Maya living in remote areas spoke only Mayan or broken Spanish, and he relied upon her to translate.

The two stonefaced Maya turned toward her. Their expressionless faces glistening with perspiration, they stood next to Dr. Burt, the tops of their heads only reaching his shoulders. Each man wore faded Levis and T-shirt with a black braid that touched his belt in the back—a Maya warrior never cut his hair.

She knew the men. Big-Beak Macaw wore the orange lifevest she had given him two years ago. With his big nose, his name was unforgettable. The other Maya, Five-Owl, claimed to be a prince. By custom, they wouldn't speak until she greeted them.

"*Hola,*" she said. "What brings you here?"

"Come with us for the feast for the day the earth makes no shadow," he said in Mayan.

"Tomorrow there will be no shadows at noon," she told Burt. The sun would cross directly overhead at this latitude, bathing the earth in white light. Astronomers called the phenomenon *zenial passage*. Her Maya ancestors calculated those dates and used them as times of festival, but she didn't know the Mayan words for it.

Last year, after her wedding celebration, Five-Owl and Big-Beak had promised to invite her to a feast. They had witnessed her ceremonial ascension to the throne and sworn allegiance to her and to B'alam Witz.

Pesh moved closer to Burt. "They invite us to a feast. They accept you as an honorary Maya, an opportunity to observe authentic Mayan culture. Want to go?"

"Absolutely!"

"Come," Five-Owl said in Mayan. "We have a temple like yours. You must bless it."

"He wants to show us another ruin," Pesh paraphrased for Dr. Burt. She moved between Mayan, Spanish, and English so often that she sometimes forgot which language she was speaking. Bless their temple: she had led them in prayer to Hun Hunahpu when they first met, two years ago.

"*Absolutamente*. I must see your temple," Dr. Burt said to Big-Beak in Spanish. "Pesh, go tell Steve we're crossing the river. I'll listen for the baby while you're gone."

Pesh took the narrow trail to the ancient plaza where Steve, the most experienced of Dr. Burt's students, had unearthed ceremonial bowls, vases, and urns—after she told him where to dig. In a vision, she had watched Mayan priests puncture each pot with a "kill hole" to release its inner spirit.

This year's archaeological dig at B'alam Witz pointed directly to the center of one face of the temple, the only structure still standing. The temple backed against a hillside hiding limestone caves and an underground river.

She liked to think of this as her temple, named for her ancestor, King Yaxuun B'alam. B'alam's throne, a stone bench with twin jaguars forming its armrests, rested on a platform eighty-nine steps above the jungle floor, the steps so narrow that Kedar climbed by placing his feet sideways.

Behind the cat-seat bench loomed a huge jaguar mouth, an opening with stone teeth taller than a man and a throat blocked by rubble where the building fused with the hill. In the old days, the king and his priests would emerge from that great mouth in a magnificent ceremony. When she sat on that throne, she looked out over the jungle canopy and imagined the cheering crowd below. This was her city, her temple, her throne.

In front of the temple, Steve, skinny and almost as tall as Dr. Burt, held a shovel and stood where citizens of B'alam Witz would have assembled to witness ceremonial functions.

"*Hola*," Pesh called out. "Find any relics today?"

"Yo, Pesh," Steve said. The three other workers looked up, taking a break from sifting gritty earth over wooden boxes. "A painted jug, broken into fewer pieces than usual."

"I'm eager to see it." Pesh would reassemble the jug in her university lab at Austin. The ceramics were delicious puzzles, forensic evidence to solve archaeological mysteries.

"Okay, tonight." Steve leaned on his shovel and wiped his forehead with his blue bandana.

"Tonight—that's what I came to tell you about." Pesh stepped into the shade. "Dr. Burt and I are crossing the river. There's a festival over there, and he said you're in charge."

"At last, a position of power." Steve laughed. "Tell him not to worry."

When Pesh returned to the fire circle, the two Maya stood drinking sodas, and Dr. Burt sent her to collect her gear. In the tent, she strapped the sleeping baby onto the Navajo-like cradleboard and packed a snack and a change of clothes for the little one. She left the digital camera because indigenous Maya believed the camera stole their souls.

By custom, she needed a gift. *What to take?* At the bottom of her shoulder pack, she had a replica of a Mayan jade turtle, carried here to show Dr. Burt her handiwork. She had modeled the turtle from resin and weighted it with black sand at University of Texas for a museum exhibit. The turtle would be a good gift for Five-Owl, who wanted her, as a Maya shaman, to bless his temple.

"I'm ready," Pesh called out. She pulled her long black braid to the front, donned the cradleboard, and suspended her pack over one shoulder. Then she remembered that Burt had never been deep within Mayan territory. "Please leave your camera here. You can't take pictures at a Mayan religious ceremony."

"Okay," Dr. Burt answered. "You know the customs."

She followed the men, picking her way down the slippery clay slope to the canoes. The macaws circled overhead. They ignored the men but scolded her for disturbing their clay-eating frenzy. One red and blue bird swooped down and combed its powerful claws through her braid—an omen. The hair raised on the nape of her neck and on her arms.

While Five-Owl claimed they had a temple, satellites had shown no Mayan white roads and no evidence of buildings. Chiich always warned her, *never go to Guatemala*, but she had been over there once before and knew the men. Intrigued by the opportunity to attend the festival, she ignored both her grandmother's words and the macaw's warning.

Big-Beak helped her with the cradleboard and seated her behind him in his canoe, and Dr. Burt rode behind Five-Owl in the other canoe. The two Maya dipped their oars in rhythm and paddled across the current on a diagonal so smoothly that she felt only a gentle rocking.

What was she getting herself into, taking her baby in a canoe? If the boat overturned, the cradleboard would sink immediately. She had purchased it online so she could put the baby in a safe place while she worked, not to carry the baby on her back. She shrugged; she knew both Maya, both skilled canoeists.

Pesh fingered her shaman's talisman; its smoothness comforted her, as did the steady progress of the canoe. She could not shirk her responsibility. To bless the temple and to ask the favor of the gods were duties of a Maya shaman.

3

Despite the macaw's omen, when the canoes reached shore, Guatemala seemed no different from Yucatán. The same heavy air carried the sound of monkeys chattering, the cries of orioles flitting about hanging nests, and the scents of vanilla orchids mingled with the cinnamon and nutmeg of an allspice tree.

Pesh and her baby followed Dr. Burt and Big-Beak single file with Five-Owl taking up the rear on a path semi-shaded by dense plant growth. They stopped in front of a tall rubble pile so overgrown by vines that at first Pesh didn't recognize it as a ruin. Its steps and walls had been split by strangler figs, its roof collapsed onto eroded rock. With that mask of vegetation, no one could see it from the air.

"Absolutely amazing," Dr. Burt said.

Pesh didn't agree with him. The ancient structure had few remaining limestone building blocks. She scraped the ground with her boot: hard-packed clay. Her geologist husband Kedar had expected clay deposits on this side of the river. She guessed the Maya had used the heavy soil to form bricks, long-since eroded away.

Glad to rest, she took off the cradleboard and rolled her shoulders. She touched her little one's hair, and the baby smiled in her sleep.

"Twin brothers once ruled here. Two temples, one on each side of the river." Big-Beak pointed to the fallen stones. "This is *B'alam Witz,* Jaguar Mountain. Across the river, that is the city *B'alam Ha,* Jaguar-Hidden-Water."

"You are mistaken," Pesh said. "Our ruin is called B'alam Witz." That name had appeared in the bark-book she had unearthed at the temple. He should remember the name from last summer. Five-Owl claimed descent from a king named B'alam—not her ancestor. She looked again at the broken stones and debris, the crumbled rock and decayed steps. Not as grand as her temple.

"The feast is tonight to join both sides of the river," Five-Owl said in Mayan. "*Ko'ox.* Come on. Hurry up."

Hungry, the baby woke, cried, and waved her hands. Pesh pushed the infant's hair back and kissed her forehead, inhaling her good smell. Her breasts were swollen with milk—her little *chaanpal* needed to nurse.

"I need to feed my baby."

"We are close to the village," Big-Beak said.

She picked up the cradleboard, heavier each time she put it over her shoulders. How did Navajo mothers hike carrying one of these?

"*Ko'ox.* Hurry." Five-Owl grasped her arm so tightly that his fingers made white marks. "We have to get ready."

"Let go of me!" Pesh slapped Five-Owl's hand.

He released her arm and glowered.

"I won't bless anything unless Five-Owl shows me some respect." Pesh rubbed her arm and stood stiff, face devoid of emotion, like the best of Maya royalty.

"Lady Queen B'alam," Five-Owl said, looking down.

Pesh matched his glower but fell in step with the men, who led them into a village plaza bordered by carved stones and surrounded by bamboo houses.

"Women go this way." Big-Beak pointed to the largest of four thatch buildings.

"Queen Mother Precious-Turtle," Five-Owl called out at the doorway. "You have a guest."

Inside the cool structure, a temporary building for the festival, Five-Owl's mother welcomed her. Pesh sat down to nurse her baby. Two other women were feeding their babies, one an infant, the other a toddler. The toddler's mother said he had three summers. Several women admired the baby-carrier and everyone wanted to touch it. They all looked forward to the evening's festivities, a welcome break from life as subsistence farmers.

Precious-Turtle said she spoke little Spanish, but her son had taken the Spanish name Abejundio the Beekeeper and he tended three hives. In the old days, trading honey had made their people rich. Then she unfolded a long skirt and a *huipil*, a traditional Mayan garment worn over the shoulders like a long blouse. This one bore an embroidered *quetzal* on its front.

The quetzal, sacred to the Maya, had long green tail plumes twice the height of the bird itself. The exquisite needlework captured the texture of feathers with brilliant blue-green thread.

"A wedding dress for a princess to marry my son." She gestured for Pesh to put it on.

"I cannot marry Five-Owl." Pesh emphasized her words by shaking her head. She forced herself to keep calm, her face without expression. "I already have a husband. Five-Owl should know—he was there."

"But you must join the royal family at the festival."

"No! I won't marry him." Pesh raised her voice.

"Not a ceremony to marry a man," Precious-Turtle said. "A ritual to bind both sides of the river in friendship."

A wedding dress—for a friendship ceremony? Pesh hadn't heard of such a ceremony, but she agreed to it. She hadn't worn a *huipil* since she had fourteen summers, and then only to church. She laid her Bermuda shorts and T-shirt on a mat and stroked the talisman she always wore next to her skin. She tied on the long skirt and pulled the *huipil* over her head, transformed into a Maya princess of the Classic Period, a thousand years ago.

Later, in the plaza, Pesh leaned the cradleboard against a tree near the royal table, where the baby could see her. Dr. Burt sat to the left of Five-Owl; she took the place between Five-Owl and Precious-Turtle with Big-Beak at the end. The royal party sat on a low bench behind a wooden-plank table. Commoners of all ages sat on the ground.

"You look great in that dress," Dr. Burt said. "I wish I had a camera to get a picture."

"Precious-Turtle embroidered it for this ceremony. It's for a wedding, but she says this is a sister-city ritual," Pesh said, a question in her voice.

Pesh wore the quetzal *huipil* over a full-length skirt, and Five-Owl wore white linen trousers and a white shirt trimmed with floral eyelet edgings. They stood and shared a double-necked wedding vase, sipping a potent alcoholic drink that burned her mouth and throat—*balche*, the sacred combination of tree bark, cinnamon, and fermented honey. She managed not to cough or choke on her first swallow and drank no more, pretending to sip.

So that's it—only the drinking of *balche* from a wedding vase? She had no speaking part, made no promises. She handed Five-Owl the turtle, and he gave her a beaded abalone-shell comb for her hair, a ritual exchange of gifts. They nodded to the throng and resumed their seats.

A white-robed shaman, solemn and stately, swung burning incense that smoked from a ceramic saucer as he entered center stage. He wore an immense headdress made of red macaw feathers and topped by two long green tail feathers from a quetzal. His jaguar mask could have been worn in 800 AD, twelve centuries—three *bak'tuns*—ago. Facing the crowd, he raised his hands above his head and then turned to the royal party and gestured toward a second white-robed Maya who carried a squawking turkey, a magnificent ocellated turkey with iridescent feathers and blue wattles. Chanting in Mayan, the shaman placed sacred pebbles at the corners of the table in front of them.

The changing colors of the bird's wing feathers in the firelight reminded Pesh of how her jade jaguar caught the sunlight along its sleek and polished body. She touched it through the linen cloth of the *huipil*. If Five-Owl's village had a shaman, why did he need her?

The helper held the *cutz*, the sacrificial turkey, on the ground below the table. The shaman, still chanting, raised an obsidian knife, cut the bird's neck, and held it by its feet, letting its blood flow into a ceramic vessel in front of the wedding party's table. The headless turkey struggled and its blood splattered on the shaman's white robe, and his helper carried the bird away. The shaman blessed the blood and offered it to the gods, holding the bowl above his head. He invoked *Chaac* the Rain God for the prosperity of B'alam Witz and B'alam Ha.

Pesh hoped he would carry the blood away, not sprinkle it like rain. In ancient times, the Maya held blood sacrifices for ceremonies of significance. Because she had grown up alone with her grandmother, Mayan festivals were new to her. She had never witnessed such a ceremony. She glanced at Dr. Burt, who appeared lost in thought, or maybe shocked into silence.

Still fascinated but uncomfortable, Pesh stretched one leg, then the other, and shifted her weight on the cold and unforgiving stone bench. The baby cried, softly at first, then more insistently.

Dr. Burt rose but Precious-Turtle loosened the straps on the cradleboard and picked up the baby before Pesh could say no. The baby cried on.

"She needs to nurse. And not with another woman."

"Okay," Precious-Turtle said, a universal word. "I'll watch her for a few minutes." She hugged the baby, soothed her, and walked to the center of the plaza where women tended cooking fires. She waved to Pesh, spooned some corn meal gruel into a cup, and helped the baby to sip the warm mixture. The baby puckered her mouth, then smiled.

Pesh kept her eyes on both of them. Her grandmother always said, "It takes a village to raise a child." *Maiz* gruel was a traditional food. Babies liked it, and she had, too.

The shaman placed the bowl of blood on the ground in front of the royal table and spoke final words of congratulations. With his palm toward his heart, he made the sign of the Mayan cross, moving his hand east to west like Great Father Sun, up to down like heaven to earth.

The shaman nodded and left the plaza as though nothing had changed here in a thousand years. His helper removed the bowl and paraded around with it on his way out of the plaza while a third Maya blew raucous blasts from a conch shell trumpet.

"Was this a wedding? Or something else?" Burt asked. "One wouldn't expect a blood sacrifice at a wedding."

"I didn't catch it all, but the shaman asked *Chaac* the Rain God to grant prosperity." Pesh sprang to her feet. "I must feed my baby. Where is she?"

Precious-Turtle returned, carrying the baby on one hip, and accompanied Pesh to the women's building where she could remove her over-the-head garments to nurse. Half an hour later, the three of them rejoined the revelers. The turkey, and its blood, had been removed.

Suddenly famished, Pesh relished the feast: a small roasted pig, tamales, squashes, spicy beans, and tortillas. Women cooked around four fire circles and served each course to the royal table first. She drank from a ceramic cup without handles and used a flat bowl carved from wood and decorated with a three-beehive design. They all ate with their fingers, wrapping food with torn bits of tortilla.

After eating their fill, the men drank and danced to the rhythm of turtle shell drums, rattling gourds, and ceramic flutes. The barefoot dancers wore khaki shorts—a curious mixture of old and new. Faces and bare chests, arms and legs, all bore elaborate tattoos of indigo blue from the leaves of the *añil* plant. The dance celebrated the sun crossing the heavens and told stories of warriors brave in battle. With more *balche* and increased tempo, the dancers moved with wild enthusiasm but without apparent pattern, as though they had lost their senses.

Pesh didn't drink her *balche* even though it tasted much milder than the beverage in the ritual vase. Instead, she poured it little by little into Five-Owl's ceramic cup whenever he looked away, in case the wedding had been more than symbolic. Drunk, the dancers dropped out, one by one. When Big-Beak passed out on the ground and Five-Owl looked ready to sleep, she picked up the baby.

"Looks like the party's over," she said to Dr. Burt.

"The men sleep over there," he said, pointing. "Are you okay?"

"I'm fine. See you in the morning."

Pesh returned to the women's building to rest on a mat, her baby lying beside her. She couldn't sleep. Five-Owl had deceived her: he already had a shaman, and the joining in friendship was a marriage ceremony. Was it only a ritual, or would Five-Owl come for her in the night?

What a fool she had been to come here. But she had to come. Big-Beak and Five-Owl had sworn allegiance to her at B'alam Witz last summer—they were adopted into her tribe. Grandma Chiich taught her that, as a Maya shaman, if she refused requests for help from her tribe, the gods would punish her, a belief instilled in Pesh's very nature.

Someone, silhouetted in the moonlight, stood in the open doorway. *Five-Owl?* Her heart hammered and blood pulsed in her temples. She pretended to sleep.

"Where's my *wife?*" Unsteady, Five-Owl slumped against the doorframe. "I want my wife."

He staggered inside and fell across Pesh's legs.

"Get off me!" Pesh made a fighting fist and delivered a hard punch. Her knuckles hit his face, a satisfying loud crunch. Her first time hitting a person—she had practiced on Kedar's punching bag.

Howling, Five-Owl raised himself and put one hand to his face.

She pushed his shoulder away and rolled him from her mat onto the floor, on the side away from the baby, who cried, then screamed. Her hand throbbed, but her successful middle-knuckle punch gave her a sense of power. She comforted her baby and Five-Owl rose from the floor.

"Hurt this baby, you die! Cimil sends the snake!" Pesh invoked the God of the Underworld and meant every word, words that pierced his alcoholic stupor.

He stood, rubbing his face.

"Get out of here." Precious-Turtle pummeled him with a broom. "You're drunk."

Five-Owl groaned. He spit blood onto the ground, lurched to the door, and disappeared into the night.

"Try that again," Pesh called after him, "I'll knock your nose off!"

Several women awakened and tittered. Someone whispered, "He's afraid to come back."

Pesh massaged her knuckles—sticky, the metallic smell of blood, like the sacrificial turkey. She cleaned them with a baby-wipe and moved her sleeping mat closer to Precious-Turtle. Her baby made soft sucking sounds.

She didn't want to name the baby *Waxak Chuwen*.

Chiich had named Pesh *Chanlajun Yaxkin*, Fourteen Sun-God-Month from the Sacred Calendar, but called her *Pex*, Little One. English speakers grappled with the idea of pronouncing "x" as "sh" and called her *Pecks*, so offensive to her ear that she changed the spelling to Pesh.

She refused to call her tiny *k'iin chaanpal* "Eight Month-of-the-Monkey," *Waxak Chuwen*. By tradition, the firstborn daughter of a shaman always became a shaman, particularly one born on an auspicious date. But this child, a citizen of the United States, belonged to the modern world where she would have many opportunities.

Sleep eluded Pesh. Five-Owl had tricked her—he wanted only to bed her. She had shamed him in front of the women. What if he refused to row her across the river?

They both were prisoners of Five-Owl.

4

Kedar Herold gripped the yoke with white knuckles and turned the aircraft toward his only landmark. The top of the temple at B'alam Witz glowed eerily in the light of the half moon. The jungle below, a green carpet by day, was a black velvet cloak trimmed with a silver ribbon under a brilliant field of stars. That silver ribbon, the Usumacinto River, separated Mexico from Guatemala. To land the plane safely, he had to see its surface. He saw only blackness.

He circled the Cessna seaplane over the ruin. Desperate to land, he had to rescue Pesh and the baby—his wife and his little Princess. Steve's call earlier from the camp's satellite phone: "Pesh went across the river with two Mayan men. They didn't come back." Pesh, missing—a knee jerk reaction—flying off after sunset with tomorrow's supply order. It was illegal to fly after dark in Mexico, as well as dangerous. Unable to see the water's surface: why hadn't he thought this through?

Calm down. Think. He had landed here a hundred times—but never at night. Recapture the feeling of landing on the river, that seat-of-the-pants feeling when everything went right. But he could see less than when he flew in a thick fog, and he had no instruments for guidance except his GPS. He lined up the aircraft with the river and turned on the landing lights.

"Come on, Cessie. We've done this before." Kedar reduced power and descended gently. He didn't want to make Pesh a widow.

At the last moment, the moon reflected on the surface and his gut feeling seemed right. When the seaplane settled smoothly on the calm waters at the bend in the river, he realized he had been holding his breath. He turned the plane diagonal to the current, the challenging moment when the aircraft changed from a free creature of the air to an unwieldy boat.

A pontoon tapped the bank and he shut down the engine. Slipping a flashlight into his pocket, he stepped out onto a pontoon and dropped into waist-deep water to guide the plane to its hitching post. He held the flashlight between his teeth to free his hands, but the wet rope slipped away twice. *Damn!*

The aircraft secured, he splashed to shore, stomped water off his amphibious sandals, and hurried toward the camp. Only an hour after the call—"Pesh has not returned"—he had taken off from Mérida. His wife still puzzled him. She believed she was a shaman and a princess, and she must have felt duty-bound to go across the river with those two Maya. Why at night?

"I made it," Kedar called out. "Let's go find Pesh."

"Wait a minute!" Steve, one of Dr. Burt's helpers, waved a coffee cup. "What are you doing here?"

"You said Pesh went off with two strangers. I was going crazy, worrying about her."

"I only called you because they didn't return." Light from the campfire flickered across Steve's bearded face.

"They? You mean—Dr. Burt went with her? You—" Kedar pointed an index finger. "You turkey! Your message sounded like Pesh was in danger."

"Hey Dude, you said to let you know if she left camp. I didn't know you'd fly at night."

"Well, I'm going after her." Kedar paced around the fire circle. "I can taxi the airplane across the river."

"No! Wait! The jungle's too dark. You'll get lost!"

"I won't get lost." Aided by moonlight, he could follow the trail from where the Maya beached their canoes.

"You're going to be a tasty snack for a hungry jaguar."

"Jaguars?" Kedar paused. His father came from Iraq: he didn't speak Mayan or know the local customs.

"Remember the name of this place? B'alam Witz means Jaguar Hill," Steve said. "Let's go in the morning."

Kedar threw his pack down. Gritting his teeth, he admitted, "I guess you're right."

"I'll help you unload tomorrow," Steve said. "Want some java?"

Settling into a camp chair, Kedar accepted the cup of coffee Steve offered: full of grounds, bitter, and from the bottom of the pot because the eggshell rattled around when Steve poured it. He couldn't keep his feet still, didn't need coffee in the middle of the night. But he'd be counting the hours until dawn anyway.

"Why does she keep wandering off?" Kedar spit a mouthful of grounds back into his cup.

"She went to see a temple or some crazy thing," Steve said, his face so dimly lit by the dying fire that Kedar couldn't read his expression. "She knew the men."

"Did one of them wear an orange life vest?"

"Yes. He had a beak-like nose." Steve drew a nose in the air in front of his face.

"Oh, Proboscis-Man," Kedar said. "Pesh gave him that vest for a canoe ride."

"One of her adventures alone?" Steve asked.

"Not exactly." He didn't tell about ditching the plane in the river—not his grandest moment. "Thinks he saved Pesh's life. What a liar!"

"He can't be trusted?"

"That other one, always with Proboscis-Man, he's worse," Kedar said, sloshing the coffee remaining in his cup.

"Pesh seems to think they're okay," Steve said. "Calls them our Maya neighbors."

"Why'd she take the baby in a canoe?" Kedar shook his head. But Burt went with her.

"Dude, she never leaves that baby for a minute. She keeps her nearby and sings lullabies while she works."

"But why does she keep going off alone?"

"Hey, Dr. Burt's with her this time," Steve said. "We'll find them in the morning."

"I guess I'm remembering two years ago when she spent the night in the cave system. An accident, she said. She came out through a different opening—lost in the jungle."

"Aha, so that's why she won't go into the cave," Steve said. "We're sending in spelunkers next year. She said she'd study their pictures and catalog the finds."

"Pesh loves to come here." Kedar balanced his empty cup on the fire circle boundary.

"She's fascinated with that temple." Steve said. "Drew it from her imagination with enough detail to use it as a blueprint."

"She'd like to restore it," Kedar said, relaxing in the camp chair. "But we'd rip up half the forest bringing in heavy equipment. Makes me wonder how the ancients built it. Those building stones weigh tons."

"But smaller than those used in Egyptian pyramids."

"Yes, but the Maya stacked their pyramids steeper and put platforms at the top."

"I bet Pesh could find a way to build either one," Steve said. "She's amazing."

"I agree with you there." Kedar rose from his folding chair and stretched.

"I've watched her work," Steve said. "Last year she studied the glyphs on the faces of the temple steps. This year she stays on the ground and draws fallen monument stones, the *steles*. Cleans off the moss, sweeps the stone with a soft brush, then draws every glyph."

"She takes them home and writes down what they mean while I watch TV," Kedar said.

"Better get some shuteye." Steve yawned. "We want to look for her at first light."

"All this talking, I've calmed down," Kedar said. "It's just that those two men make me uneasy."

5

With the rising of Great Father Sun, Pesh's long night in Guatemala ended. She awoke snuggled against Precious-Turtle, who had scolded Five-Owl last night and sent him away. *That liar!* He'd have bruises and a hangover.

While Precious-Turtle started the cooking fire, Pesh changed the baby and nursed her. Then she smoothed the quetzal *huipil* and laid it on the older woman's mat. Outside, Pesh took a cup of bitter hot chocolate and gave a sip to the baby, who licked her lips and frowned.

"Good morning," Burt said, approaching Pesh and the baby. "No sugar? This is a poor substitute for coffee."

"The baby doesn't like it either," Pesh said. "She has a full tummy. Could you please watch her for a while?"

"Come here, tiny one." Burt gathered the baby into his arms and kissed her forehead.

Pesh spooned out a cup of maize gruel from Precious-Turtle's kettle. She had taken only her first sip when Big-Beak Macaw rushed over and prattled on: Five-Owl needed help; his wife must bargain for him.

Five-Owl stood behind Big-Beak, his face bruised, one eye closed and blackened, otherwise his usual expressionless and obnoxious self.

"I'm not his wife. Why should I do anything for him after last night?" Pesh asked in Mayan. But the women always did the bargaining. Taking another taste of gruel, she ignored Five-Owl.

That peccary skunk-pig! She set the cup down next to her feet, ready to settle this.

"He was drunk," Big-Beak said.

"Speak for yourself." Pesh put her hands on her hips and faced Five-Owl.

Five-Owl hung his head. She stared at him long enough to make a normal person squirm.

"Someone wants to buy jade from the ancestors," Big-Beak said.

"Jade is sacred." Pesh transferred her stare to Big-Beak. "What are you selling?"

He held out the turtle figurine, her college classroom project, given to Five-Owl last night.

"Five-Owl doesn't treasure my gift?" Pesh made her face expressionless, but she could hardly contain her glee. The wedding gifts were pledges between the bride and the groom. Returning them meant a divorce, or at least an annulment.

"He needs money," Big-Beak said, but Five-Owl didn't look at her.

"You sell my gift." Pesh moved closer to Five-Owl, close enough that he stepped back. "Here's my abalone comb."

Five-Owl slapped the comb out of her hand.

She could out stare him any time. When he looked away, she asked, "Why doesn't the Royal Mother bargain?"

"Her Spanish isn't good," Big-Beak said.

"But certainly better than Five-Owl's manners."

As if she heard her name, Precious-Turtle joined them, carrying the quetzal *huipil.* She extended her arms to Pesh, offering an embroidered gift that took weeks to complete.

"*Dios bo 'otik utsil,* " Pesh thanked her. It was rude to refuse a gift. How kind—she'd be a good mother-in-law for someone. "May the gods repay your goodness. Why don't you bargain?"

"I can't bargain. Five-Owl scolds me."

"Then we'll do it together," Pesh said. Five-Owl had to learn respect for his mother, respect she could gain by successful bargaining. "I'll tell you what to say."

Precious-Turtle looked worried.

"Maybe you need to hit him with the broom again," Pesh whispered. She glanced down at her light-colored Bermuda shorts and jungle boots—not what any Maya would wear. She pulled the traditional garments over her clothing to play the part of the leader's wife for Precious-Turtle's sake. Taking the older woman's arm, she said, "*Ko'ox*. Come with me."

"Why are you dressed like that?" Dr. Burt, holding the baby, looked them up and down and frowned. "Aren't we going home?"

"I must look the part," Pesh explained. "Traditionally, women bargain. Especially the leader's wife."

"But you didn't marry him?" He looked puzzled.

"I'm doing it for Precious-Turtle," Pesh said. "Listen and see how we do it."

Pesh stood next to Big-Beak. He introduced her as Royal Princess Lady Five-Owl to Bartolo Cruz, a young man of slender build with no facial hair who hid beneath a wide-brimmed hat and aviator sunglasses. Cruz must have come in by way of the river—sent by a black marketer who dealt in looted Mayan artifacts, no doubt.

"And this is the Royal Mother, Precious-Turtle," Pesh said in Spanish. She held out the resin-and-sand turtle as though it were a precious jewel. The young man ran a finger across its exquisite carving. Then she whispered to Precious-Turtle, "We ask for $800. He might pay $500."

Precious-Turtle nodded and repeated $800 in Spanish.

He answered immediately, half as much.

"*Muy bonito*," Pesh said. "*Muy precioso*." She held up seven fingers and whispered, "700."

"*Setecientos*," Precious-Turtle parroted.

Cruz shifted his attention from Pesh to Precious-Turtle, then turned and looked at the sky.

The women waited. No one said a word.

"*Quinientos*. Five hundred," he said.

"No." Precious-Turtle said without prompting, "*Seis, seis cientos.*"

Cruz looked at the women, then at Big-Beak. He held out $600. Precious-Turtle grabbed the money and counted it.

"*Bueno.*" Pesh handed Cruz the turtle figurine, holding her hand over it for a few extra seconds and adding the expected curse, "*K'aas wayak' dios bo'otik.*"

"*¿Qué?* What did she say?" Cruz asked.

"*Gracias y adios,*" Big-Beak said. "Thanks. Goodbye"

"*Hach beyo!* Good job." Pesh squeezed Precious-Turtle's hand. "Come visit me across the river. I'll teach you Spanish."

Pesh congratulated herself. Precious-Turtle had $600 and the prestige that went with getting more money than usual in the bargaining game. She'd fooled Cruz and divorced Five-Owl. This was a good day.

"Cross river now," Pesh said, wearing her wooden Mayan facial expression. Five-Owl would have trouble refusing—the entire village had witnessed the sale.

Five-Owl scowled, but Big-Beak nodded.

"*Ko'ox.* Let's go, now." Pesh wanted to leave before he changed his mind.

Burt, who had packed the baby into her cradleboard, asked, "What did you really say to the young man?"

"The gods pay nightmares to he who owns the turtle. A Mayan curse for someone who steals our treasures." Her words had been much more colorful.

"My Lord!"

"My shoulders are sore from yesterday. Can you please carry the baby?"

"Sure." Burt hefted the baby, and they followed the men as far as the crumbled temple, where Five-Owl and Big-Beak stopped.

"The temple blessing," Five-Owl growled in Mayan. "You forgot."

"No. That temple is old and wants only to rest." She glared at him, determined not to do anything he wanted.

"Let's go," Dr. Burt said to Five-Owl.

"*Ko'ox.* How much longer to the river?" she asked.

Five-Owl said either "you talk too much" or "be quiet" or maybe "shut up." Did he ration his words, ten per day? *That lout, that barbarian!* She was glad last night had been only a ritual. Had she really married him, she wouldn't have the pleasure of defying him: in the world of the Maya, a woman always deferred to her husband. She fingered her jaguar talisman through the double layer of *huipil* and T-shirt and followed the men.

Five-Owl stopped so suddenly that she bumped him.

"Who's coming?" Big-Beak asked.

"Pesh! I was so worried." Kedar, with Steve behind him, appeared past a turn in the path. He ran toward her, prepared to wrap his arms around her.

She hung back and stood like a post in a cornfield. On this side of the river, she had married Five-Owl in a ritual, and no one would hug in public.

When Kedar's expression changed from joy to pain, Pesh looked down—she still wore the *huipil* and long skirt. Her face and neck, impossibly hot, tingled, and her stomach tightened. Had she the backbone of a bean slug? She would defy Five-Owl.

"*Mi esposo. Iicham.* My husband." Against Mayan tradition, Pesh hugged Kedar and kissed his cheek—with everyone witnessing. "My dear husband."

Still wrapped in Kedar's arms, she turned and smiled. "*Adiós.* Goodbye."

Surprise flickered across Five-Owl's face, only a slight change in his wooden expression.

Big-Beak watched, waiting to see what would happen.

"Good Lord!" Dr. Burt rested the heavy cradleboard against his leg.

Steve, who had witnessed the whole show, merely shook his head.

"Let's go," Kedar said. "We'll all fit in the Cessna. I can taxi back."

Pesh pulled off the *huipil* and the long skirt, worn over her *norteamericano* clothing, and stored them in her shoulder pack. One day next semester, she would wear them to class. Dressed again in her usual shorts and T-shirt, she took Kedar's hand to walk to the river and his waiting airplane.

Guatemala and the old Mayan ways were not her life. Her *k'iin chaanpal* had been born at the spring equinox, a propitious date. Grandma Chiich would have named the baby by the sacred calendar.

Pesh would break from that tradition—break from all of it. She didn't look back.

6

Savoring the moment, Chanla Pesh drew in a deep breath and smelled the sweet air—magnolia blossoms, freshly mowed lawn, wisteria—at Austin's Zilker Neighborhood Park, only two blocks from their apartment. For the past five years, her life had been ordinary, ideal: a family to love, a fellowship at University of Texas, and a job for a semester every year at the B'alam Witz ruin in Yucatán.

"Mommy, look at me!" Yash whizzed down the tall spiral slide.

"I'm watching." Pesh waved to her daughter. Six years old today. Maryam Yaxuun B'alam had been christened five years ago at St. Mary's Cathedral. Pesh had broken with Mayan tradition. Instead of naming her child from the sacred calendar, she had chosen Yaxuun B'alam for her royal ancestor and Maryam for Kedar's birth mother, who had died years ago. Pesh's father-in-law had shortened the name Yaxuun to Yash.

"Daddy, can I slide down—just one more time?"

"Not now." Kedar waited at the foot of the slide. "It's time to go to Grandpa's house."

"But it's my birthday." Yash jumped off the slide, ready to climb up for another ride.

"That's why we have to go. Come on, Princess." He swung her onto his shoulders.

Pesh threw Yash's canvas shopping bag over one shoulder. A souvenir from the Capital of Texas Zoo, it was decorated with a jungle scene featuring a pair of scarlet macaws. Yash carried it everywhere, its straps over one shoulder, its bottom barely clearing the ground. This time, it contained a birthday present from her father.

"Hurry up, Mommy. I want to show my box to Grandpa."

"I'm coming." Humming a little tune, Pesh followed them for six blocks to the ranch-style stucco house where Yash's grandparents lived. She had met her father-in-law Burt when she had eight summers; she had called him Dr. Burt then.

Kedar lowered Yash to the flagstone porch. Her long black braid hung down to her waist behind her, and she stood on tiptoes to rap the brass doorknocker.

"Let me have my macaw bag, Mommy," Yash said.

Burt opened the door, releasing the aroma of homemade bread, and inside Isolde, Kedar's adopted mother, waved from the hallway.

"Hello, Yash," Burt said, picking her up and holding her above his head.

"Put me down, Grandpa. I'm a big girl now. I'm six."

"Okay," he said, laughing. "Six, but your bag's as big as you are."

In the hallway, Pesh and Kedar hung their sweaters on the coat tree, and Kedar moved Yash's bag to the floor beside her.

"Look what Daddy gave me." Glowing with excitement, Yash pulled her gift out of the bag—a hand-carved cedar box the size of a Bible. "It's from Guatemala, and this is my mineral collection."

Her box, a replica of one used to house an ancient Mayan *codex* book, contained several small samples of minerals. She had gold in white quartz, clear quartz crystals, a green tourmaline crystal, and a turquoise pebble.

"Here, Grandpa. This one is serpentine. See, it feels soapy."

"Soapy—can I wash my hands with it?" Burt held the stone and turned it back and forth.

"You're being silly, Grandpa," Yash said, grinning. "Grandma, look at my rocks."

"Those crystals came from my mine in California. Aren't they beautiful?" Isolde, Kedar's adopted mother, had mined gold in the Mojave Desert with her first husband for thirty years. She and Burt, lonely after outliving their spouses, had met through Kedar, who had delivered supplies to B'alam Witz from its opening eight years ago. Burt joked that he married her for her homemade bread.

"Will you take me there, Grandma?"

"I'd like to, Liebchen, but I sold the mine when I moved to Austin." Isolde often called her *Liebchen*, German for sweetheart. She wore a red apron, like one she had sewn for Yash.

Yash closed the lid and hugged her cedar box. "I know how to identify all of them. When I grow up, I'm going to be a geologist like Daddy and an archaeologist like Mommy."

But not a shaman. Glad that Yash didn't know about such things, Pesh touched her jade talisman through her shirt.

"In the meantime, come and help me set the table." Isolde, six feet tall and taller than Burt, towered over Yash, who held her hand and skipped to the kitchen.

"Yash looks exactly like you did when you were a little girl," Burt said to Pesh.

"Still does," Kedar said. "That long black braid, round face, lovely almond eyes."

"We get the long braid from Kedar's side of the family," Pesh joked. His adopted mother, Isolde, wore her white hair in that same style.

"I dyed my braid white," Isolde called out from the kitchen. Dishes and glassware made tinkling sounds as she set them on the kitchen cart. Yash traced the golden rims that crowned the china and the etchings in the crystal glasses before arranging the finery on a table dressed in lace.

"Good job!" Isolde said. "For a special birthday."

After they all had enjoyed roast chicken, buttered noodles, and sliced tomatoes, Yash helped to clear away the dishes. A few minutes later, she reappeared, carrying a lopsided chocolate cake with six askew candles.

"Yash frosted it herself yesterday," Isolde said. "I'm brewing coffee for the men."

"What a lovely cake," Pesh said. How times change. Her grandmother Chiich never baked cakes; she had baked tortillas over a stone hearth. She had loved her grandmother as much as Yash loved Isolde. It's too bad that Chiich and Yash would never meet in this world.

They sang "Happy Birthday" and lingered at the table.

"I have news, big news," Burt said. "Paul Anderson, one of my archaeologist friends, has a secret project—finding the sources of ancient Mayan jade."

Wary, Pesh fingered her small jaguar amulet. She had never worried about where it came from. It came from the gods.

"He found some jade boulders in Guatemala," Burt continued, "and he sent me this map of Mayan trade routes."

"How interesting: jade, cacao, and honey," Pesh said, holding Burt's paper.

"What's a trade route, Mommy?"

"They're like highways, except they didn't have cars in the old days," Pesh said. "No carts or horses either. They traveled everywhere on foot."

"See, there, in the Motagua Valley." Burt reached over and tapped the map with one finger. "That's where Paul's looking."

"Can I see your treasure map, Grandpa?" Yash asked, looking over Pesh's shoulder.

"You may see it, but it isn't a treasure map." Burt ran his finger down the middle of the paper. "That's a valley, there, colored green. Somewhere in that river, they found jade rocks."

"Let me borrow your map to compare it with satellite print-outs," Kedar said. "I want to study geological maps of the area because jade forms around fault lines."

"Scientists know the jade artifacts in museums come from at least seven different sources. Paul wants help to locate them," Burt said. "Pesh, where did your jade jaguar come from?"

"I found it in the cave behind B'alam Witz," was Pesh's edited answer. *Jade always came from the gods, of course.* She held out her talisman, suspended from a leather cord around her neck, and turned it in the light: a reclining jaguar carved from dark green jade, about eight centimeters long. The gods had given it to her, seven years ago, the day she became a shaman.

"But who put it there and where was it mined?" Burt forked his last bite of cake.

"I don't know. It's too dangerous to go back to look around." Too close to *Xibalba*—she never wanted to go there again. Pesh had become a shaman in that holy cave. The looter she had cursed that day died by crocodile, where no crocodiles had been seen for a hundred years.

"No one knows where their mines were?" Isolde asked.

Pesh pulled her thoughts back to the dinner table discussion in time to hear Kedar say, "I don't think they had jade mines, Mother. Jade is found randomly, like finding gold nuggets."

"My grandmother Chiich called jade sacred," Pesh said. "More valuable than gold."

"But no one knows where the Maya found it," Burt said. "That's been a mystery for five hundred years."

"Chiich called it a living stone because it appears to breathe," Pesh said. "Like the winds bringing life-giving rains."

"Does your jaguar breathe, Mommy?" Yash asked. "Is that the test for jade?"

"I don't know about the breathing, but that isn't how to test for jade," Kedar said.

"You need a sample of jade for your box." Isolde pushed away from the table.

Burt turned to Pesh and looked puzzled. "What's this, jade breathing?"

"It appears to give off a vapor in the early morning sunlight." Pesh held her fork in one hand, her cake forgotten. "Maybe it's because the stone takes a long time to warm up."

Isolde returned and handed Yash a mintgreen teardrop pendant. "I never wear this piece of jade. I took it off the chain so you can have it."

"It's not the right color but it feels cold," Yash said. "Is that a test for jade?"

"That's one way to know jade," Pesh said. "It always feels cold when you first pick it up."

"Jade comes in many colors, Princess," Kedar said. "It probably has a small coefficient of thermal conductivity. We'll look it up together."

Yash looked puzzled.

"The big words mean it feels cool to the touch," Pesh said. "When you have a fever, a piece of cool jade feels good against your face. In fact, shamans used jade to treat everything from pain and fever to head fractures."

"Come now," Burt asked. "How could it cure a head fracture?"

"Probably because they believed it." Pesh shifted in her chair. Her grandmother had bright green jade in her sack of shaman's stones. "However, the shaman also used honey to heal wounds, and honey contains a natural antibiotic."

No longer listening, Yash opened her birthday box and arranged her pebbles in a circle on the table. She put the light green teardrop in the center.

"Getting back to jade and Guatemala," Burt continued, stirring cream into his coffee. "They need an archaeologist who knows Mayan languages and culture as well as someone with a background in geology."

Pesh glanced at Kedar, who grinned at her.

"It's a perfect assignment for you two," Burt said. "You have the right backgrounds. Are you interested?"

"Guatemala has a lot of jungle and remote areas," Kedar said. "They'll need a helicopter. I think I can get one."

"I must take Yash, as I've always done at the B'alam Witz dig," Pesh said.

"But she will miss school. You need me to watch her." Isolde had helped care for Yash ever since her birth. The child crawled up on her lap and hugged her.

"I could bring my books," Yash said.

"You said, Guatemala?" Pesh's heart rate speeded up, and she rethought the assignment. Phantom ants crawled up Pesh's back, fueling her apprehension. She flashed to her ritual marriage to Five-Owl and the blood sacrifice of a turkey. She had resolved never to act as a shaman again.

"We could do it, from a helicopter with state-of-the-art equipment," Kedar said. "I want to test a new instrument I developed for my geology degree."

"I need more jade for my collection," Yash said.

"Where would we stay?" Pesh, unsure about the whole project, asked, "How would we take care of Yash?"

"It sounds like a grand adventure," Isolde said. "I will watch Yash and listen to her read."

"If we go, I could talk to Maya elders," Pesh said. If Kedar and Isolde both came, surely she and Yash would be all right. "Perhaps someone remembers legends, old stories that might give us clues."

While Pesh didn't mention it, she knew how to trace her jade jaguar to the cave at B'alam Witz, a good start on finding where jade came from. But she had a tight feeling in her stomach. Chiich had warned her, *never go to Guatemala.* She had never said why.

7

Where did this jade come out of the earth? Chanla Pesh, fondling her shaman's talisman and lost in thought, perched on the edge of her desk chair in her quiet apartment in Austin, Texas. As a lecturer in Mayan Studies at the university, she had told no one that she was a shaman. She stared at the reclining jaguar carved from jade, dark chatoyant green, its luster changing like a cat's eye, and became more curious by the minute. The Maya had told no one where they found jade, but she could trace the history of her jade jaguar through a dream-walk.

In a vision years ago, she had merged with King Itzamná B'alam and watched his scribes paint glyphs in vibrant red, green, and blue onto whitewashed pages. They stored the finished book in an elaborately carved wooden box, and the king hid it from the Spaniards. She'd later found that box and the book at the B'alam Witz ruin, in a hollow temple step where he had hidden them. She had translated the book.

As an archaeologist, being a shaman had advantages. She could visit ancient buildings, the better to sketch them; she could follow long-dead persons, the better to read ancient script; and she could track down looters, the better to recover stolen artifacts.

Her talisman had been found in a cave behind that very ruin. By ancient custom, the Maya would have placed it in the grave of a king. She could look for the point of discovery again, but she had failed once before. She needed a deeper trance, the *dream-walk-while-awake*.

To enter such a state, her grandmother Chiich had sprinkled her own royal blood, a pinch of dream-mushroom, and a crumble of *copal* incense over a fire. Her visions came from breathing the sweet-smelling smoke.

Pesh didn't need all that to induce a guided daydream for a vision journey, but to trace the talisman, she had to fall into a deep trance. Her students had given her a lump of incense in a candle cup. She lit it and waited for its pungent smoke. Holding her obsidian ritual bloodletting knife, the blade so sharp it could sever a finger without pain, she nicked her left thumb. Three drops of royal blood fell onto the jade jaguar's back. Seated cross-legged on the bedroom's hardwood floor, she inhaled incense smoke.

To fix her concentration, Pesh rubbed the smooth head of her jade jaguar and closed her eyes to let pictures form on the inside of her eyelids. She fingered blades of grass toughened by the dry climate. Sunlight filtered through tree leaves and vines, and leaf ants crossed the trail in single file. She channeled the screams of howler monkeys, the smell of vanilla orchids, the feel of a fly on her nose, to a day in the jungle. She forced stray thoughts and chatter out of her mind until she was there, at B'alam Witz, sometime in the past.

The jungle then had the same heavy air, the same sweet smell. *Chanlajun Pex Yaxuun B'alam*, her Maya self, rested hidden beneath a tree at dusk. Crickets sang in the symphony of the forest and beetles buzzed in rhythm. She crushed grass-that-smells-like-lemon on her skin to repel insects and stretched the muscles in her arms and legs.

Then, a Maya man materialized and her spirit slipped into his body. She rubbed oil on her face—it was his face, his handsome face, his forehead flat and sloping back in the classic style. She/he rubbed the hard muscles in his chest, stretched his arms, and ran his fingers through his hair. She saw the moon and the white road through his eyes and smelled orchids through his nose and breathed through his mouth. She had meshed with the Maya warrior *Sac B'alam Ahau*, the white jaguar lord.

The kings and princes at B'alam Witz had taken the name *B'alam* for untold generations. Sac B'alam held the jade jaguar in his right hand and felt its smoothness. He moved the talisman across his chest in the sign of the Mayan cross—right to left as the sun moves from east to west and up and down from the heavens to the earth. He asked B'alam, the jaguar god of the underworld and patron god of war, to bless the amulet. Afterward, he placed it in his deerskin bag.

Illuminated by the moon, Sac B'alam loped along a *sacbé,* a white plastered road connecting northern Mayan cities. He had to bring the jade jaguar to his twin brother to put on their grandfather's grave, as was the custom.

The scene shifted. Sac B'alam, his brother Pakal, and four Maya warriors entered the caves. They held pitch torches and plodded down, deep into the dark. Sac B'alam led them in prayer to the gods of the underworld and Pakal placed the jaguar talisman beside the grandfather, a mummy wrapped in blue woven cloth.

Pakal reminded his brother that, on their return, he had to smash the path behind them so the spirits would remain in *Xibalba*, land of the dead.

After the first swing of his jade sledgehammer, Sac B'alam shed Pesh as though she were the skin of a snake. Separated from Sac B'alam, she drifted between worlds. The men left her there, in the dark cave—the sacred cave where she would become a shaman in a few centuries. The entire scene went black. She couldn't bring back her spirit.

"Hear me, O gods of *Xibalba*! Which way?" she cried out in Mayan.

"You—again? Needing our help to leave the cave? Ha-ha-ha!" The voice boomed out of the dark, behind her, all around her. "Why call on us?"

Pesh cringed. *Cimil*, evil god of the underworld!

"You have forsaken us for years," he bellowed. "You are a fallen *Xmenoob.*"

Pesh did not answer. Cold swept up her legs and through her buttocks and spread to her shoulders and the top of her neck. She could not move. She had ventured too close to *Xibalba*, the underworld land of spirits with no time. *Xibalba*: where the gods had claimed her as a shaman and given her the special powers of *Xmenoob*.

Forsaken for years— Did Cimil know that she had taken her baby Yash to be christened in the Catholic Church? Was that it? She had asked for wedding blessings from *Hun Hunahpu*, god of the corn harvest, at the temple at B'alam Witz, but that was before Yash but far in the future.

"Only the gods can know where jade comes from," Cimil thundered.

"Find the lost jade, your salvation," a less threatening voice. "A wager: you win if you find the lost jade."

The Trickster? A riddle? Lost jade? She trembled.

"Find where your talisman comes from," a third god roared. "Without our help."

Pesh groaned and put her hands over her ears.

"We will tell you where the jade jaguar came from," Cimil said, his voice an unpleasant cackle, "but your first-born daughter will become a shaman."

The cave returned to black. The torches were gone, not even the glow of an ember. The heavy blackness pushed her down, down to death.

"No! Never!" Screaming, Pesh emerged from the vision, her heart pounding. Sweat poured down her face. She lay in a heap on the hardwood floor, her muscles jerking. An arrow had skewered her skull, the sharp and insistent pain made worse by sunlight streaming through the window.

After the twitching stopped, she sat up, nauseated and unsteady. The room spun. What was in that incense? She held her head in her hands and swallowed bile.

Grandmother Chiich had warned her, if a shaman—especially one of the chosen ones—did not fulfill the duties given by the gods, she would suffer. Pesh suffered now, as if a knife twisted in her stomach, joining the barbed blade in her head. She steadied herself against a chair.

Yes, she was one of the *Xmenoob*, a shaman by blood, as Chiich had been before her. A fallen *Xmenoob*— What did that mean? Even though she no longer practiced the old religion, she always wore her jaguar talisman next to her skin. The lucky totem given to her by the gods in the sacred cave: she felt it now for comfort.

Pesh took out Chiich's small linen satchel, hidden at the back of her dresser, and fingered its sacred pebbles. Jade, the green of life; amber, yellow for the compass point south; cinnabar, red for east; quartz, white for north; and obsidian, black for west: the colors of the Cosmos.

Each stone, like every word in Mayan, had several meanings. The Mayan word *ya'ax* was used either for blue or for green, the colors found in the sacred quetzal's tail. Her ancestral name *Yaxuun B'alam* meant "precious-bird jaguar" or the king who had given her his DNA. And *yax* meant precious, sacred, or even jade. Would anything be different, if she knew how to use the stones?

A fallen *Xmenoob*: a disgraced shaman. Her shoulders heaved with dry sobs that became shivers. She rubbed her throbbing stomach, rocked back and forth, grieved for her loss, as though an obsidian knife had stolen a fetus. She felt a fetus kicking, a phantom fetus like an amputee's aching phantom limb. Even her jade talisman gave no comfort.

She shook her head. She was an American citizen, a lecturer at the university. She could tell no one about her encounter with Cimil—hearing voices from unfamiliar gods from a thousand years ago. But she couldn't live like this, in periodic states of anxiety. Cimil had hurled a challenge, like a jade spear lodged in her skull.

She held the jade talisman. Sunlight shimmered down the jaguar's back from its head to its tail. A man, not a god, had placed it in the cave. A man, not a god, had carved it. A man, not a god, had found the raw stone.

She would find the lost jade, herself, with no help from the gods. She would journey from Austin to B'alam Witz to wherever the talisman was carved, to wherever it had begun.

8

Everything hinged on the helicopter. Kedar applied to the Geological Institute immediately. After his experiences locating tourmaline crystals housed in caverns, he was sure they would okay his request, particularly because they added him to their very next meeting agenda.

Two weeks later, the Geological Projects Committee met in the boardroom at the University of Texas, a room with marble floor, paneled walls, and a high ceiling. Six men, all dressed in suits and ties, all with gray hair, sat along the side of a twelve-foot rectangular walnut table and faced a state-of-the art presentation wall.

Kedar, wearing an impeccable dark suit, appreciated the air-conditioning. He resisted an urge to unbutton the top button of his shirt and rubbed his sweaty right hand against his pants leg under the table.

The committee chairman, Dr. Holz, called the meeting to order. "Our next applicant is Kedar Herold, who proposes to find jade in Guatemala."

Kedar closed his eyes and took a calming breath. Then he rose. "Thank you. Gentlemen, I propose to use your helicopter and its special instruments to prospect for jade in Guatemala, part of an archaeological project to find the sources of the ancient Mayan jade."

He opened his PowerPoint presentation and brought up Slide 1. Then, careful to make eye contact, he picked out a serious-looking older man who wore thick glasses.

"The Palenque Museum houses everything found in Pakal's tomb. Pakal was a powerful Mayan king. His death mask is green jade but the source of that jade is unknown. From electron microprobe analysis, we know Mayan jade came from at least seven different places."

Slide 1
Pakal's Death Mask
Palenque Museum

The committee member nearest him interrupted. "I thought there was a recent find in Guatemala."

"That's true. But that isn't where Pakal's jade came from. We want to find other sources. Jade comes in a variety of colors; the Maya liked green. The Spanish *conquistadores* valued gold far more highly than jade, but the Maya and the Aztec called gold *excrement of the sungod.*"

Dr. Holz laughed and sat straighter in his chair.

Kedar continued, "The Spaniards didn't spend much time looking for jade, and with no more kings, the jade market dried up. In Guatemala, if you ask about jade mines, the answer is always '*No hay ninguna*,' there aren't any."

"So let's see where jade is found." Kedar showed Slide 2, which listed Burma, Siberia, Alaska, Canada, California, Montana, and Guatemala.

"As you can see, jade doesn't occur in many places. Several green stones are called jade: jadeite, nephrite, and sometimes serpentine. The stones differ in chemical composition. Chinese jade is mostly nephrite, tougher than Mayan jadeite but easier to carve. Jadeite was found in the Motagua Valley, Guatemala, after Hurricane Mitch. In 1998, landslides moved bus-size boulders and exposed veins of jadeite in bedrock."

"Then you already know where jade is found in Guatemala?" Dr. Holz asked.

"Yes, but only one location. There must be others. World wide, not many significant sources of gem-quality jade are known." Kedar tapped the projection screen with his red laser. "For example, Alaskan and Siberian jade is nephrite. Nephrite is easier to carve, but jadeite is more rare and more highly prized."

"Yes, yes. But you are applying for Guatemala."

"On Slide 4, sir." Kedar, too nervous to change the order of his presentation, positioned the next slide. "So, how do we tell these green stones apart?"

Slide 3
Jadeite vs. Nephrite vs. Serpentine
Jadeite: hardness 6.5 to 7. Specific gravity 3.28 to 3.4
Nephrite: hardness 4.5 to 6.5. Specific gravity 2.9 to 3.2
Serpentine: hardness 3. Specific gravity less than 3

"As you can see from Slide 3, jade is more than three times heavier than an equal volume of water and harder than steel. Specific gravity can be checked in the field with bromoform. Jadeite and nephrite are both dense and tough, but jadeite is harder and heavier than nephrite.

"While diamonds and sapphires are denser than jade, they are crystalline; jade is amorphous, ropy and tough. Lead and gold also are denser than jade, but they are metals. Specific gravity is a fast check to separate the green stones."

Kedar paused for effect and looked individually at each professor seated around the table.

"Those very properties of denseness and toughness are why jade cannot be mined like a vein of gold. Blasting or high heat followed by cold water causes jade to fracture, ruining the stone. Jade is tough, immutable. Jade tools, used by ancient man, were almost unbreakable. Some of these prehistoric tools are in museums—"

"Do you have a picture?" Dr. Holz asked.

"I'm sorry, sir, I don't have one." *Next time, cut out the ancient history.*

"Okay, go on." Dr. Holz nodded.

"Jade is very rare," Kedar said. "When found in place, jade turns up as masses or veins within *serpentinite*, a green rock named for its undulating, layered texture. Serpentine, found in conjunction with both types of jade, occurs near large side slipping faults. So, I will start with a geological map. Faults along the edges of the North American and Caribbean Plates are shown in the next slide."

Oh, no! Lost them. One committee member dozed and another tapped his pen and gazed into space. Dr. Holz looked at his watch.

Kedar stepped to one side and said nothing for a few seconds. The men shifted around, looking at one another.

"Now I'll show you where to find jade," he said in a louder voice. "Guaranteed to wake you all up. Okay, how will I find the stuff? The hunter has to know the habits of his prey, and jade likes to live with serpentine."

Laughter told Kedar that he had them again. He clicked the remote to Slide 4 and flashed the red laser pointer on the transform fault.

"This is where jade will hide and here's why.

"Jadeite, the principal component of gem-quality jade, is formed in the earth's crust under an unusual combination of conditions: high pressure, as encountered at depths of at least fifteen miles, and relatively low temperature, 400 to 700 degrees Fahrenheit, as compared with a more typical 1300 to 1500 degrees for such depths. Such conditions occur naturally when plate tectonic collisions push slabs of cold crust beneath an adjacent piece of crust.

"Such plate collisions occur in Guatemala as shown on Slide 4, along those transform faults." He pointed.

Slide 4
Jade in Guatemala

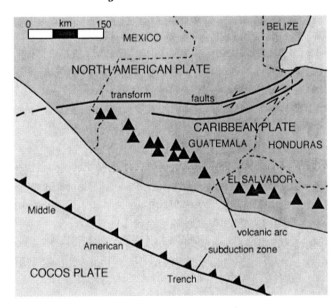

"The Motagua Valley in Guatemala follows the Motagua Fault, the major fault of the right kind in the Mesoamerican region. Somewhere in those mountains is the source of the jade that washed down in Hurricane Mitch."

"That's a large area. How are you going to find jade from that map?" Dr. Holz asked.

"I'm glad you asked," Kedar said, "because that's the most important part of this presentation." Slide 5 listed the main instruments needed to find jade: ground-penetrating radar, the gradiometer, and the electron macrophobe.

"Here's how I'll do it," he continued. "I'll use GPS, the Global Positioning System. I'll compare satellite information with the latest geological maps. The ground-penetrating radar gives images of subsurfaces, and the gradiometer measures the relative densities of that subsurface. All of these instruments are in the Geological Institute helicopter and such maps are available. To coordinate with those instruments, I will use an electron macrophobe to analyze rock samples from the air."

"Macrophobe? What's that?" Dr. Holz's tone of voice seemed a bit unfriendly.

"My new instrument." Kedar hoped he could win him over. "Archaeologists studying Mesoamerican jade artifacts can determine the composition of even a small speck of a mineral lying within a polished surface by using the electron microphobe. I have developed a more powerful instrument based upon that same technology, as part of a project for my master's thesis: an electron macrophobe. I will analyze rock samples on the ground from the cockpit of the helicopter."

"Helicopter?" Dr. Holz frowned and looked doubtful.

"Yes. I am an experienced helicopter pilot, and I have mapped ancient roads built by the Maya from GPS satellite information." He paused. "Are there any more questions?"

The committee members looked at each other. After a momentary buzz, one asked, "This new instrument. Have you actually used it?"

"Yes. I tested it for my thesis. But to calibrate it, the macrophobe must be installed in the helicopter and used in conjunction with other instruments. I can do that only while in the air."

"Sounds ground breaking," said the professor seated nearest him. Someone else added, "A terrible pun," causing laughter around the table.

Kedar forced himself to smile. He had an urge to storm out, but then he'd never get their approval.

A third committee member, the one with the crewcut, said, "Seriously, what experience do you have?"

"From the air, I mapped portions of the sea floor within the Chicxulub Crater off the Yucatán Peninsula. Your institute outfitted the plane I used." Kedar had more practical experience than any professor in the room. "I traced ancient Anasazi trails in New Mexico and reported the results to the main office of the Geological and Archaeological Institute."

"All of that from a helicopter?" the professor with the crewcut asked.

"I used one of your Cessnas, not a helicopter." *What more could they want?* "I used that aircraft's other special instruments to locate caverns laden with tourmaline crystals in the Mojave Desert."

"You will study sources of jade in Guatemala?" Dr. Holz asked.

"That is correct."

"I don't think we need any more information," the chairman said. "We'll give you our decision by the end of the week."

"Thank you for reviewing my application," Kedar said. *Don't think we need any more information*—did he mean *Yes* or *No*?

"Wait a minute," said the elderly professor, the one who wore the thick glasses. "Guatemala is a wild place, lawless. How will you keep the helicopter away from the drug cartels?"

9

From the air, Chanla Pesh saw Guatemala as a brooding landscape of pointed hills jutting from an ash-colored mist. Approaching Guatemala City from the west, the airliner crossed the ancient metropolis of Kaminaljuyú, inhabited for three thousand years, but now reduced to a few grass-strewn mounds. Their kings had gone to their graves surrounded by carved jade jewelry, ornate pottery, and other treasures. Perhaps a local descendant remembered where the ancients found jade.

Closer to the capital, the peaks beneath Pesh grew sharper and greener before being replaced by groups of flat-roofed houses. When the plane tipped its wings over the city, great ravines came into view with ramshackle houses clinging to their rugged hillsides. The plane turned and descended over yet more shacks crowded together, certainly not a city of kings, but instead a city of adobe hovels, dirt yards, and rusted-out cars.

When the captain announced the approach for landing, Pesh fastened her seatbelt, secured her six-year-old daughter Yash, and reminded her about easing pressure on her ears.

"Can you yawn like Mommy?"

Yash yawned and smiled. She hadn't complained once on the entire flight from Austin, Texas. A good traveler, she always accompanied her mother to her grandfather's dig at B'alam Witz.

Pesh had obtained an archaeological grant from the University of Texas to spend six months with Paul Anderson to learn everything she could about jade, the stone of Maya royalty:

how to recognize it in the field, how to work it, and especially where the ancients had found it.

Jade artifacts in museums came from at least seven sources. The Andersons had found one such location; Pesh and Kedar would search for others. She'd use Mayan legend and her abilities as a shaman, and he'd use science and a new instrument he'd developed. But who knew when? Kedar's request for Geological Institute's helicopter was still pending.

She stroked the small jade jaguar she always carried, the talisman given to her by the Mayan gods in a sacred cave years ago. She must find its source to appease Cimil, lord of the underworld. But what about the lost jade, ordered by the voice of the second god? Surely she sought the blue jade favored by the Olmec, a civilization from a more ancient time, before the Maya. No one knew the origin of blue jade.

But, Guatemala? A shiver swept up and down her spine, as though millipedes danced there.

The Andersons' driver met Pesh and her daughter with a luggage cart after they passed through customs. He looked at them and consulted a sheet of paper. "Chanlajun Pex?"

"*Sí.* And you are Ignacio?" Pesh knew he was Maya, both because of his prominent nose and because he didn't stumble over her name.

"I'll help with your luggage." He pointed to the door. "Follow me."

Ignacio loaded their cases into a dented white van. Pesh sat in front while Yash took a nap on the backseat. He pointed out a few local sights, but other than that, he didn't say much—too busy dodging the traffic. The entire city seemed insane: traffic congestion, armed guards in front of every bank and business, and people hanging off every form of transportation. No one paid any attention to lights—it was mass chaos. She sighed with relief when they turned onto the highway, escaping toward Antigua.

Outside Antigua, the highway crested a hill and became a tortuous, nerve-testing plunge on bad roads overlooking the Motagua River Valley—an hour's drive, according to Ignacio. Pesh gripped the seat and checked on Yash, still asleep. Somewhere there, the Andersons had found jade, washed down from the mountains in torrential rains in the aftermath of Hurricane Hugo. While she had seen a mass of green foliage from the air, this side of the mountains was dry and rocky— amazing, how the landscape had changed.

Ignacio slowed while passing through Antigua, much smaller than Guatemala City, but he did not stop the van until they came to the Andersons' gate.

"Don't let the remoteness of this place fool you. We're like an oasis." Ignacio used a remote control to open the heavy gate with its cast iron pickets topped by spear-like spikes. A colonial style house, adobe with an inviting veranda, stood shaded by several magnolia trees. Pesh had seen similar fine homes in Mérida, left there by *henequén* tycoons. This estate was a forti-fied village, the mansion and three smaller buildings surrounded by a rock wall topped with glass shards. The Andersons must be wealthy.

Mrs. Anderson ran to the van to greet them, her red hair accented against a white cotton broadcloth shirt worn loose over tan slacks.

Pesh caught herself staring at a face painted with freckles and rust-colored hair that matched the canyon walls in Bryce Canyon.

"Welcome to Quetzal Centrale." The tall woman extended her hand. "I'm Sylvanna Anderson. Everyone calls me Vanna."

"I'm Chanlajun Pex." Pesh smiled like a Texan and shook Vanna's extended hand. Living in Austin, she had learned *norteamericano* customs. Avoid staring at her hair, she told herself. "Just call me Pesh."

"And this is your little girl?" Vanna asked.

"Yes, Maryam Yaxuun B'alam," Pesh said, the name on her daughter's passport.

"My grandfather calls me Yash," the child said.

"All right, Yash. I'm pleased to meet you."

Two large dogs, Doberman Pinschers, ran to Vanna's side, their lips drawn back into a silent snarl. Startled, Yash scooted behind her mother to a place of safety.

"Let them smell you," Vanna said. "Roco, Pepe. Yash and Pesh are friends."

After a thorough sniffing session, the dogs retreated. Pesh was glad to see them go.

"Now they know you belong here," Vanna said. "Guard dogs. You can't play with them."

"This place is huge, like a small village." Pesh shifted her attention from the dogs to the fortification. "Do you need that rock fence?"

"Guatemala is a rough place." Vanna pointed out the glass shards imbedded in the top of the rock walls. "That keeps out trouble."

"What trouble?" Pesh asked.

"The locals think we're rich," Vanna said, laughing. "They know we're working jade here. They think we have a mine like King Solomon's."

They did seem rich to Pesh; they lived in a mansion.

"Can I see your mine?" Yash asked. "My grandma had a gold mine."

"I'm sorry to disappoint you, but no one has a jade mine," Vanna said. "You can't blast your way into a hill because you ruin the stone."

"Where did you find it, then?" Yash asked.

"That's enough, Yash." Pesh squeezed her hand—so grown-up for six.

"Good question, Yash. We'll talk about it at dinner." Vanna took them to their living quarters, a suite opening onto the veranda in the main house. The driver had delivered their four large suitcases to two adjoining rooms with red-clay tiled floors and high ceilings. Pesh learned that everyone took communal meals in the main house or outside in the courtyard.

After unpacking, Pesh and Yash walked around to stretch their legs. Large trees—magnolia, carob, and cashew—shaded the grounds and flowers grew everywhere. Pesh recognized the golden shower tree, *lluvia de oro*, from its blooms: delicate yellow drop clusters. Passion fruit vines with red flowers climbed the rock wall.

They wandered into the kitchen in the main house and met the Andersons' cook Zia, who spoke Spanish and K'iché, a Mayan language unfamiliar to Pesh.

"I'm from B'alam Witz in Yucatán and speak Yucatec," Pesh said. "I hope to pick up a few K'iché words from you. We're here to help the Andersons search for jade."

"They have looked for years," Zia said. "Now their jade shop gives us work."

"During my visit, I hope to learn all I can about jade and how to work it."

"Jade is history. It's part of us, part of our ancestors."

"I know," Pesh said, while Yash stood quietly, listening to every word.

"Jade protects the Maya. It protects my family. My son, he's eight, not much older than your girl, he always carries a piece of jade the size of a *centavo* in his pocket."

"I'm almost seven," Yash said.

"Then you should always carry a piece of jade."

"Can I play with your little boy?" Yash stepped closer to Zia.

"He stays with his grandmother in Antigua during the school year."

"Oh. Then he isn't here?" Yash sounded disappointed.

"He needs an education," Zia said. "The Catholic schools are the only good ones. The Andersons pay me enough to send money for his tuition."

"Doesn't he come to visit you?" Yash asked.

"Yash, don't pester Zia," Pesh said. Her daughter seldom played with other children and spent most of her time talking to adults.

"*No problema*," Zia said. "Why aren't you in school?"

"She brought her schoolwork with her." Pesh smiled at Yash and turned to Zia. "Back to the jade, do you know any Mayan legends about where it comes from?"

"My grandmother said it came from a sacred valley or a sacred mountain, I don't remember which," Zia said. "I can introduce you to the elder, Xiu. She's a shaman and knows those things."

"*Gracias.* I look forward to meeting her." This piece of luck was too easy. Was Xiu *Xmenoob*? Except for her grandmother Chiich, she had never met another *Xmenoob*.

Pesh and Yash went back to their rooms to put things away, and before long, Vanna came to invite them to dinner. In the dining room, a blond man wearing a loose fitting safari jacket sat at a table shaped like a cross. Its tips pointed north, east, south, and west, the cardinal directions favored by the ancient Maya. Pesh recognized Burt's old friend, Paul Anderson, from his picture.

Paul rose from the table—he was at least six feet tall. "You must be Burt's colleague, the young lady who translates Mayan books and returns stolen Mayan treasures."

"*Hola*," Pesh said, not knowing what else to say after hearing so much praise. She stood stiffly, holding Yash's hand, and wondered if she should sit down.

"And we're so glad you're here," Vanna said from behind her. "Paul, this is Pesh and her daughter, Yash."

"Welcome, Pesh! Let me shake your hand." Smile lines carved Paul's craggy face and his voice had a hearty, friendly tone. As an after-thought, he said, "*Hola*, Yash."

"I'm glad for this opportunity to help you find jade." Pesh shook his hand and Yash stepped behind her. "Sit here, Yash, next to me."

At first, Pesh had worried about being unable to cook her own food, but Zia's *pepian*, a sweet-tasting chicken dish, was spiced to perfection. Paul seemed friendly and she enjoyed his dinnertime conversation. He loved to tell stories and Yash listened wide-eyed.

"Never do anything to attract the attention of the rebels or government troops, *banditos*, or machete-wielding *campesinos*," he advised. "But, as a pale foreigner towering over the locals, it's not easy to keep a low profile."

"I won't have a problem like that," Pesh said, and everyone laughed. "In Guatemala, no one looks twice at a tiny Maya woman."

"Unless you wear those shorts," Vanna said.

Pesh hadn't thought of that. The stories continued.

"We were shielded by our apparent insanity," Paul said. "Everyone we came across, storekeepers, farmers, villagers, told us we were wasting our time looking for jade mines. '*No hay ninguna,*' everyone said, 'There aren't any.' Then the *campesinos* realized the truth—we were *idiotas*, outlandish but harmless."

Paul and Vanna laughed. Yash, sitting politely, looked puzzled.

"How did you find jade, then?" Pesh asked.

Paul told about prospecting around the Motagua River for a week, walking on a parched hillside about two hours north of the river. They had filed along in the heat, tapping their hammers on stones beside the trail, listening for the distinctive *ping* of a jade outcrop, but they didn't know what that would sound or feel like. Whenever a rock rang a little differently, they stopped, chipped off a piece, and dropped it into a vial of *bromoform*. All the chips floated, like the dozens of others they had tested. Jade, being heavier, should have sunk.

"What's *bromoform?*" Yash asked.

"It's a nasty yellow liquid that let's us test for jade," Paul said. "It's poisonous. It makes your nose and throat sting and burns your skin."

"I was ready to call it a day," Vanna said, "but then I hit one more boulder. The steel head bounced back so hard that my hand flew up and the rock rang like a bell."

"A jade bell." Pesh knew about that sound only from legends. "Ringing one is supposed to ward off evil."

"We'll hit a jade sample tomorrow so you can hear it," Paul said, pushing his chair back from the table. "And drop a chip into our test liquid, too."

"I didn't finish my story." Vanna leaned forward. "The chip from my rock sank, but while it still might not be jade, I loaded it into Paul's backpack. It weighed a good 20 pounds—that kept him out of trouble for a while, lugging it back to the workshop."

"She does things like that all the time." Paul laughed, a hearty laugh. "Back in Antigua, we sawed into the mystery rock and found a grayish green stone under that dull exterior. I sent a sample to the States for testing, and bingo! Jade!"

"So that's how you did it." Pesh couldn't think of another question, except when is bedtime.

"It's getting late." Vanna pointed to Yash, asleep at the table. "We'll show you the jade workshop tomorrow."

10

At Quetzal Centrale, Zia served breakfast on the veranda. Pesh enjoyed plantains and hot chocolate made properly—strong, not too sweet, enhanced with nutmeg and cinnamon. Yash had a second helping of everything, and Vanna was the one telling stories.

"Paul keeps the source of the jade a secret because people think we're rich," Vanna said. "Even though those raw rocks aren't worth much until we shape and polish them."

"Is that hard to do?" Yash asked.

"Yes. A complicated piece takes days, even months. I'm going to show your mother around the workshop."

"May I please come, too?" Yash asked. "I need jade for my mineral collection."

Vanna laughed. "Alberto will fix you up."

"Keep your hands behind your back, so you remember not to touch anything," Pesh warned, but delighted that Yash showed such an interest in jade.

In the courtyard, rocks rattled and banged and crunched, tumbling in a revolving barrel.

"We keep the noisiest machines out here." Vanna introduced the shop foreman Alberto, a K'iché Maya.

"*Hola*, Pesh. And what is your girl's name?" Alberto asked in Spanish.

"Yash."

"*Señorita Jade.*" Alberto laughed and turned toward the child. "*Yash* means jade in my language."

He pronounced *Jade* the Spanish way, "*Haa-dey.*" Yash hid behind her mother, clutched one leg of Pesh's safari shorts, and peered around at Alberto.

"*Señorita Jade.*" Alberto bent down and swept his hand toward the door. "Come into my workshop."

The jade workshop, outfitted with machinery to cut, drill, and polish jade, had a tile floor and a translucent plastic roof. The equipment's metal edges gleamed against whitewashed walls. A large diamond saw hummed and dropped a pile of jade dust and chips, a saw that "grinds through jade as fast as ice cubes melting in lemonade," according to Vanna.

"May I please have a scrap?" Yash smiled at Alberto and added, "*Por favor?*"

Pesh smiled proudly—so grown-up, so polite.

"*Sí, Señorita Jade.*" Alberto picked up a scrap smaller than Pesh's thumb, dull dirt-brown on the rounded side, dark grayish green on the flatter, cut side. "When we found this, it wore a brown rind disguise. See those white scratches from the saw? We grind them out next. It's a good specimen of raw jade."

"Go ahead." He held it out to Yash. "It's yours."

"*Gracias.*" Yash admired her new treasure and slipped it into her pocket. Then she clung to Pesh's shorts as Alberto walked away.

"You could use those scraps and jade dust," Pesh said, turning to Vanna. "Add resin and make jewelry for tourists."

"Good idea, but clearly marked souvenir," Vanna said. "We already stock jade beads and small amulets so a tourist can take home a memento, genuine and important to the Mayan culture. Did I tell you we have a retail store in town?"

"I'd like to see it," Pesh said. Yash added, "Me, too!"

"Here's a sample." Vanna held a jade disk, polished to a high luster. "Alberto will show you how we make them."

A few minutes later, Alberto brought out a small box containing jade marbles and beads. "These still need final polishing. We do the stuff for tourists by machine. Over there—Jesus will show you."

Jesus smiled. His workstation smelled like honey.

"Are you using honey—*Miel?*" Pesh asked.

"No, *señora*, you smell the wood." He held out his polishing bit made of hard, black wood—*lignum vitae,* according to Alberto. Jesus used it to rub the stone with grit, around and around.

"Okay, Yash," Alberto said in heavily accented English. "Would you like a jade bead for your very own?"

"Oh, yes, please, . . . *por favor.*" Yash watched transfixed as Alberto used the diamond saw to cut off three small cubes of jade. He let her hold them.

"Now I will turn them into beads. Hand one to me." Alberto clamped the chunk of jade over his worktable under a motor the size of a coffee mug, suspended from the ceiling by a cable. He pulled down a small drill bit attached to a flexible cable and turned on the motor with a foot pedal. The machine whined and ground like a dentist's drill and filled the air with smoke-like dust as it bore a hole through the half-inch piece of stone.

"In the old days, they used the leg bone of a bird and fine grit to drill a hole. This machine speeds it up." He drilled the other two beads-to-be and gave them to the girl. "There you go, three beads."

"But they aren't round." Yash frowned, puzzled.

"We tumble them to knock off the corners. That's what's going on in those barrels churning outside. I'll show you how to shape them tomorrow, if you bring them back."

"Okay." Yash stepped closer to him and whispered, "Can you keep a secret? I'm a princess and my Mayan name is Yaxuun B'alam."

"A princess from the north, heh?" he said.

"Don't bother him with things like that," Pesh said.

"No bother, not for a princess." Alberto took a deep breath, puffed out his chest, and drew himself up to his full five foot four. He boomed, "My name is Tz'u'utz' B'alam."

Yash stepped behind her mother and again peered around her leg.

Pesh stifled a smile—laughing would insult him. *Tz'u'utz' B'alam*—Blowing-Smoke Jaguar—he must have made it up. She stood silently, her face without expression, the Mayan custom for polite behavior.

"I'll carry these always, like you, Mommy." Yash dropped the beads into her pocket and kept them with her the rest of the day. At bedtime, she hid them under her pillow.

"May I touch your jaguar?" Yash asked as she settled in for the night. She often liked to stroke it before she fell asleep.

Pesh let her daughter hold the jade talisman to feel its smoothness. "*Find the lost jade . . .*" Could she find jade without calling upon the gods?

11

The three metal tumbling barrels on the concrete slab outside Alberto's workshop revolved and rattled and rumbled. Each barrel, half-filled with water, grit, and rocks, was connected to a belt and an electric motor and lay on its side within a box-like base. Pesh, ready for another lesson, followed Yash, who clutched her three beads and danced along the path.

"*Buenos días*. Want to see what's in those barrels?" Alberto turned off one machine, removed its cover, and emptied its contents—water, coarse grit, and jade pebbles—into a large plastic box. He washed out the two-foot barrel with a hose and poured the rock mud over a slagheap behind the building. The inside of the barrel wasn't round but ten-sided—a decagon, he said. He washed the pebbles through a colander to remove all of the mud and grit. The jade stones had become partially polished marbles.

"*Señorita Jade*." Alberto asked in softly accented Spanish, "Did you sleep with your jade so it knows you?"

Yash nodded. "Will you make them round?"

"I'll grind your beads with the next batch of marbles. That knocks off the corners," he said. "Yours are the only ones with holes through the middle."

"Can I see them tomorrow?" Yash asked.

"All right." Alberto dropped the beads-to-be into the tumbler for shaping. "But they won't be ready for polishing."

"When can I polish them?" Yash leaned over the machine's open mouth.

"In three days. Now you can help me sort the rocks." Beside the tumblers, Alberto had a wheelbarrow full of unprocessed rocks of different sizes. Covered by a dirt-colored rind, they all looked the same.

"I have to choose the real jade ones," he said, handing Yash a rock. "Is this one jade or only a copy-cat?"

Yash ran her fingers over the pebble, an ordinary-looking but heavy river rock.

"This feels like jade," she said, returning it to Alberto, who seemed surprised.

"What about this one?" He pointed to a stone of the same size and appearance.

Yash examined it carefully from all angles and lifted it with one hand, then the other.

"This looks the same but it doesn't have the same feel," Yash said, holding out the small rock. "It isn't heavy enough. It isn't jade."

"Right! I think you have a natural feel for jade."

"Let me try." Pesh recognized jade by its coolness but had to touch each stone to compare them. Yash's study of her rock collection seemed to have paid off.

"In the Orient," Alberto said, "some Chinese women wade in a murky river and find jade by the way the stones feel against their feet."

"Do I have to go into a river?" Yash asked.

"No." Alberto laughed. "But most people can't tell those stones apart."

"I like to stroke my mother's jade jaguar," Yash said.

"And what is that?" he asked.

"I must find where this stone came from." Pesh pulled out her shaman's talisman, a small reclining jaguar carved from dark green jade.

"*Muy bonita, muy preciosa*," he said, holding it in the sunlight with a hand missing its index finger. "I have not seen jade that color."

"What happened to your finger?" Yash asked.

"That's rude, Yash," Pesh said. "Please forgive her manners."

"*No problema, señora*," he said. "I am proud of my left hand. We had thieves—thieves in my workshop. Before we built the rock fence and had the irongate. I threw them out, both of them, but one had a knife. I grabbed the knife by accident and my finger fell on the floor."

"How brave," Pesh said, glad for the rock fence. Yash had retreated to a position behind her mother.

"Not to worry." Alberto invited them in and went back to work, and Pesh and Yash watched Alberto's assistant Jesus polish a green and gray jade disk to a brilliant luster.

"The ancients made the best pieces shine like a mirror," Jesus said. He gave them each a jade piece for final work and a cloth embedded with grit as fine as flour.

Later, Alberto gave Yash a quetzal note, Guatemalan currency equivalent to an American dollar bill. "This is for you, but don't spend it."

"This money has a window in it shaped like a flower," Yash said. "I can look right through it. Green and red, the colors are so pretty."

"That's how they protect it from counterfeiters." Beneath *Banco de Guatemala*, the multi-colored bill showed a red-bodied quetzal in flight. Its green tail extended behind it, the tail three times as long as the bird's body. Mayan characters filled the borders and corners.

"Those Mayan glyphs would give a counterfeiter fits," Pesh said.

"*Verdad*," Alberto said. "The quetzal is the national bird of Guatemala, and its picture appears on our money. In the old days, its tail feathers were used for money."

"Is its tail really that long?" Yash said, pointing to the bird's picture on the bill.

"*Sí, Señorita Jade.*" Alberto gestured toward the sky. "The Maya harvested only its tail feathers and released it. It was sacred. They would never have killed it. The gods would have punished them."

"Can I see a real one?" Yash slipped the quetzal note into her pocket.

"Too many people have wanted its feathers. It's nearly extinct—very few left." Alberto asked Pesh, "Have you ever seen a quetzal?"

"No," Pesh said, and Yash shook her head.

"A pity," Alberto said. "Every Mayan princess should see a quetzal at least once."

"Could I see one on Google?" Yash asked.

"We don't have Internet access here," Alberto said. "You have to go to Antigua."

On the third day, Yash was so excited about polishing her jade that she jumped out of bed before dawn. Immediately after breakfast, Pesh took her hand and accompanied her to Alberto's workshop, where everyone was already at work.

"Here are your beads, *Señorita Jade.* Now you must polish them." Alberto set out leather cloths, a dish of rendered cooking fat, and a pan of sand. "You dip the cloth into the fat, then into the grit. Then you rub the bead."

"Will rubbing fix this one?" Yash held her bead to the light— slightly translucent but foggy, not quite round, mint green mottled with white.

"The coarser grit lets you finish shaping it. Then you polish it with finer stuff. That's how our ancestors did it."

Pesh examined the marble Alberto gave her. Gray with a yellow band, definitely a jade-feel, but not the smoothness of her talisman. Touching jade always had a calming effect. She liked the feel of jade, the honey-smell of the polishing machine, and the peace of sitting there cross-legged.

"How long do we do this?" Yash asked. "It's boring."

"Not when I tell stories," Alberto said. "That makes time fly by. Do you know why beans are so many colors?"

"I never thought about that," Pesh said. "They always turned out whatever color we planted." She had played with the colored beans—red, black, striped brown ones—when she helped Chiich plant corn, squash, and beans. The beans climbed the corn stalks, and the squash spread out and covered the ground. The orange squash blossoms, the smell of fresh moist soil—

"I want to hear the story," Yash said, putting her hand over Pesh's mouth.

Pesh realized Alberto had paused.

"And so do I." Pesh hoped he hadn't found her answer rude: *beans always the color we planted.* She had loved stories when she was Yash's age.

"Okay. Once upon a time, a good man decides to sell his soul to the devil to get himself out of his troubles. He has no job, no money. The devil Kizin appears. He's short and squat with a pointed nose, and he always snarls—*grraahh!*"

Yash's eyes widened at Alberto's sudden growl.

"The man tells Kizin, face-to-face, he wants to sell his soul. The devil likes the idea, taking the soul of a good man. The man asks for five things, one for each finger on his right hand."

"One, two, three, four, five." Alberto counted in Mayan, holding out his right hand. "Kizin rubs his hands together." Alberto paused, then, high pitched and loud—"*Heh-heh-heh!*"

"Oh!" Yash jumped, her mouth opened wide.

"On the first day, the man asks for money. Right away, he pats his pockets—lumpy, heavy, full of gold coins. On the second day, he wants good health. *For the rest of your life,* Kizin said, *Ha-ha-ha!* Why did he laugh, *Señorita Jade?*"

"Because he wouldn't really do it?" Yash said.

"You're right. It's a joke. Kizin would make sure his life wasn't very long."

"But that's not funny," Yash said, frowning.

"On the third day, the man asks for fine food. Kizin gives him a banquet and fills his pantry. On the fourth day, the man wants to travel, and in a jiffy he visits a thousand places. Just think—a thousand places."

"Daddy's airplane takes longer than that."

"Not in my story, *Señorita Jade*." Alberto continued, "On the fifth day, Kizin says, *What do you want? Think carefully— it's your last day*." Alberto rubbed his hands together and cackled like Kizin, a squeaky "*Heh-heh-heh!*"

Yash covered her mouth with one hand.

"The man has one last whim: to wash those black beans until they turn white, and Kizen says, *That's too easy. I'll do it, and then I'll take you away with me. Heh-heh-heh!*"

This time Yash didn't flinch at Alberto's high-pitched cackle.

"And Kizin begins to wash the beans, but they won't turn white. He gnashes his teeth and growls. *Gr-r-rah! He fooled me!* And that's why there are black beans, yellow beans, and red beans."

Yash laughed and looked at her mother.

"I like the way you animate your stories, and I like Mayan legends about fooling the gods," Pesh said. But Kizin was only the trickster—easier to fool than Cimil, god of the underworld.

"You want another story?" Alberto asked.

Yash, sitting forward, her eyes opened wide, said yes.

"Okay, me, too." Pesh continued to smooth her gray and yellow bead. Alberto spoke in a combination of Spanish and a Mayan tongue different from her grandmother's language, but his gestures and body language made his story understandable and delightful. "Do you know any legends about jade?"

"Well, let me see." Alberto paused. "Jade is sacred and magic, and the gods threw it down into the sacred valley for men to find."

"But that isn't a story," Yash said.

"Okay. This isn't about jade, but it happened. In 1906, a Mayan family near here found a crystal skull while digging up their cornfield. A shaman said it came from the Pleiades in the sky. Carved from a quartz crystal, but no one knows how, because quartz is very hard."

"Quartz is harder than jade. My Daddy said so."

"What happened to the quartz skull?" Pesh asked.

"A traveler from Holland bought it in 1991. The skull is elongated, like the head of an ancient king. It's nicknamed *ET* because it looks like an alien."

"I saw the movie *ET*," Yash said. "I went with my grandmother."

"There are Mayan legends about thirteen crystal skulls," Alberto said, "but no one can prove whether this crystal skull is an artifact of the ancient civilization."

"Did you get to see it?" Yash asked.

"No, I only heard about it," he said.

Pesh wasn't interested in crystal skulls, only where to find jade. She listened to Alberto while admiring the mirror-like surface of her polished jade bead.

"I'd like to find that jade," she said. "Where the gods threw it down."

12

"Everyone ready?" The sun shimmered through the magnolia tree onto the front wall of the mansion at Quetzal Centrale and highlighted Vanna's red hair. "I have to visit our retail shop in Antigua, but I wanted to show it to you anyway."

"Let's go." Pesh tried not to stare. Vanna's hair, red as a fox's fur, appeared brighter than yesterday.

The Andersons' driver Ignacio pulled up to the front steps, and Pesh boosted Yash into the Quetzal Centrale van. They piled into the second seat and buckled up, Yash in the middle between Pesh and Vanna. Kedar, still waiting in Austin for his helicopter grant, would miss today's tour.

Ignacio positioned the van to pass through the automatic steel gate and looked both ways before pulling onto the highway. His mustache twitched as he reminded them they wouldn't stop before Antiqua, an hour's journey. He had a wispy black mustache, the only one Pesh had ever seen on a Maya man.

"Ignacio, have you heard anything more?" Vanna asked. "About the store next door, broken into last night."

"*No, señora,*" Ignacio said. "Next door is only the little padlock. Your store is like the fortress."

Pesh wanted to hear about the robbery last night in Antigua, but Vanna said no more.

"How often do you go to your store?" Pesh asked, noting the two-hour round trip.

"Twice a week," Vanna said. "I used to go every day, but now we have employees."

The road narrowed. All the roads in Guatemala seemed rough to Pesh. Riding over a particularly large bump, they were momentarily airborne, but Ignacio didn't slow.

"I'm sorry, *señoras*. It's dangerous to slow down and we cannot stop."

"*Banditos*," Vanna said. "They're like pirates along this stretch of the road."

"Like the *Pirates of the Caribbean*?" Yash asked Pesh.

"That's only in Disneyland." Pesh pulled Yash closer to her and asked, "Aren't there any highway patrolmen?"

"Of course not." Vanna laughed. "This is Guatemala. You hire your own protection, but it isn't a problem, unless you make yourself stand out. Driving a new Ferrari sportscar here would be a bad move."

Ignacio swerved suddenly to avoid a dead animal—large, gray and fat, maybe pregnant. Yash, who had unbuckled and stood to see out, fell into Vanna's lap.

"Yash, sit down and stay in your seat!"

"Mommy, what was that? It stinks." The dead animal, bristly and stout, had a pig's snout.

"That's *javelina,* the skunk pig," Ignacio said. "In English, a peccary. They have nasty dispositions and can rip you apart with their tusks."

"There are many animals to avoid when you venture into the jungle," Vanna said. "We've fenced them out at Quetzal Centrale."

Ignacio added, "And fire is the food of the peccary—*k'ahk' ti' chitam*—but I have never understood why we say that." Then he gave the road his full attention, and so did Pesh.

Most of the cars on the road looked old and beat up. People lived in shacks near the edge of the road. Two boys, dressed in rags, chased a mangy mutt across a dirt yard in front of a building with corrugated iron walls, weeds growing on its roof, and a new Mercedes sedan parked by the front door.

"They're gonna get robbed," Yash said, pointing at the expensive car.

"Going to be robbed," Pesh said.

"Not if he works for a crime lord," Vanna said.

They returned to silence for a while, until Yash asked, "What's *afinidad*?"

"Affinity? Where'd you hear that?" Vanna asked.

"Alberto said I have *afinidad* for jade, and my name means jade in Mayan."

Vanna laughed. "So you have a natural attraction to jade."

"I can tell which rocks are jadeite by feeling them," Yash said.

"That's a lot less dangerous than using bromoform," Vanna said. "Maybe you're a jade witch, like a water witch, only finding jade."

Puzzled, Yash looked at Pesh.

"She's teasing you," Pesh said.

"A water witch uses dowsing to find ground water." Vanna pulled out a page from the newspaper and twisted it into a Y. "She holds a Y-shaped tree branch, her hands on both horns of the Y, its leg pointing out in front. Like this."

"It points to water?" Yash asked.

"The end of it drops down over a place where they can dig a well."

"A well is like the *cenote* at B'alam Witz," Pesh explained to Yash, and turning to Vanna, said, "That's Burt's dig. He's Yash's grandfather."

"You go with your mother to B'alam Witz?"

Yash nodded.

"She always travels with me." Pesh hugged Yash, one-handed.

"I can draw my Mayan name in glyphs and write the numbers, too," Yash said.

"Oh-my-god! A Mayan scribe who's a jade witch. And you're only six?"

"Almost seven," Yash bragged.

"Well, whether you believe in dowsing or not, they still find water that way all over the world," Vanna said. "You could save us hundreds of hours if you really are a jade witch."

"I'm sure dowsing can be explained by science," Pesh said. No way should Yash waste her life being a witch of any kind. The witch conversation ended when Ignacio announced the outskirts of Antigua and the smoking volcano towering over the landscape.

"Antigua sits in the middle of *tres volcanos*," Ignacio said, holding up three fingers. "*No problema*—only one is active."

"Mommy, look!" Yash said. "That mountain's smoking! Is it talking, too?"

"The mountain grumbles and rumbles every day," Ignacio said.

"I've never seen even one volcano," Pesh said, watching a smoke plume climb higher. "Isn't it dangerous?"

"We never worry. It smokes every day like that and shows its fire at night. *Volcán de Fuego* is ten miles from here. We Maya call it *Chi Gag*, Where-the-Fire-is."

"It looks like an ice cream cone blowing smoke rings," Yash said. "Can we walk up there to see it?"

"No, it's too steep, and the ground would be so hot it would melt your shoes," Pesh explained. "You know how wax drips down a candle?"

"Like at church?"

"Melted rock runs down the sides of that volcano," Pesh said. "Like wax."

"*Volcán de Fuego* isn't as dangerous as *Volcán de Agua*," Vanna said. "*De Agua* is only five miles from Antigua, and it makes mudflows—melted rock, rocky debris, and hot water—moving at 400 miles an hour. A similar *pyroclastic* flow, along with poisonous gases and falling ash, killed everyone in Pompeii in 79 AD."

Pyroclastic—that'll be the first word Yash asks her father about. Pesh pointed out brightly painted houses—yellow, orange, rosepink, yellowgreen, blue—along the cobblestone street.

"Mommy, they're painted with crayons," Yash said, and Vanna laughed.

"We have mansions, too. We're very proud of our town," Ignacio said. "Antigua is a World Heritage site, once the colonial Spanish capital of all of Central America."

"Until they had to move it after a destructive mudflow from the volcano," Vanna said.

Then Ignacio pulled up in front of Vanna's shop, ending the conversation.

In the retail center of the city, Pesh noticed armed guards posted on both sides of the door of a bank and more guards in front of a liquor store. Another bank, one block down and on the other side of the street from Vanna's shop, also had armed guards on duty.

"All those guards have rifles?" Pesh asked.

"This is Guatemala." Vanna pulled a ring of keys out of her pants pocket. The shop had been painted jade green, and metal bars guarded the windows. Above the shop's door, a neon sign announced "*Taller del Jade Maya*" in large red letters and "Mayan Jade Workshop" in smaller green letters.

Vanna unlocked two heavy padlocks and folded back the iron grill enclosing the storefront. Inside the door, elegant wooden display cabinets held pieces of shaped and polished jade. She had displayed everything on open shelves, not behind glass, not locked up.

"Don't you have trouble with shoplifters?" Pesh asked.

"We keep the antiquities under lock and key. Tourists usually aren't thieves, and they have to pass by the cash register to leave the shop." Vanna handed Pesh and Yash each a piece of worked jade. "Feel how heavy, how smooth. I want customers to experience jade for themselves."

Yash rubbed it across her face. "It's so cool, so nice."

"Those jade pieces provide tourists with something handsome and also culturally significant, but they're pricey," Vanna said. "The green table, over there, has machine polished jade of lesser quality, jade disks on leather thongs."

"Could I buy a leather cord for my jade bead? Please?" Yash asked.

"First customer of the day!" Vanna laughed, as she often did. "Here, take it—an early birthday present."

"*Gracias*." Yash tucked the black cord into the pocket of her knee-length Bermuda shorts, pants like her mother always wore.

"You're welcome."

Vanna pointed across the room to a display on a red table, five wicker baskets each holding small items made from wire, gold beads, and fresh water pearls. "If they want inexpensive souvenirs, we have jewelry over there."

"So you make jewelry as well?" Pesh asked.

"Sometimes in the evening or when business is slow. Something for everyone."

"But you specialize in jade."

"Right. But you have to remember, we're not selling jade. We're trading on an image." Vanna liked to talk about her shop. "Diamonds glitter like nothing else, but it's not their sparkle that sells them. It's the idea: diamonds are forever. The story sells the stone."

"I know," Pesh said. "I sold tourmaline crystal jewelry when I attended college in Mérida. After I named it Mayan love-stone, my friend Jorge couldn't keep it on the shelf."

"Did that come from Grandma's mine?" Yash asked.

"Yes, it did." Pesh squeezed her hand. "She gave you a sample of tourmaline for your collection."

"That's about it out here." Vanna swept her hand toward the backroom. "Come on. We have a jade museum."

In the *Taller del Jade Maya* museum, Vanna exhibited carved reproductions of Mesoamerican figurines and masks along with several ancient jade tools. A glass showcase mounted on the wall held small objects labeled by number: a prehistoric spearhead, a jade bracelet, and a translucent green ear spool an inch across, its partner lost over the centuries.

"See that, Yash?" Pesh pointed to the jade ear spool. "It's a kind of earring to be worn by a royal child. How'd you like to wear that?"

"No, it's way too big." Yash fingered the heart-shaped gold stud she wore in her earlobe.

"Ancient peoples made tools out of jade stones," Vanna said, unlocking one cabinet. "Jade is so heavy and tough that these could be used today."

Pesh picked up what looked like the head of a sledgehammer—heavy, smooth, mottled gray jade. It fit nicely in one hand. A thrill ran through her: she was holding history, the history of her people.

"Feel how heavy, Yash."

"That's a *celt*—that's what archaeologists call them," Vanna said. "Celts have been smoothed and shaped for hammers or to grind corn or to use as who-knows-what. I have several—I use one for a doorstop. Finding celts is a bit like finding arrowheads in the North American plains."

"Is that one an ax head?" Pesh asked.

"Yes, and still sharp enough to fell a tree if it had a handle. Those notches are for binding it to a wooden handle with leather thongs."

"Don't you have any handles?" Yash asked.

"No, but we made that spear." Vanna pointed to the one mounted on the wall above the cabinet. "See the notches on this spearhead? We forced a spearhead through a green wood branch, right above the knot. When the wood dried, it shrank and hardened. It keeps the head in place, and the knot strengthens the handle."

"Oh," Yash said, and Pesh wondered how much of that long explanation the child understood.

Vanna warmed to her topic. "The Maya made spears and had a state-of-the-art weapon when they used the *atlatl*, an Aztec spear-thrower. Jade spearheads never break." She took out a shiny black object. "But this obsidian one is sharper."

Yash reached out and Pesh exclaimed, "Don't touch it! You'll cut off a finger!"

Wide-eyed, Yash held her hands behind her back, as Pesh had often told her.

"This black-green jade hatchet is only four inches long." Vanna returned to the display and took out a tool. "How much do you think it's worth?"

"A Mayan artifact is priceless," Pesh said.

"One like it sold at auction at Christie's for $5000. And a smaller piece, grayish greenveined jade, smoothly polished and pierced twice for suspension, sold for $3000."

"How can a tourist know if it's ancient or if you made it?" Pesh asked.

"They can't. But we'd never fake an artifact. If we did that and word leaked out, we'd lose our good name."

"Do you ever buy jade pieces?" Pesh still wondered where the Andersons got their money.

"Sometimes local Maya bring us a find," Vanna said. "Sometimes we buy it to keep it out of the black market trade. But sometimes they bring us an artifact stolen or looted from a grave."

"What do you do then?" Pesh wouldn't like to be the one who bought a stolen artifact.

"We play it by ear. But we don't expect a rapid response from the police."

No police, no highway patrolmen—Pesh was glad she lived in Texas.

"In fact, last year, a man was supposed to bring us an artifact, but he didn't show up. The next day, he was found murdered. The police came then—too late."

"Mommy, I have to go potty." Yash bounced from one foot to the other.

"Over there." Vanna unlocked the door. "We'll go home after dark so you can see the fire-rimmed volcano and its red lava flow. There's a flame atop the mountain, like a candle—a Roman candle."

13

Whop, whop, whop! "It's Daddy!" Yash darted away from the magnolia tree.

Pesh raced after Yash toward Paul's private helipad. That helipad, in the far corner of the Anderson's twenty-five guarded acres, had been Kedar's final argument to convince the Geological Institute's Project Committee to approve his application to take their helicopter to Guatemala, where thieves stripped aircraft as efficiently as a school of piranha pulled flesh off deer that stepped into the water to drink.

Tonight she could hold Kedar, talk to him. Pesh's pulse raced; her heart pounded in her chest. Anticipating the mini-sandstorm, she spun Yash around.

"Close your eyes!"

The hovering Bell Jet Ranger threw out a storm of pebbles and sand and then touched down. When the rotors stopped, Kedar hopped out, and Yash wrapped her arms around his legs.

"Your grandma's here, too." He hugged Pesh, the child still clinging to one leg.

"There's my *Liebchen*!" Isolde waved to Yash from the cockpit.

"Hi, Mother!" Pesh opened the passenger's door for Isolde, and Kedar, carrying Yash, helped her step out.

"Grandma, I know how to polish jade," Yash said.

"You can show us tomorrow, Princess." Kedar hoisted Yash onto his shoulders.

She leaned closer to her father and asked, "What's *pyroclastic*?"

"You've got me there. Where'd you hear that?"

"Vanna. Volcán de Agua is *pyroclastic*."

"Aha!" Kedar shifted her to a perch more comfortable for his neck. "A good word for a geologist. It means a mudflow— steaming mud, poisonous gases, and glowing red rocks hotter than burning barbecue briquettes. It moves very fast, 400 miles per hour, and gobbles up everything in its path."

"Will it eat up Antigua?"

"No one's worried about that now," Kedar said, setting Yash down.

"Daddy, Vanna has a jade ax. It's a thousand years old. Could you make it a handle? I want you to chop down a tree."

"Ask me again tomorrow, Princess." Kedar grabbed Isolde's suitcases. "I have to carry these in. You can show me where to go."

"Grandma has a bed in my room." Yash hugged Isolde. "Want to see the jade workshop?"

"You can show her tomorrow," Pesh said.

Yash ran ahead to open the door.

"There's your bed, Grandma," Yash said as soon as Kedar set down Isolde's suitcases.

"Daddy, wait! I want to show you the dollar bill with the window." Yash held out the money that Alberto had given her.

"It says, One Quetzal. That's Guatemalan money."

"I know. I want to see a quetzal. Can you find one with Google on your laptop?"

"A quetzal, huh?" Kedar said. "We can't use Google without Internet access. Tell you what, I'll copy an image of one the next time I'm at the airport."

"Your father still has to carry in his own suitcases," Pesh said. "Then we have to clean up for dinner with the Andersons. Zia has invited you and your grandmother to eat in the kitchen tonight."

Later, Kedar and Pesh sat across from Paul and Vanna at the largest dining room table Kedar had ever seen and sipped coffee spiked with vanilla.

"Burt said you found jade in the Motagua River Valley," Kedar said. "How did you know to look there?"

"We read Foshag's book on Guatemalan jade like a Bible," Paul said. "An archeaologist reported ancient jade workings above the Motagua River."

"That's a huge area," Kedar said.

"We hiked up tributaries of the Motagua and searched, many times." Paul patted his mouth with his dinner napkin and slid his chair back. "One day we struck pay dirt—a partially buried pod of jade twice the size of a living room sofa, a really big hunk of rock."

"That's unusually large for a jade deposit," Kedar said. "Jadeite?"

"Yes, the good stuff. Then the problem became, how to get it out of there. You can't break off pieces—a chisel fractures it—and it's very heavy. And more basic—how to keep it secret."

"Is that a worry?" Kedar asked, puzzled. "It's not worth much until you work it."

"It's dangerous to have anything of value—after all, this is Guatemala. So we bought the land, brought in workers and gasoline-powered drills. We hauled out the pieces on donkeys."

Kedar studied Paul's face and thought about what he didn't say. He had money from somewhere, enough to buy all that land and to build Quetzal Centrale as well.

"It took us three months," Vanna added. "We never allowed anyone to visit our source."

"However, we have to make an exception for you." Paul took a sip of water. "We'll go there, show you how to identify jade in the field."

"Paul will make you sign an oath of secrecy—in blood." Vanna looked so serious that Kedar couldn't tell if she was joking or not, but after a few seconds, she cracked a smile.

"Just kidding," Vanna said. "But you must promise never to tell where we go."

"For your own safety," Paul said. "Some thugs kidnapped Ignacio and tried to force him to tell where to find the jade mine. He really didn't know. Thank goodness, they let him go."

"Sounds like a spy story or a thriller novel." Kedar leaned forward in his chair.

"Do you know of other sources of jade?" Pesh asked.

"That's where you two come in," Paul said. "We want to find the origin of those jade museum pieces. We need another source before reporting to the archaeological world."

"So you've never reported all this?" Kedar asked.

"We kept our source a secret." Paul appeared to study his coffee. "But that led to other problems. How could an academic journal accept an article about a pre-Columbian jade mine without a location? So that's why we need you to search for sources and verify our finds."

"What did you do next, when you couldn't publish all this?" Kedar, not satisfied with Paul's answers, wondered how the Andersons funded their explorations.

"We learned how the ancients worked jade, and we opened a jade shop in Antigua—Vanna took Pesh there," he continued. "But that made things worse. Our stuff looks too good. People thought we were selling looted antiquities or carving pre-Columbian forgeries."

Paul stirred his coffee as though the whole cloves at the bottom of his cup held answers to their questions.

"Then you found a prehistoric jade mine?" Pesh asked.

"No, not exactly," Paul said. "When you think of a mine, you conjure up the image of a tunnel or a pit in the ground. But pre-Columbian prospectors must've found loose boulders or dug from an outcrop. Jade is harder than steel—how would they have mined it with stone tools?"

"Did they use *spalling*—heating the stone until it cracks?" Kedar asked.

"Heat damages the stone closest to the fire," Paul answered. "They probably collected loose stones that washed down from the surrounding mountains."

"We tried to pry out some pieces from the vein," Vanna said. "Believe it or not, when jade fractures, it sounds like a gunshot."

"Like a warning from the gods," Pesh said. "We should wait until they throw it down from the mountains."

"That's certainly simpler," Vanna said. "We'll teach you what we know."

"We can show you how it looks while still in the ground," Paul said to Kedar. "Can you fly us there in the helicopter?"

"If you can find a flat place for me to land," Kedar said. "I'd like to hover over your jade find to test my macrophobe."

"Yes, I recall you had a new instrument of some kind," Paul said.

"I developed it as a project for my master's in geology," Kedar said. "It detects the densities of rock formations."

"And jade is very dense."

"Exactly. Pesh has to go with us because she knows all the special instruments."

The next morning, Yash and Isolde had breakfast in the kitchen with Zia. Yash liked eating there because she didn't have to sit quietly through long conversations. Zia cooked boiled eggs, sapodilla, and pineapple date bread. The eggs had brown shells, and the sapodilla looked like a giant brown egg except inside it had reddish brown flesh. It tasted like a pear sopping in brown sugar.

"I'd never seen a sapodilla," Isolde said. "*Deliciosa.*"

"*Gracias*," Zia said, smiling.

Yash finished her hot chocolate and thanked Zia, but she wanted to visit Alberto.

"Grandma, let's go to the jade workshop and polish jade," Yash said. "I'll teach you how."

"After you finish your schoolwork," Isolde said. "You must do that every day."

"But you haven't met Alberto," Yash pleaded. "I'll work extra tomorrow."

Yash led Isolde by the hand past the noisily churning stones. "Can you smell honey? That means they're using the polishing machine."

After Yash introduced her grandmother, Alberto gave Isolde another unpolished bead from the same stone as Yash's other beads.

"I'll help you," Yash said. "Alberto tells stories while we work."

"You must both carry your jade," Alberto said. "Jade keeps you safe, and you and Yash will always be able to find one another. That's a Mayan legend."

"A charming legend," Isolde said. "*Muy bueno.*"

Yash gave Isolde a polishing cloth and plopped down cross-legged, ready to work.

"I can't sit that way on the ground, Liebchen," Isolde said. "I won't be able to get up."

Alberto brought a folding chair for Isolde, and Yash sat next to her feet.

"Are you going to tell us a story?" Yash asked, leaning against her grandmother's legs.

"Okay, for my good workers, but my English isn't good. *¿Habla español?*"

"*Un poquito.* Why don't I just listen?" Isolde said.

"This one's about the soul of a dog," Alberto said. "Once upon a time there was a man, always in a bad mood. He hits his dog *Tzul*. Kizin, that spirit-of-evil, says to Tzul, *Oh, you poor thing. Why so sad?*"

"*Because my master beats me.*" Alberto gave Tzul a squeaky voice and continued, "Then Kizin says, *He's an ornery man. Why don't you leave him?*"

"*But he's my master*," Alberto said in the dog's voice.

Yash giggled and Isolde smiled.

"*He doesn't deserve your loyalty.*" Again the dog's voice: "*Doesn't matter—he's my master.*" Alberto made a sad face and shook his head. "Kizin pesters Tzul, *Give me your soul. I'll give you anything you ask for.* Then Tzul says, *I want a bone for every hair on my body.*"

"Oh." Yash put her hand over her mouth.

"So Kizin counts the hairs. But when he gets as far as the tail, Tzul jumps." Alberto's hands jerked.

Yash caught her breath, and Isolde watched his hands.

"*G-r-r-r-ah! I lost my count!*" Alberto growled. Then he used the dog's voice, "*It's these darn fleas!*"

"Kizin starts again from the end of Tzul's tail. But it twitches. *G-r-r-r-ah! Stay still, Tzul!* Kizin starts a third time, on one ear. When he gets to the hind leg, the dog kicks. "*G-r-r-r-ah! I lost my count!*" The dog's voice again: *It's these darn fleas!*

"Then Kizin gives up and throws three bones at Tzul," Alberto said. "Tzul howled, *Yap! Yap! Yap! Yee-ow-ee!*"

Yash grinned and mimicked, "*Yeee-ow-eee!*" and Isolde laughed, a loud guffaw.

"So, it's harder to buy the soul of a dog than that of a man," Alberto said.

"Do dogs have souls?" Yash asked.

"Sometimes I think so," Alberto said.

"I loved your sound effects," Isolde said. "You speak with your hands."

"Next time I'll tell how *K'uk* the Quetzal got his tail."

"It'll be fun." Yash grabbed Isolde's hand and bounced up and down. "I'll teach you Spanish."

14

Pesh wanted a visual memory of exactly where the Bell Jet Ranger helicopter went in the Motagua River Valley. Paul and Ignacio sat in the rear to direct them. From the copilot's seat, next to Kedar, she studied the terrain intently. Kedar said jadeite occurs along fault lines, and the Caribbean and Central American Seismic Plates ground together here beneath their flightpath. She had seen what slippage along a fault line looked like over the Mojave Desert: fences shifted fifty feet, roads disconnected, ridgelines freshly broken. She saw no such evidence.

Along the way, from the backseat, Paul bragged that he'd purchased 400 acres from cash-strapped *campesinos* who still lived there. The peasants became loyal fans: their livelihood hadn't been disrupted and they paid no rent. In return, they discouraged outsiders and poachers. Best of all, the jade was collected on private property, and Guatemala couldn't claim any of it.

Pesh held the pen, ready to record any deep red patches that should appear on the overlay of the GPS map. Kedar had prepared blank tables for her use. She glanced at the small gray screen. Still blank, like a television set with no remote. Under the Bell Jet Ranger, a cylindrical metal box the size of a roll of paper towels housed Kedar's electron macrophobe and, next to it, an inverted circular plate fed information to the ground-penetrating radar. Excited about trying out his experimental instruments, he had thrashed about next to her all night.

"I see it, over there." Paul's voice boomed through her headset from the backseat, where he rode with Ignacio, who would guard the helicopter while they hiked.

Pesh immediately recorded their location. Within seconds, a red patch bloomed over the GPS map, and Kedar hovered over the site of Paul's raw jade. Her pencil flew over the data sheet as she tried to get all the numbers down.

"We are calibrating the instruments over your known jade deposit," Kedar said. "They measure the density of the rock formations below."

"And jade is very dense," Paul said. "You said you invented that machine?"

Pesh, thankful for her headphones, listened in.

"Previously, the electron macrophobe was used only in a laboratory environment," Kedar said. "I modified it to allow a greater range, and Pesh is gathering data."

Paul unbuckled his seatbelt to lean over her shoulder as she recorded GPS coordinates and filled out the data log.

"We need only a few more readings." Kedar moved the helicopter a few yards to catch the outcrop from a different angle. "Pesh is terrific. She has recorded instrument readings for me for years."

Hearing Kedar's compliment, Pesh swelled with pride.

"There's a flat place for landing." Ignacio pointed out an area near the river and barren from sparse rainfall.

"But we have to avoid the cactus," Kedar said. A field of candelabras—two of them as tall as a two-story building—bordered the barren area on the left. On the right, a patch of cholla cactus with white fuzzy-looking thorns stood like a line of teddy bears, and beyond, claret-cup cactus bloomed with flowers the color of arterial blood. He hovered the helicopter in preparation for landing.

Pesh felt a jolt as a sudden gust of wind caught the chopper and moved it away from Kedar's target. *Those candelabras!* She closed her eyes and braced herself, hands together on top of her head, forehead against the instrument panel. A bump, and it was over—off center but away from the big cacti. *Dios bo'otik!*

"Wait until the rotors stop," Kedar said, looking cool and professional. Paul seemed not to notice the hard landing, but Ignacio's mustache twitched, giving away his nervousness.

When Kedar gave the word, Pesh stepped out so close to a three-foot cholla that its thorns clung to her shorts. Kedar's mother called that a "jumping cactus" because its stems detach with the gentlest touch or even the air current of an animal moving past. Before she finished pulling off stickers, Paul gestured toward an animal trail.

"That's where we walked in," Paul said. "It isn't far."

Pesh hoisted her shoulder pack, ready to follow them.

"I'll wait right here." Ignacio spread a blanket over the ground in a shady spot to guard the aircraft in comfort. In Guatemala, one never left any kind of vehicle—car, truck, motorcycle, or aircraft—unattended. *Banditos* would strip it for parts and scrap metal.

They hiked a quarter mile until the rough trail passed a stone house with a rusted corrugated metal roof, its walls carefully fit together without mortar. A few trees shaded the house. Lines of broken white stones bordered its arid yard, and the Sierra de las Minas Mountains rose in the background. Laundry hung on a rope to one side of the front door. A rusted wheelbarrow rested under covered parking for a pickup truck. Several brown chickens clucked and scratched under a single bush bearing red-pink flowers, and a cock with magnificent red-brown plumage strutted nearby.

"*¡Hola!*" Paul called out.

Someone standing inside the open doorway waved him on, and that seemed to be all there was to it, getting permission to pass. Was he one of Paul's *campesinos,* watching over the trail?

Ten minutes later, they stood at Paul's jade outcrop. To Pesh, it could have been any kind of dirt-brown rock. Paul reminded them appearances counted for little because jade wraps itself in nondescript rind when exposed to the elements. Most of the exposed gemstone had been removed and carried back to Quetzal Centrale on the backs of donkeys. The jadeite vein ran under the hill and deep into the earth, and the jade pod had tested positive on Kedar's instruments and provided calibration. But that large deposit would remain buried because jade, unlike gold, cannot be mined by blasting and digging without destroying the best stone.

Pesh was eager for a turn with the hammer. The hunt for jade in the field was based upon its sound when struck. Would the feel and sound of striking jade anchored to the earth be the same as for the small samples in Alberto's workshop?

Paul, a master of the language of the hammer bounce and recoil, struck the rock with his hammer and it rang like a bell, the same sound made by a known sample. To learn the feel of the recoil, Kedar and Pesh each tried out the hammer.

The hammer made a ping like one of the bells in Rachmaninoff's symphony and recoiled with a snap that buzzed Pesh's wrist. Kedar's hammer blow sounded the same, but when Paul asked him for a test chip, he couldn't break the rock.

Paul raised the hammer shoulder-high, swung it in a smooth arc, and broke off a test chip with one glancing blow. He made it look easy.

"It takes a lot of practice," he said. With a chisel, Paul chipped off another small piece, which shattered with a sound like a gunshot. It sank when he dropped it into his vial of bromoform to test its density. As a demo, Paul dropped several other similar-looking pieces of rock into the vial. Not as dense as jade, they all floated.

Bromoform: nasty stuff, yellow and viscous. The strong smell burned Pesh's nose. It'd be a great weapon, if one of those *banditos* turned up.

"You see, that's all there is to it," Paul said. "But you need a little luck."

After two hours of instruction on identifying jade in the field, they opened the sandwiches Zia had packed.

"We almost lost Ignacio on our first helicopter trip out here," Paul said. "It was a hazy day toward the end of the rainy season. We used a charter service out of Guatemala City—they do sight-seeing tours, too.

"Our need for helicopters drove us to build the heliport at Quetzal Centrale." Talking with his hands, Paul waved the remnants of a sandwich.

"Anyway, back to losing Ignacio." Paul unpacked a second sandwich. "That helicopter was expensive, and we didn't know when we could rent one again. We wanted to check out two places, both several days' walk from any road.

"So the pilot left off Ignacio to scout up the hill, and we went on downstream. But on our way back to pick him up, fog came up."

"Flying in fog—in the mountains—that's dangerous," Pesh said. Kedar never flew in fog without proper charts and never in mountains. Paul continued as though she hadn't spoken.

"I carried this for luck." Paul pulled out a jade disk from under his T-shirt. "Ignacio had one from the same piece of rock. According to legend, two people carrying jade from the same source can communicate with each other. I held this tightly and closed my eyes and concentrated on Ignacio. I directed the pilot where to go, and we broke through the fog—and there he was!"

"No way!" Kedar said. "You're pulling my leg."

"Unbelievable, I know, but it happened."

"That's one of the magical properties of jade my grand-mother told me about," Pesh said. "But I have never tried it."

"Aha, a believer," Paul said.

Pesh didn't think Paul believed in Mayan magic, but he did love to tell stories. She finished her sandwich and folded its waxed paper cover into small squares, creasing each line with her thumbnail. When she opened it out, the creases were bright lines in the sunlight. Lines pointed in every direction like her search for jade.

"Anyway, we had to get back into the air right away, while we still had daylight," Paul said. "Before we were a thousand feet above the ground, the fog closed in again. We couldn't see the ground. Worse, we had circled around so long that we were low on fuel."

"We have to watch that, out here," Kedar said. "It wouldn't be a matter of landing safely, but surviving until someone came to get us."

"Thank God for Coca Cola!" Paul said. "Our pilot landed in their parking lot outside of Antigua."

"Did they have fuel? How'd you get home?"

"We called Quetzal Centrale for someone to pick us up. We had to truck in fuel."

Kedar has never run out of fuel, Pesh said to herself. The charter pilot had taken a huge risk, letting the fuel tank run dry. Kedar would manage the flight more carefully.

She looked forward to scouting out here alone with Kedar, without Paul's scary stories and without his nasty bromoform.

15

Kedar hovered the Bell Jet Ranger over a scrubby ridge on another hazy day toward the end of the rainy season. With Pesh in the copilot's seat and Ignacio in the backseat, he had followed a tributary of the Motagua River. The macrophobe showed rock formations, but too far beneath the surface for accurate readings.

"Keep going upstream," Pesh said. "The macrophobe senses denser rock up the hill." She trained the binoculars on a stone outcrop several hundred feet below. The barren ground gave clues to a likely serpentine deposit, where jade often lurked. "That's a good place."

Kedar landed the chopper. Ignacio climbed out and stretched, and Pesh grabbed her pack, ready for a hike. She left the bromoform packed snugly in its box in the helicopter.

"You need to carry the bromoform," Kedar said.

"No, I'm not taking it," she said. "It's heavy and nasty and I hate that stuff. Instead, can we use the handheld GPS and label envelopes for samples? You could test with bromoform later."

"Actually, you have a clever idea," Kedar said.

"I'll take pictures and record everything in my notebook," Pesh said.

"Don't worry about the helicopter, *señor*," Ignacio said. "It's safe with me."

They left Ignacio to guard the aircraft and hiked uphill along the edge of the stream through an area bereft of trees but full of small scratchy plants. From a spot on a ridge on the dry south side of the mountains, they could see for miles. Below them on the north side of the mountains, trees with pink flowers and green moss hanging like tinsel soared a hundred feet high, and beyond those, dozens of *ceibas* reached for the heavens.

"What a vista," Kedar said. "Amazing what a little water can do."

"See those *ceiba* trees in the distance?" Pesh asked. "*Ya'axche*, the sacred trees of life. They connect the earth of men with the thirteen heavens where the gods dwell."

"Thirteen," Kedar said. "Legends about thirteen appear in every mythology. There's even a word for fear of the number 13: *triskaidekaphobia*."

"All right, Professor-man," Pesh said, laughing. "I thought we were admiring *ceiba* trees."

"I count thirteen steps over to that outcropping." Kedar tried the hammer on rock that protruded from the hillside but produced only dull thuds.

"Your macrophobe didn't sense jade up here."

"Just practicing," he said. They hiked on.

Pesh liked prospecting in the comfort of the cockpit, but this groundwork was far too hot. She wore a broad-brimmed hat, necessary in midday in the full sun, and removed it temporarily to dry her forehead. Two tiny yellow and green birds chattered and chased each other in the air around a tall cactus, its stem surrounded by thorns like rolls of barbed wire—secured apartment living for birds. She thought of her own nest, their cozy apartment in Austin, out of the sun.

"How about lunch?" Kedar wiped his forehead with a white handkerchief and pointed to a shady area under a small grove of trees, all with yellow and fuzzy flowers.

"Not there. The thorns of the acacia tree house stinging ants." Pesh gestured to a stand of spiny bushes that she recognized, but could not name, and left the trail. Her hat slipped down and blocked her view—she disliked hats. Failing to look closely under her feet, she tripped over a loose stone jutting from the sandy soil.

"Look what I found!" She picked up a long thin stone, shaped by man, not by nature—perhaps the head of an ax. "A *celt!* Vanna has some in her museum."

"Oh, my! Let me hold it." Kedar turned the artifact this way and that. Then he stepped off the trail and kicked at ragged pieces of broken stone. "Did you see these?"

Jagged jade-like bits and a few stones, possibly used as hammers, littered the ground.

"Snap some pictures for Paul. This might be an ancient workshop," Pesh said, chosing some scraps for testing later in bromoform. "They'd be more comfortable working up here than next to the river."

"For sure," Kedar said. "Perhaps that's why the satellite pictures show a section of an ancient trail through here."

"Like the Anasazi trails we mapped in New Mexico?"

"Right. Except these become lost in the jungle as soon as they cross the mountains." Kedar recorded the area with his cell phone.

Pesh closed her fist around some fragments of stone and stared into the sky. She visualized faint outlines of two Maya pulling garnet-laced cords across blue-gray stone. Working first above and then below, cutting grooves until they broke it.

"Think of it!" she said, placing the fragments and the *celt* in her pack. "Right here, a thousand years ago, Maya worked for weeks to cut pieces of jade small enough to carry home to their kings."

"Let's mark the map," Kedar said. "This must be on a Mayan trade route."

Farther along the faint trail and higher on the mountain, they approached a small log house shaded by a large tree that painted the ground purple with falling blossoms. The walls of this log cabin, unlike those in the central U.S., consisted of thin branches arranged vertically and lashed together with vines. Kedar snapped its picture.

On the hillside behind the house, a cornfield grew in three terraces planted in the ancient way. Each cornstalk supported a tangle of bean vines, and squash plants grew at its base.

"*Hola,*" Pesh called out. She smelled cooking corn, *maiz tortillas.*

An old woman came to the open door. Behind her, aging wooden furniture, hammocks, and an indoor clothesline crowded the small room. An old man, eating a tortilla stuffed with beans, sat on a mat. Tortillas cooked on a hearth over three large stones. A gentle breeze wafted their aroma, the smell of Pesh's childhood home.

"We wish to pass by your house," Pesh said in Mayan, because one never went through someone's space without permission. Maybe the woman would invite them in, out of the sun.

The woman looked doubtful but said nothing.

"Paul Anderson sent us to look for jade," Kedar said. Paul's name was equivalent to open sesame, even though Kedar spoke no Mayan. Her expressionless face softened.

"*He' Le, Hola,*" she said, Mayan for "Then that's the way it will be. Hello."

"I'm looking for jade like this." Pesh held out her dark green talisman.

"*B'alam!*" said the woman, the universal Mayan word for jaguar. She reached out to touch it but waited for permission.

"Okay." Pesh nodded her head. "Have you seen any stones this color?"

The woman felt the smooth cool jade and then swept her hand towards the doorway, inviting them. She nodded and said, "Okay."

"Okay," Pesh repeated, taking Kedar's hand. "I'm Pesh and this is Kedar. You are—?"

"Chiich."

Chiich meant grandmother. The Maya gave their first names or nicknames, but telling whole names to a stranger gave away too much power. The woman reminded Pesh of her own grandmother.

Chiich gave them cups of spicy herbal tea.

"Have you seen any jade stones? *Yax?*" Pesh rephrased her question.

The woman pointed to the shelf behind the hearth, then picked up a small object. She let Pesh hold a partially carved piece of apple-green stone in the shape of a cross, about three inches long, a small artifact with the coolness and weight of jade.

"*Muy precioso,*" Pesh said. Was it jadeite? She had no way to test it.

"They search for jade," Chiich said to the old man, who stood to admire Pesh's talisman. "Did you find more?"

Through some Spanish, some Mayan, Pesh learned that the man had found the apple-green cross in the area of the ancient workshop. The old couple had no other pieces.

"*Yax* is sacred. We never sell," Chiich said. "Valley is sacred. Gods threw down *Yax.*"

"*Dios bo'otik,* the gods pay." Pesh thanked her and added, "*Vaya con Dios.*"

"*Ko'ox.* Let's go." Pesh grabbed Kedar's hand and made a polite exit. "*Xi'ik tech utsil.* Goodbye. Take care."

Afterwards, as they passed the jade workshop on their way down and while Pesh filled in Kedar on the conversation, a cloud blocked the sun and the temperature dropped ten degrees.

"Fog!" he yelled. "Run, Pesh! I can't fly if I can't see!"

Pesh struggled to run. The pack on her back held several rock samples.

She and Kedar jogged back to the helicopter to join Ignacio. Kedar started the rotors before the three of them settled in their seats, but it did no good: fog had formed everywhere.

"¡Señor! No puedo ver!" Ignacio pulled his shirt over his head and prayed, *"Madre de Dios ..."*

Fog—weather like in Paul's story about almost losing Ignacio. Pesh thought he would try to jump out, even though they were a hundred feet above the ground, now invisible.

Kedar did not answer but turned to the south, free of obstructions because they had landed on the south side of the hill. In a few seconds, they broke out into clear air.

"It's okay now, Ignacio," Pesh said. "Look out the window."

Ignacio peeped out over his shirt.

"Whew!" Kedar said. "That was close." He stabilized the aircraft at altitude and flew over fluffy rolls of fog that completely obscured the ground.

"I knew you could do it," Pesh said. "Where are we going next time?"

"We need to follow the Motagua River to look for another jade deposit for Paul."

More days hiking in the heat, carrying that dangerous bromoform, wearing that ridiculous hat. Pesh sat silently for several minutes, choosing her words.

"Let's spend several days mapping jade deposits from the air along the Motagua," Pesh said. "Just the two of us and the macrophobe. We can give Paul a marked-up map."

"Good idea," Kedar said.

"*Bueno.*" Ignacio's mustache twitched. "I never want to fly in fog again."

On their next foray, Pesh had time between recording readings to study the terrain. This time she saw evidence of the 1986 earthquake, the one that had brought Guatemala City to its knees. Rows of trees in orchards were displaced several feet, whole rows interrupted in the middle as though slid over by a giant's hand. A section of railroad had new track, but beside it, part of the old one still stood, bent into S-curves and Ws. A new bridge spanned the river, the crumbled supports of the old one still visible.

After three days of mapping the Motagua from the air, Pesh asked, "More scouting tomorrow?"

"We've already found several outcrops for Paul," he said. "Placer jade would wash down from the mountains into the valley after big storms or earthquakes, but we can't map those loose boulders."

"Then you have other ideas?" Pesh spoke into her headset microphone.

"I want to go higher over the mountains, to scout and study the terrain," Kedar said. "You can help me find evidence of fault zones."

"Oh, I know the place." Pesh had been rereading Kedar's copy of *Mineralogical Studies on Guatemala Jade*. "It's where Foshag painted the treasure-map X over the Sierra de las Minas."

"Yes, in 1955," Kedar said. "The book doesn't show a specific location, only an X over the mountains. The Sierra covers an area eighty miles long and twenty miles wide."

"I like scouting with you—from the air," Pesh said.

"I know you'd rather scout from the helicopter than prospect on foot," Kedar said. "Paul can go with me for the hot, sweaty work."

16

The Andersons' white panel truck bounced through an endless series of potholes, more potholes than road. With Ignacio at the wheel, the van leapt across a place so rough that Pesh bumped into Zia and almost slid off the seat.

"How much farther, Ignacio?" To Pesh, every road away from the main highway seemed an obstacle course. The roads in this area didn't appear on any map.

"Another half hour," he said. "Please fasten your seatbelt, *Señora* Pesh."

Pesh settled back. She would meet *Xmenoob Xiu*, Guatemala's most powerful shaman, who could see the future in the rising smoke of a sacrificial fire. Ignacio and Zia both had relatives in Xiu's small village, *Alta Altun*. The name was an odd juggling of Spanish and Mayan words meaning *high rock stone*. Because of the difficult journey getting there, they planned to stay two nights.

She worried about Kedar's safety. She saw him and Paul Anderson leave, heading for jade outcroppings along the Motagua River and accompanied by two armed guards. *Why did Paul need armed guards?*

So far, Kedar's search for jade using geological maps and science had yielded nothing new, except for the site of an ancient jade workshop. But science couldn't explain everything. She would use Mayan legend and magic to find jade, especially the origin of her jaguar talisman. Zia had promised to introduce her to Shaman Xiu, and Alberto had related some legends:

the creation story, antics of the gods, and magical uses of jade. Thinking about Alberto, Pesh broke the silence.

"Alberto has been very kind to Yash, letting her shape jade in his workshop."

"He says he's getting a second chance to be a father." Zia grabbed Pesh's arm for balance.

"Yash loves his workshop and the stories he tells." Pesh felt no guilt for leaving Yash with her grandmother and Alberto. The child wouldn't miss her at all.

"His girl was only six, like Yash," Zia continued. "There was a cholera epidemic. She and his wife both died."

"How sad for him." Pesh didn't know what else to say. These days, no one should die from cholera, with antibiotics and modern water and sewage treatment.

"That happens a lot in Guatemala," Zia said. "Many childen die as infants. I treasure my son. I want him to have a better life, so I send him to school in Antigua. That's why I work for the Andersons."

The mountain road climbed higher and higher along a canyon wall. The roadbed of potholes was connected to other potholes by humps in the middle of the road. Their route narrowed until they reached the edge of a crevasse. Where a bridge should have connected the two pieces of road, two logs had been wedged into place as a crude crossing.

"Hold on, *señoras*." Ignacio geared down. The engine whined and the van shuddered. "The big earthquake destroyed the bridge."

He steered the van so the wheels climbed onto the logs and inched across the ravine.

Pesh looked down and wished she hadn't. She caught her breath and held it—they'd have to cross again to return.

"*Santa Maria, Madre de Dios, …*" Zia closed her eyes and prayed.

On the other side of the divide, the van wobbled from one rock to another along deep ruts. After another ten minutes, they approached a small village. Cornfields filled terraces on the mountainside, and eight huts clustered together, their thatch roofs supported by adobe walls. Two small boys played ball in an open dirt yard. Ignacio parked on a flat place beneath the only tree on this side of the village.

"It's that house." Zia pointed to a rectangular dwelling with one central door facing east but without windows. Pesh recorded GPS coordinates from the satellite phone, provided by the Geological Institute as part of her grant for this trip. She might want to return to Alta Altun, a village not on any map. Then she captured the scene in a photo.

"Don't let Xiu see you do that," Zia said. "She doesn't want any pictures because they steal your soul."

"Okay." Pesh tucked the phone into the bottom of her shoulder pack and climbed out of the van. She was glad to stretch after the long ride.

"Go ahead, *señoras*." Ignacio opened the hood to add a quart of oil. "I'm going across the square to visit my family. No one at Alta Altun will bother the auto. I'll sleep here tonight."

"Will you be okay, sleeping in the van for two days?" Pesh asked.

"Of course. I brought pillows and a blanket," he said. "This afternoon, I'm going to beat my uncle at dominoes."

The women crossed the plaza and stopped in front of a hut, and Zia called out in Mayan, "*Xmenoob Xiu*. May we visit you?"

"Zia." *Xmenoob Xiu,* a small gray-headed woman, came to the doorway, exchanged greetings with Zia, and gestured for them to come in. She wore a floor-length white cotton dress, its skirt embroidered in an intricate zigzag pattern with bright red, blue, and green thread. When Zia introduced Pesh, Xiu said, "*Llámeme Xiu.* You may call me Xiu."

Her Mayan name *Xiu*, the K'iché word for plants, sounded like the English word "shoe," a slight click added before the vowel. Xiu offered them herbal tea, and they sat cross-legged on the floor out of the sun.

Her house, topped with thatch, had only one room, rectangular with rounded corners. Adobe bricks made from grasses and mud and whitened with lime formed its walls. For cooking, she had the traditional grill set over three stones. When the hammocks were hung, the single room would be converted into a dormitory. Like pre-Hispanic Mayan houses, Xiu's was built of perishable natural materials: wood, mud, grasses, and thatch. The hut had a *sacsab* floor, gravel covered with white packed soil.

Xiu spoke some Spanish but mostly K'iché Mayan. With Zia's help, Pesh asked her about sources of jade: where did the ancients find it?

"Jade comes from the sacred mountains," Xiu said. "The gods throw it down into the sacred river. But to ask the gods where to find it, I must wait for nightfall."

"*Gracias*." Pesh didn't want the gods to get involved.

After they finished their tea, Xiu said she had to visit a sick boy.

"May we go with you?" Pesh asked. "My grandmother was a healing shaman."

Xiu nodded and Pesh and Zia followed on a fifteen-minute walk to a lone hut. Inside, a boy lay on a sleeping mat, his leg purple and swollen into a weeping puddle of pus. His mother, her eyes red from crying, stood by. She looked like she hadn't slept in a week.

Xiu opened her shaman's pouch and gave the mother some herbs to use in a bowl of *chacah*, medicinal *cacao* or chocolate with hot peppers, honey, wild tobacco juice, and the bark of the silk cotton tree. She threw in a pinch of crumbled angel's trumpet flower as a sleep aid, but only a pinch.

If that had been Yash on the mat, Pesh would have rushed her to the emergency room—but not in rural Guatemala. The thought raised the hairs on her arms and made her stomach rock hard—she'd have to rely on jade and herbs. She was glad that Yash was safe at Quetzal Centrale.

Xiu asked the boy's mother to make the *chacah*. Pesh caught the K'iché expression "*x-men*," a woman who knows the connection of mind, body, and spirit. The word sounded like *shaman*.

When the mother returned with the potion, Xiu went to work as a healer. She placed a hand on the boy's brow, rested a jade pebble above his nose, and chanted a spell of healing. Then she moved the jade stone back and forth above the wound to practice *pul yah*, the removal of pain and physical ailments where they manifest. The mother helped him sip the medicine.

¡Ay Dios mios! The boy would be dead by morning! They must stop his infection. Pesh knew what to do but wanted to show respect for Xiu. She asked Zia and Xiu to step outside a moment, and through Zia, she said, "My grandmother used maggots to remove pus and then covered the wound with honey."

"Fly worms? How does that work?" Xiu had never heard of that, but she also feared for the boy's life.

Pesh explained that the maggots ate only infected flesh and did not hurt healthy tissue.

"Then let us try your grandmother's cure. I want to learn it," Xiu said.

After a Zia-translation, the boy's two brothers went searching for a dead animal. Xiu gave the sick boy more of the medicinal drink, and he fell asleep. Not long after, his brothers returned with the odoriferous corpse of a dog.

"Boys always know things like that," Zia said.

"Ask them to put the white worms into this cup," Pesh said. "We need them to remove the pus."

"Don't bring that rotted dog into the house," the mother said in K'iché.

"We need the fly-worms," Xiu said.

Working beside Xiu, Pesh placed wriggling white maggots, one at a time, directly onto the boy's wound. She had watched her grandmother Chiich do that, years ago.

"You use fly-worms?" the mother asked. "He will recover?"

Xiu nodded, and the woman's eyes filled with tears, a silent thank you.

"When the fly-worms have done their work," Xiu said, "I must drown them to finish the *pul yah.* I will return to tend the wound."

On their way to visit the afternoon's second patient, Xiu told Pesh and Zia that health was balance, whereas illness and disease were imbalance. Balance, influenced by the season and affected favorably or adversely by diet, included mind, body, and spirit. She called sleep a religious experience and insomnia the result of a lack of piety.

Pesh peppered Xiu with questions.

"You show great interest," Xiu said. "These teachings are K'iché beliefs."

Continuing in silence, Pesh pondered Xiu's philosophy of medicine. Even though she understood much of Xiu's K'iché language, she missed nuances of meaning.

In the evening in the village plaza, Pesh and Zia sat cross-legged with Xiu under a half moon and the great star Venus, *Chaac Ek.* Fifteen or twenty Maya from the village and nearby areas joined them around the fire, all of them waiting to hear Xiu's visions.

Coming in from Pesh's right, an elder wearing a white robe blew three notes on a conch shell trumpet. His masked helper handed a cup of *balché* to each woman: Pesh, Zia, Xiu, and two other supplicants. The elder signaled them to drink.

The *balche,* every bit as strong as her grandmother's, burned Pesh's throat. She managed not to choke or cough. Like Xiu, her grandmother Chiich would have seen a vision through the smoke of the fire.

Xiu nodded, and the purification ceremony began. Three Maya chanted solemnly. Their masks depicted jaguar faces and their feather headdresses were taller than a man. The elder crossed himself, east to west, north to south: the sign of the Mayan cross representing the sun crossing the sky and blessing the earth from above. He repeated ritual words in K'iché and blew copal incense smoke across each corner of a table marked with colored ribbons—red for east, black for west, white for north, and yellow for south.

The elder placed offerings of cacao beans, seed corn, and jade beads by the ribbons at each corner. He nodded and blew three notes on the conch shell trumpet. Then he and the masked men walked away into the dark.

Even though she found this part of the ceremony familiar, Pesh's breathing accelerated and she rubbed her jade talisman for comfort.

Xiu, still seated cross-legged, pulled out a small linen satchel suspended from a cord around her neck and worn under her *huipil*. Her ritual pouch held sacred pebbles—greenstone jade, yellow amber, red cinnabar, black obsidian, and white quartz—the colors of the Cosmos: green for life or for the Earth, the others for the cardinal compass directions. She arose and arranged her ritual stones at the corners of the table, beside the offerings for the gods. Breathing deeply of copal smoke and facing the fire, she chanted a wellness spell for those troubled in spirit. Her eyes turned up until only the whites showed.

"Now tell your trouble," Xiu said from her trance state.

It was as though Xiu spoke to her alone. Pesh didn't want to tell Xiu—and thus Zia and the Andersons—that she was a shaman, a fallen *Xmenoob*, or that if she didn't find where her jade jaguar came from, Cimil, that evil god of *Xibalba,* said he'd take her child as a shaman. Not sure how much of all that she believed, she answered, "I must find where my talisman came from."

Zia simply asked Xiu where Pesh should look for jade.

"The gods send jade to the sacred river, guarded by croco-diles," Xiu said in a monotone. "Crocodiles with red eyes, croco-diles larger than a man, crocodiles in a round blue lake. A red lake between two rivers."

Without interpretation, Pesh was clueless. She didn't need a translation for crocodiles or for sacred river or for the colors, but Zia had to help her with the circular lake. How could a lake be both red and blue?

After Xiu answered two other supplicants, Zia asked, "Will Pesh find jade?"

"Pesh wades in the river. Her feet know jade. She hides from the crocodile." Xiu faced the fire and chanted words Pesh didn't understand. Then she swayed and fell to the ground.

Pesh and Zia hurried to her side, and Zia asked, "Are you all right?"

After a few seconds, Xiu awoke. "The gods are displeased. I must rest."

Zia helped Xiu to her hut. While Xiu rested, Zia hung the hammocks inside the hut for the women, and Pesh checked that Ignacio would be comfortable sleeping in the panel truck.

"How'd you do at dominoes?" Pesh asked.

"I lost, but my uncle cheats," Ignacio said. "See you in the morning."

When Pesh retired to a hammock between Xiu and Zia, she lay awake reviewing the day. Xiu, as healing shaman, was the emergency room here. How lucky: the old woman hadn't been hurt when she fell.

Pesh knew why the gods were displeased—she was a fallen *Xmenoob*. She must find the lost jade at any cost.

17

Awakened by the predawn change in light, Pesh arose earlier than Zia and Xiu. She pulled a lightweight blue blanket around her shoulders, walked the trail to the spring behind Alta Altun, and enjoyed a long drink of its cold, pure water. Birds called to each other: *chirr-up*, get up, *see-you-cu-cu*, come enjoy the day. By hearing only their sounds, Kedar could identify birds; Pesh hoped he was all right, out there in the wilderness of the Motagua Valley with Paul.

She returned in time to watch Zia and Xiu stir the breakfast maize gruel over the cooking fire outside in the chilly early morning air. From their conversation, she learned Zia had been born at Alta Altun. Pesh wanted to ask Xiu about the origin of her jade talisman, but she didn't want to mention Cimil. How much should she tell about herself?

"My grandmother was a healing shaman," Pesh began. "Like you, she had a linen sack of sacred stones."

"You have learned much healing from her," Xiu said.

Pesh nodded. "*Chiich* named me *Chanlajun Yaxk'in Yaxuun B'alam*. Fourteen-month-of-the-sun-god, descendant of the northern jaguar king."

Pesh pulled out the carved piece of jade she always wore under her shirt, the talisman the gods gave her on the day she became a shaman, but she wasn't ready to tell that story. "I must find where my little jaguar came from."

"*B'alam!*" Xiu reached out to touch it. "We worship B'alam, jaguar god of the hunt."

"This belonged to a strong shaman." Xiu held Pesh's amulet with both hands and gazed into space.

Pesh waited for Xiu to continue. Did she guess the strong shaman was Pesh, or did she refer to an earlier time?

"You carry the jade B'alam, and you carry the name B'alam." Xiu saw that as an omen, because four powerful jaguars hold up the sky. "You carry power."

"I'm trying to find jade like in my little b'alam," Pesh said. "Where does it come from?"

"You belong to the village B'alam Ha, Jaguar-Water, to the north."

"Where does jade this color come from?" Pesh asked.

"Green is the color of the center of the world." Xiu added that her most powerful visions came from a cave high in the mountains, a sacred cave dedicated to B'alam the Jaguar God, where she inhaled the breath of B'alam.

Pesh didn't want help from the gods of *Xibalba*, the underground realm of spirits. Would Cimil's *no help from the gods* extend to Xiu's vision in a sacred cave?

Xiu rose and rinsed her bowl in a water bucket, and Pesh and Zia did the same.

"You must follow me." Xiu pointed to a narrow trail beside her hut and away from the village, and Pesh and Zia fell into step behind her. Xiu, an old woman, climbed as nimbly as a mountain goat, while Pesh, not used to the mountains, panted and slipped on rough pebbles.

Pesh smelled sulfur and noted the lack of vegetation. The loose rock underfoot made cracking sounds, like breaking glass. She walked over sharp obsidian shards, remnants of volcanic action. Kedar said that Guatemala had more volcanoes than any other country on earth.

Xiu paused at a branch of the trail. "That trail goes to B'alam Ha, north of here."

"How far?" Pesh's heart pounded from the unaccustomed altitude.

"Three days, five days, but we're not going there."

"Then we go west?" Pesh asked.

Xiu pointed to an opening in the mountainside and resumed her brisk stride. She stopped at the cave's entrance and indicated for Pesh and Zia to follow.

Pesh had seen only limestone caves, never one formed by a volcano. Her arms tingled and her heart beat too fast. Was it the altitude—or her fear of caves? She swallowed hard and felt faint, like there wasn't enough air.

Inside, the cool cave smelled like almond blossoms, but unpleasantly so. Inhaling the strange odor, she felt a revolt in her stomach and hoped she wouldn't throw up. The limestone caves in Yucatán were wet and led to *Xibalba*, but this cave was dry. In the flat Yucatán, the Maya built high temples like artificial mountains to be closer to the gods. Pesh was intrigued both as an archaeologist and as a descendant of a king.

Zia lighted a pitch torch and carried it while they followed Xiu through a second opening. Using the flickering light from the torch, Xiu pointed out a mural, a wall of hunters and jaguars hunting for game.

"What is this place?" Pesh looked right and left, up and down. She rushed to the mural, its colors still vibrant, its details clear. Maya in feathered red and green costumes, their skulls elongated in the fashion of the classic period, hunted beside jaguars. But jaguars wouldn't hunt with men—the mural must depict a legend. She had seen Mayan murals portraying battles and kings, but never one of hunters.

"This is B'alam's sacred cave," Xiu said. "I must breathe the breath of B'alam."

Zia mounted the torch in a sconce on the wall. The dancing light illuminated a stone bench behind a small table that held a single object. Pesh picked it up, a skull carved from apple-green stone, not the green of her talisman but the same color as the cross she had seen in the Motagua Valley. A thrill ran up and down her whole body. The center of the stone skull had been carved out, leaving a translucent shell like a gruesome green jack-o-lantern. Alberto had told her about a crystal skull found near Antigua, but not one of green stone. Was it jade?

Xiu took the skull from Pesh and positioned it over a lighted candle. Green light shone through the open eyes and mouth and fluttered throughout the head.

Xiu straddled a stone bench and hung her head over a crack in the floor, a crack that vented almond-like fumes.

"Was my jade talisman blessed here?" Pesh moved closer to Xiu.

"The breath of B'alam." Xiu recited nonsense, but perhaps Pesh didn't catch all the words.

"Did my jade jaguar come from here?" The sweet fumes repelled Pesh.

Xiu said nothing. Zia then asked if Pesh would find jade in the mountains, find jade in a river valley, find jade at all. Xiu, as rigid as the stone bench, seemed not to hear.

Pesh was unable to learn more from Xiu. She returned to the mural, splendid in the dim flickering light. She placed a hand on the painted image of a jaguar and stood still, very still. She tried to evoke a vision of the painters, and a mental image formed of two Maya wearing loincloths. One painted the eyes of the jaguar with a fine brush while the other mixed ocre and charcoal in a mortar—

"It's Xiu!" Zia cried out. "She fell off the bench!"

The Maya disappeared, and Pesh hurried to where Xiu had collapsed on the floor, her face turned away from the rising fumes. She was cold, unresponsive.

Pesh held her jade talisman against Xiu's forehead and crooned a healing lullaby for a sick child. When the jade warmed to body temperature, Xiu awoke in a confused state.

"B'alam doesn't speak," Xiu said. "Not a propitious date for prophecy."

"Can you ask the Daykeeper for a better day?" Pesh asked. Daykeepers, who specialized in counting days on the sacred calendar, often served as priests.

"*Ah-K'in*, the shaman-priest who kept the days, has died," Xiu said in Mayan. "But 1000 Daykeepers live nearby in Momostenango."

"Would a Daykeeper know legends about jade?" Pesh asked. Nearby could mean anything from a day's travel to a week's.

"Of course not. They keep only the sacred days."

"Is there anyone else who could help me?"

"Go to the Land of Mam," Xiu said, again in her oracle-state. "Ask a favor of Maximón."

On the long ride back to Quetzal Centrale, Pesh mulled over what Xiu had said.

"Who is Maximón?" she asked Zia.

"Some faithful Maya who live in remote mountain areas bring Maximón gifts—cigars, money, or liquor—and ask for favors," Zia explained. "He's part of the Holy Week carnival rituals, and his effigy resides in a different house every year."

"Oh." Pesh couldn't think of a verbal response. She had never heard of such a custom.

In her mind, Pesh replayed the cryptic messages from Xiu. B'alam Ha: somewhere to the north. B'alam's sacred cave: a mural on one wall. A thousand Daykeepers in Momostenango: nearby. The Land of Mam: Maximón. A round lake: both red and blue. The clues led nowhere, her reasoning as circular as the red and blue lake.

She was no closer to finding Cimil's lost jade or the origin of her talisman.

18

Kedar, comfortable with the clear skies, refolded his charts and stored them in his flight bag. Not a cloud in sight, triple digit temperatures in the arid valley. No aviation weather information was available here in Guatemala, but, unlike in Texas, he didn't need it: clear and hot. Eager to start today's flight to the Motagua Valley with Paul, he packed sandwiches and plenty of water and sunscreen.

When Kedar went to the heliport on the compound to ready the Bell Jet Ranger, a burly Maya carrying a rifle stood by. *What the devil did he want? Where did he come from?*

"That's my helicopter. Who are you, and why the gun?" Kedar asked, guessing that Spanish was the *lingua franca.*

"I am Arturo and I guard *Señor* Anderson today."

Kedar didn't notice a second Maya, also armed, until he stepped forward.

"I am Cesaro."

Kedar considered asking if they were guarding his helicopter or hijacking it, but decided against that idea. *Paul must have hired them.* He finished checking out the aircraft and left Arturo and Cesaro at parade rest.

Back in the dining room, Paul still worked on his tortillas and scrambled eggs. He had spread out yesterday's newspaper on the table on both his right and his left. The Andersons usually read the news a day late because Quetzal Centrale was too far from Antigua to have the paper pitched onto their porch, but the news seldom affected them directly. Except for earthquakes, and those announced themselves.

Kedar took a seat across from Paul but a little far for comfortable communication. The Andersons' dining room table was large enough to seat sixteen people.

"Good morning again," Kedar said, when Paul didn't look up. "You need bodyguards for this trip?"

"This is Guatemala. The crime lords think I'm rich."

"Well, aren't you rich?" Kedar poured himself a second cup of coffee.

"That's rich." Paul laughed at his own joke, but Kedar didn't see the humor.

"Only because Vanna's such a good businesswoman." Paul rearranged his tableware. "We came here as archaeologists searching for the lost jade of the ancient Maya. We wanted to find their source. Where did the Maya find all those riches buried with their kings?"

"That's what Pesh and I are trying to discover."

"At first, no one bothered us. We were *locos, idiotas*. After finding the first jade source, and an ancient workshop to boot, a good archaeologist would have reported it. We didn't."

"Why not?" Kedar sipped his coffee, anticipating a good story.

"I looked at that big beautiful boulder, and I wanted to learn to work jade. How did the ancients do it? I could put Guatemalan jade into the world market."

"So that made you rich?"

"Not yet, not in twenty years. The only change is that we've been blackballed by academia." Paul laughed and pushed back from the table. "I sold everything I owned in the U.S. and borrowed money from investors. Everything here is in overhead—the land, the equipment, the store, the factory."

"So you've invested your heart and soul in Guatemalan jade."

"That's right. We do everything legally. We've spent years building this business, started two other retail outlets, but we haven't finished paying off the loans." Paul's voice trailed off and he seemed to focus on a point twenty feet behind Kedar.

"You seem to have a good business and treat local people fairly," Kedar said, trying to understand. "Then why were you blackballed?"

"Our jade products are too good." Paul looked pained. "Other archaeologists thought we were making forgeries or selling artifacts on the black market."

"Pesh and I have located new sources of jade for you," Kedar said. "How does that fit into the picture?"

"With new finds, I'll report the first ones." Paul chased the tortilla crumbs on his plate with a fork. "We've removed most of the jade from them already."

"Okay. But I still don't understand, why the armed guards?" Kedar pushed away his cup of cold coffee.

"Drug lords and other thieves watch us closely—especially one called Crocodile. Sometimes I think they know more about my money than I do. I'm going to buy land from *campesinos*—in cash. If Crocodile finds out I have cash, I will need the guards."

"I've seen the iron grill gates around businesses in Antigua and the guards at the bank," Kedar said. Guatemala must be even tougher than he'd been told.

"I want to put claims on the areas that promise jade. After it's all registered, the Guatemalan government will help me to prosecute poachers."

"Poachers? Help from a corrupt government?"

"That brings us back to the beginning of the discussion," Paul said. "Now I can't let poachers know the source of our raw material. And *El Cocodrilo*—the Crocodile—he's the worst of the bunch. He watches my every move. I swear—he's stalking me."

"I see. Are you ready for today's adventure?" Kedar asked, his curiosity satisfied.

At the heliport, Kedar loaded Arturo, Cesaro, and the rifles in the back of the Ranger and stationed Paul on his right in the co-pilot's seat.

"Keep your seatbelts fastened," he announced through the intercom system. "We'll hit rough air when we descend into the Motagua Valley."

The guys in the back didn't look like they had a clue, and they weren't buckled in.

"Paul, please give Arturo and Cesaro my safety announcement in Spanish. Everyone must keep his seatbelt fastened." Kedar noticed the rifles propped against the side of the cabin. "Tell them that goes for rifles, too. Put the safeties on and lay the guns across the floor."

When they complied, Kedar took off. The helicopter rose, rotors thumping rhythmically.

Kedar had no weather report, but common sense dictated turbulence over the southern slopes of the Sierra de las Minas. That was the only arid region in Guatemala, with temperatures in the triple digits. He directed Paul to follow the GPS coordinates on the map and to double check the macrophobe readings over their target.

"See that outcropping? This is it," Paul said.

Kedar landed near the rock outcropping. Pesh had marked it on the map as a probable source of jadeite. The three passengers disembarked. Paul went to work, pinging his hammer, and the two guards watched him until Paul told them to go sit down.

Glad he'd remembered his broadbrimmed hat, Kedar stood beside Paul in the full sun. Arturo and Cesaro napped in the partial shade of scraggly bushes.

"This is the real thing, all right," Paul announced, after an hour of tapping and testing. "We're going to buy all the land near this jade strike."

Paul woke up Arturo and Cesaro, and he and his bodyguards hiked to nearby dwellings where peasants lived. He left Kedar to guard the helicopter in the heat.

Kedar had nothing to do—except wait. *Thank God for the helicopter's shade. And for this, he had a college degree in geology?*

When Paul returned—near sunset—he explained that he had purchased land from *campesinos* for cash: another 400-acre chunk.

"Only three or four dwellings left to visit," he said. "We need to return in a couple days."

Kedar took off with enough daylight to make Quetzal Centrale before full dark. He knew why Paul carried money.

Paul said Guatemala would have no claim to his jade after he registered ownership. He could report the location of the first jade he had found—now mined out—as well as the ancient jade workshop. Perhaps he would again be accepted in archaeological circles.

Kedar could hardly wait to tell Pesh—he had solved the mystery of where Paul got his money. And why Paul had wanted them to look for jade. And why he had bodyguards. The danger in searching for jade came only after finding it. It didn't pay to stand out with a nicer car than the neighbors or by seeming to have money. That must be why Paul never polished his van.

The menace in Guatemala came not from bad water and earthquakes but from gangs of thugs and crime lords. Perception was everything, and Paul appeared to be rich by owning a jade mine. If crime lords thought you were wealthy, then the thieves and kidnappers came out in droves.

But Kedar had nothing to fear. He had nothing the gangs could turn into money, and he could hold his own in a street fight.

19

"Remember—no stopping until Antigua." Ignacio, the Andersons' driver from Quetzal Centrale, parked under the magnolia tree and waited for everyone to load: Pesh, Isolde, Vanna, and Yash.

"Here, sit in the front where you can see the sights," Pesh said. She held the door for Isolde and climbed into the middle seat with Vanna and Yash.

"Kedar's not coming?" Isolde asked.

"Next time," Pesh said. "He's delivering supplies to B'alam Witz today."

Yash stood and leaned forward to whisper in Isolde's ear: "Ignacio drives really fast because there are *banditos*."

Overhearing Yash, Pesh said, "But I have never seen any." The Andersons kept their white van in top running order but left it battered and unwashed so as not to attract *envidia*, envy. According to Vanna, to appear wealthy in Guatemala was to paint a large red target on your car door.

"I'm looking forward to showing off our jade shop," Vanna said.

"She has a museum and a very old ax with no handle," Yash said.

"If I'm going to work part time in the shop," Pesh said, "I need to find out how to deal with difficult situations. What if someone brings in a carved piece of jade?"

"If it's ancient, find out where it came from. They'll want money. Bargain, and if the price is less than $5,000, tell them I'll buy it. That keeps it off the black market."

"What if it's stolen?" *Bargaining—with looters?*

"That's tricky." Vanna flipped her long red hair away from her face and seemed to consider her answer. "Then it's a police matter, but good luck on getting a response."

"If they bring in a river stone, I'll get you and Paul to test it." Pesh wondered if those purchases accounted for the Andersons' mysterious wealth. "How do you price raw jade, if top quality?"

"What the market will bear." Vanna became more serious. "Per ounce, jade's right up there with gold and diamonds. But only after it's worked."

"Like dealing in gold, then," Pesh said. "The Maya always valued jade more than gold, and the Aztec called gold the excrement of the sun."

"Sun poop!" Vanna roared with a belly laugh as loud as Isolde's guffaws. "Gold shit!"

"Those are bad words," Yash said. "Grandma says you can't ever say them."

Isolde turned to stare at Yash, and Vanna convulsed with mirth.

Yash looked down and bit her lip.

"Oh, Honey!" Vanna stopped snorting and touched Yash's shoulder. "I wasn't laughing at you. It's that, you looked so absolutely serious."

Yash smiled but didn't answer.

"Your grandmother taught me about words a lady should never say," Pesh said.

"It's a matter of good manners, *Liebchen,*" Isolde said. "You have to be old enough to know when it's all right to say bad words."

"I'll be seven tomorrow. Is that old enough to say … you know?"

"We'll talk more tomorrow," Isolde said.

Pesh mused, a whole year since they first planned this trip to Guatemala. Getting grants to use the helicopter and permission from the university had been a slow process.

Upon reaching the outskirts of town, Yash jumped up between the seats and pointed at *Volcán de Fuego* towering over Antigua. "Vanna, tell her about the volcano!"

"I have never seen an active volcano," Isolde said.

"After dark, it belches fire and puts on a show," Vanna said. "We'll watch it on the way home."

Pesh saw children peddling produce on the sidewalk. *They should be in school.*

Ignacio parked by the shop's front door and Vanna unlocked the chain wrapped about the entrance to her business, *Taller del Jade Maya*. She gave Isolde and Yash a tour of the shop and the small jade museum while Pesh talked to tourists and manned the checkout station.

"You should see the tourist area," Vanna told Isolde. "You could get Yash an ice cream cone at the bus station."

"Come on, Grandma." Yash yanked Isolde's arm. "It'll be fun."

"Don't pay attention if people stare," Vanna said. "They won't mean any harm. They have never seen such a tall woman. Especially one with a long white braid in the back, the same hairstyle worn by many Mayan women."

"Don't worry about us. Come, Liebchen."

"Have a good time. The bus station is eight blocks, to the right." Vanna sent them on their way and returned to the retail area. "Any problems, Pesh?"

"Not yet. This is fun. I sold a $100 jade carving."

"Then you won't mind running the shop while I tend to errands." On her way out the door, Vanna said, "I'll be back in a while."

Two American tourists, dressed in white running shoes and shorts bulging at the waist, came into the store. The man looked bored, as though waiting for his wife to make a purchase so he could get out of there.

"Do you have children?" Pesh asked. "These jade disks will keep them safe."

"Really?" the woman asked. "How does that work?"

"Mayan jade is lucky," Pesh said. "Maya warriors wore a disk like this when they went into battle. A boy would like one."

"We don't have any boys, but I'd like to wear one for fun," the man said.

"These two are a pair. Notice that they come from the same piece of jade," Pesh said. "If two lovers wear them, they can communicate with each other."

The man, whom Pesh had thought bored, bought the pair. The woman bought two carved figures, a rabbit and a monkey. As Vanna had said, a good story makes a good sale.

After only a few minutes, a Guatemalan woman—a Maya dressed in traditional long skirt and sandals—came into the store and glanced around in every direction, as though lost.

"How may I help you?" Pesh asked, first in Spanish, then in Mayan.

"I want to sell this jade mask." Whispering, the woman pushed a lifesize greenstone mosaic mask, its eyes and mouth inlaid with shell, almost into Pesh's chin. She gripped the mask so tightly that her knuckles had gone white and looked behind at the doorway. "*Por favor.*"

"Let me see it." The mask felt like serpentine, not jade. Pesh had seen its picture in the newspaper only last week—stolen from a museum. Excavated at Monte Alto, a Pre-Classic site. The paper described it only as "greenstone." *¡Ay caramba!*

"Where do you think the mask is from?" Pesh had a bad feeling in the pit of her stomach.

"The south coast," the woman said, shifting her eyes here and there as if she looked for the answer on the ceiling. "That's where we found it."

"On the beach? Where, near La Democracia?"

"That's it," the woman said, gazing at the ceiling.

Big coincidence: she's lying. Pesh asked, "Do you think it's old?"

"Old—it's Pre-Classic." She checked the doorway behind again.

"Old indeed," Pesh said. Archaeological jargon. How would the woman know, unless she had stolen it? She lied about finding it, but she's worried about something outside.

"What do you think it's worth?" Pesh asked.

"I want thirty thousand American dollars."

"I can offer you three thousand. It's serpentine, not jade." Pesh recalled that Vanna said not to pay too much. However, a serpentine mask, if carved by the ancients, was priceless.

"My husband wants $30,000." The woman looked toward the door. She had a purple bruise on her cheek. "He's right outside."

"I can promise $5,000, *no mas*. I only work here." *A stolen mask!* She couldn't let her get away with it, even though the woman was only a pawn. The husband did it, and he hit her, too. But a crime lord surely owned the husband.

Clutching the mask to her bosom, the woman shook her head.

"Then I must call the owner of the shop." Pesh retreated to the office and called the police instead. They put her on hold. *¡Dios en cielo!*

She could hang up now, as though nothing had happened, but this was a stolen Mayan artifact! Vanna said the police were corrupt—would they respond?

"*Hola. ... Sí, Taller del Jade Maya.*" Finally, the police were coming. How could she entice the woman to stick around until they came?

Standing at the front of the shop, the woman flicked her eyes from the door to the mask.

"I'm sorry," Pesh said. "You'll have to wait for Vanna. Would you like a cup of tea?"

The woman didn't answer but took a seat on the folding chair Pesh offered.

"Do you have children? I have one, a girl." Pesh poured tea into two cups from the small thermos behind the counter.

"I have three." The woman seemed to relax but said, "I have to go soon."

"Did your husband hit you?" Pesh asked.

The woman's eyes filled with tears.

"This tea is *maté*, from Argentina." Pesh was sorry she had notified the authorities—too late to take it back. Not knowing what to say, Pesh changed to small talk.

The woman sipped the tea. Pesh swallowed one mouthful—too hot, too sweet, awful stuff—and deserted her cup when three tourists came in. She talked to Vanna's customers and sold a few trinkets, but time was passing. Were the police ever going to come? Pesh's heart raced and her stomach clenched. She needed to give the woman an opportunity to leave or at least to explain.

When the shoppers finally left, she confronted the woman, who remained on the chair and clutched the mask.

"I don't know where Vanna is, but that mask looks like a stolen one," Pesh said. "I read about it in the newspaper."

"No. We found this one." The woman looked toward the ceiling.

"But it looks so much like the stolen one pictured in the newspaper." Pesh drew in a deep breath. The only way to handle this—be honest and direct. "I called the police."

"¡No! No policía!"

"I'll give you a choice," Pesh said. "You can either leave it here and walk out the door, or you can wait for the authorities."

"I have to ask my husband." The woman jumped up, her face blank in typical Mayan fashion, and ran to the door, the mask cradled in her arms.

With incredible timing, the police pulled up to the curb. Two uniformed officers—guns in their belts—grabbed the screaming woman. The husband sped away. One cop held the woman's elbow and escorted her back into the store while the other stood by.

"Is this the stolen mask?" the policeman asked.

"Yes, I think so." Pesh's heart beat as fast as a hummingbird's. That poor woman, the bruise on her face, stood glaring. Pesh's hand shook when she signed the statement. "Will I have to testify in court?"

"*Sí, señora, si dice usted verdad.*"

"*Sí,* I have given you the truth." Pesh answered with great apprehension, not looking forward to appearing in court. The husband who sped away—where did he fit into this? A crime lord must be involved.

The cops led away the handcuffed woman, who turned to face Pesh one more time.

"You'll be sorry!" she yelled in Mayan, struggling to free her hand.

"*¡Vámonos!*" The officer on the other end of the handcuff yanked her arm and shoved her into the back of the police van.

From the open door, Pesh watched them drive away. She felt like crying. While she tried to calm herself, Vanna turned the corner and hustled toward her.

"You'll never guess what happened while you were gone," Pesh began.

"Oh-my-god!" Vanna said before Pesh finished her story. "What were you thinking of? This is Guatemala. There will be reprisals—it's like you painted a big red bull's eye on your forehead!"

"Let's not worry Isolde." Pesh's stomach knotted, but she lifted her chin in an attempt to look confident. She had done the right thing.

As though Pesh had called her, Yash skipped through the front door, six steps ahead of her grandmother.

"Come here, Sweetheart." Pesh hugged Yash and wiped ice cream off her chin. "I can tell you had chocolate."

"Let's read, Grandma." Yash led Isolde to a chair in Vanna's office.

Pesh forced her clenched fists to relax. It wasn't fair for the woman to go to jail for what her husband had done. Maybe she could voice that opinion in court.

Pesh bit her lip and fought an urge to twist her braid. She told herself to stop overreacting.

A few days later, when Pesh and Kedar entered the Anderson's dining room, Paul had spread yesterday's newspaper across one end of the table.

"Listen to this!" Paul called their attention to an article in *Prensa Libre*, the Guatemala City newspaper.

"*Profesor* Carlos León de la Barra, *El Museo Nacional Arqueología*, announced the return of the funeral mask stolen last month from *El Museo de La Democracia*. This exceptional greenstone mask was part of the funerary offerings uncovered in the grave of a nobleman buried in 527 AD. The Mayan artifact was turned in to the police by *Chanlajun Pex de Taller del Jade Maya en Antigua*."

"Well, you're in the news now, Kiddo." Paul dropped the paper onto the table.

"That's terrible news," Vanna said. "Thank God they didn't run your photograph."

Pesh wanted to curl up into a little ball. Her stomach convulsed with worry. She hoped Guatemalan crime kings didn't read the paper.

"Don't worry, Sweetheart." Kedar handed her a glass of red wine. "Anybody bothers you, I'll clean their clocks. I didn't train in martial arts for nothing."

"What if they have guns?" Pesh drew in a deep breath.

"Just stay where there are lots of people," Kedar said.

"That's why the fence at Quetzal Centrale." Vanna went on, reporting that Guatemala City had more than forty murders every week, and El Salvador, Honduras, and Guatemala constituted the most violent area in the world outside of actual war zones. "But Antigua is a safe place for tourists."

Pesh sipped her wine, then had another. Maybe Guatemalan crime lords couldn't read at all. *Hay no problema*, as Alberto would say. *Don't go alone to Antigua.*

20

A circular red and blue lake: what could that mean? Perhaps Alberto could interpret Xiu's mysterious messages. Pesh invited him to share a pitcher of pineapple-guava juice with her and Kedar in a shady spot under the magnolia tree in front of the Andersons' mansion.

"Maybe you can help us, *por favor,*" she said, handing Alberto a glass of juice.

"Anything for you, *Señora* Pesh."

"Zia introduced me to *Xmenoob* Xiu, and we asked her where to find jade." Pesh positioned herself between Alberto and Kedar.

Leaning back against the tree trunk, Alberto said, "Xiu knows those things."

"But I didn't understand her answers." Pesh quoted Xiu's cryptic Mayan words. "How can a lake have the shape of a circle and be both red and blue?"

"Hm-m-m." Alberto looked toward the sky. "A red lake—red means east. Maybe Xiu's lake is to the east."

"To the east?" Kedar opened his geological map. "Many areas have incomplete maps, but to the east of Guatemala City, there is a circular lake. Nearly a perfect circle on the map."

"Of course! A lake, in the shape of a circle—that has to be *Laguna Lachuá.* It's worth a visit, jade or no," Alberto said. "You might see a quetzal or a crocodile."

"It's the only lake like that on the map," Kedar said.

"And famous for its bad smell, like rotten eggs," Alberto said. "In K'iché, *la chu ha* means fetid water. It cures skin diseases—scaly white patches, hives, or warts."

"The Maya would have known that," Pesh said.

"Laguna Lachuá lies within a national park, here." Kedar pointed to a spot on his map. "Within dense jungle."

"Go there like tourists," Alberto said. "The bus is cheap. You won't need a car."

Three days later, Ignacio dropped Pesh and Kedar at La Termina in Antigua. He indicated the once-a-day bus for the five-hour trip to Laguna Lachuá National Park and waved goodbye.

La Termina smelled like tamales intermingled with stale urine and strong body odor. The building buzzed with vendors selling hats, sunglasses, and snacks. Babies cried, childen ran about, and a seated beggar playing a guitar called out for coins. Pesh shook her head *no* to the guitar player but purchased two mangos from a ragged boy who looked no older than Yash.

Kedar paid for their tickets at a booth watched by an armed guard, as on every occasion where money changed hands, and Pesh stood behind him. While walking to their bus, Kedar pointed to a fleet of multi-colored vehicles, independently owned local buses, some bound for Guatemala City.

"Check out the chicken buses," he said. "That's what Ignacio called them."

Pesh was so busy looking that she didn't wonder about the name. The polished buses, like peacocks fanning bright feathers, parked in a long line by the fence while their *ayudantes* strutted and screamed, "*¡Guate! Guate!*" Each driver stayed in his bus while his partner, the *ayudante,* sold tickets, loaded passengers, and piled luggage onto the roof.

Each polished bus wore flambouyant colors and bore a brightly painted name. *La Cometa Dorada* (Golden Comet) was lime green and mango orange; *Estella Blanca* (White Star) was blue, fluorescent pink, and white; and *Primorosa* (Exquisite) was red, yellow, and black. She didn't have time to look at all the pictures on even one rolling bulletin board.

"Come on. It's time to load," Kedar said.

Pesh pushed into the line, scrambled onto the bus, and slid into a window seat. Kedar struck up a conversation with the Canadian students Brad and John seated behind them.

"Did you notice the chicken buses?" Kedar asked. "Why are they called that?"

"How could we miss them?" Brad said. "They bring live chickens aboard, and everyone's packed in like chickens on the way to the slaughterhouse."

"No, that's not it." John leaned forward and laughed. "You'll find out why if you ride one from Antigua to Guatemala City."

"Don't you recognize this bus?" Brad asked.

"No. Should I?" Kedar asked, gripping the bar above the seat in front as the bus lurched out of the parking lot.

"We rode to elementary school in this old relic, or in one like it," Brad said.

"What happens is, the U.S. and Canada send their outdated school buses here and to other places in Central America," John said. "To the Philippines, too."

"That bus didn't turn into the 'Magic School Bus' when it got older," Brad said. "It became a drag queen and moved to Guatemala."

John slapped his thighs and roared with laughter, but Pesh didn't get the joke. She had never ridden in a school bus. She had run for half an hour every morning to be early enough to help Madre Magdalena, her elementary school teacher, and Kedar drove Yash to the Catholic school every day. She fell into her own thoughts.

The red and blue bus to Laguna Lachuá whined and wobbled like a washing machine with an uneven load on its climb on the dry side of the mountains. The area was arid because the Sierra de las Minas formed a barrier to winds bearing rain.

The tourists rode quietly, some of them trying to read, some taking a nap. How could anyone read, while the bus negotiated such curves?

After the bus crossed the summit, it dropped down on the north side of the mountains, the rainy side, into a lush cloud forest. Outside the window, mist shrouded rolling mountains and evergreen trees, and hundreds of *ceiba* trees poked up out of the rain forest in the distance.

"What a view!" Pesh pointed from the half-open window. "I can see why the ancients called this land *guatemala*, the land of trees."

"It's good to have someone else do the driving." Kedar grasped her hand. "I'm so glad to have you to myself for a few days."

The touch of his hand sent a tingle from her fingers all the way up her arm to her shoulder.

"We never seem to have time for the two of us," he said. "Do you realize this is the first time we've gone away together without Yash?"

Pesh squeezed his hand.

"Let's make the most of it, a mini-vacation."

"And a chance to talk," Pesh said. "I haven't told you everything I learned from Xiu."

Pesh reviewed everything she could remember about Xiu's visits to the sick and ended her report with, "She rubbed a piece of jade on an old man's stomach—he had kidney trouble—and gave him a potion to ease pain."

"Most of the cure, you know, is because they believe it," Kedar said. "Here's a tidbit of word history. Because of its supposed beneficial effect on the kidneys, the stone nephrite was called *lapis nephriticus*, from Greek for kidney. And of course, nephrite is a form of jade."

"Now there's a conversation stopper," Pesh said. "But go back to the part about believing it. Xiu treats the whole person, body, mind, and spirit, and much of her healing techniques are like my grandmother's. Besides, she's *Xmenoob*, a shaman who sees visions in the campfire. She said I have a troubled spirit."

"Do you?"

"I need to tell you. Remember, last year, when Burt asked me where my jade jaguar came from? I tried to find out by traveling to the cave at B'alam Witz in a vision."

"No! You promised—no more dabbling in the black arts." In a voice loud enough for other travelers to hear, Kedar said, "You frighten me with your spells. It's like you had a hotline to Beelzebub."

"Beelzebub?" Pesh turned around to see who was listening. "He isn't a Mayan god."

"He's a fallen angel," Kedar said, "Second only to Satan. A devil of the Philistines."

"Oh, you mean like in the Bible." Pesh lowered her voice. "I've been trying to tell you, I'm a fallen *Xmenoob*."

Pesh explained, instead of helping her trace her jade talisman, the lord of the underworld Cimil called her a disgraced shaman. She could redeem herself if she could find her jaguar's origin without calling upon the gods. But she couldn't bring herself to add Cimil's price for failure: to claim Yash as a shaman.

Kedar frowned and said, "I see," but from the way he set his chin, he didn't understand. She did feel better, having talked to him. She had told no one about her encounter with Cimil. *Why would a lecturer at the university be hearing voices from unfamiliar gods from a thousand years ago?*

A fallen *Xmenoob*—maybe she wasn't a shaman any more. She felt suddenly lighter.

The locals left the bus at wide spots in the road, leaving aboard only those traveling to the park. The students, mostly from the U.S. or Europe, had backpacks large enough to crawl inside. They reminded Pesh of turtles. The man with wooly-camel hair and a blond fellow with a carefully trimmed mustache spoke French loudly and nonstop. Three men and a woman, dressed identically in black shorts and athletic shoes, spread out across the rear seat, drinking beers and becoming more raucous with every mile. Preferring to be left with her thoughts, Pesh didn't communicate with any of them.

At the entrance to the park, Kedar took her hand.

"Let's start the day over and just have fun," he said.

"I'd like that," she said, squeezing his hand.

As Pesh had expected, the rustic hotel had rough lumber walls and a thatch roof, and visitors brought their own food. The lobby had comfortable-looking bamboo cane chairs, but they wouldn't have time to use them.

The clerk at the check-in desk gave them a room key and a warning: "Don't leave any food out overnight in our kitchen." Spreading his hands out twelve inches, he added, "The Guatemalan rats are this big, and they eat everything."

"I hope you aren't measuring them between their eyes," Kedar said, and the two men enjoyed a good laugh.

Kedar's exaggerations amused Pesh, and their spotless room showed no signs of rats or insects. She had packed fruit and beans and tortillas as well as drinking water. A potted plant hung from a hook over a desk in the corner, and a brochure listing activities for tourists and information about the area lay on top of the double bed.

"In case a critter comes looking for food." Kedar took down the plant and set it under the desk, then wrapped his belt around their bag of food and hung it from the hook. "This is what to do when camping if there are bears around."

"The only bears in Guatemala are in the zoo," she said.

"Who knows? The room looks neater now." Kedar flopped onto the bed and opened the brochure. "Want to go for a midnight swim, in the crystalline waters of Laguna Lachuá?"

"I'm more interested in the evening boat ride to explore Río Ikbolay."

"Then let's take a walk."

Pesh's feet crunched on limestone pebbles and she smelled sulfur stink. Closer to the water, a sign posted along the boardwalk warned against stepping on what looked like white sand. The beach was a dangerously thin limestone shelf, limestone mire, not sand. From the white bank of the turquoise circular lagoon, the forested peak of La Sultana dominated the horizon over the Ixcán jungle, and below the surface, red, blue and orange fish swam in the warm, clear water.

While they stood enjoying the view, Kedar opened the park's information packet. The brochure showed the national park as a square patch of forest floating on an area of deforestation caused by illegal logging operations. Razor-sharp park boundaries stood out from quilt-like fields that surrounded a giant mirror in the middle of nowhere. Reading on, Laguna Lachuá was 173 meters above sea level and 220 meters deep with a surface area of 4 square kilometers.

"That means," he said, "the lake floor is 47 meters below sea level. That's about 150 feet below sea level. I always do better with feet and yards. A *karstic* lake, three miles across, 720 feet deep."

"Sometimes it's hard to have a husband who's a geologist. What's *karstic*?"

"Well, the lake is a type of *cenote*, and it's deep—too deep for a scuba diver to explore," Kedar said. "If jade artifacts were thrown into this *cenote* like the one at Chichén Itzá, nobody would ever recover them."

"Maybe *Xmenoob* Xiu predicts a deposit of raw jade." She wondered, had they come to the right place?

"Very unlikely in this terrain," he said.

They took a path away from the lake. Pesh smelled vanilla and picked a white blossom for Kedar. Vanilla orchid vines wrapped themselves tightly around tree trunks and climbed up to reach the top of the canopy for rain and light, vines hundreds of feet high with green pods eight inches long. Many tree trunks had thorns, their branches covered with phosphorescent green moss. With so much calcite in the water, tree branches that fell into the lake became calcite skeletons. A lone crocodile splashed into the water, and howler monkeys called one another.

"Howler monkeys, all noise and no bite," Pesh said, laughing.

"The first time I heard one of those in the night," Kedar said, "I pictured a seven-foot creature with big teeth—coming to eat me!"

"Closer to one foot," Pesh said. "They're tiny."

Around a bend and at the edge of the forest, they came across the Ikbolay, a green river that ran underground through the hills and emerged blue on the other side. It had left dry caves as it changed course over the centuries.

"There's your blue," Kedar said. "And there's where your jade is hidden, deep, deep down. Or in those caves."

"No, no caves today." Pesh didn't like caves. "No Mayan ruins here. This can't be where Xiu meant."

"Maybe, in the old days, they visited the lake to cure some disease," Kedar said. "Bathing in a spa or drinking mineral water, like in Europe."

"Alberto said the water cures skin diseases. They might have come here to cure people, but not to bury a king with his jade treasures." Pesh bent over and picked up a discarded plastic water bottle. "My ancestors respected the earth. I'll recycle this."

"I want a sample of that water for Xiu," Pesh said. "This bottle's the right size." She removed her boots and socks and waded into the lake holding a white tree branch for balance. The shallow water was warm from the sun and white slime dripped from the branch. When she returned, she worked her wet feet into her socks.

"At least you won't get athlete's foot," Kedar said, "pickling yourself like that."

Her hand dried in the warm air. Covered by a thin film of calcite precipitate, it looked like she wore a single white glove. Any jade pebbles here would be painted white. But how would jade get here?

"Couldn't the river carry jade stones and drop them into the lagoon as it slowed?" she asked. "Like gold nuggets travelling downstream?"

"No, the geology is wrong, and you'd never find it there." Kedar pointed to the lake's edge. "It'd be coated in white, like that dead tree."

"Xiu said I'd find jade with my feet."

"You already did." Kedar laughed and shook his head. "Remember—you tripped over a *celt* when you happened upon that ancient jade workshop."

"I thought Xiu meant I'd wade in a murky river, feel jade with my feet. Hide from the crocodile."

"This looks absolutely clear," Kedar said, lifting her sample of lake water and holding it in the sunlight. "But this place stinks like rotten eggs. The high level of sulfur indicates the possible presence of petroleum under the lake."

"Too bad jade has no odor," she said.

"That figures. Look there," Kedar said. A red macaw landed in a tree above them, and he imitated its call. When he answered another birdcall, a yellow and orange bird flew by his head. "Want to see a quetzal?"

"Where?" Pesh looked into the trees overhead. "I've never seen one."

"I'll call one for you. They sound like this on the Internet: *See-woo, see-woo, scee-eet.*"

"There, look!" Pesh held her breath and her heart skipped a beat. Such a long green tail, it had to be a quetzal. "This is the first time I saw a quetzal! The first time ever!"

"They don't call me bird caller for nothing." Kedar captured the bird with his camera.

Afterwards, they returned to the hotel to dine in their room and get ready for the evening excursion on Rio Ikbolay.

At ten o'clock, they walked over the edge of the lake on a wooden ramp supported by piers white from calcite and waited in a cabana ten feet above the water. Soon they boarded a black rubber Zodiac pontoon-boat to travel down the blue river. The guide spotlighted wildlife with his flashlight beam—red-eyed crocodiles, their eyes a brilliant ruby-red.

"There's your red," Kedar said.

Red— Pesh shuddered at a memory that popped up out of nowhere. She had seen red blood bubble up in the river when a crocodile took a man. She grabbed Kedar's arm.

"Are you okay?" Kedar held her by the elbow.

"Just thinking about those red hungry eyes." *Xiu had warned, hide from the crocodile.*

After midnight, they picked their way to their hotel room by flashlight: no electricity after eight o'clock. Kedar lowered the bag of food for a snack, removed two mangos, and then hoisted the bag back onto the hook. He handed Pesh a mango and upended the flashlight to shine a cone of light. They sat on the end of the bed, there being no chair. Mango juice ran down Pesh's arm and dripped on the sheet.

"This is messy." Pesh tried to clean herself with a paper towel. She wrapped the used towel around the mango skins and seeds and placed the refuse package into the wastebasket.

She turned out the light and snuggled in next to Kedar. "Do you remember the time you fell out of the hammock when you tried to kiss me goodnight?"

"Look where that got me!" Kedar laughed and pulled her closer.

Later, Pesh awoke because something scurried across her toes. She shot up, pulling the sheet off Kedar, and shook his shoulder.

Kedar grabbed the flashlight and spotlighted an animal that disappeared through a gap under their door. "The biggest rat I ever saw!"

"It's as big as a cat!" Pesh said.

"It must have smelled those mango seeds." Kedar flashed their hanging pack. "I'm glad I hung up the food."

"It could have bit my fingers." Pesh pulled the sheet up around her shoulders until only her chin stuck out. "I smell like a mango."

"It's gone now." Kedar jumped out of bed and placed the wastebasket and the mango pits outside their door in the hall. "Go back to sleep."

"What if it comes back?"

"Don't worry. I'll chase it away." Kedar climbed back into bed, his flashlight still illuminating the room. "Cuddle up close."

The cuddling was nice but the rat was not.

"We've seen enough," Pesh said. "Let's get back on the bus in the morning."

"Okay, but not back to Quetzal Centrale. They don't expect us for two more nights. Let's go to Guatemala City for a night on the town."

"I feel guilty, leaving Yash for us to have fun."

"She's a big girl now, seven years old. She likes Alberto's stories, and she's trying to teach Spanish to her grandmother. She won't miss us."

"What about our search for jade?"

"Oh, come on." Kedar hugged her and turned off the flashlight. "We deserve a day off."

21

Early in the morning at Lake Lachuá, Pesh and Kedar boarded the red and blue bus to return to Antigua and mostly slept along the way, a five-hour bumpy trip following lumbering semi-rigs. At La Termina, they stretched their legs and shopped for a chicken bus to Guatemala City.

"How about that one?" Kedar pointed to *el Cometa Esmeralda*, painted emerald green with yellow flashes and sporting lots of chrome. The random flowers and jungle animals on its front and sides had nothing to do with comets, and neither did the orange spots on the tire rims.

"Let's sit by a window," Pesh said.

The *Green Comet*, growling in low gear, lumbered to the Las Cañas summit in the mountains surrounding Antigua. When it increased speed on the downhill trip to Guatemala City, Pesh felt every curve. The entire bus body rattled about and threatened to lose a side panel.

A second chicken bus, travelling even faster, passed them on a blind curve as though this were their personal racetrack.

"I see why they call this a chicken bus," Kedar said. "It's the Roller Coaster of Doom."

White-knuckled, Pesh looked out the window at the steep drop-off only a few feet away. Kedar called it a roller coaster—she had never ridden on one and never wanted to. Too much like the *doom* part.

Pesh stepped off the bus after sunset. Even the fried chicken joint at the crowded bus station employed an armed security guard. Ragged children, no older than ten, peddled fruit and snacks, and one pleaded with Kedar for a dollar.

"We're not eating here," Kedar said. He returned to *la Cometa Esmeralda* and gave the driver, who called himself *el piloto*, a ten-dollar bill to drop them in the tourist section on his way back to Antigua. The driver loaded his bus, took the detour, and let them off in front of the Holiday Inn.

"Let's pretend we're American tourists," Kedar said. "See how the other half lives."

Inside the elegant lobby, the hotel clerk, dressed in slacks with a white shirt and tie, looked Kedar up and down. Pesh glanced at her rumpled shorts and muddy jungle boots—Kedar looked equally grubby and disheveled.

"We spent a week back at Lake Lachuá National Park," Kedar said. "We need a room for two nights."

The clerk looked doubtful until Kedar spoke to him in English and whipped out his Visa card. Payment in hand, the young man gave Kedar a key.

Their room looked like it belonged in a palace. It had all the conveniences expected by Americans, including air-conditioning, which Pesh turned off. They showered and changed and took a taxi to Restaurante Tua, recommended by Google as one of the best restaurants in Guatemala City. At the restaurant, the *maitre d'hôtel* wore a tuxedo and escorted them to their table with a grand flourish.

"This is first class." Kedar grasped Pesh's hand under the table. "The trip took the whole day, but worth it."

"And no rats," Pesh said, laughing.

They clinked glasses of red wine, and two guitarists came by to serenade *la Señora Pesh*.

"You put them up to that, didn't you?" she asked.

Kedar only smiled. A waiter appeared, bearing their plates on a silver platter, delightful food from the first bite.

"This *Chipotle Pollo* is perfect—the flavoring, the color, the presentation," she said.

"So is my *Tuna Tataki*," Kedar said. "Now this is the way to look for jade."

"Jade—that's why I want to go to the *Museo Nacional de Arqueologia*." She had seen ancient jade in Palenque, master-pieces like Pakal's death mask. The museum in Mérida had several jade sculptures, including the copy of her jade talisman she had donated. The National Museum of Anthropology in Mexico City displayed jade treasures as well. None of those museum treasures matched the color of her jaguar talisman.

Scientists had analyzed those jade museum pieces and concluded that they originated in seven different locations, but no one knew where. However, Paul had not reported his finds in the Motagua Valley. At least local jade should come from there. Pesh expected to find some clues at the museum.

"Maybe if we see some artifacts from the K'iché Maya, we'll get some ideas of where to look for jade from the museum labels." She hoped for a signal, a vision maybe, or stone the same color as her little B'alam.

The next morning, they took a taxi to the National Museum and arrived right after it opened. A pottery vessel decorated with three scarlet macaws, their colors still vibrant, presided over the entrance hall. Its sign announced, "From the tomb of Lady Une' B'alam, Tikal."

"Your relatives really get around," Kedar said.

"My ancestor lived far from here," Pesh said. "Let's go over there to exhibits of jade from royal tombs."

Pesh looked at every display and took copious notes, but nothing matched the dark green of her talisman.

To Pesh, the most striking piece at the *Museo* was a pair of Mayan ear spools from that rarest of jade, translucent imperial green. The ceremonial earrings had ornate carving around their circumference and sculpted flowers on the flanges. The plaque said, "The *arêtes* have 2 centimeter diameters in the central part that fits into the pierced ear." The earrings, shaped like spools of thread, had holes larger than her entire earlobe.

Kedar asked, "Did the Maya pierce the ears and gradually stretch the lobe with larger and larger spacers? Or did they slice open the ear, insert the spool, and let the wound heal?"

"No one knows. Either way, uncomfortable for sure," Pesh said. "The plaque says, 'the king's ear spools were a cultural marker of the bodily receptor of speech and song.'"

"No one other than an archaeologist would know that," Kedar said. "Why didn't they just say ears?"

"Treasures, from the tomb of a king," Pesh said.

"The weight of royalty, hanging in his ears." Smiling, Kedar touched his own earlobe.

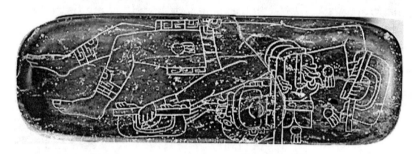

"Look there!" Kedar pointed to the next display. "One of your *celts*, with a star map carved on it. That's what it has to be. See, the fat figure lying on his back, over the three stars in Orion's belt. What's he doing—swimming along the Milky Way?"

"Your Orion's belt is in the turtle's stomach—see the turtle—there?" Pesh wondered at the beauty of the blue-green-gray jade *celt* with white scratched drawings on it. The display included no description, not even where the piece had been found, but it did seem to be a star map. Kedar's photo, taken through the glass case with his smartphone, lost detail. She tried to memorize the design to draw it later.

The museum had many jade pieces, none of them dark green, none with a luster that changed in the light with the angle of viewing. She placed one hand on the glass case. Nothing in the display made her fingers tingle.

"You shouldn't touch the glass," Kedar said, but Pesh saw no docents or guards.

"If I could hold one of those, I might find its story in a vision." Except that hadn't worked for her jade talisman.

"You said Cimil would be after you, if you used magic," Kedar said.

"Don't remind me!" Pesh shuddered and calmed herself by fingering B'alam. *Why could she find no jade matching hers?*

"I don't know what to do next," she said in a small voice. "I don't have time to waste."

"Why don't we visit a ruin?" Kedar suggested. "Didn't you say you spotted a big one from the air when you flew in from Austin?"

"Oh, Kaminaljuyú," Pesh said. "Not much left except an interesting story. The Maya built the whole city with adobe, and it weathered and crumbled into mounds. Invaders who came from central Mexico—Aztec lands—lived here for several centuries."

"You could talk to an archaeologist," Kedar said. "We have the whole afternoon."

Kedar rented a car he could return in Antigua. The ruin of Kaminaljuyú, converted to a city park less than five miles from the city center, had only a self-guided tour identifying those stone monuments remaining. The oldest one translated to "January 3, 878: Fire-is-Born arrived from the north" and showed the king's glyph, a smoking frog. However, the signpost displaying the site map directed visitors to Museo Popol Vuh in central Guatemala City.

"Come on," he said. "We have time if we hurry."

Museo Popol Vuh housed a major collection of Mayan art including ceramics and portable stone sculptures, all attractively displayed behind clear glass walls. A sand-colored pottery bowl (circa 600 AD) featured a scarlet macaw, its red paint still bright, and bore the plaque, "Macaws, important in Mayan mythology."

Pesh and Kedar started with the special exhibit of funerary ceramic art. She recognized many figures from mythology and stopped to admire a ceramic *incensario*, a bowl used for the ritual burning of incense. An effigy of a small furry animal stared with large eyes into the center of a brown bowl.

"What's that?" Kedar asked. "Looks like a cross between a mouse and a cat with large eyes like an owl's."

"A *cacomistle*," Pesh said. "It's a nocturnal mammal with a ringtail, but I don't remember any legends about it."

"You know all about every animal. How do you do it?"

"No different from your large repertoire of birdcalls," Pesh said. "I must have seen a hundred bowls but not one piece of jade."

"There's a docent tour in half an hour," Kedar said. "Let's keep looking around."

In the next room, Pesh found the museum's only jade artifact, a necklace with a carved owl pendant. It was carved from green jade like her talisman except a lighter shade, and the luster didn't change with the viewing angle.

Owls: messengers of the underworld. She consulted her talisman. No heat, no tingle, no sign of recognition.

Pesh and Kedar followed the docent past funerary art, small statuary, and polychrome ceramic vessels painted with mythical beasts.

"Found right here, in Kaminaljuyú." The docent stopped in front of the jade owl necklace.

"Do you have other jade artifacts here?" Pesh asked.

"Many others are in *Museo Nacional de Arqueologia.*"

"*Gracias.* We were there this morning. Do you know where the ancient Maya found their jade?"

"No, but it didn't come from China as conjectured by some foolish persons," he said.

"Just between you and me, do you have any hunches?"

"I heard a rumor," he said, "that jade has been found in the Motagua River Valley."

She thanked him again. Perhaps the Andersons' source wasn't as secret as they thought, but she was no closer to finding the lost Mayan jade. Perhaps B'alam Ha held that secret, but the old shaman had been wrong about Laguna Lachuá. What else had Xiu said—1000 Daykeepers?

On the way back to the hotel, Pesh asked Kedar if they could keep the rental car for an extra day.

"Of course, Princess," he said. "What's up?"

"I have to go to Momostenango." Pesh related Xiu's cryptic messages about Maximón and the Land of Mam. "I think the Daykeepers could help me find Maximón."

"Who, or what, is Maximón?"

"According to an old legend, he slept with all of the wives *at once* while the village men were off working in the fields," Pesh said. "When the men returned, they were so enraged they cut off his arms and legs."

"I'm surprised they didn't cut off something else."

"But Maximón didn't die," Pesh said. "The gods forced him to repay men with favors."

Kedar's road map showed Momostenango in the mountains 70 miles west of Guatemala City, nestled next to Quetzaltenango and not far from Xiu's village Alta Altun—as the crow flies. The road, surely laid out by a snake, had so many hairpin curves that their travel time was more than two hours.

Quetzaltenango, the second largest city in Guatemala, was known locally as Xela. Like Antigua, Xela was surrounded by mountains and volcanoes and laced with narrow, cobblestone streets. Unlike Antigua, Xela was a university town, with one large state university and six private universities. Xela's bustling downtown sported modern banks, grocery stores, hotels, Internet cafes, bakeries, movie theaters, and restaurants.

"Let's stop at the Internet cafe," Pesh said. "So many students attend university, we'll find someone who speaks Spanish or English."

Pesh and Kedar had coffee at a friendly table of college students eager to practice their English. The only girl there suggested not to waste time going to Momostenango.

"Everyone there speaks only the Mayan language Mam," she said. "They're deeply involved in Mayan religion and they're secretive. They aren't likely to answer your questions."

The rest of the students agreed that Maximón had many shrines, the biggest in San Andrés Xecul, "down the road a few kilometers."

"Maximón takes the place of Judas Iscariot in Holy Week celebrations," the girl added.

"*Gracias*," Pesh said, noting the curious blending of Catholicism and ancient Mayan religion.

"Better bring a gift for Maximón," the student wearing coke-bottle lenses advised. "Get him a cigar."

Kedar and Pesh drove another twenty miles to Xecul, much smaller than Xela but steeped in Mayan culture. The Church of San Andrés Xecul dominated the downtown with a dome painted in green, red, yellow, and blue sections like a beach ball. Painted sculptures of human figures, angels, monkeys, and quetzal birds danced in multicolored chaos on its bright yellow west façade. From the top, two jaguar statues looked down at the town's market square.

"Is this a Catholic church? With jaguars?"

"They represent the hero twins of Mayan scripture, from the *Popol Vuh*," Pesh said. "We could stand here an hour, picking out symbols, but we have to find Maximón."

Inside the church, Pesh saw dozens of burning candles, gory images of Christ, and chandeliers made from glass stones, coins, and rosary beads, but no shrine for Maximón.

Three blocks farther from the market square, smoke rose from an outdoor altar beside another yellow church. An arrow labeled "Maximón" pointed to the right. Pesh and Kedar found his shrine, located behind a grocery and with an admission charge as well as a fee for taking photographs.

"This is so commercialized. Do you want to go in?" Kedar asked. "I did buy a cigar."

"I need to see this through," Pesh said.

Inside a small room elaborately decorated with garlands of flowers and rows of burning votive candles, Maximón rested on a wicker chair. He was attended by two of the Cofradia Brotherhood. The effigy wore a black suit and tie, but dark sunglasses and a red bandanna obscured his face. The arms of his suit dangled, and a crimson and seagreen woven blanket covered him from the waist down. Max had a lighted cigar in his wooden mouth, and his attendants helped him to puff.

Pesh coughed and choked on the heavy smoke while Kedar placed a cigar in the offering basket. Max's gifts included a gold coin, a bottle of French Grand Marnier, and a fistful of crumpled Quetzal notes.

A woman, speaking Mam, asked Max for a favor, and two tourists asked for riches in English. Pesh asked in Yucatec, because she didn't speak Mam, for his help finding the source of her jade talisman, so Cimil wouldn't win.

The attendants said Maximón linked *Xibalba,* the underworld, and *Bitol,* the heart of heaven, so prayers for revenge or success at the expense of others were likely to be granted. Max would listen to any request in exchange for a suitable gift.

Max's expensive tastes in alcohol and tobacco made him more a sinful human character than a saint, surely not a Mayan god. *Max was a sham.* Pesh slowly shook her head.

Outside, Kedar said he thought she couldn't get help from the gods.

"Max isn't a real god," Pesh said.

"Then why did you ask him?" Kedar asked.

"It can't hurt, and we're already here," she said.

"Oh. Hedging your bets," he said.

She didn't know what that meant. In no mood for light-hearted jokes, she plodded behind Kedar, her shoes weighing twenty kilos each. *How dare they sell religion, mock Mayan beliefs?* Marketing Mayan culture to tourists—as wrong as stealing treasures from an ancestor's grave. Maximón was a fake, no jade at Laguna Lachuá. Were any of Xiu's words worth hearing?

"I must go to B'alam Ha," Pesh said. "That's the only remaining clue."

22

"Grandma, it'll be fun." Yash grabbed Isolde's hand and bounced up and down, on one foot and then the other. Vanna had invited her and Isolde to spend the day in Antigua while Pesh and Kedar scouted for jade from the helicopter. "I want to show you the jade museum again."

"All right, Liebchen," Isolde said. "You have worked on your studies every morning."

Right after they arrived at *Taller del Jade Maya*, Yash wanted to walk to the bus station to get an ice cream cone.

"It's only ten o'clock," Isolde said. "You won't want your lunch."

"Please, Grandma," Yash said. "I promise, I'll work on reading when we come back."

Outside the store, Grandma squashed her broad-brimmed straw hat, with its red paper flower and blue ribbon, and yanked it down to cover her ears.

Yash skipped along next to her grandmother, but she didn't wear a hat. She wore light colored knee-length trousers like her Mommy's and the new pink plastic shoes that Daddy gave her for her seventh birthday. Daddy said she'd have a party in Austin next year. Zia had baked her a pineapple cake, but she didn't have any birthday candles.

The bus station smelled like tamales and exhaust smoke and tobacco and people who needed a bath. Yash watched everybody load onto a pink bus, bright pink like her shoes. The bus had a running spotted cat painted on its side, a jaguar—*b'alam*, like her name. It was noisy—babies cried, adults yelled, children wailed—and people crowded in everywhere. Cages filled with chickens were tied onto the top of the bus, also a large dog that stuck its nose out over the railing. So many people pushed onto the bus that more were standing than sitting. Yash tried to count them but they moved around too much. She stood watching until the bus pulled away.

Yash finished her ice cream cone and took her grandmother's hand to walk back to Vanna's store. A white-paneled van screeched to a stop so close that she ducked behind Grandma. Two big, tall men jumped out and grabbed Grandma.

"The kid comes with us." One of them snatched Yash.

"Let me go!" Grandma screamed. "Help! Help!"

The man with yellowed teeth had a gun. He hit Grandma's head, like on TV in Texas.

Grandma fell down, blood on her forehead. Her hat blew way.

"Grandma! You killed my Grandma!" Yash tried to go to her, but the other bad man, who had a large black mole on the tip of his nose and really big ears, held her above his head.

"No! Put me down!" she screamed in English and kicked his face.

"Shut up that damn brat," Yellow Teeth said in Spanish.

"Stop kicking and quiet down," Black Mole growled.

Yash stopped kicking and struggling because it did no good, not because Black Mole said to. She didn't want to do anything he told her to do.

The other people walking by paid no attention. Not even to an old lady lying on the sidewalk. Not even to a little girl screaming.

"Shut up!" Yellow Teeth slapped her face.

No one had ever slapped her, *ever*. It hurt and it made her mad. She held back tears—she'd tell her Daddy on them. Didn't they know she was a Maya princess like Mommy?

Black Mole dropped her into the back of the van and locked the door. The men talked about her as though she wasn't there. She pretended to be a spy, like on Grandpa's TV in Texas. She'd learn their names and where they lived and she'd tell the police. The police would throw them into jail and take her home.

The two kidnappers drove a white van with closed panels and windows only in the front. She couldn't see out and she couldn't tell where they were going. She twisted her braid and tried to think, what would Mommy do? If they stopped, she could run away and hide.

Before they went very far, they asked for her name in Spanish. She answered in English, "You want my name?"

"Name," Yellow Teeth said.

"Liebchen." Mommy told her never to tell her real name to a stranger. She asked for their names, but they only laughed at her. She spoke in English. If they didn't know she understood their Spanish, maybe she could get some clues like on TV.

They stopped the van and stepped outside and Yellow Teeth called Vanna's shop.

"We have your little Liebchen," he said. "If you want to see her alive again, we need $50,000 by this time tomorrow." He smiled and waved to the other bad man.

Maybe they were mad at Mommy for telling the police on them, for stealing the mask from the museum, like the story in the paper. Maybe she could get out while they weren't looking. Yash pulled the door latch but then Yellow Teeth turned toward her and glared.

"Not there? Well then, you'll just have to tell her," Yellow Teeth said. "We'll call back in an hour, and she better be there."

He returned his cell phone to his pocket, pulled himself into the driver's seat, and slammed the door. When he turned the key, the engine made knocking noises and rumbled. Then the van lurched, and they were underway again on a smooth road.

"There's a banana plantation off to the right," Black Mole said.

Yellow Teeth turned the van so quickly that Yash slid across the back seat. She fingered her jade bead, hidden under her T-shirt. She hoped Daddy would find her, but she didn't hear any helicopters. After a long time, she couldn't hold it any longer.

"I have to pee," she said. "Toilet. *Baño*."

"Let her out. She'll stink up the car." Yellow Teeth stopped on the edge of a road.

The men stood outside and turned away when she pulled down her trousers. When she finished, Black Mole grabbed her braid and held it like the leash on a dog. She wished she were a dog, a big mean dog. She'd bite off his hand and tear one of his big ears.

Back in the van, she squinted her eyes shut and rubbed her magic bead. She wished she had given one to her mother because Mommy knew about magic. She thought about her mother's jade jaguar, and how she liked to touch it when Mommy told her bedtime stories.

Daddy knew about science, not magic. Would he ask his jade bead where she was? Daddy could beat up Yellow Teeth and Black Mole. Why didn't he come?

Maybe Grandma would answer her bead and tell Daddy where to find her. But Grandma had blood on her forehead. She didn't move after she fell down and no one stopped to help her. Did that mean she was dead?

Yash bit her lip so she wouldn't cry.

23

"Here's Alta Altun, Xiu's village." In their room at Quetzal Centrale, Kedar tapped the satellite image on his laptop with his index finger. He compared his geological map of the Sierra de las Minas with printouts of satellite pictures of the area and drew a red X at the GPS coordinates that Pesh had given him.

"Look at the detail." Pesh leaned over his shoulder. "You can see the houses."

"Great, isn't it? Over here, see that trail?" Too excited to sit, Kedar stood. "I think that's the one to B'alam Ha. It seems to be on an ancient Mayan trade route."

"That fits with everything we've been doing," Pesh said. "Looks like what Xiu showed Zia and me."

"Remember when we traced ancient Anasazi trails across New Mexico using satellite images? This would be the same—except the region is so mountainous and overgrown with vegetation. We won't be able to see the trail from the helicopter. And so rugged—we'd have a devil of a time trying to hike there."

"The ancient Maya managed it, without help from devils," Pesh said. "Xiu said it'd take five days."

"This is so exciting!" Kedar waved one hand and pointed to the map. "The cave you told me about, behind Alta Altun, it's at the juncture of a strange alignment of tectonic plates. Xiu's village sits on a fault line, and those shifting plates could have caused jadeite to form."

Pesh straightened up, then sat on a chair beside the table. "I didn't find any jade there, only obsidian. Xiu calls the cave a sacred place. She sees visions when she breathes the breath of B'alam."

"That could well be," Kedar said. "A similar formation in Greece vents hydrocarbon gases, including ethylene, which can induce a trancelike euphoria and hallucinations. Like inhaling fumes from glue."

"All of this geology-speak." Pesh laughed. "The fumes smell like almond blossoms, and Xiu did have a vision."

"That's ethylene," Kedar said.

"Ethylene doesn't have the magic or mystery of *the breath of B'alam*."

"True, but I've read that the ancient Greek oracle of Delphi sat over such a vent."

"And Xiu's answers were every bit as cryptic, Professor-man."

"I want to carefully map and document the area," Kedar said without a smile. "We may find another unexplored Mayan ruin. Maybe even your jade."

"So, we're going there this afternoon?"

"Actually, no." Kedar smiled and pointed to the map. "I found B'alam Ha here."

"That's a resort area for rich American tourists, called the Mayan Riviera," Pesh said. "Shouldn't we pay attention to business?"

"I can deliver supplies to B'alam Witz on the way so I can log the helicopter hours. We can load up today."

"You have enough helicopter hours, but I have only a month left on my grant," Pesh said.

"Only two nights. Come here, spoil sport." Kedar hugged her and nuzzled her hair. "I want to have my beautiful bride all to myself."

"Okay," Pesh giggled. "I'm ready."

"Then come away with me on my magic carpet."

Late on the next afternoon, Kedar landed at the heliport at the resort B'alam Ha, near the Mayan ruins Tulum and Cozumel, and a Mercedes limousine ferried them to the hotel. Pesh and Kedar checked into a magnificent room fit for a queen and king. The hotel was a white stucco building with a thatch roof. It was part of a *faux* tropical village encircling a man-made, perfectly round *cenote*. The bar stood outside in an open gazebo, its conical thatch roof supported by large timbers finished for posts.

After dark, they perched on stools around the bar to watch the *Folkorico Troupe* from Mérida dance on the walkways around the deep-blue pool.

"This place is fancier than the Holiday Inn in Guatemala City." Pesh eyed the sign above the posted drink menu that named this place *Xibalba en Balam Ha*, written in a carved-stone font. She translated, "Land of Spirits at Jaguar Hidden-Water." An interesting play on words, but not punctuated properly. The cocktails had English names—Jaguar Juice, Monkey Business, Blue Heaven—followed by a list of sodas like Coca Cola.

"Two Jaguar Juices," Kedar said.

Their drinks came in round glasses like goldfish bowls with long curled orange peels hanging over the sides and dark blueberries imbedded in crushed ice and orange juice.

Pesh sipped her Jaguar Juice, her first cocktail; it tickled her tongue with zippy soda.

"*El jugo de jaguar.* Did you know, *jugo* also means meat juice?" Pesh swallowed a longer drink, numbing her lips, and felt as though she watched a scene through a glass window. The music washed over her and bathed her with rhythm and made her shift back and forth, tapping one hand on the counter.

"Don't drink it so fast," Kedar said. "The barkeep put three shots into each glass."

Stronger than *balche*, but at the moment, Pesh didn't care. So colorful, so charming, so captivating—she danced her fingers on the counter and swayed side to side on the barstool. The women dancers wore embroidered white linen *huipil* dresses with graceful *rebozo* shawls, dangling fold filigree earrings, and long rosary beads. The men, elegantly dressed in white straight shirts and slacks, all sported white straw hats. Pesh watched red lights circle back and forth over the water, painting the pool in rose hues.

Kedar leaned closer. "There's Xiu's red and blue, and the *cenote* is mostly round."

"Xiu couldn't have meant this place, a modern resort for American tourists."

"Who knows?" Kedar stood and signaled the waiter. "Over here!"

"*Para la señora.*" The waiter held a gold-rimmed plate—with an orange-flavored cupcake bearing one lighted candle and surrounded by swirling chocolate and raspberry sauce.

"*¿Para mi?*" Pesh asked. "I love chocolate sauce!"

"A pretty good birthday surprise for my dear wife." Kedar kissed her cheek and resumed his perch on the barstool.

"Thank you. I had forgotten." Pesh blew out the candle and played with the sauce and took a taste. Perhaps eating the cake would lessen the bite of the jaguar.

"Sweet things are better shared," Pesh said, feeding Kedar a bite of cake.

"U-m-m-m. Good if I do say so myself." Kedar laughed, swaying with the music.

"The dancers remind me of Mérida and the archaeology conference," Pesh said.

"Where we met." Kedar slid his hand over one of hers.

"I had only my work pants and boots and the *huipil* my grandmother made." Pesh stared into space, remembering the blue *cotinga* flowers bordering the white skirt. "She worked on that embroidery for a month so I'd have one nice dress."

"I remember you in a blue dress. The prettiest girl I had ever seen."

Pesh blushed and giggled, then grabbed his thigh under the counter.

"I think I should give you more jaguar blood," he said. "I like you this way."

"I think these drinks are stronger than *balche*."

"That blue dress, the one you charmed me with, wasn't a *huipil*," Kedar said. "Is there a story there?"

"Dr. Burt gave Mary Anne—she's his niece—his credit card and told her I needed some clothes. The first time I ever went shopping, and the first time I wore a zipper. Mary Anne had to help me because the zipper stuck."

"Where's Mary Anne now?"

"Teaching in Boston." Pesh became pensive. "You know, the day I wore the blue dress, my whole life changed. A college scholarship, and I met you. The room faded away and I saw only you."

"I love you, too." Kedar squeezed her shoulders.

After the music stopped, he said, "I thought the day your life changed was when you became a shaman."

Pesh wanted to tell him she had to find where her talisman came from—or Cimil said he'd take Yash as a shaman. But she didn't want to spoil this romantic evening.

"I'm pretty good at bewitching you," she said.

Kedar laughed and pulled her up from the stool.

"Come and show me," he said.

The next morning, Pesh and Kedar strolled hand in hand on the beach at the B'alam Ha Resort. Kedar pulled her close with an arm around her shoulder and they watched a glowing pink sunrise and smelled the fresh sea air.

"What a relief to leave that pesky cell phone in the cockpit. I refuse to check the messages," Kedar said. "For once, I have you all to myself."

"I love it here." Pesh snuggled against his shoulder. "It's like the sun is putting on a show for us and for us alone."

When the sunrise had faded, Kedar asked, "Ready for breakfast, Sweetheart?"

"I'm always ready for a cup of hot chocolate," she said. "This being Yucatán, I'm sure they'll fix it the way I like it."

They seated themselves at the outside bar around the breakfast buffet. Pesh enjoyed tropical fruit and beans wrapped in corn tortillas. She didn't want any of the American-style breakfast, but Kedar ate two pancakes with syrup and a boiled egg. She took a second cup of the hot, spicy drink in a Styrofoam cup and walked with Kedar around the perimeter of the pool and to the parking lot, exploring.

A rock fence, overgrown with plum pink bougainvillea, separated the buses from a wildlife preserve. Beyond the thorny vine barrier, hundreds of red macaws perched in palm trees. The birds squawked and begged to a dozen tourists who laughed and clicked their cameras.

"They're smart enough to know tourists mean food," Kedar said.

"My Maya ancestors believed red macaws have great spiritual power."

"You told me—omens," Kedar said. "Birds that pretty have to be a good omens."

"Come here, you." Kedar plucked three deep pink flowers and tucked them into her hair. "Now tell me, who is the fairest of them all?"

Pesh touched the bougainvillea blossoms and laughed—until a red macaw swooped down and stole a flower from her hair.

"Shoo!" Pesh batted at the bird and sucked in her breath. *Bad omen!*

"I didn't know they were so big," Kedar said. "Must have a six-foot wingspan."

"I thought they flew down only for food," Pesh said, trying to slow her racing heart.

"Let's get out of here," Kedar said. "How about a swim?"

At the hotel shop, Kedar bought a bright red swimsuit and Pesh decided on blue.

"Blue's your color, Sweetheart, but you're cuter naked," Kedar said while they changed in their room.

"I'd rather wear only my skin but not with tourists around." Padding to the pool barefoot, she stepped on a hard object, a key ring with a jade disk dangling from it.

"You found jade with your foot, like Xiu said."

"No, it's plastic. It says '*Hecho en Mexico*' in white letters."

"Are you sure, not made in China?" Kedar asked.

After a hearty laugh, Pesh said, "Xui didn't mean this place."

"Don't worry. We'll go to the other B'alam Ha when we return. We have plenty of time."

"Yash would have loved the dancers last night," Pesh said. "All that color."

"She's fine," Kedar said. "My mother and Alberto took good care of her when we went to Lake Lachuá. She didn't miss us at all."

"This is the best mini-vacation ever," Pesh said. "We can bring Yash another time."

24

"Sit down, Brat!" Black Mole frowned, angry, like he would slap her, and Yellow Teeth drove and drove.

Yash couldn't see where they were going. Whenever she tried to stand to look out, Black Mole pushed her back down.

Yellow Teeth drove over a bumpy road. When he parked under some trees, she closed her eyes and lay still until they climbed out, hoping to hear what they said. The men stood outside the van and smoked cigarettes, but Yash didn't hear them call Vanna about the money.

With nothing else to do, she pretended to train binoculars all around outside from the front windows of the van. Blue, green, and red parrots squawked at one another in a tall cedar tree. A strange tree had hands for flowers—five pointed fingers came out of the center of each red flower. And there were many banana bushes. Hungry, she wanted to eat a banana. She could pick one, if she could escape from this jail-on-wheels, but they'd catch her for sure. As a distraction, she entertained herself by looking for hidden animals.

Over the driver's head in a tree, a big snake hid, coiled around a branch. Its colors made it blend into the background. It had gold eyes and a yellow chin and a black collar behind its eyes down to the edges of its mouth, and it had a black tongue that moved in and out. It spoke in a hissing way.

The snake said it would help her. She had asked it in her mind.

The snake dropped down onto the driver's shoulder. Yellow Teeth turned his head and tried to push it away, but it moved so fast she couldn't see it. The snake bit him on his throat, where a vein throbbed.

"Help me! *¡La barba amarilla!*" Yellow Teeth screamed. He batted at the snake, and it dropped off. "*¡Ayuda!* I'm a dead man. *¡Muerto!*"

"Come on, you yellow bastard!" Black Mole approached the snake with a machete. The snake reared up and made its body into an "S" shape and struck Black Mole's leg so fast that he missed it with the machete. Then it bit his hand.

"Take that, Devil Snake!" He made another pass with the machete and cut its head off.

Yash gasped and covered her eyes. She hadn't wanted the snake to kill Yellow Teeth, even though he deserved it for slapping her. The men made terrible noises and yelled bad words. Hearing more cries for help, she looked again.

Yellow Teeth lay on the ground. He groaned, clutched his stomach, and threw up.

Black Mole cut open his own leg with a knife and squeezed out blood. He said more bad words and let it bleed. Then he cut his hand and sucked it.

Yellow Teeth groaned again and threw up blood. Then he went to sleep, and Black Mole threw up and curled up into a ball on the ground.

Yash felt like throwing up, too. She had grabbed the edge of the seat so hard that her knuckles turned white. When she let go, her hands shook. She looked away from the sick men. She wanted to run, run anywhere, run away from here, but she had nowhere to go.

She wanted Mommy. Mommy would hug her and smooth her hair and tell her it was okay.

Chir-roop, chir-roop.

Yash sat forward and looked for what had called her. A bird with green tail feathers, its tail longer than it was tall, perched in the cedar tree. It wore its green feathers like a cloak over bright red chest feathers.

Chir-roop, chir-roop. Soo, soo. Soo, soo.

A *quetzal*—Yash recognized it from Alberto's tales and from a picture on her father's cell phone. The bird told her to stay in the van, but hungry, she looked all around.

She ran to a banana bush, grabbed two bananas, jumped back into the van. The bird said to roll up the window, so she did. It was hot and stuffy in there. She found some stale tortillas and a mango and felt better after she ate.

Right after sunset, Venus, the evening star, came into view. She rolled the window down a crack for air, and a chorus of crickets chirped and sang. Later, the moon rose and she picked out the man in the moon—her mother called it a rabbit. She slept but woke up to chattering sounds, coming from all around the van.

In the moonlight, large animals ran around and grunted, *huh, hunk, click click, huh,* like they were going to eat one another, like teeth clattering together when somebody's cold. They had a strong, bad smell and wore black fur and white smiles that went from their chins to their shoulders. They stank.

They must be the skunk pigs Ignacio told them about, on that good day when she and Mommy went to Vanna's shop and they saw the volcano's red fire at night. Ignacio said skunk pigs tore animals apart with their tusks.

Yellow Teeth and Black Mole lay on the ground. They didn't move. The skunk pigs used their tusks to rip up the men's arms, but they still did not move.

More skunk pigs. Eleven. They squealed and fought. *Wee-ahh! Wee-ahh!* Rattle and chatter. *Woo woo woo heh heh heh!* The animals tore up the men's clothes. *Crunch, crunch! Slurp, slurp!*

The pigs were eating Yellow Teeth and Black Mole!

Yash's teeth chattered and her shoulders shook, but still she stared out the window.

The skunk pigs grunted and sniffed and ran away when there was nothing left except bones and empty pants.

She curled up into a little baby-ball and hid on the front seat. How much longer before Daddy found her with his helicopter? Exhausted, she fell asleep.

At first light, Yash lifted her head enough to peer out the window. She saw and heard nothing moving. Cautiously, she opened the door to go pee. She tiptoed past the men, who looked like soup bones. She jumped to break off a yellow banana and it squished in her hand.

Several large birds came, circling. She ran back to the van and locked herself in. The birds, three of them, had big curved beaks and bald necks with no feathers. They picked the rest of the meat off the men's bones and cracked the bones open and ate the insides. Eight more large black birds came, all squawking and cawing and screeching and fighting over the bones.

She couldn't get out, but she was safe in the van. Nothing could get her. Then she heard, "*Grrr-aah-a-woo.*" She covered her ears and scrunched down in the seat. Then she remembered the sound that only howler monkeys make. She looked high in the trees and spotted one, grave and solemn, its red-brown, long hair around its neck like a scarf. Alberto said they were gods, divine patrons of the scribes in the old days long ago.

She spent the morning looking for hidden animals through the windshield and counting each kind of creature. She rubbed her jade bead: *Daddy, please come!* Mommy could help him with the magic—Mommy would hug her.

Her stomach rumbled and she eyed those bananas, some yellow, some green, growing in bunches like green fingers pointing upward. The clumps of bananas in two of the rows were tied with blue plastic ribbons and others had blue plastic bags around them. They must belong to somebody, but no one was here now.

She got out again to pee. This time, she snuck close to Yellow Teeth. Just bones. Bloody bones. He couldn't get her. She snatched up his machete and jumped back, her heart pounding. It was heavy, hard to swing. She was hungry. She swung, tried to cut down a banana. Then she heard that awful *huh, huh, click, click.*

"The skunk pigs are going to get me!"

She ran to the van. Opened the door. Tossed in the machete. Pulled herself up over the high step. Scrambled in. Slammed the door.

Two pigs crashed into the side of the van and chattered like evil things. They were bad and they'd eat her but she was safe in the van.

She drank the last of the water.

At dinnertime, Yash found no food, not even crumbs, but she saw no pigs. She ventured out, only far enough to pee against Yellow Teeth's rear tire. It felt good to make his car stink even though he couldn't smell it.

Yash climbed back into the van and locked the doors against skunk pigs and whatever else might come in the night.

25

A vehicle rattling over the gravel road awakened her. At first, Yash didn't remember where she was. She had dreamed about Daddy, and now here he came. She had to pee. She jumped out of the van and ran into the forest, limping because one foot was bare. She'd hide and surprise Daddy.

A pickup stopped.

Yash peered out from behind a tree. She didn't see Daddy. Four men piled out and one of them opened the driver's door on the white van.

"The brat isn't here," he said. He threw her other pink shoe into the bushes. Another man, taller than the others, found the kidnappers' bones.

"Look at this!" The tall man held up a bloody boot. "Only bones left. They're dead."

Yash cringed and clung to the far side of a tree. Those bad men looked meaner than Yellow Teeth. What would happen if they found her? She pulled her shoulders in and tried to look smaller.

"They don't need *el coche del Cocodrilo*," a third man said. "I'll drive it and follow you."

Yash listened from behind the tree. *The crocodile's van*? Maybe *cocodrilo* had another meaning in Mayan. She'd ask her mother— But those men weren't Maya. They were Spaniards.

"What about the brat?" the man who discarded her shoe asked.

"When those pigs come through, there's nothing left," the tall one said. "She's dead, like the others."

"*Vámonos*. Let's go."

When she was sure they were gone, Yash retrieved her pink plastic shoe. She had survived because she had left the van and hidden, but it would be harder for Daddy to find her. He had told her and Mommy, if there's an accident, we stay close to the airplane so rescue workers can find us. Daddy would look for a white van because Grandma would tell him— Was Grandma dead?

She couldn't hide in the van, like the quetzal had advised her. She looked high in the trees, but she didn't see the quetzal. Where could she go? She needed a place to hide, away from jaguars and snakes and skunk pigs. She climbed the big tree where she had hidden, up to a broad Y where she could lie down and see everything, like a lookout for spies.

"When will Daddy get here?" she asked her jade bead. "Tell Mommy he needs her magic."

No answer, only branches crackling. Hidden in the tree, she stayed very still, heart hammering, watching the path below.

Someone was coming—a Maya boy about ten, no one with him. He carried a machete and a big bunch of bananas that made her mouth water.

"*¡Hola!* What are you doing up there?" he asked in Spanish.

"Hiding from jaguars." She had thought no one could see her in the tree.

"That's a bad place to hide. Jaguars climb trees. Come down from there."

"No."

"I don't see any jaguars," he said. "Climb down."

"No."

"I'm Pedro." He bent his head back, looking up at her. "Who are you?"

"Yash." He seemed friendly. He could kill skunk pigs with the machete. The men drove away with her machete.

"Are you going to sleep up there?" he asked.

"I live here now." She thought about the van, its safety gone, and about her comfortable room at Vanna's.

"It isn't safe at night." He sounded like he knew what she should do.

"Can I have a banana?" Looking at the yellow fruit, she salivated. Her stomach growled so loudly that Pedro would hear it.

"Come down," he said. "I'll give you a banana."

Yash looked all around. No pigs hiding, no snakes, no bad men. Pedro had a machete and that made them safe. She jumped down and grabbed the banana. She wolfed it down but eating so quickly made her burp.

"Sorry." She sat down on a big flat rock. He must think she had no manners—she hadn't thanked him for the banana.

"*Gracias*," she said.

"Do you want to feed my kitten?" he asked, smiling.

"Where is it?" Puzzled, she looked all around.

"Waiting for me at home. Do you want to see it?"

She nodded, and he pulled her to her feet.

"Come with me." Pedro hoisted the bunch of bananas over one shoulder and pointed the way with the machete. "*Ko'ox. Let's go.*"

Birds called one another and the sweet smell of vanilla filled the thick jungle air. A troop of monkeys, howling and growling, scrambled through the treetops. Yash followed him through such thick vegetation that she wondered if he had lost the path.

Pedro backed against the bushes, opening a hidden pathway, like parting a curtain to a garden. On the other side, blue morph butterflies flitted around yellow flowers on vines that climbed a large tree.

"We stop here." He nodded toward a rock on the side of the trail and set down the machete and the bananas. They drank from a spring, and Yash climbed up on the rock. Pedro cut off two bananas, handed one to her, and scrambled up beside her.

"Sh-h-h." He waved toward a dead tree and they stared silently at a hole in the tree trunk above them.

A small brown bird stuck its head out of the hole and perched at the edge. The bird's brown feathers matched the color of the tree trunk. It cocked its head and regarded Yash with large yellow eyes set under feather eyebrows.

"An owl," Yash said. How did Pedro know it was there?

"Sh-h-h. She will hide if she hears too much noise."

The bird closed her eyes and seemed to sleep.

"She likes to sleep on her porch. She has a nest inside."

Pedro cut off a yellow vanilla orchid for Yash's hair, like she was a fairy princess.

"*Ko'ox*. Let's go."

Yash followed him home to see his kitten. Did he have his own room, like she did? She pictured a fluffy white kitten sleeping on a small red cushion beside his bed. That's where her kitten would sleep, if she had one.

Maybe she'd go back to Vanna's tonight. Pedro's mother could telephone Vanna's shop.

26

"Something's wrong!" Pesh yelled while Kedar landed the helicopter at Quetzal Centrale. Alberto ran to greet them, but without Yash.

"*¡Gracias a Dios!*" Alberto called out. "Thank God, you're back."

"Where's Yash?" Pesh hit the ground before the rotors stopped. The expression on Alberto's face scared her.

"That's what we all want to know." Alberto's face fell and he looked ready to cry.

"Where's my daughter?" Kedar grabbed Alberto's upper arm.

"*No se, señor.* After you left, Yash and Isolde went to Antigua with Vanna." He choked over his next words. "Vanna says they went for a walk but never came back."

"Yash is gone?" Pesh's heart speeded up and her mind shut down. *Should have checked messages on the cell phone.* "We have to find her!"

"*Sí, señora.* My little friend *Señorita Jade* is missing."

"Then Vanna must have seen where they went."

"*No, señor.* And Isolde doesn't know either. She's in the hospital."

"*¡Dios mio!*" Pesh grabbed Kedar for support. A pain crumpled her stomach, like she had been kicked.

"My mother, in the hospital?" Kedar asked.

"*Sí.* Someone mugged her." Alberto hunched his shoulders and looked down. "I am sorry to give you so much bad news."

"Did Vanna call Burt?" Kedar asked.

"*Sí, señor.* He is many miles from here."

"Where is my mother now?"

"In Antigua," Alberto said. "Ignacio can drive you there in the van if you give him thirty minutes."

"We'll be ready." Kedar smoothed Pesh's hair. "It's my fault. I was selfish. We should have taken Yash with us."

"How could you know?" Pesh said, but she struggled to say it. She felt so guilty for having so much fun that she wanted it to be someone else's fault, not her own. Kedar looked so pained, his mother injured, too. She said only, "Let's go! Now! We have to find her."

Kedar carried their bags to their room so they could freshen up.

Pesh splashed her face with water and put on a clean shirt, but she couldn't think of anything except that her baby was gone, stolen by someone evil—she'd curse him but she had no name, no way to target him. But Kedar had the bead.

"Are you still wearing Yash's bead?" Pesh hugged Kedar, then pulled the cord on the jade bead, drawing it to the front of his shirt.

He stared at the bead.

"It's supposed to connect you," Pesh said. "Hold it tightly, close your eyes, and focus on Yash. Is she all right?"

Kedar squinted his eyes shut and concentrated, but he didn't see anything.

"Maybe it takes longer or maybe you don't believe," Pesh said. "It won't work for me—she gave you the bead."

"And one to Mother. Maybe she can make it work."

After the longest drive ever to Antigua, Ignacio parked outside the small hospital, which turned out to be a rural medical clinic. The clinic, primarily for emergencies and general care, had only six beds.

Kedar and Pesh found Isolde in a room shared with a man on a ventilator. She had a bandage around her head and lay on an adjustable bed. She looked very pale.

"Mother. What happened?" Kedar rested his hand on her shoulder.

Pesh had never seen Isolde lie so still. Her chart said only "concussion."

"Kedar, you're here. I'm so glad." Isolde opened her eyes. "I'm so sorry! I lost the baby! They took her!"

"Who took her?"

"I couldn't stop them. They hit my head. They grabbed Yash. O-o-oh! My head hurts!"

"Mother, who took her?"

"Two big men wearing dirty clothes. They had a van. They hit me with a gun and grabbed Yash, my little Liebchen." Isolde gulped, then sobbed.

"Mother, don't cry," Kedar said. "That's not good for your head."

"Don't worry. It's not your fault," Pesh said, touching the talisman for luck. "We'll find Yash."

"The men called Vanna, said they wanted $50,000, but they never called back." Isolde looked ready to cry. "Does that mean Yash is dead?"

"I think she's all right," Pesh said, not sure she believed it. She held Isolde's hand because she needed to be in peace to heal properly. "Do you have the jade bead she made for you?"

"Yah, yah, right here," Isolde said, fishing the bead from under her hospital gown.

"You need to use it. You're the only one who can," Pesh said. "Remember the legend? The jade connects you."

"This can call Yash?"

"Hold it tight and close your eyes. Concentrate on Yash."

Isolde shut her eyes and tensed her face.

Kedar stared at them both.

"It doesn't talk to me," Isolde said.

"Try one more time. Close your eyes and think about Yash, what she looks like, what she sounds like," Pesh said. "You can do it, because you love her."

Isolde appeared to sleep for so long that Pesh feared the nurse would send them away.

"She's talking to a boy, and she's happy," Isolde said, eyes still shut. "She's holding a kitten, tan with black spots. The biggest kitten I ever saw."

"Yash is alive!" Pesh covered her mouth with one hand. The only cat with black spots she knew was a jaguar.

"Where is she?" Kedar asked.

"I don't know. Oh-h-h, it hurts too much." Isolde's head sank back into the pillow and she looked ready to sleep.

"Do you remember anything else, anything at all?" Kedar said. "What the car looked like?"

"A white panel truck with one front fender missing. They didn't speak English," Isolde said. "It happened so fast I can't remember. Oh-h-h! My head!"

"Mother, may I have your jade bead?" Pesh squeezed her arm, hoping Isolde would know she loved her.

"Of course, Liebchen." Kedar's mother still called her that sometimes. Hearing the term of endearment brought tears to Pesh's eyes.

"Let me hold your hand, the one with the bead, and tell me I can have it." By using both jade beads, Mother's and Kedar's, perhaps she could help Kedar contact Yash.

"Here it is, Liebchen," Isolde said.

"Please tell me I can have it," Pesh said.

"I give it to you." Isolde's eyes closed and her head sank into the pillow.

"Visiting hour is over." A nurse dressed in a starched white dress stepped into the room. "She needs to rest."

"We'll be back tomorrow night," Kedar said to the still figure on the bed.

"Goodbye, Mother. We love you." Pesh squeezed her hand and the bead. "Your bead will find her."

"We'll search for Yash tomorrow," Kedar said as the nurse pushed him out the door.

"No! Right now!" Pesh wanted action.

"Sweetheart, I'd like that, too. But it's too late in the day and we'd run out of gas.

27

Yash followed Pedro through the brush until he stopped and pointed to a very small house. The house was built of stacked stones with one wall of rough lumber and a tin roof. The yard was all dirt and rocks but vegetables grew along one rock wall.

Pedro fitted the machete across two pegs on the wooden wall and said to come in with him. He put the bananas on the table and greeted his mother in Mayan. Pedro's mother looked like her mother but she held a baby and wanted to know, "Who is she? Where's she from?"

Pedro said he found Yash in a tree and she was lost. He gave his mother the vanilla orchid from Yash's hair, and she nodded at Yash.

Yash didn't understand everything they said because they spoke Mayan, like Alberto. But she remembered that one always gave a gift before asking for a favor. *How could his mother call Vanna? She didn't speak Spanish!*

Pedro said, "My mother says you may call her Maria."

"I'm happy to meet you," Yash said in English. Maria probably wasn't her real name, only what to call her. *Would she stay here tonight? Pedro's father could call Vanna.*

"Would you like to see my kitten?" Pedro bent down over a basket in the corner.

Yash smiled and nodded, glad they both knew Spanish. She could see he didn't have his own room—the house had only one room. The kitten, as big as her neighbor's cat in Texas, was tan with black spots shaped like small roses. It had really big paws and blue eyes.

Pedro picked up the kitten from its nest of blanket scraps in a wicker basket. He pointed to the floor and said, "Sit there and you can hold him."

Yash sat cross-legged on the dirt floor, and the kitten filled her lap. She petted his soft fur and rubbed her cheek against his back. His purr sounded like a buzz saw.

"I love him," she said. "What's his name?"

"*Jaguarcito*, because he's a baby jaguar."

"Where'd you get him?" She nuzzled the jaguar cub.

"Someone shot his mother, and I found her den." Pedro showed her how to hold a plastic baby bottle filled with canned milk and water.

The hungry kitten sucked the nipple and kneaded the bottle with his front paws. His nails needed cutting because he made big scratches in the plastic.

"I have to get rid of Jaguarcito before my little sister starts to crawl," he said.

Yash stared. *Get rid of this wonderful kitten?*

"My mother says Jaguarcito might hurt my sister." Pedro looked sad. "My father says he'll turn him loose in the jungle. But he won't live because his mother didn't teach him to hunt."

"Oh." She didn't know what else to say. The kitten missed his mother, like she did. Then Yash couldn't hold it anymore. "Where is your toilet?"

"I'll show you," Pedro said. "It's in the back."

Yash followed him outside to a small room with a half-door. Someone standing outside could see her feet. There were two feet painted on the concrete floor and a drain hole.

"You pee into that," he said.

"What if I have to, you know …"

"We poop in there." Pedro showed her a little room with a bench that had a hole in it.

"Oh." It stank. *What if she fell in through the hole?*

"Come back when you finish." Pedro went back into the house.

She tried peeing into the drain hole. If she squatted, she had good aim—more fun than using a real toilet. Where did Maria cook dinner, with no kitchen? Maybe outside, like camping.

Pedro's father came home in time for supper. He looked like Alberto, and he asked in Mayan, "Who is this?" and "Where did she come from?"

Yash tried to tell him. Bad men took her away. A snake killed them. Her Daddy would come to get her in a helicopter. He didn't understand her Spanish and she didn't know enough words in his language.

Pedro said she was lost. Her father needed to find her.

"Where does she live?" Pedro's father wanted to know.

"Austin, Texas," Yash said.

"Texas is in the United States," Pedro said. He asked Yash, "How did you get here?"

"I went on a walk in Antigua to get ice cream. Then two bad men grabbed me and took me away in a white van."

"Where in Antigua?" Pedro asked.

Yash knew the name of Vanna's shop. *"Taller del Jade Maya."*

Pedro's father sounded excited. *"Jade. Yax.* They have lots of money to pay a reward. Ask her where that is."

"Where is the shop?" Pedro asked.

"I don't know but I can get there from the bus station." *He said he'd get a reward—it was fun knowing some Mayan!*

That night, they hung a hammock for her. They all slept in hammocks and she liked rocking back and forth. The next morning they had corn meal gruel and bananas for breakfast, and Pedro's mother Maria said they needed a bath, but Yash hadn't seen a shower.

Maria poured water from a bucket into a metal tub outside in the side yard and warmed it with boiling water from a metal teakettle. She washed the baby and dried her with a towel. Then she said, "Now it's your turn."

She set out clean clothes for Pedro and an outgrown pair of his pants and a shirt for Yash. Maria said she'd wash their clothes, and Yash and Pedro got into the tub together.

"You look different from me," Yash said.

"Haven't you ever seen a boy before?"

"I don't have a brother."

"Well, you do now," Pedro said. They shared the baby's towel and Maria dried their backs.

"What's that you're wearing?" Pedro asked.

Yash held out her mint green and creamy white jade bead, polished to a high sheen. "It's magic. I made one for my father so he can always find me, but it isn't working."

"Jade. That's jade. Where'd she get it?" Maria helped Yash step into the tan pants. They were too long, so she rolled them up to make a cuff above the pink shoes.

"You made that bead?" Pedro asked.

"Alberto cut it in his jade workshop. I polished it."

"I'd like to do that," Pedro said.

Later, while Yash fed Jaguarcito, she told Pedro, "My Mayan name is Yaxuun *B'alam*. Jaguar."

"My Mayan name is 15-*Lah-mat*," he said.

Yash knew her numbers but not the other word.

Pedro drew loops in the air over his ears. She couldn't guess until he knelt on all fours and hopped around.

"Rabbit!" she said, but Pedro didn't know the English word. They laughed so hard that Jaguarcito stopped nursing.

"Is 15-Rabbit your birthday?" Yash asked. Part of her mother's Mayan name was a day on the sacred calendar, where animals named most of the months.

"It's just my name," he said.

"Then when is your birthday? My grandmother bakes cakes for my birthday."

"I don't have a grandmother," Pedro said.

When Jaguarcito had a full tummy and fell asleep, Pedro took Yash to the jaguar's den, a nest of leaves and branches lined with feathers between large tree roots.

"She had only one cub. Weak and very hungry, and his eyes weren't open yet."

"Can't you teach him to hunt so he won't die when your father turns him loose?"

"I don't think so." Pedro frowned and looked down. "He's going to weigh a hundred kilos and he'll be taller than my father. He'll need a lot of food."

Yash couldn't picture a cat that big—bigger than her father. Still worrying about the jaguar kitten, she asked, "How do they hunt?"

"They leap down from a tree onto the back of an animal and kill it with one bite," Pedro said. "That's why you couldn't stay in a tree overnight."

"Oh. I guess you couldn't show him how, then. But I don't want Jaguarcito to die."

"I'll give him to you. You can take him home."

"Really? I love Jaguarcito."

Later, after dinner and after dark, Pedro grabbed her hand and pulled her to her feet. Outside, the moon was full.

"*Lamat*. Rabbit in the moon," Pedro said, pointing up and using Yash's word.

"That's the man in the moon," Yash said, but it did look like a rabbit.

"*Ix Chel* the Moon Goddess put her pet rabbit there."

"Pedro, what are you doing out here?" Maria came up behind them in the dark. "Get back in the house this minute."

"We must go to bed now," Pedro said.

Yash swung gently in her hammock. Maria didn't like Jaguarcito and she didn't like Pedro. She was mean like the stepmother in *Cinderella*. Yash could save Jaguarcito from Maria—except when would her father find her? Would she ever get home again?

On Sunday, Pedro's father drove them all to Antigua in his faded blue pickup, Maria and the baby in the front. Pedro and Yash rode in the back in the truck bed. Yash liked the wind in her hair and she liked having a brother. Pedro knew everything. She tried to talk to him, but her words blew away.

They stopped at the bus station and had ice cream cones. Yash had strawberry. She had no trouble showing them the way to Vanna's shop.

Pedro's father parked in front of *Taller del Jade Maya*, but a padlock held the iron grill shut. The sign on the door said, "*Cerrado*. Closed."

"It says come back in the morning," Yash said. They had to come back! Where was Vanna? Her stomach felt as though she had swallowed a bird that flapped and scratched.

"I can't come then," Pedro's father said.

She couldn't stay here and sleep on the sidewalk, but she didn't want to go back with Pedro's family. What could she do? The brown paper napkin left from her ice cream—

"Pedro, do you have a pencil?"

He found a pencil stub in the glove box, and Yash wrote, "Y - A - X," her Mayan name in English letters, and under it, she drew a jaguar head, *B'alam*. "What's your phone number?"

"We don't have one," Pedro said.

She hadn't seen a phone in his house. His father must not have a cell phone. They didn't have a street address. How would Daddy find her?

"What's the name of the road we came here on?" Yash would make spy clues, her favorite game with her father.

"Highway 14."

Yash wrote capital "B" and added two bars and four dots under *B'alam*'s head, because road is *beh* in Mayan—like the alphabet letter B—and the number she wrote was 14. Highway 14: Daddy would like her clue. Then she slipped her small hand through the iron grillwork and slid the napkin under the door.

Her note would give Daddy enough clues, that and the jade bead.

28

Hours and hours and hours. The headset pinched her ears and the engine thropped on. Days and days and days. Armies of *pe'epen* moths battled in her stomach. Where was Yash?

Pesh flew search patterns with Kedar, trying to get an answer from Yash's beads and looking for a white panel truck. They had scoured both sides of the highway from Antigua to the north, back and forth over forty miles, as well as roads south, east, and west. Dense vegetation obscured the ground. Few roads crossed the north-south two lanes serving Antigua, only footpaths too narrow for a van.

Where to look? Unable to stay still, Pesh shifted in her seat, crossed and uncrossed her legs, and swiveled her head until her neck stiffened. Her stomach seemed ready to explode. She fingered B'alam, told herself to calm down, and concentrated on the view below.

"We're looking for a white van?" One dirt road led to a banana plantation, but off the main highway. Pesh saw no vehicles of any description.

"Our only clues are a white van and a large kitten," Kedar said.

"A jaguar cub," Pesh said into her microphone. "Black spots—it's a young jaguar."

"No. Where'd she find that?"

"Who knows?" Pesh answered, glad for a diversion. She rocked back and forth and drew in a deep breath. Isolde saw Yash when she used the beads—her baby had to be okay. "But Yash is alive. I'm sure of it."

"Complete with kitten," Kedar said. "I'm out of ideas and out of gas."

"*Xmenoob* Xiu knows about jade. She might read the beads." Pesh needed hope—she'd try anything. Xiu didn't have a strong score so far—no jade at Laguna Lachuá, that fake god, Maximón. But Xiu was *Xmenoob*. "Let's go to Alta Altun tomorrow morning."

"Sounds good to me," Kedar said. "We're getting nowhere here."

The helicopter needed a flat place to land. Alta Altun, high in the Sierra de las Minas, nestled amongst rocks and steepness. Kedar finally set down about two nautical miles from Xiu's.

"A little walk will feel good." Pesh needed to stir around, to get her mind off Yash, to concentrate on the task at hand. "I try not to worry, but I'm beside myself."

"So am I." Kedar took her hand. "Yash, and my mother, too."

Pesh didn't answer. Kedar's hand comforted her, but she worried about Yash, worried about Isolde, worried she'd lose to Cimil.

Xiu's village sat on the other side of the mountain, two miles in a straight line. Who knew how far with up and down? Weeds and bushes grew waist high, as though they waded through green water. After the weeds, they crossed an area of devastation where nothing grew. The ground glittered with black mirrors and sounded like her feet were smashing dishes. Kedar stopped in front of her.

"This is incredible! I never thought I'd hear it."

"I don't hear anything." Pesh looked all around.

"The sound of advancing obsidian lava is unlike anything on earth," Kedar said.

"You mean the breaking dishes?" Pesh asked. Fracturing sounds—as if a bowl of her homemade rice crisps with its usual snap, crackle, and pop also contained thousands of fragile plates, each breaking. Yash liked that cereal and she liked to watch the dried rice pop like popcorn. Yash—her baby—lost.

"I'm sure we're standing on a slow moving lava flow," Kedar said. "It's creeping down the volcano's slopes as it slowly cools from the outside in."

"This shimmers in the sunlight." Pesh picked up a sample of black obsidian showing conchoidal fracture, a shell-like break. "Yash will want it for her collection. Look at those lustrous, changing colors."

Pesh teared up. Would she ever see her baby playing with her rocks again?

"Striations like in tiger-eye," Kedar said. "I should buy her a sample in a rock shop. Tiger-eye is a golden-brown chatoyant stone formed by the alteration of *crocidolite*. Changes its luster like the eyes of a cat."

"In Guatemala, it should be jaguar-eye. Yash'd love it." Pesh paused, afraid to picture Yash. She choked out, "We have to find her."

"Better get a move on," Kedar said. "Unless we're going to spend the night with Xiu."

"No!" Pesh shook her head. "I don't want to do that. We must look for Yash."

"It takes an hour to walk to Alta Altun," Kedar said. "An hour in, an hour back, fly to the heliport before dark. We don't have much time."

From the west, Alta Altun looked like most Mayan villages, a few modest huts with bare dirt yards, children playing, a lone red rooster strutting. Pesh pointed across the plaza. "That's her house."

From the front door of Xiu's hut, Pesh called out, "*Xmenoob Xiu!* May we visit you?"

"*Pex!*" Xiu answered. "What a delight. Do come in."

"This is my husband, Kedar."

Xiu nodded, invited them into her one-room hut, and offered herbal tea. Pesh recognized all of what Xiu said. *Dios bo'otik*, she didn't need Zia to translate.

"How did you come?" Xiu asked. "I see no van."

"Kedar flies a helicopter—an airplane." Pesh wondered if Xiu had ever seen a helicopter, or an aircraft of any kind. "We left it on the other side of the mountain."

"You could leave your carriage where Ignacio parks the van."

"Thank you. It's too far away for Kedar to move it—another time." Pesh signalled A-OK to Kedar with her hand.

"Zero is a strange thing to say," Xiu said.

"In America, that means okay." Okay—the one word understood in every country.

"Kedar speaks no Mayan?" Xiu asked.

"Only a little Yucatec."

"Then I can speak freely," Xiu said. "Welcome, *Xmenoob Pex Yaxuun B'alam*. I recognized you as a shaman when you ordered the maggots for the sick boy."

"He recovered?"

"He has a scar but he plays with the other boys."

"I brought you a gift." One always came with a gift, especially if one wanted to ask a favor. Pesh handed her the bottle of water from Laguna Lachuá and explained about its healing qualities. "Of course, for a severe skin problem, the patient should go to Lachuá and bathe in the waters."

"*Dios bo'otik*, the gods pay," Xiu said, thanking her. "We went there in the old days. Patients with severe skin sores— pale-colored, lumpy, ugly—made pilgrimages to Lachuá. They cleansed themselves by fasting and drinking the water of Lachuá for the five holy calendar days. They threw jade pebbles into the lake, gifts for the gods."

"*Leprosos*. The disease is called leprosy in English," Pesh said. "Did the treatments cure them?"

"I do not know but many took the cure," Xiu said.

"Doctors would like to know that cure," Pesh said. No wonder she didn't find jade at Lachuá. Those pebbles, thrown into the water long ago, would have turned white.

"I sense you are troubled," Xiu said.

Pesh told her that Yash had been kidnapped but the jade hadn't helped them find her.

"Yash polished these beads, and she wears the third one," Pesh said, handing them to Xiu.

"Such an easy problem." Xiu clapped the two beads together. "Jade is lazy, and being old, sleeps a lot. We will wake it up."

Xiu held the beads in one hand and took Kedar's hand with the other. The three of them—Xiu, Kedar, and Pesh—held hands, closed their eyes, and concentrated on Yash. Xiu saw her eating dinner with a Mayan family.

"Ask her where," Kedar said.

"Seek and let the jade direct you," Xiu answered, but Kedar didn't know enough Mayan to understand.

"Don't worry," Pesh said to Kedar. "Now I know how to use the beads."

Then Xiu asked Pesh in Mayan, "Did you find the origin of your jade talisman?"

Pesh shook her head.

"Your jaguar charm belonged to a *Xmenoob* before you. Did you go to B'alam Ha?"

"Not yet." Pesh knew Xiu meant a village nearby, not a rich person's resort.

"My shaman's amulet is the firebird." Xiu showed Pesh a talisman carved from black obsidian, an owl with iridescent feathers. "Firebird lets me see visions in the smoke above the flames of a fire, but it wouldn't let me see you finding the jade of your jaguar. The gods are displeased."

Pesh knew why.

Xiu continued, "I sense there is something you haven't told me."

"I am a fallen *Xmenoob*." Pesh hung her head and her stomach tightened.

"That is surely a mistake," Xiu said, putting down her empty cup. "So few of us are left."

"I must find the source of my talisman without asking the gods for help." Pesh took a deep breath and noticed that Kedar had nodded off. *What a relief to talk about it.* "Cimil will claim Yash as a shaman."

"I see why you are troubled," Xiu said. "But Cimil's power comes from believing in him. Less people believe—he's weaker now."

"I don't want my daughter to become a shaman." Pesh swallowed but her mouth was dry. Her heart pounded the way it always did whenever she thought about Cimil's threat.

"Is it so bad to be a shaman?" Xiu asked. "You can help people—just don't let them take advantage of you. Helping is not doing things for people. You must discern what they truly need. Teach them how to help themselves."

"I will think on your words." The last time Pesh had acted as a shaman, at Five-Owl's festival across the river from B'alam Witz, she had rushed to help him but he had deceived her—he hadn't needed a shaman. But she taught Precious-Turtle to bargain in Spanish. So, that's what she did wrong with Five-Owl but right with his mother.

Pesh was glad Kedar knew no K'iché. He found her role as a shaman disquieting, especially if she made a curse. *Voodoo*, he called it. She touched her jade amulet. She had worn B'alam next to her skin since the day she became a shaman.

"Why do you hide?" Xiu asked. "You tell no one you are *Xmenoob*."

"I am an instructor at an American university. No one there believes in shamans."

"So they do not understand," Xiu said. "But here, a shaman is respected. You must thank the gods for the special gifts they have given you and use them for good."

"I will think on your words," Pesh said. "We must return to look for Yash."

"And I must think about your problem."

"Thank you, the gods pay," Pesh said in Mayan, and added, "*Vaya con Díos.*"

"Hurry." Pesh grabbed Kedar's hand and pulled him up. "We must search for Yash in the morning."

"*Xi'ik tech utsil.*" Xiu waved goodbye. "Good luck!"

On the way to the helicopter, Kedar asked, "What was that about Yash and Cimil?"

"I should have told you." Hot blood rushed to her head and her temples throbbed. "It's too painful."

Kedar put his arms around her.

"Cimil wants Yash to become a shaman." Tears started and her chest heaved.

"Well, then." Kedar cleared his throat. "I don't understand. Surely everything will turn out okay."

"Only if I find the source of my talisman."

Kedar landed the helicopter at Quetzal Centrale while the setting sun still glowed red on the horizon. "I need to fill the gas tank before we fly looking for Yash tomorrow," he said, "but if we leave here at sunrise, we can stop at Guatemala City on the way."

"I'll be up before the sun," Pesh said. "I'm too stressed out to sleep."

"Xiu said it'd be easy to find Yash now," Kedar said. "But I still don't know how to use the jade beads."

"But you have me. Xiu saw her, and you will, too."

"You're right about Xiu," Kedar said. "She's amazing—the mayor, the doctor, the priest, all-in-one."

When they arrived at the house, Vanna met them at the front door, and Pesh asked if she had contacted Burt.

"Of course. There's an update on Isolde," Vanna said. "She has bone pressing on her brain and needs surgery. She can't travel far in a car on poor roads. They said she needs an airlift."

"Airlift—that would be me," Kedar said. "I need gas in Guatemala City, too."

"Ground support. That would be me," Vanna said. "I'll close the shop tomorrow. Ignacio and I will meet you in Guatemala City."

Early the next morning, Kedar landed in a city park near the Antigua Medical Clinic. Two male nurses from the clinic moved Isolde. She was strapped to a stretcher and wore a halo collar around her head and neck to prevent movement. The male nurses carried her to the park and loaded her into the back of the helicopter. Kedar thanked them and Pesh made her as comfortable as possible.

"You look so amazing in that headgear," Kedar said. "I'm taking a blackmail picture."

"They gave me so much pain medicine, I don't care how I look," Isolde said.

At the hospital in Guatemala City, a green "H" on the roof marked special parking for helicopter ambulances. Kedar set down in the center of the "H." Two orderlies carried Isolde inside, and he moved the helicopter to the airport. Then he and Pesh hailed a taxi to rejoin Isolde at the hospital.

Kedar stopped at the admissions desk to get directions to Isolde's room. They needed money up front, and he didn't know how to make payment arrangements for her surgery, scheduled for tomorrow morning.

"I'll bring her husband here tomorrow," Kedar said.

"I'm going with you," Pesh said. "I haven't been to B'alam Witz in months."

Pesh felt torn in every direction at once. They needed to find Yash but they had to bring Burt to Isolde as well. If Xiu saw Yash, her baby must be all right, and the jade beads would guide them. But Pesh worried nonetheless. She must find Yash. She must find the lost jade.

29

When Pedro's father drove away from Vanna's shop, hot tears welled in Yash's eyes and her stomach hurt, but she didn't want Pedro to see her cry. She drew up her knees and put her head down against them. *Why didn't Daddy come? Would he see her note? Would she ever go home again?*

"Don't worry." Pedro, sitting next to her in the back of the pickup, ruffled her hair. "My father takes us to the Mayan market in Antigua every week."

"What day is that?" she asked over the noise of the traffic.

"Thursdays. Or Sundays."

Yash didn't know if this was Sunday. His family didn't have a calendar. At home, she went to church with Grandma on Sundays. *Was Grandma all right?*

The pickup pulled into a crowded, dusty parking lot.

"*Ko'ox*, come on," Pedro said, and she followed him through crowded walkways. Music and singing, people everywhere. All the women wore full length skirts and cotton *huipils* bordered by intricate zigzag designs. She saw fresh fruit and vegetables, embroidered dresses and lace scarves, handwoven blankets and shawls, baskets and straw hats, and food stands.

Maria bought them snacks from a woman in a royal blue dress with red flowers on it. She gave Yash a paper cone filled with salty roasted treats, crunchy and shaped like grasshoppers, and with a slice of lime to squeeze over them.

"These are *chapulines*," Pedro said. "Roasted locusts. Grasshoppers."

"Real grasshoppers?"

"*Sí*. Maria fries them with hot peppers."

Yash had never tasted bugs, but Pedro ate one. She put one in her mouth, ready to spit it out, but it tasted salty and good like tortilla chips.

Yash did feel better after eating. She watched Maria spread out her handwoven straw hats on a yellow cloth; she sat on the ground selling hats, her baby in her lap. Pedro's father talked to the men and drank beer.

"*Ko'ox*." Pedro pulled her up by one hand. "They have folk dancing now."

He led her to an outdoor stage and they sat on the ground in front of the crowd so she could see. To one side, musicians played the flute and the marimba and kept time with gourd rattles—Pedro called it "*Xeet Kewel*." Then men wearing white pants tied with red sashes came onto the stage and stomped feet in time with the gourds. Women whose shawls were tied with red, yellow, orange, and green tassels joined them. They all moved in time with the music and passed the shawls around. The women had flowers in their hair, one black braid pulled back and twisted up. They all were young and beautiful like her mother.

The dancers dropped red flowers onto the floor, and Pedro snatched one of them.

"Let's dance," he said.

"I don't know how."

"You don't have to know anything. You feel the music." Pedro tucked the red flower into her hair. "Come over here and let's copy what they do."

Behind the crowd, Yash and Pedro twisted and turned like the dancers. People nearby turned to watch and clapped when they stopped.

"I had so much fun!" Yash loved the music and the dancing. She still wanted to go home but Austin was far away. She'd be happy at Vanna's and she could work on jade with Alberto, if Daddy ever found her.

Instead, she went back to Pedro's parents' home.

The next day Pedro showed her how to catch grasshoppers for dinner—harder than it looked. Every time she dropped a fist full of bugs into the bucket, some jumped out. Yash laughed and chased grasshoppers and ran after Pedro until they filled the bucket.

Yash helped Maria fry *chapulines* with chili peppers and garlic over the cooking fire in the front yard. Maria said to cover the pan as soon as she dropped in the grasshoppers, but Yash was too slow. Then her job became catching the bugs that hopped out.

At bedtime, Yash climbed onto her hammock. *Maybe Daddy would come in his helicopter tomorrow.* Every night she rubbed her piece of jade and wished for him to answer her, but this time, when she reached for her bead, it was gone. Her heart pounded and she couldn't lie still.

"I lost my jade bead." She shook Pedro's hammock.

"I'll help you find it in the morning," Pedro whispered in the dark.

"But it's magic. Now Daddy will never find me!" Yash rubbed her knuckles across her cheeks, wet with tears.

"S-s-sh. Everyone sleeps now."

Everyone but Yash slept. She tossed and turned and worried all night. How would Daddy find her?

As soon as they finished breakfast and fed Jaguarcito, Yash and Pedro searched everywhere they had gone the day before, but they couldn't find the bead.

"I polished it myself and gave it to Daddy." Her eyes filled with tears and she choked out, "Now he can't find me."

"Don't cry, Little Sister," Pedro said. "I'm sure we'll find it tomorrow."

At dinnertime, Jaguarcito toddled out of his basket, ready to explore.

"Jaguarcito has learned to walk," Yash said. "He's so cute!"

Pedro shook his head and sucked in his breath. "He'll be needing his first meat soon."

"What if he eats the baby?" Maria said in Mayan. "He can't stay in this house any more!"

"Yash and I will take turns watching him," Pedro said. "I'll make him a sandbox."

Yash helped Pedro cut down a cardboard canned milk carton and they filled it with dirt from the yard.

"Why doesn't Maria like Jaguarcito?" Yash asked.

"She doesn't like me, either." Pedro shoved the box against the wall next to the kitten's basket. He petted Jaguarcito's head, and the kitten purred.

"That's too dirty to keep in the house," Maria said, her hands on her hips. She had a big, round stomach.

"But he won't mess up your floor if he uses this," Pedro said.

"I don't like that animal in my house." Maria glowered.

30

On the morning of Isolde's surgery, Pesh, Kedar, and Burt sat in the hospital cafeteria drinking coffee and picking over stale sweet rolls. Pesh sipped burnt coffee and nibbled a few sliced almonds and a pineapple chunk. The rolls were not at all like Isolde's wonderful breads—wonderful, like her mother-in-law. Isolde had had a concussion once before—an accident, in her mine. Wasn't a second one more serious?

Pesh swallowed hard and tried to relax her stomach muscles.

"I'm glad you're here," Kedar said to Burt. "I couldn't have handled this for Mother."

"It's a long surgery, and afterwards, I'm the only one they'll allow in ICU," Burt said. "Why don't you call me tonight and come back tomorrow?"

"That's sensible, except we're too worried." Pesh twisted the end of her braid and wiggled more than a small child. She wanted to leap up and search for Yash—but where?

"We could look for Yash," Kedar said. "They won't need the helicopter until the doctors release Mother, a week or more."

"But we still don't know where to look," Pesh said. "At least, we know she's okay, and the jade beads work. Or at least they did for Mother and Xiu."

"What's this about jade beads?" Burt asked, his coffee cup poised midair.

"Yash is fascinated with jade," Pesh said. "Alberto calls her *Señorita Jade*, and she's been spending hours in his workshop, learning to work jade and polishing it."

"Our amateur mineralogist," Burt said, smiling.

"She polished beads." Pesh held out a mintgreen and mottled white bead suspended on a leather cord. "She gave this one to Isolde, and another like it to Kedar."

Burt cupped the bead in his right hand while Pesh explained the legend, how they were connected to Yash through jade cut from the same stone.

"Isolde saw Yash holding a kitten, so we know Yash's all right," Pesh said. "But we can't find her."

"Isolde saw her with a kitten?" Burt asked. "Are you sure that's not from being hit in the head?"

"Our friend Xiu saw Yash, too, having dinner with a Mayan family," Pesh said. "But in Guatemala, that could be anywhere."

Kedar's smart phone rang.

"Vanna," he said. "Yes, surgery scheduled for nine o'clock. What—a note from Yash?"

"What is it?" Burt and Pesh chorused.

Kedar signaled them to be quiet and turned on speakerphone.

"Y, A, X. Next, a drawing of a jaguar's head. Then a capital B, two bars and four dots," Vanna's voice said.

"Her name in Mayan!" Kedar said.

"Fourteen!" Pesh yelled. "Capital B—*beh* is road in Mayan. Highway 14 is the highway running north and south through Antigua."

"Now we know where, and we know how to make those beads talk to us," Kedar said. "Let's go!"

"Then use your phone to call a taxi to the airport," Pesh said. "I can be ready in five minutes."

Even with all the hurry they could muster, Pesh and Kedar used most of the morning to get to the helicopter. Once in the air,

Pesh felt more comfortable—finally looking for their lost baby. While both of them held the jade beads, Kedar flew search grids centered on Highway 14, five miles on either side, until they were 50 miles south of Antigua. No white van—except for those traveling on the road.

"Are you feeling anything from Yash's jade?" Kedar asked.

"No, but we've been flying for hours." She should have felt a tingle, seen Yash's face, or heard Yash speak. *Nada.*

"No trace of Yash. No message from the jade," Kedar said. "What's wrong?"

"I wish I knew." Pesh, as a fallen *Xmenoob,* felt as though part of her had been cut off, like an amputee suffering pain from a phantom limb, except she had lost her identity. She hadn't found the source of her jade talisman, and now she couldn't even picture Yash.

"We've burned a lot of gas," Kedar said. "We need a fuel stop for helicopter and pilots."

"Good," Pesh said. "I need a break before we fly north looking. If she isn't south on Highway 14, she must be to the north."

"Here—drink some water. We still have a few hours of daylight," Kedar said.

Pesh spent more hours trying to call Yash's image with the jade. Xiu saw the child with no problem, and Isolde reported that Yash held a kitten.

Why weren't the jade beads working?

31

Yash and Pedro searched for her lost bead all day. They couldn't leave the kitten with Maria, so they carried him with them, and Jaguarcito watched from his basket.

Later, at dinnertime, Maria had a rapid-fire argument with Pedro's father: The jaguar will eat the baby. ... The box of dirt smells bad. ... I don't want that animal in my house.

Pedro's father didn't eat his dinner.

Yash didn't get every word but she understood Maria's angry tone. She relaxed when Maria took the baby outside to feed her.

Pedro had a conversation with his father. Yash had lost her magic bead. Her father can't find her. She needed to go to Antigua—there would be a reward.

Yash didn't get the rest of it. She didn't know anything about a reward.

Pedro's father started to eat his dinner, so Pedro and Yash did, too.

"We're going to Antigua tomorrow," Pedro said. "Very early so my father can go to work. It's harvest time and he needs the money."

Yash's spirits soared. Too excited to eat, she suppressed a giggle and picked at her food. Then Pedro cleaned their wooden plates, all except for Maria's.

Before dawn, Maria cooked corn-meal gruel. After they drank a little of the hot, cinnamon flavored beverage, they loaded into Pedro's father's pickup, Yash and Pedro in the front, Pedro holding Jaguarcito in his basket. Maria stood there, baby on one hip, and waved goodbye.

"We can't leave Jaguarcito with Maria," Pedro said. "I'll stay with you and help until he learns to use a sandbox."

Yash petted Jaguarcito's soft fur and pictured the jade workshop at Quetzal Centrale. She felt like singing.

Pedro's father pulled up in front of Vanna's shop, early enough that the gate still wore a padlock. "Be right back," he said. He climbed out and slammed the door so loudly that Jaguarcito jumped out of the basket. He talked to the man unlocking the store next door and they both waved their hands around. Then Pedro's father walked back to his truck.

"*Taller del Jade* opens every day," he said, climbing back into the driver's seat. "The man doesn't know why they closed last week."

Pedro glanced at Yash and then looked back to his father, who said, "You know how to find my brother Cuxil?"

"I can find Cuxil's house," Pedro said.

"If you have any trouble, go to Cuxil. I'll leave you here," Pedro's father said. "Take good care of Yash and tell her mother I need the reward. You can find me at the Mayan market."

Yash and Pedro, holding Jaguarcito, got out and stood on the sidewalk. Then Pedro's father gave him a handful of coins.

"*Ka'ah dios kala'anteech.* May the gods protect you," he said and waved as he drove away.

"Is he coming back?" Yash asked.

"I told him I'd stay with you," Pedro said.

"Who's Cuxil?"

"He's my uncle," Pedro said. "Let's find breakfast."

Yash looked both ways along the street. "Nothing's open."

"Let's go to the bus station. It never sleeps." Pedro carried Jaguarcito in his basket.

After a few steps, Yash froze in place. Her chest tightened and her breathing came too fast.

"What's wrong with you?" Pedro asked.

"I'm so hungry my insides are quivering and my stomach hurts."

"You'll feel better if you eat," Pedro said.

Yash remembered the smell of cooking tortillas at the bus station and the taste of their ice cream. "I want a tamale," she said.

Pedro bought them both tamales, and when they finished, ice cream bars.

"It's kind of crazy to eat ice cream for breakfast," he said. "I don't know if we have enough left to buy milk for Jaguarcito."

The chocolate ice cream comforted Yash, but before she finished it, a noisy van that needed a muffler roared past. She flinched and her heart thumped. She turned to look behind her at a white van with a crumpled front fender. She flashed a picture of Grandma: *The gun hit Grandma, blood on Grandma's head, Grandma on the sidewalk.*

Yash dropped her ice cream and it went splat. She grabbed Pedro.

"What's wrong, Little Sister?" Pedro set Jaguarcito down and put his arms around her.

"Right here," Yash said in between sobs. "The attack happened right here. Yellow Teeth had a gun and they took me away."

32

The bells at the cathedral in Antigua rang nine times. Yash couldn't remember what time Vanna unlocked her business, but the shops across the street hadn't opened either. Seated on the sidewalk, she leaned her back against the wall in front of *Taller del Jade Maya* and held the jaguar kitten in her lap.

"The milk isn't sour," Pedro said, handing her the bottle. "You'll feel better if you feed Jaguarcito."

"This is the last of yesterday's milk." Yash rubbed her face on the jaguar's soft fur and cuddled him in her lap. She moved the bottle closer to the kitten, and he sucked the nipple enthusiastically. "We have to get more this morning."

"I hope I have enough money left."

Yash concentrated on feeding the kitten until a van pulled up to the curb, the van from Quetzal Centrale, with Ignacio behind the wheel.

Vanna climbed out, turned, and stared. Her face turned white and her mouth dropped wide open. Then she rushed over. "Yash! Yash! Honey, we've been worried sick!"

"Pedro brought me back." Yash held Jaguarcito, who was so long that his tail brushed the sidewalk.

"I'll hold Jaguarcito," Pedro said.

"Oh, Honey, I didn't recognize you at first." Vanna hugged her. "You look like a street urchin."

Yash liked being hugged. She didn't know what an urchin was, but she hadn't had a bath for days and her hair hadn't been combed either.

"What happened to your clothes?" Vanna asked.

"I was climbing trees." Yash looked at her too-big pants. She still wore her pink birthday shoes, muddy and coming apart. "Pedro's mother gave me these pants."

"And this is Pedro?" Vanna asked.

"He gave me Jaguarcito." Yash noticed Pedro's hair needed combing. "Pedro, this is *Señora* Anderson."

Pedro said, "*Mucho gusto, señora,*" but Vanna didn't greet him. He stood in the same place and didn't move one inch. Jaguarcito's tail slapped the sidewalk.

"Oh-my-God!" Vanna squeezed Yash's shoulder. "I can't believe you're here. Your parents have been looking everywhere. What happened?"

Yash didn't know where to begin. Feeling guilty over causing so much worry, she blurted out, "Some bad men hit Grandma on her head and grabbed me and put me into a van and drove into the jungle and got bitten by a snake and died and then the skunk pigs came and ate them up."

"You must have been scared to death." Vanna hugged her again. "Thank God you're safe."

"Pedro took care of me," Yash said.

"For heaven's sake, let's go inside," Vanna said.

"Do you have any milk for my kitten?" Yash asked.

Vanna laughed and that meant things were all right. She asked Ignacio to buy canned milk and two combs and bananas or *burritos* for the kids to eat, and they went inside.

"I'll call your father on his satellite phone. He and your mother are out looking for you." Vanna touched Yash's head and smiled at Pedro. "Your parents have been worried sick."

"My magic jade bead didn't work," Yash said.

Vanna gave the children foil-wrapped moist towelettes to clean their faces and stationed them in her office. They fed Jaguarcito, who was always ready for more milk.

"I have to pee," Pedro said.

Yash moved the kitten's basket out of the way but where he could look through the open doorway. She showed Pedro how to use the toilet. She came back in time to see two American tourists come into the shop, an overweight man and a woman wearing a floppy straw hat.

"Your kitten is *so cute*," the woman said. "Can I pet him?"

"He's a baby jaguar, but he likes people," Yash said.

"A jaguar-cat? I've never heard of that breed." She stroked Jaguarcito's head and he purred his buzz-saw song.

Later, a Mayan woman entered the shop. Through the open doorway, Yash saw her look all around. Then she whispered to Vanna, "*Quiero vender jade.*"

Yash watched: the woman wanted to sell jade.

"Let's see it," Vanna said.

"May I hold it?" Yash said, standing beside Vanna.

The Mayan woman looked from Vanna to Yash and handed it to the girl.

"It's serpentine, Vanna," Yash said after examining the green carving of a rabbit. "It isn't heavy enough, it isn't cold enough, and it feels soapy."

"How does that child know anything?"

"She's a jade witch." Vanna sounded serious, but she looked like she wanted to laugh. "And she's always right."

"She's magic?" The woman's eyes widened. Then she looked at Yash. "No, she's too young to know anything."

"Under the circumstances, I can offer you only $100," Vanna said.

The woman looked all around, shoved the money into a pocket, and hurried out the door.

After she left, Yash asked, "What will you do with it?"

"The style is modern, but I'll give it to a museum if Paul thinks it's ancient," Vanna said. "Otherwise, I'll label it serpentine and sell it online."

"Did you call my father?" Yash asked.

"I couldn't get him on his cell phone, but he always returns before dark," Vanna said.

"Did you give him my note?"

"Yes, I found it the next day. We closed for three days when Isolde went to the hospital—I guess you don't know."

"Oh, no! Is my Grandma okay?" She remembered—*Grandma's head, bloody, after Yellow Teeth hit her.* She bit her lip to keep from crying.

"Well, I think so. They hit her so hard that they fractured her skull, and a piece of bone pressed on her brain. She went to the big hospital in Guatemala City."

"Is she going to … die?" Yash's voice broke. She had insisted on going to the bus station for ice cream. Grandma, hurt, and she might die. She blubbered, "It was my fault."

"I'm sure she'll be fine." Vanna hugged her. "It wasn't your fault."

"Can I see her?" Yash's face was wet from crying.

"That depends on what the doctor says, but she's going to be okay." Vanna dried Yash's tears with a tissue. "Don't cry, honey. She's has good doctors, and she'll be all right."

Yash returned to the office and Pedro, who had been listening, asked how she knew it wasn't jade. She told him about jade: its weight, its hardness, its smooth, cool feel. She let him hold pieces of Vanna's collection.

Pedro hefted a *celt* and traced with one finger the lines etched on its surface.

"Where did you learn all that?" he asked.

"My daddy's a geologist and I have a mineral collection," Yash said. "Besides, Alberto showed me his jade workshop and he said I have *la afinidad* for jade."

"What's that?" Pedro seemed unsure of the big word.

"Vanna says that means affinity," Yash explained. "Mommy says it means kinship."

Pedro frowned. She had forgotten he didn't know English. In Spanish, she added, "It's like jade is a member of my family."

"But jade's a rock. It can't be your uncle."

"Alberto says I can always pick out the jade from the similar rocks in his shop," Yash said. "I hold it, and I know."

"And he lets you polish it?"

"I work there every day, and Alberto tells me stories."

"I want to learn about jade, too," he said.

Vanna closed the shop early. Yash, Pedro, and Jaguarcito piled into the Quetzal Centrale vehicle with her. Vanna told them to wait in the van when they arrived at the electric gate.

"I have to tie up the dogs," she said. "They'll go nuts when they smell that jaguar kitten."

Then Vanna said they had to stay in Yash's room and they had to clean up. Yash showed Pedro how the shower worked and handed him a towel. Afterwards, he had to wear the same pants, but Yash gave him a *Laguna Lachuá* T-shirt, too big for her, exactly right for him. He stood in front of the mirror and combed his hair until he looked nice. Then he cleaned up Jaguarcito with the wet washcloth.

"The kitten needs a sand box," he said. "I'll teach him to use it so you won't have to wipe up his behind every day."

Jaguarcito explored the room and went back to his basket for a nap, and Yash took her turn in the shower. She needed to wash her hair; Maria hadn't helped her with it. Her hair was so matted and grubby that she removed the hairclasp Pedro gave her at the Mayan market and unraveled her braid. She enjoyed the warm water, dried her hair with a towel, and dressed in clean clothes.

Yash stood in front of the closet mirror. Her untamed hair made her look like a wild animal, a porcupine. She used her new comb to remove tangles, beginning at the bottom like Mommy did, but she couldn't reach the back of her head. She couldn't see it either.

"I can't go to dinner," Yash said, close to tears. "I can't comb my hair."

"Here," Pedro said, grabbing her comb. "My father said I must take good care of you."

"Ow! Don't pull!"

Pedro finished combing out her snarls, but she didn't look like herself without the braid down her back. She couldn't see her hair in the back—how did Mommy do it?

"I'll braid it to the front so you can see how it's done," Pedro said. "I watched Maria when she did her hair."

Yash admired Pedro's handiwork, a braid over one shoulder and hanging in the front. It had a crooked place, but she liked her new look.

"We'll go to dinner when Daddy comes back," she said. "Vanna doesn't have picnics at dinnertime like your mother does. We all sit at a big table and use knives and forks. I'll sit next to you and you can watch what I do."

"Okay," Pedro said. "What about Jaguarcito?"

"I think he can stay here if we give him some milk and close the door. I'll be right back." Yash found Zia in the kitchen.

"Yash!" Zia dropped the frying pan she held with the dishtowel. "I'm so glad to see you."

"Sh-h-h. Vanna told me to stay in my room until my father comes. Do you have any canned milk for my kitten?"

"A kitten?"

"You can see him in my room," Yash said. "He needs a sandbox, too."

Zia came to see the kitten, and Pedro seemed happy to see someone he could talk to in Mayan. Zia said she'd ask Alberto about a sandbox and bring a towel for the basket.

After Zia went back to the kitchen, they fed Jaguarcito. Yash asked Pedro where he went to school. He said it was too far from his house, unless he stayed with *mi tío Cuxil.*

"Can you read Spanish?" Yash asked.

"No. I wish I could."

"Then I will teach you." Yash opened her beginning Spanish reader and began showing him the alphabet.

"I know that part," Pedro said.

"Then you can read," Yash said. "The words always sound out the same way."

Whop, whop, whop—

"Daddy's helicopter!" Yash jumped up so quickly that she knocked over her chair. "Daddy's coming. Please watch Jaguarcito until I come back."

33

Hours and hours: Pesh and Kedar had circled Highway 14 in careful search grids, back and forth, over and over, until everything below looked the same. They didn't stop to eat, but Pesh had no appetite. She'd lost weight in the two weeks since Yash had been stolen. She pulled off her headset to rub her aching temples. Would they ever find Yash? Would she ever see her baby playing with her pebbles again? *Not rocks, Mommy— they're my mineral collection.* She unbuckled her seatbelt in the helicopter and closed her eyes to rest them from the glare, only for a moment.

"Wake up and fasten your seatbelt." Kedar tapped her arm. "We're close to landing."

The sun rested on the horizon, and the green painted "H" at the Quetzal Centrale helipad came into view directly below her. Someone stood too close to the helipad!

"*¡Ay ay ay!* Go around!" Pesh yelled.

"What?" Kedar added power and lifted up and turned to the right.

Drawing in her breath sharply, Pesh screamed, "It's Yash! It's Yash!" Tears welling up, she couldn't say more.

"What! Are you sure?" Kedar hovered and swung the helicopter around so he could see the tiny figure on the ground. "My God, it is Yash! My little princess!"

"She knows to stand well back. I'll try again."

"She's clear," Pesh said. "*Dios Bo'otik!*"

Kedar landed the helicopter. Pesh jumped out before the rotors stopped, ducked under the blades, and ran to her daughter.

"Yash! I was so worried!" Pesh hugged her baby. "Are you okay? How'd you get here?"

"Pedro's father took me to Vanna's shop," Yash said.

Before Pesh could ask more questions, Kedar scooped Yash into a bear hug. "My little princess! I'm so glad you're all right."

"Daddy!" Yash squealed in delight, then said, "Don't squeeze so hard. Why are you crying?"

"It's because I love you so much." Kedar released her and swung her up onto his shoulders. "Sometimes that's what daddies do when they're really, really happy. I thought I'd never see you again."

"Let's sit in the shade of the magnolia tree," Pesh said.

"Daddy, can I have a kitten?" Yash clung to his neck the way she always did when she wanted something. "Pedro gave me a kitten."

"A kitten? Let's talk about that later." Kedar usually bounced her around like her horse, but not this time.

"Where's Grandma? When can I see her?"

"You can see her right now, Princess." Kedar stopped in the shade, stood Yash on the ground, and pulled out his smartphone with its photos. "She has a medical halo and she's sewn together with black string."

"Does it hurt?" Yash asked, looking at her father.

"That funny-looking hat is halo traction to keep her from moving her head."

"When's she coming home?" Yash asked.

"I don't know, but Grandpa Burt is with her," Kedar said. "She's going to be okay."

"Your Grandma told us two men took you away in a white van." Pesh encircled Yash with her arms. *Was her little girl really okay?* "Did they hurt you, sweetie?"

"They slapped me, and that made me mad," Yash said. "I had to sit there for a long time and they wouldn't let me see out."

"They didn't do anything else?" Pesh held her breath. "They didn't touch you, except for the slap?"

"No, but they said I was a brat."

"Oh, Honey!" Pesh squeezed Yash tighter. "I was so worried!"

Yash wiggled away and faced her father. "I wanted you to punch 'em out, Daddy. Why didn't you come?"

"I couldn't make the jade work," he said.

"Let's sit on bench on the veranda," Pesh said. "How did you get away?"

"The men got out to smoke cigarettes. They stood under a tree with a snake hidden in it. They didn't see the snake, but I asked it to help me. The snake bit them and they died."

"You talked to a snake?" Pesh asked. *Hurt my baby, you die by venomous snake*—the curse she had given Five-Owl. *Cimil did it!*

"Mommy, I saw a quetzal," Yash said. "He told me to stay in the van."

"A quetzal?" Pesh asked. *A snake, a quetzal, both holy to the Maya—¡Ay caramba!*

"How'd you get back?" Kedar asked.

"Pedro found me, and his father drove us to Vanna's shop." Yash frowned. "I called you with the jade bead. Why didn't you come?"

"I'm sorry, Princess. I didn't know how to use it."

"Mommy's magic," Yash said. "Why didn't you ask her how to use it?"

"I had to get help to learn to use the bead," Pesh said. "You gave jade to your Daddy and Grandma—they could use it, not me. But Grandma saw you right away. You were holding a kitten."

"Mommy, Daddy, come see my kitten!" Yash grabbed Pesh's arm and pulled her along, and Kedar followed one step behind.

Back in her room, Yash introduced her parents to Pedro and Jaguarcito.

"That's not a kitten," Pesh said. "It's a baby jaguar."

"His mother died and he loves me. Pedro gave him to me," Yash said.

"And this is the young man who brought you back?" Kedar asked.

"I'm pleased to meet you," Pedro said in Spanish.

"Let me shake your hand, young man." Kedar extended his right hand.

Pedro stepped back. In true Mayan fashion, he didn't take Kedar's hand.

"It's okay, Pedro," Yash said. "Shaking hands means he likes you."

"Where did you meet Pedro?" Kedar asked.

"Pedro found me in a tree and brought me home."

"*Gracias,* Pedro." Kedar smiled and clapped Pedro on the shoulder.

Pesh noticed Pedro wore clean clothes and had combed his hair, and Yash's braid hung down one side in the front, not in the middle of her back. *Who had helped her with her hair?*

"Pedro's my big brother now and he knows about everything," Yash said.

"I think we should hear all about this over dinner. You're all slicked up, but we aren't," Kedar said. "I'll call you when Zia says it's ready."

Kedar and Pesh went to freshen up in their room, and Yash cuddled Jaguarcito and held his bottle for him to nurse. When he released the nipple, a few drops of milk ran down his chin and he closed his eyes.

"Jaguarcito thinks you're his mother," Yash said to Pedro and nestled the kitten into his basket. "He's afraid you're going to desert him."

"How do you know that?"

"Because he told me."

"Animals can't talk," Pedro said.

"I hear him in my head. When we go to dinner, tell him you're coming back and leave your shirt by his basket so he smells you."

"What's this about having a jaguar in your room, young lady?" Paul asked as soon as Yash entered the room.

"Here, sit next to me." Pesh pulled out chairs for Yash and Pedro across the table from Kedar and Paul. *Paul didn't say hello or glad to see you or where have you been.*

"They had the kitten when they came to the shop this morning," Vanna said. "We brought it here temporarily."

"He's sleeping in his basket," Yash said. "We told him to stay there."

"That's no kitten! It's a jaguar!" Paul slapped his water glass against the table. "Do you know how big they get?"

Yash cringed and Pedro stared at Paul.

Good thing that glass isn't stemware, Pesh thought. *He's a grump tonight.*

"A hundred kilos," Yash said.

"That's 220 pounds. One big cat, one mighty killing machine," Paul said. "They're hunters. They go after chickens, goats, pigs. Farmers shoot them."

"Somebody shot his mother so Pedro took him home so he wouldn't die," Yash said.

"Pedro is kind-hearted," Vanna said. "Jaguarcito's cute now but he'll be dangerous when he grows up."

"But he likes people," Yash said. "Pedro is teaching him to use the sandbox."

"We know you love Jaguarcito, and Pedro does too," Pesh said. "But where is he going to go? Pedro can't take him home. You can't take him into the United States. Paul and Vanna have no place for him here."

"I've been calling around," Vanna said. "I have a friend, a vet who treats exotic animals, and he said the Guatemala City Zoo wants baby jaguars."

"But he'll have to live in a cage," Yash said. "No one will love him."

"Good. We'll be rid of him then," Paul said. "A rescued, wild-born jaguar brings valuable new genes to the zoo population."

The conversation stopped when Zia served lemon chicken with rice and beans, already loaded onto plates. They ate quietly, and Pesh hoped Paul's mood would improve when he had a full stomach.

"You'll never believe it," Vanna said, scooting back in her chair. "The Woodland Park Zoo in Seattle shows videos to their jaguar cubs. They all watch the Cheetah show on a big screen."

"Let me tell Pedro." In Spanish, Yash told him about the movies for cubs. He whispered that he had never been to the movies.

"You can rent a car in Antigua," Vanna said. "Take the animal to the zoo."

Stirring milk into his coffee, Paul said, "Do it before he gets any bigger, while you can still handle him in a vehicle. Jaguars are incredibly strong. I heard that one hauled the carcass of a young cow up into a tree."

Pedro's eyes lit up and he grabbed Yash's arm. "Tell him in English, jaguars like to swim. They have long tails, and they skim the surface of the water with them. That makes fish come up, and jaguars jump in and grab them."

Yash translated, everyone laughed, and Zia passed around pineapple upside down cake.

Kedar said to Yash, "You haven't told Paul about how you got away from the kidnappers. And Pedro found you?"

"The bad men drove to a banana plantation. They slapped me and told me to shut up," Yash said in Spanish so Pedro would understand. She explained that, when the men were outside smoking, a snake dropped down from a tree and bit them. They got sick and then they died.

"Weren't you frightened?" Vanna asked.

"No, because I stayed safe in the van. But the skunk pigs were worse. They're ugly and make scary noises and they stink."

"They could have eaten you!" Pesh interrupted.

"Peccaries!" Paul said from across the table. "They're mean."

"My God! What happened then?" Kedar pushed aside his dessert, uneaten.

"The skunk pigs came and ate the bad men until they looked like soup bones." Yash waved her hands and pointed like Alberto when he told a story. "They go *huh-huh-huh* and *click-click-click,* and they stare at you with little beady eyes."

"*¡Ay, caramba!*" Pedro said.

"Then what did you do?" Pesh asked.

"A quetzal told me to stay in the van," Yash said.

"You talked to a quetzal?" Pesh asked to get her back to the main story. Yash seemed to believe she could talk to animals. *A snake, a quetzal, both sacred to the Maya: surely Cimil's work.* "And you hid in the van?"

"I stayed there so the skunk pigs wouldn't get me. Then a car was coming, and I thought it was you, Daddy," Yash said, looking at Kedar.

"Who was in the car?" Pesh sucked in her breath.

"More bad men. I sneaked out and hid behind a tree. They held up a bloody boot and said the pigs ate the other men. They took the van away so I went to live in a tree."

"And that's where Pedro found you?" Pesh asked.

"I was hungry. Pedro gave me a banana and brought me home with him."

"And Pedro's father gave you a ride to my shop?" Vanna asked.

"Pedro, you're a hero," Kedar said. "*El héroe.*"

"I am eternally grateful," Pesh said. She added in Mayan, "*Dios bo'otik*, the gods pay," and touched her jaguar talisman through her shirt. Getting Yash back was all she cared about. Her search for jade could wait a while, now that they had an extra child and a jaguar.

34

Traffic clogged Guatemala City's main thoroughfare. Its glass skyscrapers, painted blue, pink, and orange, towered over sprawling slums. Potholed streets, choking fumes from rasping buses, street people dressed in rags peddling cigarettes—Pesh understood why Vanna said tourists avoided this city. At two million residents, it was the largest city in Central America but without the charm of Antigua or the beauty of Mérida.

Pesh looked back at the children and their kitten. Pedro held it and its bottle while Yash stroked its head and talked to it. Everything looked normal, except the kitten was a young jaguar and Yash insisted that it talked to her.

Kedar, driving the rental car, broke the silence. In Spanish, he said to Pedro, "I'll take you in a helicopter another time. The noise would hurt Jaguarcito's ears."

"*Gracias, señor*," Pedro said.

"Is this the first time you've gone to a big city?"

"*Sí, señor.*"

"Please, call me Kedar."

"*Sí, Señor* Kedar."

"He means call him Kedar *solamente, no señor*," Pesh put in. "And call me Pesh."

"When I was your age, I lived in a large city," Kedar continued. "Los Angeles in California, crowded and noisy."

"California. Is that in Hollywood?" Pedro asked.

"No. California is *mucho grande*," Kedar said. "Los Angeles is near Hollywood, where they make movies."

"Vanna said Jaguarcito would get to watch movies," Yash said, and Pedro added, "I have never seen a movie."

"We're getting close," Kedar said. "Everybody, help me watch for signs pointing to the zoo."

"You look, too," Yash said to Pedro. "Zoo is an easy word—Zeta, Oh, Oh."

When they left downtown and turned onto Boulevard Liberacíon, everything outside the window on the right side changed to green landscaping, trees, and flowerbeds, all secured by chainlink fencing. They parked beside Área verde near the administration building at La Aurora Zoo, and Pedro carried Jaguarcito in his basket.

Over the zoo entrance gate, a large sign painted with brightly colored cartoon animals—deer, parrots, monkeys, and a giraffe—read, "La Aurora Guatemala Zoo," the word ZOO in orange capital letters. A yellow and black jaguar peered out through the middle "O." The gatekeeper took one look at Jaguarcito and asked them to wait outside for a zoo attendant. Then an armed guard escorted them through a restricted area to the veterinary, where a locked metal door without windows blocked access and a brass plaque announced, "CBT Camal, DVM."

Kedar rang the bell.

The vet, Cit-Bolon-Tum Camal, introduced himself as CBT and invited them in. Shorter than Kedar, he wore a white lab coat and had a stethoscope around his neck. He looked enough like Pesh to be her brother, but without the braid down the back of his head. His black hair was trimmed in a modern style.

"You're named for one of the gods of medicine and healing," Pesh said.

"I like to think that helps me to care for my patients." CBT asked Pedro, "May I pick up your jaguar cub?"

Then, gently lifting the cub, he said soothingly, "I won't hurt you, little one." CBT held the animal next to his chest and stroked its head with one finger. Jaguarcito relaxed and closed his eyes.

"He likes people," Yash said.

"Where did you find him?" CBT asked Pedro.

"In the jungle near my house," Pedro said. "Someone shot his mother and I found her den. The cub was little and helpless and blind. He was so hungry that he tried to suck my finger. I brought him home and gave him canned milk and water."

"Aha! So, he thinks you're his mother," CBT said. "You were the first living being he saw when he opened his eyes. Let's weigh him, shall we?"

CBT said Jaguarcito weighed 13 kilos. "The female jaguar weans her cubs when they're about this big, but I will continue his habit of taking canned milk and water a little longer to let him adjust to his new environment."

"I thought he was getting heavy," Pedro said. "May I feed him one last time?"

"Good idea." CBT set the jaguar kitten on the examination table and put the stethoscope against its back. "His heart and lungs sound healthy. Would you like to listen?"

"*Sí, señor*." Pedro donned the instrument and grinned. "I hear his heart beating!"

"Next I must give him his shots to prevent illnesses," CBT said. "I need you to keep him calm. It will not hurt, but he might be frightened."

The vaccinations took only seconds while Pedro comforted the kitten.

"He wasn't scared," Yash said.

"Now put his basket into this enclosure so he knows it belongs to him," CBT told Pedro.

"You need a helper. Could I work for you?" Pedro put Jaguarcito onto his blanket and held his bottle through the open door. "I could clean all the cages."

"I'm sorry," CBT said. "The zoo could not hire someone so young."

Petting the little jaguar, Yash told CBT, "He likes you and he isn't afraid."

"What will you do with Jaguarcito?" Pesh asked.

"He will stay here in isolation for a few days," CBT said. "Pedro has done a good job with him—he seems very healthy."

"And after that?" Kedar asked.

"Three zoos in the United States have requested a jaguar," CBT said. "Jaguar births are becoming quite rare."

"Will they show movies?" Yash asked.

"Can I send him a birthday present?" Pedro asked.

"I think that's only in Seattle," CBT said, smiling. "All the zoos these days provide a pleasant place with lots of food and toys so he won't get bored."

"Could you let us know where he goes?" Kedar asked. "The children love him."

"¡Seguro! Give me your address." CBT handed Kedar a scrap of paper and a pen.

"Can you send him to Austin, Texas?" Yash asked. "That's where I live. Maybe I could go see him sometimes."

"I will give Austin preference," CBT said. "Have you seen our zoo?"

"No," Yash said, but Pedro didn't answer.

"You'll feel better when you see how well we provide for our animals," CBT said.

Pedro had never been to a zoo, but Yash filled him in on her visit to the Austin Zoo. CBT had suggested a tour, so the four of them joined a group following a guide.

In *Región africana*, they saw animals from the largest desert in the world, *el Sahara*, and from the longest river, *el Nilo*. Two *hipopótamos* swam in an artificial river. Three *elefantes* shared the largest cage—not really a cage at all, but landscaped to make them feel at home and to keep tourists away from them. Four *léones* lay lazily napping until the male with the tawny mane roared. The tallest animal in the world, *la jirafa*, fed from hay on a high shelf. The guide said *la jirafa* was 6 meters tall and his neck, 2 meters long.

"That's nineteen feet tall," Kedar said. "I still think better in feet and inches."

"But Daddy, nobody uses those any more," Yash said. "At school we learn the metric system."

Pedro nodded and said he knew about meters.

"See?" Pesh said. "You're out-numbered."

"Very punny," Kedar said, laughing, but Yash and Pedro didn't get the joke.

Next, their zoo guide brought them to the *Región asiática.* "Asia is the largest continent. It contains the highest mountain, *el Everest*, and the largest lake, *el mar Caspio*."

Pesh, standing between the children, rested her hands on their shoulders. "Back at Vanna's, I'll show you where all these faraway places are on a map."

The guide pointed out the python and the bearcat and stopped in front of *el tigre* to give the tourists a toilet break. "Those fences are there to keep tourists away from the animals. If you feed them junk food, they get sick—like people do."

Several people tittered and then the group laughed, but Pesh found his statements factual rather than funny.

"Tourists sometimes want to touch the tiger," the guide continued. "A good way to lose an arm. Wild animals are cute when they are babies, but they grow up powerful and unpredictable."

Kedar pulled Yash's braid. "You see, Princess, that's why you can't keep a jaguar."

"But Jaguarcito would never hurt me," Yash said.

"Not while he's a baby," Kedar said.

At their final destination, *Región americana,* Pesh said, "That's where we live."

The guide held up his hand for silence and waited until he had everyone assembled. "South America contains the widest and deepest river, *el Amazonas*, and the driest desert, *el Atacama*. Right here in Guatemala, we have the most volcanoes of any country in the world, and the most diverse animals."

While listening, Yash stood on one foot and then the other and played with a pebble with the toe of one shoe. After they passed *el tapir* and *la marmoseta*, she asked, "Don't you have any jaguars or a quetzal?"

"No quetzal. But you can see the jaguar over there." The guide pointed to a wide path.

"Let's go, Daddy," Yash said, and Pedro added, "*Ko'ox!*"

Down the way, they came to a landscaped pit as large as a schoolyard with a stream running through it and rocks good for climbing along its sides. A jaguar napped on a sturdy branch of a dead tree, its trunk shredded from the big cat's claws.

"They should throw fish in there," Pedro said. "He could go fishing."

The lone jaguar, a carbon copy of Jaguarcito except older, stretched and yawned.

"He's happy here," Yash said. "Maybe Jaguarcito will like the zoo, too."

"I'm sure he will," Pesh said.

The next enclosure, equally spacious, held a black panther— a black jaguar. It chased a blue ball the size of a watermelon, batting it with one powerful paw and then pouncing on it.

"Look! I can still see his spots," Yash said. "Why don't they put them into the same place so they can play?"

"Jaguars like to live alone," Pedro said. "When they're two years old, they leave their mother and live on their own."

"Seeking their fortunes, like in fairy tales?"

"Something like that." Kedar said. "Hey, Princess, this is the last of the row of big cats. Time for us to go."

A little later, on the return trip to Antigua in the rental car, Yash and Pedro fell asleep on the back seat.

"Looks like we wore them out," Pesh said. "Visiting the zoo was a great idea. I think the kids are comfortable with leaving their kitten with CBT. Thanks for asking him to let us know where they send Jaguarcito."

"Got us off the hook. I didn't want to tell Yash we don't want any pets, when we had just found her again."

"Sh-h-h. She'll hear you."

Pesh found Yash's comments about animals disturbing: "A quetzal told me," "Jaguarcito likes …," "I asked the snake to help me." *Could Yash really communicate with animals?* Pesh fingered her jaguar talisman through her T-shirt, as though it had an answer.

"Sometimes I think Yash has ears in the back of her head," Kedar said. "And she knows she can get me to do almost anything."

"I'm glad for the almost," Pesh said.

"You know, Pedro's a fine young man. I really like him, and he's been good for Yash."

"I like him, too, but we're losing a lot of days here," Pesh said. "You don't know what day to pick up your mother, and we don't know when Pedro's father will come for him."

"That's easy," Kedar said. "We need to visit Xiu to thank her, and we need to hike to B'alam Ha, wherever that is. We can't leave the kids. Let's take them along."

Pesh asked Kedar, "What about your mother?"

"Burt's with her. If they can't reach us, she'll have to stay a couple of days longer."

"What about Pedro's father?"

"Vanna can have Ignacio talk to him, pin him down to what day he'll pick up Pedro."

"Sounds like you've covered all the bases," Pesh said. "We're on the way to B'alam Ha."

35

"It's my very favorite place," Yash said. Now that Jaguarcito lived at the zoo, she could leave her room at Quetzal Centrale and show Pedro around.

At the magnolia tree, Vanna's two large black Dobermans blocked the path. They snarled and pulled their lips back in ugly smiles.

"Stand still," Yash commanded. "Roco. Pepe. Friends. Pedro is a friend."

Pedro froze in place.

"Let them sniff you," Yash said. "They think your pants smell like Jaguarcito."

Satisfied, the dogs left as quickly as they had appeared.

"How'd you make them go away?" Pedro asked.

"I heard Vanna tell them 'Friends.' Come on. The jade shop is over there." She led him by the hand past the rumbling rock-tumbler to where Alberto stood by the open front door of the jade workshop.

"Ah, *Señorita Jade*. My helper has been gone a long time. And who is this?"

"Pedro. He found me after I was kidnapped."

"Welcome to my workshop." Alberto greeted the boy in Mayan. "You kept Yash safe."

"It is my job," Pedro said.

Yash showed Pedro the polishing machine that smelled like honey, the tumblers that rumbled and knocked off rough corners, and the drilling machine that buzzed and dug a tunnel through beads. They finished the tour next to a box of unworked jade of various sizes, where Yash saw a mint-green piece with cream-colored streaks running through it, like hers.

"I lost my magic jade bead," Yash told Alberto. "May I make another?"

"You need to carry it always to keep you safe."

"It worked with the kidnappers. I lost it chasing grasshoppers with Pedro."

Alberto had several disks aleady cut from the original stone and ready for final polishing. He handed one to Yash, one to Pedro.

"*Gracias*," Pedro said. "Is this one magic like Yash's bead?"

"All jade is magic. That's why it's a sacred stone."

Yash thanked Alberto and turned her disk this way and that. "Will this work with the bead I gave my father?"

"*Sí*. They are cut from the same stone." Alberto set them up with some polishing powder in the shade of the big magnolia tree, and he brought out his experimental piece, a dark green turtle the size of Yash's hand. They all worked in silence until Yash told Alberto, "Pedro's Mayan name is 15-Rabbit."

"That's his special date on the sacred calendar," Alberto said. "I was first called 9-Owl."

"What's your calendar name?" Pedro asked Yash.

"I don't have one. I'm MaryamYaxuun B'alam."

"Everybody has one," Alberto said. "Your mother will remember."

They all went back to work. Yash polished Pedro's stone, and he polished hers, and Alberto worked on his turtle, until a hummingbird came their way, flashing red, green, and blue.

"I'll show you a secret," Alberto said. "You must be very quiet."

He crouched down and tiptoed, and he looked so funny that Yash almost laughed. She held her hand over her mouth to stay quiet and followed Alberto and Pedro to a large bush next to Vanna's house.

"Look there," Alberto said.

Yash didn't see anything.

"I see it," Pedro whispered. "There, in the 'Y' between two branches. A nest."

At first, the bush seemed to have a bark knot on the side of the branch. The knot held a small cup—a penny would fill it—the size of a walnut shell boat like her grandmother made for her. Inside the nest were two white pea-sized eggs. Yash reached out to point—

"Careful. We can never touch a hummingbird's nest. She took a week to build it." Alberto explained how the bird gathered feathers, bits of willow fuzz, and small plant parts and glued them together with spider webs.

"Will there be baby birds?" Yash asked.

"In a few days," Alberto said. "We can watch them grow." He escorted the children back to the shade and their polishing jobs.

"Well, now, where were we?" he asked. "Ready for a story to make your work go faster?"

"¡Oh, sí!" Yash loved his stories. *Pedro would, too.*

"Do you know where *Tzun-tzun* the Hummingbird got her feathers?"

"No," Yash said, and Pedro shook his head.

"Okay, then," Alberto said. "Everyone likes *Tzun-tzun* the Hummingbird. She's the only bird who can fly backwards and hover in one spot."

Yash fixed her eyes on Alberto's hands, fluttering, then hovering like the bird.

"Her feathers have no bright colors, but she doesn't mind. She is happy with her life. Then *Tzun-tzun* falls in love. She wants to get married, but she has nothing pretty to wear. So her bird friends want to surprise her with a wedding dress. What do you think they do?"

Alberto looked first at Yash, then at Pedro, and waited for them to answer.

"Go shopping?" Yash asked.

"They can't do that in the jungle," Pedro said.

"They all give her gifts. *Ya* the Vermilion-crowned Flycatcher wears crimson rings of feathers around his throat. He tucks a few red plumes in his crown and gives the rest to *Tzun-tzun* for her necklace. *Uchilachil* the Bluebird donates blue feathers for her gown, and blue-crowned *Motmot* offers turquoise blue and emerald green. Then, *Yuyum* the Oriole sews all the plumage into a wedding gown, and *Ah-leum* the Spider creeps up with a fragile web of shiny gossamer threads for her veil."

"Spider web, like in her nest," Yash said.

"*Sí, Señorita Jade*, but they need to plan the reception, too," Alberto said. "*Canac* the Honeybee tells his friends. The bees bring honey and nectar and *Tzun-tzun*'s favorite blossoms. *Haaz* the Banana Bush, *Op* the Custard Apple, and *Pichi* the Guava Bush offer their ripe fruits for refreshments, and a band of butterflies promises to dance and flutter around."

"I wish we could see that," Pedro said.

"Back to the story," Alberto said. "On her wedding day, *Tzun-tzun* is so surprised she can barely twitter her vows, and the Great Spirit says she can wear her wedding dress for the rest of her life. And that's where the hummingbird got her feathers."

"I love your stories," Yash said.

"Me, too," Pedro said. "Do you need an apprentice? I would work very hard."

"You need to finish school first," Alberto said.

"I must go to work when I am ten, but I don't want to be a day laborer like my father."

Alberto shook his head and looked sad.

"He knows his alphabet already and how to sound out." Yash wanted to take him home to Austin. He could go to school with her. Maybe they'd see Jaguarcito at the zoo.

36

Every night, the Andersons discussed the events of the day over dinner like Grandpa Burt did at his house. Yash usually had her evening meal in the kitchen with Zia, but tonight she and Pedro were invited to dinner with the grown-ups.

After spending all day in Alberto's workshop, Yash and Pedro went to her room to clean up. Pedro dressed in the new pants and T-shirt that Vanna bought for him. Yash put on a bright pink shirt and clean Bermuda shorts.

"Do you really have to go to work when you're ten?" Yash asked.

"*Sí*. Maria is not my real mother." Pedro sounded sad.

Yash noticed his worn out shoes and stepped into her old pink plastic ones.

"Maria wants me to go to work to bring home more money," Pedro continued. "She's going to have another baby. She wanted you to babysit."

"When is your father coming to get you?" Yash would hate babysitting every day.

"I don't know."

"Doesn't he want the reward?" Yash wondered how much and who would pay it

"I only told him that so Maria would let him take you to Antigua," Pedro said. "He's ashamed to ask for a reward for doing what is right."

How strange: Pedro left on the sidewalk in Antigua. Her mother and father would never leave her alone on a city street.

At dinner, Yash and Pedro stayed for dessert and the grown-ups lingered over coffee and talked about crime lords. Yash hadn't said a word all evening. She didn't want to talk to Paul—he didn't like Jaguarcito—but Paul asked her, "What did your kidnappers look like?"

"They were both tall," Yash said. "Spaniards. One of them had a black mole on the end of his nose, a big ugly mole with a hair growing in the middle."

"My god!" Paul said. "That sounds like *El Cocodrilo*! The Crocodile is one of the nastiest guys in Guatemala. Then he's dead, for sure?"

"A snake bit him, a yellow snake," Yash said. "It had gold eyes and a yellow chin and a black collar behind its eyes. He screamed '*¡Muerto!*' and called it a devil."

"The *fer-de-lance*!" Kedar drew in his breath and his face paled. "The most deadly snake in Central America."

"*La barba amarilla*, a really mean snake," Pedro said, grasping Yash's arm. "Tell them in English. Most snakes want to hide but this one goes after you, and he kills. He hunts in banana plantations, and workers fear him."

Kedar gasped at Yash's translation but Paul only grunted.

"Did the snake come after you?" Pesh asked.

"No, Mommy, because I hid in the van. The quetzal told me to stay there."

"A quetzal talked to you?" Pedro asked.

"Why not? Daddy talks to birds all the time."

"Those are birdcalls," Kedar said. "The bird actually talked to you?"

"Yes, Daddy. I talk with animals whenever I want."

"Animals, talking to you. Horse feathers!" Paul said. Then he cleared his throat and asked, "How did you know *El Cocodrilo* was dead?"

"Because skunk pigs came and ate him up. They ate Yellow Teeth, too."

"How awful! And you watched that?" Pesh asked.

"Skunk pigs are scary," Yash said. "And they stink."

"Well, then. *El Cocodrilo* won't be around any more," Paul said. "I'm happy to hear that. He and his men have been stalking me."

"Then no more hiding from The Crocodile," Pesh said, remembering Xiu's words: ... *she hides from the crocodile.*

"But the crime lords are like snakes on Hydra's head," Paul said. "Whenever you cut off one, two more appear."

No one answered that, and Zia brought in fruit custard with vanilla ice cream.

After dessert, Kedar asked about Pedro's father.

"I don't know when he's coming for me," Pedro said.

No one answered.

"*Señor* Anderson," Pedro said. "I want to work for you. I can do anything. I work really hard."

"You should be in school," Paul said. "You're too young to be looking for work."

"I have to go to work when I am ten," Pedro said.

"I hear that's common among *campesinos*," Paul said. "Laborers who harvest produce get $100 a month."

"I don't want to be a laborer like my father," Pedro said. "I want to go to school."

"Don't you have a relative in Antigua?" Pesh asked.

"*Mi tío Cuxil*. He's my father's brother," Pedro said. "But I can't stay unless my father pays for my room."

"That isn't fair," Yash said.

"You need to go to school," Kedar said.

Paul looked at Pedro but didn't say anything.

"Then let's go visit Cuxil," Pesh said. "Perhaps he'll help us see what to do."

The next day, Pesh and the children went to Antigua while Kedar delivered supplies to B'alam Witz. Vanna's burly bodyguard Arturo, wearing a military-style uniform with a holstered pistol at his waist, stood by as she unlocked *Taller del Jade Maya*; he had become a fixture there since Yash's abduction. Ignacio stayed with the van, Pesh helped greet customers, and the kids sat in the office reading.

"Vanna says it's time for lunch," Pesh said. "Ignacio knows where we can get tamales."

Always ready to eat, Yash and Pedro scurried out.

"Can we have ice cream?" Yash asked.

"I can't risk losing you again," Pesh said.

"I know a place with ice cream, *Señora* Pesh." Ignacio drove them to a restaurant popular with tourists and with a guard posted outside. He said he'd wait for them in the vehicle, and Pesh promised to bring him lunch.

"Can you find your Uncle Cuxil's house?" Pesh asked Pedro. She flashed back to when her grandmother Chiich had died. When she had no family and no home, Burt had set her up at the dormitory at University of Mérida. Pedro needed the same kind of assistance.

"I think so, but it has been a long time," he said.

Ignacio drove them there and ate his lunch while he waited outside. Pesh rang the bell, a button at the side of a steel grate guarding the entrance. The stucco house was surrounded by a rock wall topped with jagged glass shards and had no windows facing the street.

No one answered. Pedro offered to go around to the back, but that gate also was locked.

"Can Cuxil read and write?" Pesh asked.

"Of course," Pedro said. "That is how he can afford such a house."

"What is his last name?" Pesh pulled out her notebook and pen to record the street address.

"Manu. That's my last name, too," Pedro said. "Lots of people in Antigua have that name."

Pesh tore out a page and wrote that Vanna Anderson at *Taller del Jade Maya* knew where to find Pedro Manu. She hadn't met Cuxil, but Pedro said he had once stayed with his uncle. She offered to pay room and board if Pedro could live there and go to elementary school. She signed it Chanlujun Pex B'alam, Archaeologist, and slipped the note behind the locked steel grill that blocked Cuxil's entryway.

"Is this a Mayan market day?" Pesh asked Pedro, who nodded.

"Then let's go," Pesh said. "*Ko'ox.*"

Pedro and Yash grinned and climbed into the van. Ignacio dropped the three of them at the Mayan marketplace and promised to return in an hour.

"Where does your father go at the market?" Pesh asked.

"He drinks beer and Maria sells hats. This way." Pedro led Pesh to an area where Maya women sold hats, scarves, and needlework, but Maria wasn't there.

"I don't see my father's truck." Pedro's eyes looked sad. He had the characteristic Mayan habit of hiding emotions behind a blank face.

"Don't worry. We'll come again on a Sunday." In a way, Pesh was glad because Pedro could be company for Yash on the trip to B'alam Ha tomorrow. When would she meet his parents? Why had they abandoned him? Would Cuxil answer her note?

"Can we have *chapulines*?" Yash asked.

"Hungry again? You just had lunch," Pesh said. "Okay. I know Pedro likes them, too."

Yash pulled her by the hand to the snack vendor, and she and Pedro gobbled them down as though they hadn't seen food for a week.

"Kids in Austin would say, 'Yuck! Fried bugs!' But I love them," Yash said.

"Tomorrow you'll meet *Xmenoob Xiu*," Pesh said. "What can we bring her for a gift?"

Yash and Pedro asked her to buy more *chapulines*, and Pesh added a large cantaloupe and half a dozen fresh sweet-lemons, both fruits she hadn't seen growing at Alta Altun. And a large sack of corn meal—Xiu had to grind her own.

When they joined Ignacio in the van, Pesh puzzled over how to find Pedro's relatives.

"I need to meet your father or your uncle," Pesh said. "If we drive down Highway 14, could you find your house?"

"I don't think so. I always ride in the back of the truck." Pedro paused as though trying to remember. "I don't know where I am until after I've been there."

"Lots of people don't know where they are," Pesh said, chuckling.

"I mean I always face the back," he said. "I don't know any landmarks."

When Pesh asked him how long to drive to Antigua, he said he didn't have a watch.

Back at *Taller del Jade Maya*, Pesh sent the children to the office to resume reading in Spanish. She used the quiet time to talk to Vanna.

"I haven't found Pedro's father or his uncle," Pesh said. "I want to arrange for Pedro to go to elementary school in Antigua. May I use a piece of your paper?"

"Here you go," Vanna said, handing her paper and pen.

Pesh wrote a letter on *Taller del Jade Maya* stationery to Cuxil Manu to explain the situation, and Vanna said she'd mail it tomorrow.

"One more problem," Pesh said. "Pedro doesn't have a birth certificate, and I would like to invite him to visit us in the States. Can you help me there?"

"I'm sure Paul knows somebody who knows somebody," Vanna said. "We need to give details—date of birth and place, names of parents—and probably $500."

Pesh stepped to the office door and asked Pedro for his date of birth. He gave 15-Rabbit, a date on the sacred calendar. His family didn't celebrate birthdays, but he had nine summers and would soon be ten. His mother had been dead for a long time.

"The 15 is good," Pesh said. "But you need a Spanish calendar month."

Pedro didn't answer, so she suggested *Septiembre* and asked for his father's name.

"Maria calls him *husband* and *Manu*," Pedro said.

"Then what does Cuxil call his brother?" Pesh asked.

"*Ak Perezoso. Turtle*. They aren't good friends."

Lazy Turtle: not a compliment. *Turtle* as a nickname meant *slow*, at sports or in learning to read, a mocking name, even though the turtle, important in Mayan mythology, had a constellation named for it. Combined with *lazy*, the name was an insult.

"Do you know your father's first name?" Pesh asked. "His *nombre*, not his *apellido*?"

"Maybe it's Pedro, like me. I call him *Paapah*." He went back to reading with Yash, and Pesh returned to the front of the store.

"I guess we have to make it up," Pesh said, sitting on a stool next to Vanna. "I had to invent the entries for my own birth certificate years ago."

"Okay. Run it by me," Vanna said.

"Child's name, Pedro Manu B'alam. Born September 15, nine years ago. Mother's age: 16. Mother: Chanlajun Pex Yaxuun B'alam."

"But that's you, isn't it?"

"That's how old I would have been. Among the Maya, girls marry at fourteen."

"Why are you listing yourself as his mother?"

"Then I can link Pedro to me and my passport," Pesh said. "I can truthfully say he was born before I married, and no one will ask more, especially with all the Mayan names."

"You'll have to check the spelling. Place?"

"B'alam Witz, Guatemala—they'll never find it."

"But where is that?" Vanna frowned and tapped the ballpoint pen.

"It's a misnamed ruin across the river from Burt's dig: B'alam Witz, in Yucatán."

"What about the father? Kedar? Turtle Manu?"

"Not Kedar; his name isn't Mayan. Not Turtle Manu; that name's an insult." She listed the Maya prince Five-Owl, her ceremonial husband. How appropriate: a mock birth as well. *"Ho' Muwan Pedro Manu."*

"Here," Vanna said, handing her the pen. "I can't spell all that. What does it mean?"

"Ho' Muwan means Five-Owl, from the Mayan sacred calendar. The father needs a Mayan name."

"Mayan names are something else," Vanna said, shaking her head.

"If I used *owl* in Yucatec, it would sound even stranger to your English ear. *Tun-ku-lu-chu-ku*. Stone bird, because the owl sits so stiffly on his perch, and the owl's call, *who-who-who*."

"What a hoot!" Vanna laughed at her own joke, but Pesh didn't get it.

When Pesh finished recording the needed information, Vanna promised to look into how to obtain travel documents and closed the shop an hour early.

While riding in the van on the way back to Quetzal Centrale, Pesh had time alone with her thoughts. Would justice outweigh the crime of getting a false birth certificate? Then Pedro could visit them. Surely Kedar felt that way, too—she'd talk to him tonight.

B'alam Ha: she had to go there, the last place to search for the origin of her jade talisman. They'd hike who knew how far on a mountainous trail. Would Yash and Pedro be able to keep up? She couldn't leave them at Quetzal Centrale, not without Isolde to watch them. Pedro's father hadn't given permission— would that matter? In the States, taking an unrelated child across statelines was kidnapping. But this was Guatemala, a land of no rules.

"No, Pesh! We can't do that!" Kedar said later in their room. "We must find Pedro's father. And before Sunday, the next Mayan market day—we don't have much time left."

"But Pedro doesn't know where his house is."

"Then it's time for sleuthing." Kedar opened the road map. "Didn't he give Yash a banana? Look near a banana plantation."

"But which one?" Pesh noticed how far north and south the road extended.

"Remember how we scoured Highway 14 looking for Yash? Did you record coordinates?"

"Of course. We flew over three banana groves—there." Pesh marked the map with red Xs.

"We'll visit all three." Kedar refolded the map. "And hope Pedro recognizes a landmark."

"What if we don't find his father?" Pesh asked.

"Let's worry about that later." Kedar sounded unconcerned, but she hadn't mentioned the birth certificate.

"Remember the difficulty getting my birth certificate? Because no one filed it when I was born?" Pesh eased into her plan for bogus paperwork. "Well, Pedro faces the same situation."

"So? How do you know?" Kedar lined up his shoes under a chair.

"Logic. His parents are illiterate, and the Maya see no sense to it. They name babies later, not when first born, and there's a fee for filing late."

"Aha! You tried to get him a birth certificate."

"He needs one if he comes to visit us in Austin."

"But you'll have to tell him goodbye when we leave."

"Wouldn't you like to have him visit us?" Pesh asked. *Say yes! Say yes!*

"Of course. I like the kid," Kedar said.

"Well, Vanna's going to file Pedro's papers." Pesh knew he'd get used to the idea.

"You'll have to leave him in Guatemala. How's he going to get a visa?"

"Let's worry about that later," Pesh said.

"You stole my line," Kedar chuckled. "But we absolutely need to talk to Pedro's father."

37

Standing beside the van under the magnolia tree at Quetzal Centrale, Kedar spoke to the Andersons' driver Ignacio. "We had to postpone our trip to B'alam Ha. We're so glad you could be our driver today to help us look for Pedro's home."

Pesh and Yash waited in the backseat of the Quetzal Centrale van with a picnic basket while Kedar, Ignacio, and Pedro discussed how to find Pedro's father.

"Here's where we're going." Kedar unfolded the map onto the fender and bent over. "South on Highway 14, exploring backroads near banana plantations."

"Okay," Ignacio said. "I'm familiar with that area. Just tell me where to turn."

"This is a picture of roads?" Pedro asked, looking over Kedar's shoulder.

"You read it like this. We leave Antigua on Highway 14." Kedar tapped the map. "This is a side road, on the right because we're going that way."

"And the red marks are the bananas?"

"Right," Kedar said. "You can help keep track. Follow the roads from the map, and I'll tell Ignacio where to turn."

"Why are we going to see bananas?" Pedro asked. "My father doesn't live there."

"But you picked bananas," Kedar said. "One of those roads must lead to your father's house."

Soon they were underway, Ignacio behind the wheel, Kedar and Pedro next to him. Pedro followed the route with his finger all morning but didn't recognize anything. When they arrived at the third red mark, Ignacio parked near a fenced banana plantation, and they all shared the sandwiches Zia had packed for them.

"So far, no luck," Kedar said. "Let's try the roads closest to where we turned before."

"That'll take all day," Pesh said. "Pedro, if we turn back towards Antigua, could you look for landmarks again?"

"I could do that, but over there is a place I climb the fence," Pedro said, and two nearby roads later, he recognized his father's turn.

"This is it!" Pedro and Yash said together.

Ignacio parked behind a pickup on a goat-trail road near a small stacked-stone dwelling with a tin roof, Pedro's home.

"The women stay here." Kedar followed Pedro and Ignacio through the open door.

"*Paapah!*" Pedro rushed to his father, who sat cross-legged on the dirt floor next to an empty bottle of Ron Zacapa Centenario, premium Guatemalan rum.

"*Hola, Paal.* Hello, my son." Pedro's father Manu looked up, his eyes bloodshot, his nose red, and his speech slurred. He did not rise from the floor.

"Why don't you work in Antigua?" Manu asked. He and Pedro conversed in Mayan, and Ignacio translated for Kedar.

"I work for Pesh," Pedro said. "Where is Maria?"

"Maria is with her mother," Manu said. "She says this house is unlucky."

"Why unlucky?"

"Your sister died. The blue death."

"I better get Pesh." Kedar rushed outside.

"Cholera—from contaminated water," Pesh said. "They die with grayish-bluish skin."

Pesh entered the house, Yash behind her, and warned, "Don't touch anything."

"I am Pesh, Yash's mother." In Mayan, she told Manu, "You must clean everything to make this house lucky. Did Maria burn the sick child's blankets?"

"No. I don't know."

"Tell Maria not to use any of that child's blankets when she has the new baby."

"I do not see her."

"Tell her this house is not unlucky if she boils the water."

Pedro, his head bowed, stood near Manu, who paid his son no attention.

"I am sorry your baby died," Pesh said. "May I pay respects at her grave?"

Manu looked up but did not speak.

Outside, Pesh and Kedar found the child's grave, a sad little mound. Pedro and Yash joined them for a few minutes of silence, but Ignacio waited in the van.

"I didn't ask him about Pedro," Pesh said. "I have to go back." Inside, she asked Manu, "If I pay Cuxil, can Pedro stay there to go to school in Antigua?"

"Pedro must go to work."

"Going to school is work. I will pay him. Can you help me set it up with Cuxil?"

"You must ask Cuxil."

"All right." But Pesh wanted permission for Pedro to go with them tomorrow. "Can Pedro work for me until I find Cuxil?"

Manu nodded. Permission enough?

38

Pesh and Kedar loaded Yash and Pedro into the back of the helicopter for the flight to Alta Altun to visit *Xmenoob Xiu*. Kedar inspected every control surface outside the aircraft and Pesh helped the children put on headsets.

"Cup these over your ears and turn them on here," Pesh said. "Yash can show you how they work."

"I'm going to fly with the birds," Pedro said, grinning.

"My pleasure." Kedar settled into the pilot's seat and checked the cockpit instruments.

"Buckle up," Pesh said. "If you wish to speak, click that button."

"Don't hold it down or the radio screeches," Yash said.

"All right, passengers. Sit back and enjoy the sights." Kedar took off smoothly from Quetzal Centrale and set their course for Alta Altun.

Yash and Pedro looked around as though their heads were on swivels.

Pesh relaxed; she had nothing to do until they neared their destination. Kedar's helicopter contract would end soon. Would she find the source of her talisman at B'alam Ha? While the evil spirit Cimil had hung over her like a thunderbolt ready to strike for months, he seemed distant and unimportant today. Xiu had said he was weaker now, and Pesh was confident she would win.

"It's over there," Pesh said, pointing below to the goat trail driven by Ignacio the first time she had visited Xiu. The log bridge still spanned the ravine at the crossing where Zia had prayed to the Catholic saints.

"Xiu said to park where Ignacio left the van, so that's where I'll land." Kedar set down at Alta Altun in a stone-paved area ringed by eight nondescript adobe dwellings.

Children came running, attracted by the chatter of the rotors, and stood watching.

In the instant quiet after Kedar killed the engine, Pesh helped Yash and Pedro remove their headsets and unbuckle their seatbelts. They climbed out, surrounded by the children of the village.

"*Hola.*" Pesh waved and said, "We come to visit Xiu."

The throng of children followed them until they stopped in front of Xiu's humble dwelling.

"*Xmenoob Xiu,* may we visit you?" Pesh called out.

"*Xmenoob Pex,*" Xiu said from her doorway. "What a delight! And Kedar. Do come in."

"This is my daughter, Yash, and her friend, Pedro." Pesh put one hand on each child's shoulder.

"Come and sit with us. You may call me Xiu." She invited the children in with a sweep of her hand and offered all of them juice, fresh guava pulp.

"Pedro brought Yash home after she was kidnapped," Pesh said.

"Where the jade beads saw her eating dinner," Xiu said, stated as a fact. "Kedar left your carriage by the road. No one will disturb it there."

The conversation changed from Spanish to Mayan, and Pesh asked if Xiu could help them go to B'alam Ha.

"It is far for the children to walk," Xiu said.

"Kedar said Yash could ride on his shoulders."

"It is a difficult journey. Let them stay with me."

"That's too much to ask," Pesh said.

"Yash will be safe here," Xiu said. "The whole village will welcome the children."

When Pesh repeated Xiu's offer to keep Yash and Pedro, Kedar said, "Pedro's like an Australian sheepdog guarding its flock. He won't let anything happen to Yash."

"The children brought you a gift from the market in Antigua," Pesh said, presenting the bag of snacks to Xiu.

"*¡Chapulines!* Favorites of mine! I haven't had them in years."

"We also picked out some fruit." Pesh gave her the melon and the sweet lemons.

"*Dios bo'otik,* the gods pay."

"And I brought you corn meal so you wouldn't have to grind it while we are here."

"What luxury," Xiu said.

After more negotiation, Pesh agreed that Yash and Pedro would stay, sleeping in Xiu's hut but grazing around at mealtimes like the other children. Xiu promised someone would guard the helicopter and two strong men would accompany Pesh and Kedar to B'alam Ha in the morning.

"You will not find where jade comes from," Xiu told Pesh. "The gods throw it down from the mountains, from no one knows where, but your jaguar talisman has been to B'alam Ha."

"May we go outside to play?" Yash asked. She and Pedro had been quiet all this time.

"Stay in the plaza," Xiu said.

Yash and Pedro crossed the plaza to stand in the shade. The other children weren't in sight.

"Xiu called your mother *Xmenoob,*" Pedro said as though sharing a secret. "She's a shaman, like Xiu."

Yash shrugged. "I know she's magic."

A strange animal, as big as a Siamese cat, waved its tail like a flag atop a long pole and crossed the plaza. Its brown tail, longer than its body, had black rings around it.

"What's that?" Yash said, pointing.

"He's a *coatimundi*," Pedro said. "He eats fresh fruit and small lizards. He looks like he's waiting for a handout."

"He says his name is Racki," Yash said.

"*Hola.*" A village boy kicked a blue rubber ball in their direction. He threw a mango pit to the animal; it picked up the pit with its hands and nibbled the edges.

"He's Racki, our village mascot," the boy said. "I'm Marcos. Who are you?"

"I'm Pedro and this is Yash. We visit *Xmenoob* Xiu.*"

"Want to play ball?" Marcos picked up the ball and threw it to Pedro.

Later, Pesh, Kedar, Yash, and Pedro shared a communal evening meal with Xiu in the plaza, ringed by many cooking fires. Afterward, when her fire had died down, Xiu stared into the smoke.

"My talisman is Firebird," she said. "I fly with Firebird in the smoke. Firebird sees those things that will happen."

"Yash communicates with animals," Xiu said, grasping Yash's wrist.

"The coatimundi said his name was Racki," Yash said.

"Pedro knows all the animals," Xiu said. "He wants to go to school but something stands in his way."

Pedro seemed to study Xiu's face, and she placed her hand on his forehead.

"Your *wayob* is a deer," she said. "One with many prongs on his antlers. He is wise and fights for his family. He travels quickly through the forest. He knows all the animals."

"What's a *why-ohb*?" Yash asked.

"*Wayob*. Magic animal spirits. The gods send your *way*-animal to guide you," Pesh said in Spanish so Kedar would understand. *Wayob*—superstition and magic. "People say you can travel as your *wayob* while you sleep."

"Like an *avatar*," Kedar said. "Hindus believe the avatar descends from the gods for guidance and to facilitate communication."

Amazing, Pesh thought. India, one-fifth of the earth's population, eighty percent Hindu—that meant one billion Hindus, all believing in magic animal spirits.

"I saw the *Avatar* movie," Yash said. "Do I have a *wayob*?"

"You have met your *wayob*," Xiu said. "The quetzal. He lets you speak with animals."

"Does Daddy have a *wayob*?" Yash asked.

"He is Maya by adoption." Xiu held Kedar's arm and studied his hand. "His *wayob* is *Chuyum-thul,* the hawk who soars above the earth and sees everything below."

"She says your animal spirit is the hawk," Pesh said, putting her hand on Kedar's knee. "I'll tell you more later."

"Kedar will have a son," Xiu said.

Pesh wondered about that prophecy. She wasn't pregnant, but Kedar did want a son. How did Xiu know Kedar was adopted Maya? That Yash had spoken to a quetzal? That Pedro wanted to go to school? Then Xiu touched her shoulder.

"Pesh will find a place where her talisman has been but never the source of its jade."

"Does Mommy have a *wayob*?" Yash asked.

Pesh could tell that Yash loved the new word. She remembered her grandmother Chiich's legends about the *wayob*—old superstitions. But if one billion people believed in them—

"Pesh's *wayob* is the jaguar," Xiu said. "She can travel in the night and follow visions over great distances. Jaguar is *wayob* of a brave man or a king or a strong woman."

Xiu nodded her head and gestured for them all to rise.

"How do you sit in that position for so long?" Kedar asked. "My knees are stiffer than rusty hinges."

"I have done it since childhood," Pesh said. "My grandmother sat that way. She had a one-room house. Like this one, but built on a platform."

"Did you have sleeping mats like Xiu?" Yash asked. "Pedro's family sleeps in hammocks."

"My grandmother had hammocks, but no more stories tonight. We have to get up early tomorrow."

"I like hammocks," Xiu said. "I haven't enough for so many people." She gave them each a sleeping mat, and they spread out on her floor.

Pesh made sure that Pedro and Yash were comfortable, then lay down next to Kedar.

"I hope you didn't feel left out, not knowing the language," she said. "Xiu said your animal spirit is the hawk who soars above the earth and that you will have a son."

"I've always wanted a son," Kedar said.

"I'd like to have a son, too." Pesh felt crowded but cozy. Their five sleeping mats filled the floor space in the small room. Tomorrow, B'alam Ha: Xiu said she'd find where her jade jaguar had been, but not its origin.

Before dawn, the village women had prepared a chocolate drink, strong and bitter, without sugar but with cinnamon and cloves. Pesh and Kedar, their supplies already in backpacks, wore long pants and jungle boots for hiking. Pesh looked up when she heard voices.

"*Xmenoob Xiu*, we are here." Two Maya stood outside the door. Xiu introduced the men as Lalo and Volcy.

"Can I come, Daddy?" Yash popped up.

"No, Princess. You and Pedro will stay here with Xiu."

"Be good," Pesh said to Yash. She felt a tug of anxiety—leaving Yash, again. But Xiu would keep her safe. "Do what Xiu tells you and stay with Pedro."

"Here's a goodbye gift for my Princess." Kedar handed Yash a package of multi-colored balloons to share with the other children. He blew into a long red one and tied it off for Yash and inflated a round blue one for Pedro.

"We'll tell you all about it when we get back," he said.

39

At the trailhead to B'alam Ha, Pesh followed Kedar and the two burly Maya commissioned by Xiu through what soon became dense vegetation. The wet side of the mountains was lush with plant life, and they refilled their water bottles from mountain springs. While travelling, they didn't speak. Their guides Lalo and Volcy preferred to listen to the sounds of the jungle.

Maya are not known to be garrulous, but Lalo and Volcy seemed worried, their gazes flitting around, never settling on an animal or an object. They cleared the trail by smacking away vines with machetes and moved through without stopping. At a particularily overgrown area, they paused to drink from a spring.

"We must move quickly to our next point of safety," Volcy said, wiping his mouth.

"Looters use their machetes for weapons," Lalo said. "They lop off heads of interfering *indígenas.*"

Pesh understood their apprehension—a looter had once tied her up at knifepoint. Kedar frowned and looked to her for interpretation.

"He says looters are dangerous, and we must avoid them." Pesh felt no need to worry him about encounters with machetes.

"*Ko'ox*, hurry up," Volcy said, turning to lead them on.

They traveled at a frantic forced march, the pace challenging even though Pesh was an active person. Uphill, downhill, mostly downhill—her calves ached. When they stopped at a clearing, she had no energy left for talking, not even for thinking.

"We rest here." Lalo stopped by the open door of a thatched lean-to and called out, *"Xmenoob Xiu* sent us."

A Maya extended his open hand. Lalo gave him some *quetzales,* Guatemalan money. Pesh didn't see how much. Everyone in Guatemala seemed to know Xiu.

For spending the night, the keeper of the lean-to offered the four of them a hunter's hut near a bubbling clear spring. Three Mayan dwellings, made of local plant materials and clustered together, faded into the jungle background, camouflaged as neatly as a hummingbird's nest.

"We will rest next at B'alam Ha," Volcy said, his words music to Pesh's ears. B'alam Ha, tomorrow night!

At sunrise, the group set out again. Volcy and Lalo again cleared the trail and urged them faster, faster. This time, they piled cut vines behind them to disguise the trail.

Alone again with her thoughts, Pesh tried to block out sore muscles. Legend had it that ancient Maya ran along paved white roads, the *sacbes* connecting their city-states, feats that rivaled records set by Greek marathon runners. True or not, the Maya, without horses or carts, ran on the pancake-flat land of Yucatán, not over this torturous uphill and downhill.

Volcy and Lalo were tireless. Pesh and Kedar struggled to keep up, but Pesh would not admit defeat by asking them to wait. Not even when drenched by heavy rain—she had forgotten the ponchos. The men didn't seem to mind the rain. Nothing slowed the two Maya.

When the sun sagged low over the treetops, they reached B'alam Ha, a community of a dozen dwellings arranged around a central square. The ramshackle dwellings, constructed of organic materials, sat in the shadow of ruined mansions of stone.

Lalo and Volcy led Pesh and Kedar to the front of the hut belonging to the village shaman, *Xmenoob Ix Chel.*

"What will you do while we visit here?" Pesh asked.

"See friends," Volcy said. "Three days. Bring you back to Alta Altun."

"*Xmenoob Ix Chel,* we are here," Lalo called out.

"*Xmenoob Xiu* said, expect you." Ix Chel, a woman who seemed older than Xiu, invited Pesh and Kedar to enter and rolled out two mats for sitting.

"You may call me Chel. Welcome, *Xmenoob Pex*," she said. "Xiu sent a runner with a long message."

A runner, here in less than a day! Pesh felt pride in her Mayan heritage.

"Do you speak K'iché or Spanish?" Pesh asked. Chel's Mayan language differed from K'iché as well as from Pesh's native Yucatec, but it didn't seem to matter.

"No. I speak Mam." Chel moved one hand as though plucking words from her mouth. "Speak slowly."

"Okay," Pesh said, wondering if this was Xiu's Land of Mam. She saw Kedar's head start to nod.

"Xiu tells you are a healer," Chel said. "Use fly-worms to clean infected wounds."

"I walked with Xiu to visit the sick." Pesh could make out Chel's meaning because she spoke slowly and clearly. "My grandmother taught me much healing."

"Xiu says to trust you," Chel said. "You must tell no one location of B'alam Ha."

"Kedar and I will tell no one," Pesh said, a hard promise to keep. "I bring a gift, jade marbles from Antigua."

"The gods pay," Chel said, thanking her in Mayan. "Unusual shape. Not round."

Chel fingered one marble and held it up to reflect the light from the coals in the hearth, built over three stones like the hearth stones in the constellation Orion.

"My daughter polished them. She likes the irregular shape." Pesh shifted position on the mat, trying to ease her sore legs.

"And your daughter?" Chel asked.

"Yash. She has seven summers."

"I have no daughter." Chel held up one of Yash's stones, a cube with rounded corners and edges. "I treasure these marbles."

"I also treasure jade." Pesh handed Chel her jade jaguar. "My shaman's talisman."

"B'alam." Chel ran her fingers across the jaguar's sleek body, admiring.

"I'm looking for the source of that jade." Pesh leaned forward, closer to Chel.

"Green, favored by kings," Chel said.

"I need to know where the jade in my talisman came from." Pesh shivered, thinking about Cimil. "It's important, to keep my daughter safe."

"Men cannot know where the gods hide it." After a pause, Chel said, "Maya blessed by gods made pilgrimages to our sacred valley to get jade."

Quite a complex sentence—had she heard it correctly? Pesh knew no way to explain how jade formed in mountains where tectonic plates ground together, or that Kedar used modern science to search for jade from the air. Sacred valley—did Chel speak of the Motagua Valley?

Chel continued to examine the jade jaguar, and Kedar napped, his chin on his chest.

"Carved here, your little b'alam." Chel returned Pesh's talisman. "B'alam Ha. Best jade-carving workshop of all Mayan kingdoms."

"May we see your workshop?" The word *b'alam*, jaguar, was common to all Mayan languages. Pesh relaxed. She understood what Chel told her.

"Maya trained in jade carving here. Our workshops not used in a *bak'tun*. No kings after Spaniards came." Chel's sentences became longer and more complex. "No one told Spaniards about B'alam Ha. You must not tell."

"We will keep your secret." A *bak'tun*: four centuries. Chel's request made sense, but it would be hard to keep such exciting news from Burt. Perhaps she could tell him without revealing the location.

"Xiu says show you." With no mention of an evening meal, Chel lay down on her mat. "Go tomorrow morning."

Pesh, too tired to eat dinner, stretched out next to Kedar and tried to explain everything to him. With his nap and his minimal knowledge of Mayan languages, he'd been cut out of her conversations with Chel.

Pesh luxuriated in the chance to rest her overused muscles. Nothing could keep her awake, not even her excitement anticipating the visit to the ancient workshop, not even her worries about Cimil's threat. She fell asleep.

40

After breakfast at Alta Altun, Yash and Pedro helped the other children gather firewood and ripe mangos. They spent the remainder of the afternoon playing ball until Xiu gave them tortillas and beans with fruit juice for supper. The full moon rose, and the man in the moon winked at her. Sitting by Xiu's fire, Yash could hardly wait for story time.

"Do you see the man?" Yash pointed up. "My father says his face is drawn by shadows in valleys on the moon."

"Oh?" Xiu looked up and cocked her head. "I think I see a man's face when I twist my head, but we Maya know that is the pet rabbit of *Ix Chel* the Moon Goddess."

Yash wanted more of a story but none came.

"I'm a descendant of the great king Yaxuun B'alam," Yash said. "Did you know him?"

"No. He lived long ago in the north. I am a descendant of the great court astronomer for 18-Rabbit at Copán."

"I'm not related to anyone famous," Pedro said.

"But you are Maya," Xiu said. "We are a proud people. We had whole libraries of written knowledge until the Spaniards came. They gathered up our books and burned them all."

"Why did they burn books?" Yash asked. *Why would anyone burn a book?*

"They didn't want us to remember the old stories."

Xiu stirred the coals and threw on another corncob. "Would you like to hear about where you came from?"

Yash and Pedro nodded, and Xiu said her story came from the *Popol Vuh*, a book as important to the Maya as the Bible was to those devil Spaniards.

"In the first creation," she said, "the yellow god made men out of clay, but they dissolved in water and could not stand upright. They all perished in a great flood.

"Then the red god made a man out of wood. He took a branch from a tree and carved it into a human shape. It stood upright with no problem whatsoever, and it floated in water. But when the gods tested the men with fire, they burned.

"Next, the black god made a man out of gold. The gold man shone like the sun. He survived the tests of fire and water, but he was cold to the touch. He could not speak or feel or worship the gods." Xiu talked with her hands and told stories as well as Alberto.

"I know," Pedro said. "The yellow god is god of the south, the red one the east, and the black one, the west. The white god of the north made men."

"That's right," Xiu said. "You know a lot about this."

"My mother told me stories every night," Pedro said. "But she died."

Yash had never seen Pedro so sad. His chin quivered when he spoke of his mother.

"Oh, I see." Xiu clasped his shoulder and in a soft voice said, "I'm sorry you lost your mother."

Pedro nodded and swallowed hard.

"I will share my mother with you," Yash said.

"Ready for more story?" Xiu asked.

"I want to hear the rest of the story," Pedro said. "I don't remember all of it."

"Did they create the earth in seven days?" Yash asked.

"The *Popol Vuh* doesn't say." Xiu paused and stared at the fire. "But I didn't tell you why we are the Corn People.

"The fourth god, the colorless lord of the north, made humans out of his own flesh. He mixed the blood of the gods with *maiz* corn dough to fashion men, and the gods blew the breath of life into them. The men of flesh worshipped the gods and filled the hearts of the gods with joy. So *maiz* is the gift of the gods, and the Maya are the Corn People."

"Weren't there any girls?" Yash asked.

"Of course, Child. They meant all of the people, not just the men."

"Can you tell us another story?" Pedro asked.

"Tomorrow night." Xiu rose from her cross-legged position in one graceful motion. "It's time for bed."

"Will Daddy and Mommy come back tomorrow?" Yash asked.

"No. They are far away," Xiu said.

"Can my jade bead see where they are?" Yash asked, trying for another story.

"Of course. Give me your beads." Xiu clapped Yash's bead against Pedro's, making a bell-like sound. "You first must wake them up."

Xiu held the beads within one fist, her hand wrapped around them. Then she lifted her shaman's talisman above her head so that the light from the fire rippled down it and said, "I see them resting in a hunter's hut."

"Can I do that?" Yash asked.

"Of course. Close your eyes." Xiu returned the beads to the children, saying, "Hold these tightly and concentrate on Pesh and Kedar."

Yash saw them but Pedro did not.

"You can do it," Yash said. "Hold my hand, try again."

"I see them," he said, "sleeping on blue striped mats."

After supper on their second night at Alta Altun, Yash and Pedro sat by Xiu's fire and waited for tonight's story. Eager to get Xiu talking again, Yash told her about Jaguarcito.

"Pedro saved a baby jaguar. He found him and took him home and fed him milk."

"Pedro is kind." Xiu patted Pedro's shoulder.

"I didn't want the kitten to die," Pedro said.

"We had to give him to the zoo." Yash hoped he'd go to Austin so she'd see him again. "I think he's happy there."

"The gods reward kindness," Xiu said, turning to Yash. "What do you say when someone gives you something?"

"Thank you." Yash remembered her grandmother and wondered if her head still hurt. "My grandmother says that."

The surprised look on Xiu's face told Yash she had spoken in English by accident.

"*Gracias*," Pedro said.

"Spanish is the devil-language of the *conquistadores*," Xiu said. "We Maya say *dios bo'otik, the gods pay.* Do you know why we say that?"

Yash and Pedro looked at each other and said no.

"I told you about gold man, who couldn't speak or feel or move," Xiu said. "The gods left him on earth. One day the men of flesh found the man of gold. He was cold when they touched him, silent when they spoke to him. But the kindness of the men of flesh warmed the heart of the man of gold, and he came to life. With his first words, he offered praise to the gods for the kindness of the men of flesh."

"Where is the man of gold now?" Yash asked. "Does he walk the earth?"

"No one knows, Child," Xiu said. "But his words of praise woke the gods. They looked down on earth and saw that the men of flesh were poor and hungry."

"Like my father," Pedro said.

"That's why the maize god *Hun Hunahpu* told the man of gold, you are rich. You must look after them. So it was.

"*Dios bo'otik, the gods pay,* means the gods reward kindness and reminds us to be kind to one another." Xiu nodded, showing she had ended the story.

"I think my father never met a rich man," Pedro said.

"But the gods will reward him for his good heart."

"My father says he's a rich man," Yash said, "because his two Maya princesses are worth more than gold."

Later, Yash lay quietly in the dark and swung in her hammock. With less people in the small room, they each had one. She asked her jade bead, where is Daddy, and saw him sleeping.

41

At daybreak in B'alam Ha, Pesh stretched her stiff legs and rose from the sleeping mat. Today she would find the source of her jade talisman. Kedar and *Xmenoob Ix Chel,* already up, sipped hot chocolate outside at the cooking fire. Chel, a Maya born to be a shaman, was as powerful as Xiu and as gracious. She handed Pesh a cup of cocoa.

"The chocolate is perfect, exactly how I like it," Pesh said to Chel. "Do you grow the beans near here?"

"The gods provide everything we need," Chel said, smoothing her hair. "Cacao grows in our jungle. We use it for trade, now that we have no jade business."

"You said, the best jade in the Mayan kingdoms was carved here?"

"I can take you to where our ancestors once worked jade," Chel said. "Everything is covered over by jungle."

"Xiu said they carved my jaguar amulet here."

"Of course. We were the best," Chel said, stirring a pot of cornmeal soup.

Pesh accepted a small serving of the maize gruel and told Kedar, "Chel will show us the ancient jade workshop."

After breakfast, Pesh and Kedar carried wooden water buckets and followed Chel to an area of vine-covered hills, everywhere green, green of every hue.

"Old city, there," Chel said, pointing to several large mounds of vegetation.

Green vines with large leaves and stems as thick as her arms camouflaged the building stones. Pesh uprooted an armload of the smaller vines and uncovered two stone steps. Many odd shapes hid under the vegetation. This ancient city, an archaeologist's dream discovery, must be at least as large as Chichén Itzá. Filled with excitement, Pesh thought about taking pictures and telling Burt, but Chel wanted no one to find B'alam Ha.

"I want to spend more time here," Pesh said in Mayan. She leaned down and scraped moss off the lower stone's vertical face, then turned to Kedar and pointed. "Look at this stone step, with glyphs carved on its surface."

"What does it say?" he asked.

"I don't recognize the glyphs." Pesh asked Chel if she knew their meaning.

"No one can read ancient writing," Chel said.

"I usually can, but not this time." Pesh took out her small notebook and a pencil to draw what she saw carved into the step. After making a quick sketch, she placed one hand onto traces of red paint, closed her eyes, and envisioned past splendor—a tall stone building, crumbled into ruin—

"It's limestone," Kedar said, after scratching the stone with his knife and running a finger over it. "Is a source of limestone nearby? Caves, perhaps?"

Pesh asked Chel, "Where did this building stone come from? Do you have caves?"

"We have caves," Chel said.

"Where are they?" Pesh didn't think Chel knew anything about limestone.

"Caves hide behind waterfalls. Our Sacred Cave is guarded by *X-Sac-Sáasil*, sent by the gods of the north."

X-Sac-Sáasil. Pesh hadn't heard of *Lady White-Light*, and she didn't want to visit a sacred cave. She had avoided caves since the day she became a shaman. She didn't like to be reminded— tied up at knifepoint by a looter, left to die in the dark—

"Chel says the caves are guarded by Lady White-Light," Pesh said to Kedar. "Does this area rest upon a limestone shelf?"

"Not this far south of Yucatán." Kedar patted the limestone building stone. "Ask Chel if this came from nearby."

Pesh relayed Kedar's question but Chel answered, "No one knows," and continued her tour.

"This is one carving place," Chel said. "I will rest here. You can look."

In the small clearing, a few rock chips on the ground and two *celts* testified to its former use. The workshops, made of natural materials, had decayed eons ago. The *celts*, pieces of low quality jade, had been smoothed and shaped into hammers or to grind corn or to use as who-knows-what—Vanna used one like them for a doorstop. None of the chips had the color of her talisman. Someone had scratched a crude jaguar head onto the surface of the smaller *celt.*

"An early trademark for B'alam Ha," Kedar said.

Pesh slipped the *celt* into a pocket and sat cross-legged at the edge of the clearing. With her eyes closed, she grasped her jade jaguar and concentrated. She had nothing to set the date, only earlier than 1562. She tried recalling the honey-smell from Alberto's workshop and the rumble of tumbling rock, but his machines were modern. Instead, she fixed her mind upon the soft scratching of a cord dipped in fat, rolled in garnet grit, and pulled across a piece of jade. Her fingers felt leather, polishing stone with grit as fine as flour.

She sensed faint shadows, three Maya carving jade, two polishing. But her jaguar gave her no sign, no tingle in her fingers, no strong emotion. She gave it up and moved closer to Chel.

"Is this the only place they carved jade?" Pesh asked.

"Heavens, no." Chel pointed right, then left. "There were many workshops, all along this road. You can explore tomorrow."

Pesh wanted to see more, but Chel urged them onward.

"Many springs are there," Chel said, pointing to the west. "We need water now."

Pesh and Kedar followed Chel to the closest source of water to fill the buckets. On the way back, a waterfall of warm rain cascaded across their heads.

"Every afternoon this time of year," Chel said.

Later, sheltered from the weather and snug in Chel's hut, Pesh listened to the rain smattering the thatch roof and puzzled over how to discover if her jade talisman came from B'alam Ha—Xiu said it did. She and Kedar sat on mats while Chel made herbal tea.

"Do you have any samples of jade carved here?" Pesh hoped to match hers, or perhaps to clang jade pieces together to call up a vision.

"No. All sold to kings or put into their graves."

No ancient samples, nothing to guide her for a visit in a vision. No matter: perhaps she would find a clue while exploring tomorrow.

The next day, Kedar chopped a trail into the ancient city through overgrown vines. They reached a crumbled staircase with glyphs carved onto its bottom step, but Pesh knew they were looking in the wrong place.

"We need to find the hidden water," Pesh said. "Let's start at Chel's spring. She asked us to fill her buckets."

"Okay. But first, I want a picture of the writing on that step." Kedar dug around in his shoulder pack, then lifted out his Smartphone.

"Don't let Chel see that!" Secretly, Pesh wanted a picture to show to Burt.

"I'll be quick." Kedar snapped three photos, including one of Pesh standing by the stone. He took another at the remains of the jade workshop. They ambled on and stopped where they had filled the buckets yesterday.

"Chel said more springs are that way." Pesh, eager to continue exploring, pointed to the west. After walking a short distance, they came to a larger spring where water gushed out of the hills and two women filled water jugs.

"*Hola*," Pesh said from the bank of the waterhole. "We visit Chel. Please tell me, which way are the caves?"

The women looked back and forth at each other.

"Bad luck. Entrance to *Xibalba*," one of them said.

"Bad luck." The other woman shook her head and went back to filling water jugs.

"*Dios bo'otik. Adiós.*" Pesh waved her thank you.

"Come on," Kedar said. "Let's look for a waterfall. They often hide caves."

They left Chel's buckets and followed the water downstream to where it joined another rivulet. The terrain leveled out and the stream, much wider now, meandered. No waterfall seemed likely.

"I know," Kedar said. "We'll follow the larger waterway to its source."

After what seemed miles, mostly uphill, a waterfall gushed out of the mountainside.

"You mean—you're going in there?" Pesh asked.

"We won't get any wetter than we will walking back to Chel's in the afternoon rain." Kedar scrambled over wet rock to a shelf behind the waterfall and pulled Pesh up there beside him, both instantly covered by spray. They stepped farther back where it was drier but darker. Kedar pulled a flashlight from his shoulder pack.

Pesh hugged Kedar. "What else do you have in your bag of magic tricks?"

"Telling spoils the surprise." Kedar held her closer and stole a kiss. "Come on—I want to see that White-Light Lady who guards the entrance."

"But it's close to sunset*!*" *Bad luck*! Caves usually were bad luck.

"Don't worry, Sweetheart. I'm with you."

Despite her pounding heart, Pesh followed him.

"There's the lady who guards the entrance." Kedar's light shone through the cave entrance onto the calcified skeleton of a woman whose bones had a sparkling, crystallized appearance, as though she had been sprinkled by fairy dust. "Those are calcite crystals."

Pesh rubbed off a handful of tiny glittering granules. The skeleton with its cracked skull stared up with a calcified gaze, her eye sockets empty, her hipbones jutting. The cave felt haunted, a wild portal to a time of human sacrifice.

"I think they killed her with a club." Pesh envisioned the woman screaming, trying to escape, her captors attacking her. She swallowed and tried to control her breathing. "This is creepy. I've seen enough."

"Only a little more." Kedar used the flash and snapped several portraits of Lady White-Light. Behind him, spring water rushed from a black void. His flashlight flickered and pushed shadows off the walls, and skulls and broken pots lined a corridor that faded from sight into the darkness.

"I won't go farther," Pesh said, chin and lips quivering, the sound of her heartbeat thrashing in her ears. She grabbed Kedar's arm. "Too close to *Xibalba*!"

"Think of it this way," Kedar said, pulling her close. "The Lady probably guards the exit from *Xibalba* and keeps the evil spirits inside."

"She's locking *me* inside. I want out!" Pesh bumped the flashlight in her panic, knocking it from Kedar's hand. It dropped to the cave floor. Rattled into instant blackness.

"Here, I'll get it—Damn! Oh!" A thud. Silence.

"Kedar! Where are you?" Did he fall? She heard only the waterfall's muffled roar.

Lady White-Light's bones gleamed ghost-white. Pesh stepped into a veil of sticky spider webs that hung down and led to glowing worms, like white moving matchsticks. She stumbled and crumpled to the ground.

42

On her fifth morning at Alta Altun, Yash again followed Pedro and the village boys. This time before lunch, they pulled weeds in the *milpa* cornfield, and in the afternoon, they climbed trees and swung from the branches.

Yash like to climb trees. Her mother said not to swing on the branches, but the boys did it. Anything they could do, she could do. This was something she loved.

Yash moved out on a branch, hand over hand, ready to swing. Her movement shook water off the branches above and the cool drops felt good on her face on the hot afternoon. The farther out the boys moved, the more they could swing—only a little farther out. Her hand slipped—

She was airborne, crashing through limbs and leaves.

She landed on one hand and one knee. Her arm hurt so much her head spun.

"Are you okay?" Pedro touched her shoulder.

"Sure." She wasn't going to cry. She would not cry. "I need to see Xiu."

Pedro held her other elbow and guided her back to Xiu's hut.

"Xiu! Yash is hurt," Pedro called out by the doorway.

"What happened, child?" Xiu popped out and touched her shoulder. Then Xiu hugged her, asked if she could move her arm, and fingered its length.

To Yash, Xiu's light touch said love, and she felt better already.

"The bone is cracked." Xiu sent Pedro for willow branches and walked with Yash to the spring. When Yash plunged her aching arm into the cold water, the pain lessened. Then Xiu put her arm around her.

"Chew on these, but don't swallow them." Xiu gave her some leaves from the shaman's satchel. "Tell me when your mouth tingles."

Yash chewed the sweet-tasting but tough leaves. She felt warm and happy and the ache in her arm went away.

"Now let's clean your skinned knee." Xiu sponged it with a wet scrap of white cotton skirt, and Pedro came back with willow branches.

"My mouth tingles." Yash felt only a slight ache in her arm, no pain in her knee. She yawned and wanted to sleep.

Xiu cut a branch about the length of Yash's arm from hand to elbow and removed the leaves and twigs. She gave the willow stick to Pedro. "Trim like this. Six more."

Yash felt as though Xiu and Pedro had stepped to the other side of a window. *Did Xiu command those branches to do magic? Is that how to fix a cracked bone?*

"I must set the bone," Xiu said. "It will hurt but the coca leaves will help."

Xiu pulled Yash's hand and straightened her arm.

"Oh!" Yash gasped, holding back a scream. *That hurt!* She clenched her teeth and watched Xiu work.

Xiu moved her fingers up and down along the bone. Then she tore pieces off her skirt and lined up willow sticks around the injured arm. Pedro helped her to wrap strips of skirt around the arm to hold the sticks in place. Then she ripped out a square piece of the white fabric, folded it into a triangle, and tied the ends around Yash's neck.

"My arm doesn't hurt," Yash said. She had seen slings like that in cowboy movies on TV. She admired the willow branch cage encasing her arm all the way back to Xiu's house.

"You were very brave," Xiu said.

"You tore up your skirt," Yash said.

"It was an old one." Xiu unrolled Yash's sleeping mat. "Here, spit those leaves into my hand. You must rest now to mend your arm."

Yash couldn't hold her eyes open. She fell asleep.

Sometime in the night, she fondled her jade bead and tried to locate her mother, as she had done every night since her parents left. She couldn't see her mother. She was someplace very dark, too dark. Too scary: her mother was frightened. Yash's heart pounded, as if she awakened from a nightmare. She was on a mat, not in the hammock. In the dim light, she saw Xiu to her right, Pedro to the left. She shook Xiu's shoulder.

"Xiu! I need you," Yash whispered in her ear.

"Come here, little one." Xiu raised her sleeping blanket to let Yash lie next to her. She smoothed the child's hair and asked, "Your arm hurts?"

"No. Mommy's in a dark place." Yash held back sobs. "She's scared."

Xiu held the jade bead and said, "I see only darkness."

"Mommy needs help." Yash gave in to tears.

"Don't cry." Xiu hugged Yash. "She needs your help."

"We will send Firebird to give light." Xiu grasped Yash's good hand and squeezed it around the bead. "Go to your mother."

Yash shut out everything but Mommy.

Holding Firebird with her other hand, Xiu chanted something in Mayan that Yash didn't understand.

Mommy had light behind her, light shaped like a Hallowe'en skeleton.

43

Lady White-Light's skeleton glowed between Pesh and the exit from the sacred cave. Expecting a shimmering spirit to arise at any moment, Pesh moved away from the phantasm. She backed into Kedar's body on the ground and fell on top of him.

"Kedar! Wake up!" She shook his shoulder. "Are you all right?"

"Where are we?" Kedar wobbled to a sitting position. "I feel dizzy."

"We have to get out of here." Pesh clung to his arm.

"O-o-oh! My head hurts."

"Here, I'll help you get up." *Can he walk? What if we can't leave?*

"Wow! White-Light Lady!" Kedar sounded like he had been drinking.

"Is it a ghost?" Pesh shuddered, even though she knew ghosts didn't exist.

"Relax. It's only calcite phosphorescing," Kedar said. "Damn camera—battery's dead!"

"You mean—the white glow has natural causes?" *Not a trick from Cimil?*

"That glowing skeleton would have awed the Maya," Kedar said.

"What is it, then? It awed me."

"The calcite absorbed my flashlight beams." Kedar sounded back to his usual self. "But I am surprised by its brightness."

Those glimmering bones— Pesh bent down and rubbed off a handful of small, salt-like granules. They did emit light. Now that she knew the secret of the skeleton, she put the glowing crystals into a pocket to show Yash.

Kedar stood and seemed to stare at Lady White-Light.

"What are those white things on the ceiling—spiders?" Pesh asked.

"Only a type of glowworm," Kedar said, his professor-self again. "Probably the larva of an insect that catches its prey on those sticky lines."

"Glow worms, glow bones, glow spiders." *Not ghosts. No reason to fear X-Sac-Sáasil.*

"Amazing! She glows so brightly." Kedar continued to stand, fixed in place.

"Then use its light! Come on!" Pesh dropped to her knees. Searching for the flashlight, she crawled around and felt every object that cast a slight shadow.

"Found it!" Pesh waved it and light from the bones reflected off its metal case.

"Don't turn it on until we have a plan. It'll affect your night vision."

"Let's leave." The cave smelled of damp, but no longer scared her. "I need fresh air."

"Careful—don't slip."

"Come on." Pesh stepped out behind the raging water. She couldn't see the bank in either direction. "Where did we come in?"

"Along the side somewhere. I'll take the light."

"I'll hold rocks as I go." Pesh held her breath and moved forward. The rushing water battered her head. Past the torrent, she dared to breathe but fell into the cold water.

"I've got you!" Clenching the light between his teeth, Kedar stepped into the stream, pulled her out, and stood her onto the bank. "I learned this trick moving the airplane around at B'alam Witz."

"Thank you!" Pesh hugged him while water ran down their bodies. "How long were we in there? The sun is down!"

They picked their way along in the dark and in the rain and found the path they had used earlier, downhill this time.

"There's the spring," Kedar said, beaming the flashlight off to the right.

"And the buckets," Pesh said. "We promised to carry water for Chel."

Back at the village of B'alam Ha, Chel scolded them for returning after dark. "Why do you come so late?"

"We were lost in the cave of *X-Sac-Sáasil*," Pesh said. "We saw Lady White-Light."

"Bad luck." Chel shook her head and handed them towels. "You're soaked!"

Pesh changed into dry clothing, hung up their wet garments, and warmed herself by Chel's hearth.

"I've been saving this for hours." Chel handed them each a bowl of hot bean soup.

"Soup has never tasted so good." Pesh sat on a reed mat next to Kedar, who smiled at her over his bowl.

Afterward, Pesh lay back, but she couldn't sleep. *Had the jade talisman been carved here?* Both Chel and Xiu said so, but they hadn't actually visited this place in ancient times. She fingered grains of calcite in her pocket, but when she examined a pinch of it, the crystals no longer glowed.

She had collected those crystals for Yash. Could she make them glow later, at home? She missed Yash, and that gave her an idea.

"Please give me the jade Yash polished for you," Pesh whispered to Kedar, who reclined next to her on a mat.

"Sure. Here you go." He pulled the bead out from under his shirt and put it into her hand.

She held Kedar's jade from Quetzal Centrale and added her piece polished by Yash and clapped them together. She saw Yash, sleeping safely—*that's odd*—*she was curled up against Xiu.*

Xiu had said she must wake up jade. Why hadn't she thought of this before? The talisman, the two pieces from Yash: she clapped all three together and heard the lovely ringing sound of jade.

Her talisman warmed and vibrated as if trying to get her attention. Her earlier vision from the workshop returned. Three Maya carving jade and two other men polishing came to her as a focused picture, a cameo from the last *bak'tun*. The clearest vision she had ever had: bright sunlight, clear sound, visual details down to each lock of hair on each head. The carvers held jade the same color as the talisman.

"Special order for King B'alam's grave," the head carver said, holding an object out for the others to admire. The sunlight rippled down the muscled back of a small reclining jaguar, dark green, so polished that it reflected his face. "His grandson paid a handsome tribute."

The carver is holding the talisman! A jolt of electricity shot through her body from her heels to the top of her head.

"For Yaxuun B'alam, the great king of the north," the polisher said. "The grandson comes tomorrow."

Carved for King Yaxuun B'alam! Pesh watched for ten minutes or ten hours or ten centuries. Returning from that far away time, Pesh grasped Kedar's arm.

"My jade jaguar was carved here," Pesh whispered. *X-Sac-Sáasil* couldn't stop her. Cimil couldn't stop her. *No longer afraid of caves, no longer afraid of Cimil.* "I'm not a fallen *Xmenoob* after all."

"Tell me tomorrow, Sweetheart," Kedar said.

Exhausted but jubilant, Pesh closed her eyes, and her chin dropped to her chest.

"You need sleep, my darling." Kedar drew her close.

His warm arms felt safe. He lay down beside her.

The next day, as usual after she travelled in a vision, Pesh awoke hungry enough to eat her sleeping mat. She drank two cups of bitter chocolate, swallowed two portions of cornmeal gruel, and ate a mango before she said good morning, but Chel seemed to understand her fatigue and hunger.

"My talisman was carved here," Pesh told Chel.

"I told you we were the best," Chel said.

"I'd like to explore the cave of *X-Sac-Sáasil*," Pesh said. "Maybe next year?"

"Bad luck," Chel said, but she didn't say no.

"*X-Sac-Sáasil* is a trick from Cimil," Pesh said.

"Don't let him hear you say that!"

"May I spend more time at the jade workshops next year?" Pesh asked, pulling on her boots.

"I'd like to study the area, too," Kedar said.

"Of course. I enjoy your company," Chel said.

"*Xmenoob Chel*, we are here," Volcy called out.

"Volcy is here," Chel said. "You need an early start."

"*Dios Bo'otik*," Pesh said. "Thanks so much, Chel."

"*Dios Bo'otik*," Kedar parroted.

Pesh and Kedar followed the two Maya to the trail, beginning two hard days of travel to Alta Altun, mostly uphill. All while wearing wet boots.

Pesh couldn't wait to see Yash again, and she couldn't wait to talk to Xiu about Cimil.

44

The morning after she broke her arm, Yash woke up snuggled next to Xiu. She held her jade bead to check on her mother because of her dream last night, about Mommy being scared and in a dark place. She saw Mommy drinking hot chocolate. Xiu would give her chocolate, too.

Xiu sent her to the river to bathe with her new friend Rolana. Rolana helped her and braided her hair a new way with colored glass beads from the Mayan market. When Yash shook her head, the beads tinkled.

After breakfast, Xiu said not to play with the boys, and Rolana took Pedro and Yash to one of the houses where the girls learned handcrafts. Everyone wanted to see Yash's sling and the willow branch cage for her broken arm, but Yash wanted to learn to weave like the other girls. The girls wove baskets but they used both hands.

"I'll be your other hand." Pedro held the frame and she pulled the bamboo strips through with her good hand, so involved in the basket and its intricate pattern that she forgot her arm ached.

Yash asked the girls where they went to school. Alta Altun had no school. Rolana said she couldn't read, but that didn't matter because next year she would be old enough to get married. Rolana, only six years older than Yash, didn't seem like a grown-up, and Yash couldn't imagine her getting married before she grew up.

The next day, the girls learned to make straw hats, and Yash and Pedro joined them.

"Is he going to come every day?" one girl asked.

"Boys don't come here," another said.

"Maybe he doesn't want to be here, either," Yash said. "But he has to. My mother told him he had to stay with me."

Pedro looked away like he wanted to be anywhere else.

"Pedro found me after I got kidnapped."

"Kidnapped?" They all looked at Yash.

"The men had a gun but I got away. Pedro gave me a kitten, a baby jaguar."

The girls stopped working. Everybody looked at Pedro, and one girl asked, "A real jaguar? Where did you get it?"

"I found him in the jungle," Pedro said. "His mother died. I didn't want him to die."

"Pedro named him Jaguarcito," Yash said. "But my mother wouldn't let me keep him."

"What did you do with him?" one girl asked.

"We gave him to the zoo in Guatemala City." Yash wondered if they had ever been that far from home.

"What's a zoo?" Rolana asked.

"They put animals in cages," Pedro said. "Tourists like to watch them."

"That sounds sad," one girl said.

"Jaguarcito is happy there," Yash said. "In the U.S., they show movies to jaguar cubs."

"I've never seen a movie," Rolana said.

"They tell stories with pictures that move, and people talk and sing." Yash had seen lots of movies, downtown in Austin and on TV, too. There were no TVs in Alta Altun.

"Can any of you speak Spanish?" Yash couldn't believe it. No school, no TV, no movies.

"Why should we learn that devil tongue?" Rolana asked. "Did you know we used to have books, lots of books, but the Spaniards burned them?"

"Why would anyone burn a book?" *No books and no school.* Yash loved to read, and she missed her school in Austin. She wouldn't like living at Alta Altun.

45

Soon after the sun set on the second day of hiking uphill, Pesh and Kedar and the two men who guided them reached the trail-head at Alta Altun. Aided by the full moon, they made their way to Xiu's house. Pesh found her outside by her cooking fire.

"*Hola,* Xiu. We're back with much to tell you."

"Sit with me," Xiu said. "I have hot tamales."

"Where are Yash and Pedro?" Pesh asked.

"They're eating with their friend, Rolana," Xiu said.

Tamales and beans were Pesh's favorites, but she was more interested in resting her feet after two days of hiking.

"I know what you need." Xiu gave them each a bottle of beer, chilled in the spring.

"The gods pay," Pesh said in Mayan.

Xiu only nodded, and Yash and Pedro ran full speed toward Xiu's fire circle.

"Mommy! Daddy!" Yash rubbed her face against the back of Kedar's neck and grabbed Pesh's shoulder with her good hand.

"Come here. Let me look at you." Pesh hugged Yash.

"*Hola,*" Pedro said.

"*Hola.* Did you take good care of Yash?" Pesh asked.

"*Sí.* That is my job," Pedro said. "I missed you."

"Oh, Pedro, I missed you, too," Pesh said. "You are such a good friend."

"What happened to you, Princess?" Kedar touched Yash's sling. "Are you okay?"

"Oh, that. It doesn't even hurt." Yash looked at the willow sticks encasing her arm. "I fell out of a tree."

"You broke your arm?" Kedar asked. "You need a doctor and an x-ray. I'll take you to the clinic in Antigua."

Pesh immediately replied, "Xiu knows as much about setting a broken limb as any doctor there. Yash is fine."

"Let's get it x-rayed anyway," Kedar said.

"You know," Pesh said, "I used to climb trees. Yash, did you go too far out on a branch?"

"The farther out, the better you can swing," Yash said.

"She didn't cry when Xiu set her arm," Pedro said.

"And did you help Xiu?" Pesh knew that he had.

"I made the willow sticks and helped Xiu tie them together," Pedro said. "Except for falling, Yash climbs trees better than the boys."

"What's that in your hair, Princess?" Kedar asked.

"Oh, this?" Yash fingered a string of multicolored glass beads woven into her long braid. "Rolana fixed it."

"She's right over there." Yash dashed out into the moonlight and pulled the Maya girl towards the fire circle. "This is Rolana. She helped me bathe in the river."

"How kind," Kedar said. "Thank you."

"You're supposed to say *dios bo'otik*, the gods pay," Yash said. "Xiu says that."

"*Dios bo'otik*," Kedar said. "Were you good for Xiu?"

"All children are good," Xiu said. "Sometimes we must guide them."

"Is this our last night here?" Yash asked.

"Yes," Kedar said. "We need to fly back to Quetzal Centrale in the morning."

"Can we visit Rolana until bedtime?"

Kedar looked to Pesh, who nodded. "Okay."

With his approval, the children disappeared as quickly as they had arrived.

"I can't believe how stiff my legs feel," Kedar said, taking a few steps and rubbing his thighs. "I'm going to the helicopter to call Vanna. I want to check on my mother."

Pesh was left alone with Xiu, which was good because she needed a heart-to-heart talk.

"What is this, *with much to tell you?*" Xiu asked.

"Chel showed us the ancient jade-working place where my jaguar talisman was carved. She said B'alam Ha had the best jade-carving workshop of all the Mayan kingdoms."

"I told you to go there," Xiu said.

"Chel said you told her to help us look for the source of my jade jaguar. No telephone—how did you tell her?"

"Sometimes I send a runner whom I trust," Xiu said. "Our runner is so fast he travels to B'alam Ha in one day."

"Chel said men cannot know where jade comes from." Pesh twisted her braid. Took a deep breath. Tried to slow her hammering heart. She had found the jade carving site, but not where it had originated. She had difficulty mouthing the words: "Chel says Maya warriors blessed by the gods made pilgrimages to the Sacred Valley and came home with jade."

"That is true," Xiu said.

"I didn't learn where this piece of jade came from or where it formed in the mountains," Pesh said, struggling to find the right Mayan expression.

"The gods made it. They tell no one where."

"I didn't find the lost jade," Pesh said.

"What lost jade is this?"

"The Trickster said I must find the lost jade to redeem myself." Finding that jade had been on her mind for months. She had failed. *What would happen to Yash?*

"And why is he called The Trickster?" Xiu asked. "Do you think any Maya would ever misplace jade?"

"Well, then, did I lose to Cimil?" Pesh held her breath, afraid to hear Xiu's reply. *Was Yash cursed to follow Cimil?*

"Of course. Those jokesters are laughing right now." Xiu leaned on one arm and shifted her cross-legged position. "Only the gods know where jade comes from. You cannot find lost jade because none is lost."

"But what does it mean, losing to Cimil?" Pesh's insides quivered. Heat flashed over her. She rocked in place and bit her lip. "I don't want Yash to become a shaman."

"Ask Cimil to let her choose."

"But her blood is only half Maya," Pesh said.

"Is it so bad to be a shaman?"

This isn't my world anymore. Pesh pondered her answer. She didn't want to insult Xiu or hurt her feelings.

"Yash has a good mind," Pesh said. "There is so much more she could do in the States."

"The gods have already sent a snake to help her."

Pesh shrank back, frozen to the spot, unable to speak. The hair on the nape of her neck lifted. She remembered how she had cursed Five-Owl: *Hurt this baby, die by venomous snake!* Yash said the kidnappers slapped her.

She grasped her jaguar talisman for comfort. The stone felt hot and throbbed in rhythm with her racing heartbeat. She licked her lips and drew in a deep breath.

"Can't I do anything?" Pesh held back a scream.

"Yash must choose when she has fourteen summers. All humans have their own lives to live."

Pesh didn't answer. *What would Yash choose?*

"Remember how you spent the night in a sacred cave and emerged a shaman?"

"I fell into the cave," Pesh said. "By accident."

"But you asked the gods to help you," Xiu said. "In fact, you made a curse."

How did Xiu know about the crocodile?

"You bound yourself to Cimil by asking him for help," Xiu said, staring into the smoke. She fingered her Firebird talisman as though it held an answer. "I am *X-Dzac Ya*, she who medicates pain. But a shaman can be *X-Pul Ya*, she who throws pain. You are *X-Pul Ya* if your curse kills a man."

"The looter died by crocodile. The kidnapper by snake." Pesh drew in her breath. Was she *X-Pul Ya?*

"Then you are more closely bound to Cimil."

"I want to unbind myself."

"That is never done," Xiu said. "Teach Yash well."

There must be a way. Pesh had more questions, but Xiu nodded off.

46

At Alta Altun, Pesh awoke feeling rested, but when she stretched, her leg muscles screamed in complaint after the long hike from B'alam Ha. Already up, Xiu heated water outside the open door for cornmeal gruel. Kedar slept on the floor next to Pesh, and beyond him, the children, so innocent, peaceful.

Caressing her jade jaguar, Pesh prayed to her patron god, *Hun Hunahpu*, and thanked him for their safety and health. What should she teach Yash, about becoming a shaman? *Stay away from caves. Never spend the night in a sacred cave.*

"Good morning, Beautiful," Kedar said, smiling but with his eyes still closed.

"Good morning. How's your mother?" She hadn't talked to him since he called Vanna last night.

"She's going to be fine. Burt took her home to Austin."

"Good news—she's recovering." *But bad news about her return to Texas.* That meant Pesh had to take both children everywhere she went—and Pedro a stowaway. *Where was his father, anyway?*

"But I haven't told you everything," Kedar said. "Burt needs you to go to B'alam Witz. He wants you to close up the dig for the season."

"What about Pedro?" B'alam Witz was in Mexico. Pedro, *indígenas de Guatemala*, was not only undocumented but also unwanted in Mexico. But, in all the years she had worked there, the Mexican authorities had never come.

"You have to take him," Kedar said.

Back at the Andersons' compound Quetzal Centrale, Pesh had two days to pack for B'alam Witz, but her most pressing concern was to seek out Pedro's father Manu and his uncle Cuxil. Vanna had heard from neither man, so Pesh and the children hitched a ride to her jade shop in Antigua.

Burly Arturo, wearing a freshly pressed khaki uniform, sat in front with the driver. His rifle rested against one knee.

"Arturo goes with you now?" Pesh asked Vanna.

"All the time," Vanna said. "Every shop on our street has armed security by the door. A new drug lord took over from The Crocodile. *La Barba Amarilla*. Barba for short."

"Yellow Beard, named for the deadly snake?"

"Undoubtedly," Vanna answered. "Barba dyes his beard orange, and he's even meaner than *El Cocodrilo* was."

In Antigua, Ignacio dropped Vanna and her bodyguard Arturo at her shop and again drove to the house belonging to Pedro's uncle. "Cuxil Manu" still appeared in small letters on a bronze plaque above the mail slot, but no one answered the bell.

"*Mi tio Cuxil* isn't here." Pedro frowned and bit his lip.

"Don't worry. We'll send him another letter," Pesh said to soothe him.

Back at Vanna's shop, she again wrote to Cuxil on letterhead paper. She had to keep Pedro with her until she found his uncle or his father.

"Can you please post this for me?" Pesh asked Vanna.

"Of course. Go, do your errands. Just keep Ignacio with you."

"Want to go shopping?" Pesh asked Yash and Pedro, who had been quietly reading in Vanna's office. Yash liked to play teacher and made sure they read Spanish lessons everyday. Pedro was an enthusiastic student.

Always ready to go, Pedro smiled, and Yash danced around, asking for ice cream.

"Not now. Pedro needs new clothes before school starts. I saw a department store right down the street."

"You can't walk there, *Señora*." It seemed strange to drive such a short distance, but Ignacio insisted that he must keep them safe from crime gangs.

In the store, Pesh purchased school clothes for Pedro: shirts, pants, underwear, and a pair of new shoes as well as a suitcase to store them.

"What if we don't find *mi tío* Cuxil?" Pedro looked worried. "Can you get your money back?"

"Then they are my gift to you. You're outgrowing everything anyway," Pesh said.

"The gods pay," Pedro said in Mayan, grinning.

Next, Ignacio drove them to the Antigua medical clinic for Yash's appointment to x-ray her arm. They had only a short wait, and the nurse and the doctor on duty admired the willow branch splint that Xiu had made.

Pesh and Pedro watched quietly.

"Someone knew exactly what to do." Doctor Garcia, a young Caucasian MD, showed Yash her x-ray on a screen. "Your broken arm is healing quickly."

"Xiu did that," Yash said. "She's a healing shaman."

"Bush medicine." Garcia shook his head and frowned. Then he and the nurse went to work on a white plaster cast to enclose Yash's arm from wrist to elbow.

Pesh bit her tongue to keep from making a sarcastic reply. The Maya had healing secrets, natural herbs and salves, to equal much of his medicinal arsenal—without two pages of warnings about side effects.

When the doctor asked, "Pink or green," Yash chose fluorescent pink. The nurse wrapped her arm and the cast with pink gauzy tape until only her fingers stuck out.

"Come back in three weeks to have the cast removed," the doctor said. "Don't put any pressure on the arm until after it heals."

"*Gracias*," Pesh said. *Bush medicine, indeed!* "That means you can't use that arm for a while."

"*Gracias*," Yash said, and "*the gods pay*" in Mayan.

Afterward, Ignacio accompanied the three of them to the Mayan marketplace for fresh fruit and for the remote chance that Pedro's father would appear. They looked everywhere.

"Your father isn't here," Pesh said in Spanish. "Do you have any guesses why?"

"Maybe Maria had the baby." Pedro looked at the ground. "I don't think he wants me to come back."

"Of course, he wants you. I'm sure he loves you."

"It isn't that. It's time for me to strike out on my own," Pedro said. "He said you were rich, had a jade mine. If I took good care of Yash and showed you I'm a good worker, you might give me a job."

"It's the Andersons who have jade—I'm not rich. I'm a teacher and Kedar is only starting out, so in Austin, we aren't rich, but we're happy."

"Maybe you can come visit us," Yash said.

"We can send money to Cuxil so you can go to school," Pesh said, and Pedro mumbled, "*Gracias*."

They met Ignacio and picked up Vanna, who was ready to lock up for the day. The van was full for the ride back to Quetzal Centrale.

Seated in the middle seat, Pesh mulled over the day's conversations. Her heart went out to Pedro, and she'd take him home to Austin if he didn't have to battle immigration. Pedro still had no birth certificate, but beyond that would be bureaucratic paperwork: visas, passports. How could she leave Pedro here, with nowhere to go, nowhere to live?

In Guatemala, peasant boys went to work at age ten. On those dangerous streets, children were raped or beaten. Crime lords enslaved handsome boys like Pedro to steal and peddle drugs. A child without parents had few opportunities for success.

If Kedar flew them to B'alam Witz, there would be no border patrol, but if an official from Mexican immigration came to B'alam Witz, she would need a birth certificate for Pedro, her stowaway child.

47

The temple at B'alam Witz jutted above the forest in the distance, but Pesh saw it only because the GPS indicated where to look. Although she had flown here a hundred times with Kedar from Mérida, she had come from the south only once and had no landmarks to guide her.

Pesh smiled to herself. Pedro, who always rode facing the rear in his father's truck, claimed he didn't know where he was until after he'd been there—exactly what she experienced now.

B'alam Witz felt like home. She had come here every year since Burt opened the excavation of the ruin. This time, she'd supervise closing up for the archaeological season. Before she expected it, she saw the wide spot in the river.

"Landing in five minutes," Kedar said. "Buckle those seatbelts."

Pesh turned to check that Pedro and Yash were strapped in, then tightened her own belt. Kedar set the chopper down on the wide sandy beach next to the river.

"I'll start unloading supplies," Kedar said. "Steve can put them away. You and the kids can help by carrying in your personal gear."

Yash grabbed her duffle.

"No, little sister. Let me." Pedro took Yash's bag with one hand, his bag with the other, and lumbered up the hill like a mule carrying an oversize load.

"*Ko'ox!*" Yash ran ahead. "I'll show you around."

"No, you won't. Not until we finish unloading." Pesh followed the children up the path to the archaeologists' encampment. She smelled vanilla. Two red macaws, chasing each other and squawking, brushed her hair with their feet. Her tent had been erected in her favorite spot, shaded by two ficus trees with hammock hooks still attached.

"*Gracias*, Pedro. Just put everything outside the tent."

"Can we go play?" Yash asked.

"Not yet. Don't you want to say goodbye to Daddy?"

They walked back down to the river, where Kedar had stacked boxes of supplies on the bank beside the chopper.

"I'll ask Steve to carry them in," Pesh said.

"Have your satellite phone?" Kedar asked.

"Of course." Pesh hugged Kedar, and Yash hugged his right leg. "We'll be fine."

"When are you coming back?" Yash asked.

"I'll bring supplies next week," Kedar said, then shook Pedro's hand. "I'm glad you're here to keep Yash safe."

"That is my job, *señor.*"

The rotors began their throp-throp-thropping, and the helicopter lifted off. The three of them waved goodbye from the beach.

Pesh was eager to visit the excavations, especially the trench that opened a direct line from the temple to the center of the ancient plaza. Under the temple last year, Burt had discovered a secret chamber and a mural. What new relics had they unearthed?

"*Ko'ox.* Let's go, this way." Yash pranced with excitement and Pedro followed her on the trail to this year's dig, where Steve stood in a trench. Pedro stared at Steve and whispered to Yash, "He has a beard."

"Sh-h-h." Yash put a finger over her mouth. "Haven't you seen a beard before?"

"Hi, Steve. How's it going?" Pesh called out, hurrying to catch up with the children. Steve had helped open B'alam Witz nine years ago and had become Burt's right-hand man.

"You'll like the ceramics we found." Steve gazed at Yash and Pedro. "Aha. You brought two helpers."

Pesh introduced Pedro and said, "Kedar left the supplies by the riverbank. Could you please put them away?"

"Glad to," Steve said.

"*Hola.* Can I help you? I am very strong," Pedro said.

"*Gracias*," Steve said, smiling. "*Después del lonche.*"

Only a gringo would say "after lunch" that way, Pesh thought. It looked as though Steve and the other students had a meter more to dig to reach this year's goal. And, of course, they still had to push back the loose rock to refill the trench. Burt would never let them leave such a mess.

"Burt asked me to supervise the closing of this year's work," she said. "Tonight you can help me list what needs to be done."

"Sure. I'm glad to see you, but I was sorry to hear about Isolde being injured," Steve said.

"I'm taking the children to the temple for a picnic. Pedro can help you when we come back."

"Okay. We're going to work another hour or so. *Hasta luego.*" Steve turned back to his chore.

Pesh and the children rested in the shade on the third step, a good level for watching the work in progress, and she handed out the sandwiches packed last night.

"Why don't we eat from the top?" Yash asked. "We could sit on the throne. You said I could this year."

"That was when you had two good arms," Pesh said. "You can't climb temples or trees until you heal."

"Pedro could help me," Yash said.

"In a few days. But there are 89 steep steps. Pedro and I will have to help you on every one."

Yash didn't say okay and she set her mouth in her stubborn expression.

"Pedro, don't let her climb up there," Pesh said. So far he hadn't said anything beyond hello to Steve. "It's dangerous, and she can't use her bad arm."

"*Sí.* I will take good care of my little sister."

After lunch, Pedro wanted to watch the men work on the trench, and Yash wanted to stay there, too.

"I don't mind sidewalk superintendents," Steve said. "Later, Pedro can help me bring in the supplies."

"Only watch," Pesh told them. "Don't pester Steve." She could work much faster, with Pedro keeping track of Yash. "Don't go any farther away from the tent."

She couldn't resist peeking at a container the workers had filled with labeled ceramic fragments, beige and decorated with red and blue designs, pieces of a bowl. She put on work gloves and held the largest piece, and with her forefinger, traced a drilled hole in its center: a kill hole, to make a ceremonial offering to the gods. *What a treasure!*

That evening, Pesh warmed canned stew and cut up the fresh fruit she had purchased at the Mayan marketplace. She hated canned stew; she'd open canned beans tomorrow and cook some rice. The children ate from metal camping plates, and she let them each have a can of lemon soda. She always enjoyed sitting around a fire in the evening, a time to relax and discuss the happenings of the day. She had missed her time here this year.

"Steve let me carry supplies," Pedro said. "He said we could help him tomorrow."

"Just don't get in his way. He'll tell me if you do."

Pedro smiled and nodded.

Yash asked her mother for a story. "Tell about when you were a little girl."

"All right. I lived with my grandmother Chiich," Pesh began, even though Yash had heard the story. "She spoke only Mayan and followed the old ways. We lived next door to a ruin—not this one—and I liked to play there. One day when I had eight summers, Burt—I called him Professor Wallace then—"

"Was that Grandpa Burt?"

"Yes. He was the first person I ever saw who had blue eyes. He came to my ruin as an archaeologist. He always wore light-colored full-length pants and a funny-looking hat like a bowl upside down that didn't keep his nose from getting sunburned."

"Does Grandpa still have his funny hat?" Yash asked.

"Why don't you ask him? Do you want to hear the story or not?"

"Please tell us," Pedro said.

"Burt couldn't speak Spanish, and I couldn't speak English. He had an English-Spanish phrasebook, written for tourists. I memorized it and taught myself English."

"Do you still have that book?" Pedro asked. "Could I borrow it?"

"Sure. I'll have to look for it," Pesh said. "Well, Dr. Burt came there for several years. Chiich and I showed him how to read the numbers on the *stone trees*, that's what my grandmother called the monuments at the ruin.

"After I learned how to read some of the glyphs, Burt brought his students—and me—to an archaeology meeting in Mérida, my first time in a big city, and I met Kedar." Pesh smiled, remembering. "He was a pilot, and so handsome!"

"Like the movies," Yash said. "Did he kiss you?"

"That came later."

"Is Mérida big like Guatemala City?" Pedro asked.

"Much smaller, but the biggest place I had ever been," Pesh said. "I wanted to go to school there."

"Did Chiich say you could go?" Yash asked.

"No. She died before I could ask her. She wanted me to become a healing shaman, a *Xmenoob* like Xiu." But, in a vision, Chiich had told Pesh to follow her dreams.

"I had fourteen summers, too young for university but old enough to get married in my village. When Chiich died, I packed everything I owned—a Catholic Bible from my teacher, my clothing, my grandmother's tortilla griddle—into a wheelbarrow and hung my hammock at Burt's ruin."

"Did you live in a tree, like Yash wanted to do?" Pedro asked.

"No, because Burt took me to Mérida. I lived in a dormitory at the university and he arranged for a tutor."

"How did you come here?" Pedro asked.

"Burt won a grant to excavate B'alam Witz, and I have worked here every season."

"How did you meet Daddy?" Yash asked.

"I told you he was a pilot," Pesh said. "Kedar won the contract to bring in supplies to B'alam Witz. Every week or two, he came in a floatplane and landed on the river. I flew away with him to Mérida one day, and that was the beginning."

"I want to go to school, too, like you did," Pedro said.

"We'll work on it, okay?"

Yash looked ready to ask more questions, anything to postpone bedtime, but Pesh saw her rubbing her eyes to stay awake.

"Let's go try out those hammocks," Pesh said. She could hardly wait to begin an inventory of this year's finds, especially that sacrificial bowl.

48

At B'alam Witz, Steve stood in a trench that led from the pyramid to the center of the plaza, the navel of the ancient city. He shoveled gravel into a wheelbarrow while two helpers sifted loose sand through a screen into a box. He was too busy to notice Yash and Pedro.

"What are you looking for?" Pedro asked.

"Buried treasure." Steve brushed the sweat off his forehead with a red handkerchief and leaned on a shovel. "But I might let you help."

"I could dig," Pedro said. "I'm really strong."

"Okay, here you go." Steve handed him a shovel and explained how to push dirt back into the open trench.

"I want to help, too." Yash stood beside Pedro.

"Hm-m-m." Steve scratched his head. "How to put a one-armed, really short girl to work?"

"I'm not little any more. I'm seven."

Steve grinned and gave her a pair of work gloves.

"Your mother told us that the Maya often smashed ceramic ritual pots and buried the fragments in a line near the center of the city. That's why we are looking for small pieces." Steve showed her how to sift the dirt to find any scraps of pottery or other small objects.

At high noon, Steve sent the children to have lunch with Pesh.

"It's siesta time," Pesh said. "They don't work in the middle of the day. I brought your books so you can read."

"Pedro is learning fast," Yash said.

"Could I get a job here, working for you?" Pedro asked. "I'm almost ten and Steve showed me how. I'm a good worker."

"I'll ask Dr. Burt," Pesh said. "For next year. But you need to go to school."

"I want to, more than anything. But *mi tío* Cuxil hasn't said I could stay."

"Don't worry. We'll look for him again in Antigua." Pesh frowned. *What was the matter with Cuxil?* No one had heard from him or from Pedro's father.

That evening, the three of them sat on camp chairs near the fire circle and shared canned beans and tortillas. Pesh showed Yash and Pedro how to roast marshmallows and gave them a damp cloth to clean up sticky fingers.

Pesh had forbidden climbing the temple but the caves were more dangerous, so dangerous that she had never accompanied the spelunkers hired to explore them. The sacred cave was even more dangerous for Yash; spending the night there was the shaman's initiation rite. *Xmenoob Xiu* had said to teach Yash well; Pesh decided to tell the children the truth.

"Are you ready for story time?" she asked.

Yash and Pedro gave enthusiastic yeses and pulled their chairs closer together.

"I'll tell you a story about what happened to me, right here at B'alam Witz. I liked to watch the bats rise into the night sky and wondered where they came from. One day, I found their opening in the hill. I grabbed a flashlight and stepped through into the cave. I thought only a little peek wouldn't hurt."

"Can I see the bats?" Yash asked.

"Tomorrow night. They come out at sunset."

"Can we see their cave?" Pedro asked.

"Too dangerous." Pesh started to sweat, remembering Cimil's threat. "The trails are broken, and the Maya made booby-traps to keep the spirits of the ancestors from wandering away from *Xibalba*."

"What's *Xibalba*?" Yash asked.

"That's where you go after you die," Pedro said. "Maria said she'd send me there if I didn't do the chores."

"*Xibalba* isn't quite like the Hell you hear about at church," Pesh said. "The gods of the underworld rule there."

"Then what happened to you in there?" Pedro asked.

"I slipped at a broken place. The flashlight flew out of my hand and rolled away. I slid down, in stinky bat guano. It was dark, completely dark. I couldn't see anything, anything at all."

"I can see things in my room after dark," Yash said.

"Yes, because there's always some light—the moon, a street light, the stars."

"Let her tell the story," Pedro said.

"I fell down, down, down," Pesh said slowly for emphasis. "All the way to an underground river. I saw my light, but I couldn't reach it. Then something glowing moved in the river. A ghost! A were-jaguar! A shape-changer!"

"Oh-h-h!" Yash put her hand over her mouth.

"A monster, coming to get me!" Pesh shivered. "I wanted to run away, hide. I had nowhere to go."

"Was it a ghost?" Yash asked, and Pedro added, "What did you do?"

"Worse than a ghost. A scuba diver with a headlamp."

"What's a scuba diver?" Pedro asked.

"They wear black rubber suits with masks for air and swim underwater." Pesh relaxed, glad for the momentary diversion. "He had a can of air strapped onto his back."

"He swam under water in the river?" Pedro asked. "Why didn't he use a boat?"

"Good questions," Pesh said. "Not the river where the macaws have their clay lick. There's an underground river down there, below us."

"What was he doing there?" Yash asked, swinging her feet in the too-big chair.

"Looking for Mayan treasures. The Maya left gifts for the gods in the graves."

"Steve is looking for buried treasure," Yash said.

"Sh-h-h! I want to hear the story," Pedro said.

"The diver had a knife. He wanted me to show him where to find ancient artifacts. I said *no,* and he slapped me. Then he tied me up and left me to die in the dark. I screamed a Mayan curse: *Crocodiles tear off your balls!*"

"Ow!" Pedro exclaimed. "Don't talk like that."

"What are balls?" Yash looked puzzled.

"It's not polite to say that. Balls are men's private parts," Pesh explained. "I had heard the boys taunt each other at school."

"They didn't let anyone speak Mayan at my school," Pedro said. "I went there for a year."

Pesh nodded. "We were punished for speaking Mayan, too."

"How'd you get out of the cave, Mommy?" Yash crossed her legs at the ankle and leaned forward.

"I squashed my hands together like this." Pesh folded her thumb and little finger under her palm. "Then I pulled one hand out of the rope, but I scraped off a lot of skin and it really hurt. When I untied the other ropes, I had to rub my feet to wake them up. They tingled and burned, like I had stepped on needles.

"I could see the flashlight. I had to get it. I climbed on my hands and knees. The rough wall scraped my legs. When I got to the ledge, I was too exhausted to move, and I stank like guano, bat shit. I had to turn off the flashlight to save its batteries."

Pesh paused, reliving her time in the cave. "It was dark, so very dark."

"What'd you do then?" Yash sounded worried.

"I prayed to the gods of the underworld. Xiu told you stories about Mayan gods."

Yash didn't respond. Pesh had expected her to say, *but you have to pray to God.*

"I couldn't sleep. The rock floor was cold and hard. I couldn't see. Water dripped, drip, drip, drip. The river gurgled, gluk, gluk, gluk. If a bat had squeaked, I would have screamed.

"Then my hand felt something small and smooth. My jade talisman, this one." Pesh pulled out her jade jaguar.

"I like to touch B'alam when I go to sleep," Yash said.

"You showed that to Xiu," Pedro said.

"I flashed the light to see the talisman. Next to me, I saw bones! A skeleton!"

"O-o-h no!" Yash shook her head.

"This is a good story," Pedro said.

"But real. The bones belonged to an ancestor, his blue mummy wrappings in tatters. I was in someone's grave!

"I couldn't go anywhere else, so I rested next to those bones, without light. I put the jade jaguar under my shirt and it calmed me.

"I knew I had to climb higher. The flashlight flickered. I held it between my teeth and climbed to another ledge but just then my flashlight gave up."

"In the dark," Yash said. "I don't like the dark."

"I don't either. Especially with skeletons." Pesh hoped Yash understood that caves were dangerous places to go. "I couldn't see, but I could feel the rough wall. I felt my way until the trail branched. I called out, *which way?* even though there was no one to hear me.

"Then Cimil laughed, a terrible laugh. The chief god of the underworld! I was so scared I couldn't speak. Couldn't move. Couldn't breathe."

"Does Cimil cackle and snarl like Kizin, like Alberto told us?" Yash asked.

"Cimil is worse," Pesh said. "But he did help me. He told me to use the path on the right. I rubbed my hands along rough rock until I turned a corner. I saw a sliver of light.

"When I came out, the sunlight was so bright that I had to close my eyes. Grandma Chiich had told me I'd become a shaman if I spent the night in a sacred cave, but I didn't feel different."

"Xiu said you were a shaman," Pedro said.

"Is that where you got your magic?" Yash asked.

"That was the day I became a shaman, but I didn't know it until later," Pesh said. "I was lost in the jungle. I travelled north by keeping the sun on my back, but I had no water. After a while, I couldn't think clearly.

"Finally I heard Kedar—your father, only we weren't married then—calling me. He gave me water and carried me on his back because my bare feet and knees were bloody and I had lost my shoes."

"You tell stories better than Alberto," Pedro said.

"Thank you."

"If you didn't know you were a shaman, how did you find out?" Pedro asked.

"Well, this part I'm not proud of. A crocodile did kill the scuba diver, here at B'alam Witz, in our river where no crocodiles had been seen for a hundred years."

"Does that mean you killed him?" Yash asked.

"He died from my curse, and I knew I was a shaman. I had nightmares after that, the crocodile thrashing about, taking the looter away in its jaws." *How to explain to children?* "A shaman has to be careful what she says. Being a shaman is a heavy responsibility."

"Why don't you quit?" Pedro asked. "Tell Cimil to give someone else the job."

"Xiu didn't think I could unbind myself from Cimil," Pesh said. "Look, this is serious. When Yash was a baby, I visited Precious-Turtle—she lives across the river. Someone was going to hurt Yash. I yelled, *Hurt my baby, you die! Cimil sends the snake!*

"Yash, you said the kidnapper slapped you?"

"He slapped me and told me to shut up," Yash said. "Yellow Teeth was mean."

"Do you remember how he died, like magic?"

"The snake said he'd help me," Yash said.

"The gods sent the snake," Pesh said.

"So Cimil's real?" Pedro asked.

"To me, he is. But some people say the Mayan gods live only in the minds of those who believe. And Catholics don't believe in them at all."

"Then be a Catholic," Pedro said.

"I had Yash christened in the Catholic Church." Pesh wondered if becoming a Catholic would help. At church with Isolde, she always prayed silently to her patron god, Hun Hunahpu. If there was one supreme God, did his name matter? "I don't know if that helps. But I do know I could have died in that cave. I'll show you how dark it was."

Pesh and Pedro carried two camp chairs to the clearing away from the fire circle. Yash and Pedro sat there, and Pesh tied a bandana around each child's head, covering their eyes.

"No fair peeking." Pesh guided them to the other side of the clearing and then asked them to find their chairs again. "First one back wins."

They stumbled around. She helped them feel the chairs and checked that their blindfolds were still in place.

"I don't think anybody won," Pesh said to the seated children. "Now get up and stand on one leg."

Yash lost her balance right away and giggled, and Pedro did, too.

"Now you know what it feels like to be blind." Pesh untied the bandanas. "In a cave, you see even less."

On the third morning, the children were full of energy and wanted to help Steve again. They seemed to have forgotten last night's story, but then, hot chocolate could fix anything.

While they were finishing breakfast, Steve called out that a canoe was approaching.

Pesh went to the head of the river trail to watch the action. Big-Beak Macaw rowed his canoe with Precious-Turtle as his passenger.

"¡Hola!" Pesh cried out.

Precious-Turtle waved and even smiled. She had changed so much over the last seven years, but Big-Beak still presented his frozen face to the world. They joined Pesh at the fire circle.

"How nice to have company," Pesh said. "I want you to meet my children. You remember Yash, of course. This is her friend Pedro."

She found a beer for Big-Beak and an orange soda for Precious-Turtle. Big-Beak leaned back against a tree in the shade, Precious-Turtle joined her at the fire circle, and the children went looking for Steve.

Speaking in Mayan, Precious-Turtle thanked Pesh for helping her with Spanish. Now that she could bargain, Five-Owl was much more respectful.

"Remember the time you chased Five-Owl away with the broom?" Pesh didn't tell her almost-mother-in-law that she had used Five-Owl's name on Pedro's birth certificate. They laughed together.

At midday, Big-Beak signaled: time to cross the river.

"So soon?" Pesh asked.

"I come at full moon," Precious-Turtle said.

"I must leave before then, but I'll be back next year."

Pesh walked with them to the canoe and waved goodbye from the bank. On her way back to the fire circle, she heard something ringing. At first she didn't recognize the sound—her satellite phone. She fumbled, almost dropped it, then turned it on. "Pesh here."

"Hello, Heart-of-My-Heart," Kedar said. "Guess what? I'm coming tomorrow."

"You're several days early." Pesh's heart sped up as it always did when she talked to him on the phone.

"I have to take you to Alta Altun tomorrow."

"To Xiu?" Pesh couldn't believe her ears. She had work to finish here for Burt.

"Xiu is very ill. She's asking for you," Kedar said.

That evening, Pesh went over the list of closing duties with Steve; he didn't need reminding. When she told the children to pack up, they both wanted to stay at B'alam Witz.

"I like to help Steve," Pedro said, and Yash added, "You didn't let us climb the temple."

"No climbing with that arm in a sling!" Pesh said.

"You said we could stay a week," Yash said.

"I know, Sweetheart. We're going to visit Xiu one more time." *No sense worrying the kids.*

49

At B'alam Witz, Pesh stood where she had a good view of the sandy riverbank where scarlet macaws squawked and chased one another, competing for space at the clay lick. She heard the *whop-whop-whop* of the helicopter before she saw it through the trees.

"Daddy's coming!" Yash ran up behind her, Pedro not far behind, while Kedar hovered over the sand spit and prepared to set down.

"Careful." Pesh grabbed Yash's arm. "It's slippery."

Pedro stayed by Pesh, but Yash dashed toward the helicopter and interrupted the macaws' clay-eating frenzy. A scarlet, green, and blue bird, its wingspan greater than two meters, swooped down and combed through Yash's braid with its feet.

"No! Go away!" Yash waved her arms and screamed, "Mommy!"

Pesh shooed the parrot-like bird away and hugged her daughter while Kedar landed. Grandma Chiich would have seen this as an omen, something dire.

"You're okay, Princess!" Kedar jumped out and rushed to Yash. "You came between the birds and their clay."

"Why did he choose you?" Pedro asked Yash. The birds hadn't bothered anyone else.

Yash said she didn't know.

Kedar climbed the path to the archaeologists' camp to get the duffle bags and Pedro said he'd help carry them. Pesh followed with Yash clinging to one hand.

"Yo, Kedar." Steve, seated on a camp chair at the fire circle, was finishing his morning coffee.

"Hello, Buddy," Kedar said. "I'll be back in a few days to relocate you and the crew to Mérida."

"Pesh told me." Steve saluted with his empty cup. "Everything's under control."

"I can hardly wait to show Burt this year's treasures," Pesh said. "I'll teach you to reconstruct that marvelous piece of pottery you found when we get back to Austin."

"I won't let you forget," Steve said. "Let me give you a hand with those bags."

Pedro helped Kedar load the bags and Steve lifted Yash aboard. Pesh told Steve goodbye, and he stood on the path and waved.

En route, Pesh asked Kedar for any updates on Xiu.

"She's weak and has a fever, according to Zia. Ignacio said he'd drive you to Antigua this afternoon. He said you'd want herbs from the Mayan market."

"He's right. And today is a Mayan market day." Pesh glanced at Pedro, who looked outside the window. The children couldn't hear her over the engine noise. "Maybe we'll see Pedro's father there."

"Ignacio says he's vanished like smoke," Kedar said. "No one has seen him at the market. And your letter to Cuxil came back, marked deceased."

"What will we do about Pedro?"

"I'm afraid that's your problem."

"I can't abandon Pedro in Antigua," Pesh said.

"In a perfect world," Kedar said, "you'd buy him a ticket and take him with you."

"Would you like that?"

"Yes, I would—he's a great kid. But you'd never get him through immigration in Texas."

"My stowaway child," Pesh said. "Could you take him to Texas from Mérida like you did me years ago?"

"How would he hide in the ladies' restroom?"

Pesh laughed, remembering, and changed the intercom to include passengers. The children had been unable to hear their conversation.

"This is your captain speaking." Kedar deepened his voice. "Next stop, Quetzal Centrale, fifteen minutes."

"We'll visit Xiu tomorrow," Pesh said. "She's sick."

"I know. The macaw told me," Yash said.

"I wondered why he chose you," Pedro said.

Pesh broke out in a cold sweat and the hair rose on the back of her neck. She hadn't told the children Xiu was ill. Did the macaw choose Yash to give her a message?

"Xiu's illness is so unexpected, and I should visit her with you," Kedar said. "But I have to make another trip to the Motagua Valley with Paul to finish my contract."

"So you won't visit Xiu with us?"

"Sorry, Sweetheart," he said. "I hate doing it this way. I can drop you off tomorrow, but then you and the kids are on your own."

The macaw singled out Yash. Pesh's heart raced, nearly exploding. *Xiu: very ill. Pedro: no place to go. The macaw's omen—what did it mean?*

50

Pesh shook out sand from the children's socks, muddy from the clay riverbank at B'alam Witz. An omen: what did the macaw portend?

She loaded the two machines behind the kitchen at the Andersons' compound, Quetzal Centrale, and flashed to her grandmother, rubbing laundry over rocks and rinsing it in the river. Modern conveniences: *Dios bo'otik!*

The washers burbled and beeped, and she stepped into the kitchen for a moment with Zia.

"Pesh! You're back," Zia said, drying her hands with a towel. "I'm so glad."

"I'm glad to see you, too, but I won't be here long. I heard your message, that Xiu is ill. Do you know any more?"

"It's serious," Zia said. "She sent for *Xmenoob Pex*. Why didn't you tell me you're a shaman?"

"I guess I should have."

"That's so wonderful!" Zia said. "Not many people follow the old ways. Our *Xmenoob Xiu* knows more about healing than all the doctors in Antigua."

"You regard me much more highly than I deserve," Pesh said, avoiding eye contact. Now that Cimil, the god of the underworld, had won, was she still a *Xmenoob*? She didn't know enough; her grandmother had died before teaching her how to use her powers as a shaman. "I'm still trying to learn some of those secrets."

"Ignacio says he's taking you to the Mayan market in Antigua," Zia said. "Xiu needs medicines for fever and for pain in the stomach."

"We need to rush there before the sellers leave for the day," Pesh said. "Please remind Yash and Pedro to fold the clothes if they forget."

"Pedro won't forget," Zia said. "I have never met such a fine young man."

At dinner, the Andersons, Pesh, Kedar, and the children sat along one long arm of the over-sized table, the better to share the news of the day. Zia brought platters of turkey tamales and fresh fruit, bowls of black beans, and a plateful of corn tortillas. Pesh hadn't realized how hungry she was after subsisting on canned foods at B'alam Witz.

Vanna told Pesh that she had obtained a Guatemalan birth certificate for Pedro.

"I guess I owe you $500." At last, papers for Pedro.

"No such thing. It didn't cost half that much." Vanna laughed, one of her contagious laughs.

"About the birth certificate," Paul said. "Nothing black market about it. I went directly to the Office of Registry. I told them you were the one who recovered the mask stolen from La Democracia Museum, and they said: *It is Guatemala that owes la señora Chanlajun Pex.*"

"For me, a birth certificate?" Pedro asked. "You gave me a birthday, but you put Chanlajun Pex Yaxuun B'alam on the line for mother."

"So you might be able to visit us in Texas," Pesh said.

"But that is not true." Pedro frowned. "Father … Who is Ho' Muwan Pedro Manu?"

"I listed myself as your mother so I could argue with officials. Your father has to have Mayan name; Ho' Muwan is Five-Owl from the sacred calendar."

"Why didn't you make Kedar my father?" Pedro looked at Kedar.

"I'm only an adopted Maya," Kedar said, "and that's only a piece of paper you need to get travel documents. I'd like to have you visit us in the United States. The only trouble will be getting you through immigration."

Pesh had no idea how to handle U.S. immigration.

"This changes the subject but I have to know more." Vanna pointed her wine glass toward Pesh. "Zia says you are a Maya shaman."

"That's true."

"I'm a great admirer of the Mayan civilization," Vanna said. "Their astronomy—they predicted eclipses of the sun and cycles of Venus. Their mathematics—they used zero before the Europeans. Their libraries—they developed a complete system of writing rivaling that of the Egyptians."

"Mayan books were works of art," Pesh said. "Burt and I translated a complete manuscript."

"And that made Burt famous among archaeologists," Vanna said. "Did you know I came to Guatemala as an archaeologist before I married Paul?"

"I was an archaeologist before I became a shaman," Pesh said. "I followed Burt around ruins from the time I had eight summers."

"If this is not too personal, how did you become a shaman?" Vanna asked.

"I was born to it, but I didn't want to do it." Pesh wondered how much to tell. "I wanted to join the modern world and go to the university."

"You've certainly done so," Vanna said, hoisting her empty glass. "So what happened?"

"All right. One day, I went exploring by myself behind the B'alam Witz ruin." Pesh told them how she slipped and fell in the cave; how she caught a looter stealing treasures from the ancestors; how he tied her up and left her to die.

"My God! How did you escape?" Paul asked.

"His knots weren't very good. I got my bearings from his light. When he left, I knew I had to climb a rough rock wall." Pesh shuddered, remembering. "I was afraid, but it was die while climbing or die while crying about it."

"In the dark!" Paul whistled. "You have true grit."

"How did that make you a shaman?" Vanna asked.

"I spent the night in a sacred cave." Pesh pulled out B'alam, her small jade jaguar. "The gods of the underworld guided me and gave me this talisman. So, without planning it, I became a shaman."

"An exquisite piece." Vanna leaned over Pesh's shoulder to admire more closely. "That's high quality jade."

"Mommy always wears that," Yash said.

"I feel naked without it," Pesh said.

"So that's your interest in jade," Paul said. "Are you a healing shaman?"

"My grandmother was a healing shaman," Pesh said. "She taught me many things."

"I hope you're recording the secret Mayan formulas for medicines," Paul said, twisting his napkin. "The jungles of Guatemala have many plants never studied. Perhaps you should come back next year."

"Thank you for all you have done for us," Pesh said. "Way more than required for the archaeological grant."

Paul poured more wine all around.

"We were honored to have your company." Paul raised his wine glass. "Here's to a delightful search for jade."

"Hear, hear," Kedar said. "Maybe more next year."

Kedar and Pesh clicked glasses with Paul and Vanna and took sips. Yash and Pedro looked at one another, then clicked their water glasses together and sipped.

"And next year, young lady." Paul looked at Yash, but he smiled. "No animals in your room. Okay?"

"Okay," Yash said, slipping down in her chair.

"Thanks for everything," Pesh said. "Tomorrow the children and I will visit Zia's sick friend, Shaman Xiu. She asked for me."

51

The helicopter circled lower and Pesh watched Alta Altun come out of hiding. The mountain to the west poked out above the mist that covered the jungle and disguised the ravine and the dirt road. They crossed the town plaza, and Kedar settled the helicopter onto the road at the edge of the village.

Rolana and a group of village children waved and yelled greetings.

As soon as the rotors stopped, Pesh and Pedro jumped to the ground and Kedar lifted Yash out of the aircraft.

"Xiu said Yash and Pedro should visit me today," Rolana said to Pesh.

"Thank you. I'll stay with Xiu."

"*Ko 'ox.*" Rolana invited the children to follow.

Kedar stood by Pesh, one hand on her shoulder. He had one more trip with Paul Anderson to the Motagua Valley to finish his Guatemala contract. Afterward, he would move all B'alam Witz personnel to Mérida, ending this year's archaeological season, and he would return the helicopter.

"It's goodbye until Austin, my love." Kedar pulled her close. "You and Yash have to find your way home alone."

"I know. We'll be fine, but what about Pedro?"

"He's such fine young man—not suited to life on the streets in Guatemala." Kedar's voice caught. "But Pedro's his father's responsibility. You'll have to visit him."

"What if I can't find him? I can't drop Pedro on a curb in Antigua."

"Pedro's situation's impossible, any way you look at it." Kedar looked on the verge of tears. "I know what he's going through. I was an orphan until Isolde took me in. He can't live on the streets, but you can't just take him without his father's permission."

"Just for a plan B. Would you mind if Pedro visited us for a while?" Pesh asked.

"And how would you get Pedro through immigration?"

"I'll think of something."

"You know I'd like him to come, but it's impossible." Kedar hugged her. "Sweetheart, you have the satellite phone. Take good care of Xiu, and call Ignacio when you want to return to Quetzal Centrale."

Pesh waved until the helicopter became a speck on the horizon.

Pesh entered Xiu's dwelling without waiting for the usual formal invitation. Xiu lay still on her sleeping mat, her face pale and etched by pain lines. Her body seemed smaller; Pesh, shocked at her friend's condition, wanted to appear strong and confident for Xiu.

"Xiu, I am here." Pesh placed a hand on Xiu's forehead: she indeed had a fever.

"*Xmenoob Pex.*" Xiu lifted her head.

"Chew this while I brew herbal tea. It helps with pain." Pesh gave her a piece of willow bark and brewed tea with the herbs purchased at the Mayan market.

"This tea will treat your fever and make you sleep." Pesh helped her to sip.

After a few swallows, Xiu sank back on her mat.

"May I touch your abdomen?" Pesh asked. "Does it hurt when I press here?"

Xiu groaned her answer. The muscles in her abdomen contracted so much it looked like a washboard. It must be her appendix.

"Do you have any coca leaves?" Pesh saw that Xiu needed a painkiller stronger than the aspirin in the willow bark, and probably a doctor, too. She bit her lip and tried to be brave for Xiu.

"I gave them to Yash when she broke her arm."

"You have nothing else for pain?" Pesh asked.

"It doesn't matter. I am old."

"The jade will pull out the pain." Pesh rubbed her jade jaguar on Xiu's stomach and chanted one of Chiich's healing spells. She had sung it once years ago to heal Kedar's knife wound, but he had been young and strong. Jade couldn't heal anything, but if Xiu believed, it could ease her suffering.

"My time is ending. I want you to have these." Xiu gave Pesh her shaman's pebbles in their small linen satchel and her obsidian firebird talisman.

"You have no family?" Pesh pushed away tears; the pebbles were Xiu's most precious possessions. Firebird vibrated in her hand as though trying to tell her something.

"Alta Altun is my family."

"Then I will keep your treasures for now, until you are well." Pesh slipped Firebird over her head to wear it under her shirt, along with B'alam.

"You put Firebird next to B'alam." Xiu squeezed her hand. "Did you find his source at B'alam Ha?"

"No, only where B'alam was carved." Pesh sighed. "Cimil has won."

"You're wrong. The gods of *Xibalba* tricked you," Xiu said. "Cimil cheated. He asked for what no man can know."

"But I didn't find the lost jade either." Pesh leaned closer to Xiu to hear her voice.

"Did you not find Yash when she was lost? Is she not called *jade* in our language?" Xiu wheezed. "You need not fear Cimil."

311

"The gods pay. You take away my fears even though I am here to heal you." But Pesh recalled how her curse had killed the looter and how Cimil favored dark uses of magic.

"Your love is my greatest gift," Xiu said.

Too choked up to answer, Pesh held Xiu's hand.

"My linen shroud is over there with my ceremonial urn," Xiu said, as if only passing the time of day. She pointed to a brick-red ceramic urn about 20 centimeters tall and 15 centimeters in diameter with a separate knobbed cover. Cream-colored bands top and bottom bordered its body, painted with disembodied eyes and black markers resembling the rosette spots of a jaguar.

"That's an exquisite piece." Pesh recognized it as an artifact from the Classic Period. It would have belonged to a powerful shaman or to a king.

"That ceramic vessel will hold my ashes. You must place it beneath the mural of the hunt in the Cave of B'alam." Xiu's voice sounded weaker.

Pesh remembered the crystal skull and its green light. She must force herself to go into the cave one more time, alone. She must avoid breathing the breath of B'alam. She shifted on the floor, unable to get comfortable.

She helped Xiu to sip more herbal tea and held one of her hands. While Xiu slept, Pesh opened the linen bag that held the precious pebbles. She took out the four most basic shaman's beads: yellow amber, red coral, black obsidian, and colorless quartz, the colors of the four gods of creation. The amber encased a mosquito, its lacelike wings and hair-like legs perfectly preserved. The coral branched like a fern. The black obsidian pebble had been smoothed by the action of water in a stream; Kedar would call it an *Apache* tear. The quartz crystal had a pyramidal end atop a six-faced prism.

The pouch contained more treasures: a rare piece of Aztec green obsidian to make strong healing spells; a green stone the color of new corn to symbolize life; two grayish-blue jade pebbles to heal diseases of the stomach, the kidneys, and the spirit.

Pesh didn't know how to use Xiu's magic stones. Without Xiu, who could teach her? Holding the small satchel of ritual stones, Pesh prayed for more time.

A little later, Xiu opened her eyes and rallied.

"You must commit my spirit to the gods to travel to *Xibalba*." Xiu sat up to sip water. "There is no other *Xmenoob* and no one else of royal blood."

Pesh held back tears and patted Xiu's arm, but Xiu again weakened.

"I have lived too long."

"No, you can't leave. Your village needs you." Pesh's heart broke into sharp chips of ice that burned into her soul.

"Firebird will belong to one who sees him fly in the smoke of my funeral fire." With those words, Xiu stopped breathing.

"No!" Pesh covered her face with her hands and wept great convulsing sobs that shook her shoulders.

Later, how much later she didn't know, Pesh walked to the house of the village elder. He sat outside by his doorway and rose as though he expected her. Then he said, "The *Xmenoob* is dead. I have sent for the Daykeepers."

Pesh remembered the custom in Yucatán, where one couldn't speak the dead person's name for a year. She went back to the *Xmenoob* and wrapped her body in the linen funeral shroud and placed a jade bead from Alberto's workshop into her mouth.

"Goodbye, Dear Friend." Pesh ground away her tears with one fist. She remembered her grandmother Chiich's cremation and how she had burned their house down in her grief. She shuffled, head bowed, to Rolana's house.

"The *Xmenoob* has died." Pesh tried to explain that they must aid her spirit on its voyage to *Xibalba*.

Rolana covered her face with her hands and her shoulders shook with silent sobs.

"Will her *wayob* fly to *Xibalba*?" Yash asked.

"The Firebird?" Pedro added.

"Firebird will guide her to *Xibalba*."

Pesh wondered who would see the firebird. "The *Xmenoob* asked me to say the sacred words."

They hugged each other and cried together.

Would the Daykeepers guide her? Pesh couldn't let the *Xmenoob* down, not on her voyage to *Xibalba*.

52

As advised by two Daykeeper priests from Momostenango, the village men built a funeral pyre behind the houses at the edge of the cornfield at Alta Altun. They placed Xiu at its top. The Daykeepers, Maya priests who kept the Sacred Calendar, helped Pesh plan the ceremony, a symbolic ritual to please the gods. She had a small speaking part to praise the gods and to send Xiu's soul to *Xibalba*. She was too choked up to eulogize Xiu, but the funeral ceremony didn't include such speeches.

Pesh had difficulty with the language of Xiu's village, although she had spoken freely with Xiu and with Chel, their ease of communication a secret of the sisterhood of the *Xmenoob*. She would use her native Yucatec for the ceremony and to commune with the gods. The mourners would appreciate the ritual, whatever the words she used to show respect for Xiu.

After nightfall, the entire village—and Zia and Ignacio and a runner from B'alam Ha representing *Xmenoob* Chel—assembled around the pyre. Yash, Pedro, and Rolana stood by Zia. The two Daykeepers, wearing masks and dark blue robes, lit the funeral fire and ignited copal incense in coconut half shells suspended by cords. A conch shell trumpeted a single forlorn call. Drums, whistles, and flutes began their lament.

The two masked Daykeepers wended their way among eighty assembled villagers, swinging the burning incense back and forth and chanting the funeral dirge. They arrived at the front of the group and purified themselves by praying to the maize god and to the gods of the underworld and sipping ceremonial *balche*.

Pesh, as the only one having royal blood, officiated. She held Xiu's obsidian bloodletting-ritual knife above her head, the blade reflecting the flickering firelight. Slowly, she pulled it across the pad of one thumb, cutting herself, the blade so sharp she didn't feel the wound until she squeezed it to sprinkle drops of royal blood over the fire.

She swayed from side to side and hummed, "*H-m-m-m-m-m, o-o-o-o-o, h-m-m-m-m-m,*" while the Daykeepers chanted the words, prayers to aid Xiu in her descent into *Xibalba*, land of the honored dead. The rhythm of the funeral dirge pulsed through Pesh's entire body.

At the Daykeepers' signal, Pesh laid a white napkin across a small table to one side of the pyre. She raised her hands toward the heavens and praised Xiu's patron god *Itzamná*, the god of learning and medicine. She held out the amber with a flourish and placed it on the southern corner of the napkin while the Daykeepers called upon the yellow god with reed whistles and three beats on a turtle carapace drum.

Pesh repeated the ritual, praising the red god, the black god, and the colorless god in turn, and placed the stones to mark the cardinal directions. With ceremonial dignity, she delivered offerings of corn, copal, cacao beans, and vanilla pods to the center of the napkin. Then she turned toward the blazing funeral pyre and bowed her head.

"Oh, mighty gods of the underworld, the village of Alta Altun commits *Xmenoob Xiu*'s spirit to you for safe guidance to *Xibalba*." Pesh added a personal plea to Cimil in Yucatec as privately as though they spoke alone because the crowd could neither understand her dialect nor hear her words above the funeral dirge.

"You have won our wager." Pesh heard Cimil's evil laugh. "But *Xmenoob Xiu* told me your secret. You are losing your power."

Cimil replied with a growl. He did not speak.

"I am not a fallen *Xmenoob* and you cannot afford to lose a follower." Pesh felt a strange compassion for the old god whom no one worshipped.

"You saved my life in the sacred cave when you gave me the little B'alam. And you helped Yash when she was kidnapped." Pesh added "Thank you" in English because how could she give thanks in Mayan, "The gods pay," to a god? And to address him in Spanish would be an insult.

Cimil laughed, but this time his laugh was not an evil one. Perhaps he got the joke, that she couldn't thank him in the usual way.

"Yash will not be a shaman unless she so chooses." Pesh finished her conversation with Cimil. He didn't answer, but she didn't care. She no longer feared him.

Pesh belted down her third *balche* and threw the gods' offerings onto the flames, first the copal incense, then cacao and vanilla beans, and last, a handful of corn kernels. With a final flourish, she tossed red feathers from a macaw over the hungry fire.

Dizzy from *balche*, she sank into a cross-legged position and joined the other mourners. Tears streamed down her face. She smelled the stink of burning flesh, that odor partially masked by the heavy sweet smell of copal, and watched flames lick the night sky. She grieved for Xiu and thought of what Xiu had taught her, how to balance her life in academia and as *Xmenoob*.

The corn popped and snapped and shot out bright embers. In the shimmering heat above the flames, a bird rose into the air, a bird with glowing red and green feathers and the hooked beak of a hawk. Firebird!

Pesh, like a stone monument dedicated to Xiu, sat without moving until the flames died down. Then she cooled a dish of ashes and the Daykeepers carried them around for the adults to mark their foreheads with the Mayan cross. Then the Daykeepers agitated Xiu's bones and added more fuel to burn the pieces of bone to ash.

Pesh and the men sat crossed-legged and stone-faced for the funeral vigil, where they would remain until morning. Rolana took Pedro and Yash home with her for the night, and mothers put their children to bed.

Pesh remained by the fire until it burned down to glowing embers. Only then did she rise and visit the spring to drink water. She joined her sleeping children at Rolana's.

In the middle of the next morning, the two Daykeepers delivered the ceramic urn containing the *Xmenoob*'s ashes to Pesh outside Rolana's hut.

"You must remain here," the first Daykeeper said. "Alta Altun needs a *xmenoob*."

"No. This is not my village," Pesh said. "I honor the Maya by teaching at the University of Texas."

He understood only her "no."

"Alta Altun has no Daykeeper. You must remain."

The Daykeepers looked at each other as if they understood, but, with their stiff Mayan faces, Pesh couldn't tell how they felt about it, or if one of them would stay to serve Alta Altun.

Pesh left Yash and Pedro with Rolana and carried Xiu's ashes to the Cave of B'alam as Xiu had directed. She used Kedar's powerful flashlight to find the mural in the dark cave and placed the urn beneath the image of a jaguar poised to leap. Holding a damp handkerchief over her nose to avoid the breath of B'alam, she carried the greenstone skull to place it next to the urn and lit a candle within it. Green light flickered in the cavern and elongated shadows shivered across the painted hunters and their feathered costumes.

What legend did the mural portray? Jaguarcito wouldn't have hunted with men—cats didn't behave that way. She held her jaguar talisman in both hands and said another prayer to the gods of the underworld. She dropped B'alam back under her shirt next to Xiu's Firebird, sipped the last of Xiu's ceremonial *balche*, and knelt to meditate.

Later, she rose to her feet, unsteady from kneeling so long on the rock floor, or maybe from the *balche*. The jaguar's eye followed her, whichever way she turned.

She let her mind travel in a vision-journey and two Maya dressed in loincloths appeared in front of her, one painting the jaguar's eye with a fine brush, the other grinding charcoal and mixing pigments, the colors brilliant blue, red, and yellow in the light of the pitch torch. The jaguar's black rosette-spots moved over its flexing muscles. She saw the painters stand back, admire their work, and turn to walk deeper into the cave.

Pesh's jade talisman, hot next to her chest, pulsed in rhythm with the flickering shadows, as though it had a message. In her trance, she followed the men into the dark until they disappeared. What was she thinking, going alone into a cave?

Her heart hammered as though it would leap out of her chest. She placed her hand on the cave wall to steady herself. What was this? The wall was smooth and cool, smooth and cool like jade. A wall of jade, but Kedar said jade could not be mined. Was this where the gods found the jade they threw down into the sacred valley?

She turned away from where the men had vanished. Cimil laughed, but not a cruel laugh. The gruesome green light from the skull led her back and the vision-trip ended.

Pesh smelled almond blossoms, the fumes from the volcanic vent. Green light flickered from behind where she lay on the ground. She rose from the floor next to the funeral urn, picked up the flashlight, and extinguished the candle, leaving the greenstone skull to guard Xiu's ashes. As always after a vision, Pesh felt hungry enough to eat jaguar kill. She walked back to the village and hoped that Rolana's mother tended her cooking fire.

After dinner, Pesh and the children gathered around the glowing embers in front of Rolana's place. Pesh had a package of marshmallows to toast, but the children were more interested Xiu's trip to *Xibalba* than in dessert.

"I saw a red and green bird fly above the smoke," Yash said. "Was that Firebird?"

"I saw it, too," Pedro and Rolana said together.

Puzzled, Pesh didn't answer. Xiu said Firebird would belong to one who saw him fly in the smoke of her funeral fire. She didn't say it would belong to four persons or to which one, but Xiu had given Firebird to her.

"Could I become a shaman like you?" Rolana asked.

"You would devote your life to being a shaman at Alta Altun," Pesh said. "Do you feel the calling?"

"I felt it when I saw Firebird."

"Alta Altun needs you." Pesh wondered, was Rolana the one whom *Xmenoob* Xiu had chosen? "You would study with the Daykeepers and pray to the gods. When you were ready, you would spend the night alone in the Sacred Cave of B'alam."

"I could do that," Rolana said with enthusiasm. "I have fourteen summers and I want to be just like the *Xmenoob*."

Rolana was a charming mixture of child and young woman, old enough to marry at fourteen per Mayan custom. At fourteen, Pesh had cremated her grandmother and moved to Mérida—and fallen in love with Kedar.

Pesh chose her words carefully. "You can become a shaman, but I don't know if you could become *Xmenoob*. That usually passes from mother to first-born daughter. My mother and my grandmother were *Xmenoob*."

Rolana's face fell and she bit her lip.

"Don't worry. Become a shaman first." Pesh hadn't meant to discourage her. "Let yourself grow into the job. *Xmenoob Ix Chel* knows these things. She has no daughter. Perhaps she will adopt you. You must visit her."

"I will visit *Xmenoob Ix Chel*," Rolana said.

"I saw Firebird, too," Yash said. "I helped Xiu carry Firebird to bring light. You were in a dark cave."

Pesh swallowed hard. Yash helped Xiu work as a shaman. *Not good! Yash belonged in the modern world—she mustn't become a shaman!*

"The *Xmenoob* said my *avatar* ... *my wayob* ... is the quetzal and I can talk to animals," Yash said. "I want to be a shaman like Rolana."

"But you don't have fourteen summers and you don't live at Alta Altun." Pesh forced herself to speak as though discussing a matter of no consequence, but the veins in her temples pulsed and she had to swallow. She breathed deeply and stroked her talisman B'alam to calm herself. However, Cimil had agreed that Yash could choose.

"I have a *wayob*," Yash said. "Does Rolana have one?"

"The *Xmenoob* gave me the owl," Rolana said. "Owls sleep during the day and can't see in bright light, but after dark, they see what others cannot."

"The owl is a good *wayob* for a shaman who travels in the night with visions. The gods will give you a talisman when you become a shaman—they gave me this one." Pesh showed B'alam to Rolana.

"Here are the *Xmenoob*'s stones." Pesh handed Xiu's satchel to Rolana but not Xiu's talisman, Firebird. "*Xmenoob Ix Chel* will teach you how to use them. And for luck, here's a jade marble that Yash polished."

"I have one just like that already." Rolana pulled out a bead she wore suspended on a cord around her neck. "Green and white. Yash gave it to me."

"I'm wearing one, too," Pedro said.

"That's so we can be friends forever," Yash said.

It became clear to Pesh why all three children had seen Firebird rise from the flames: all three wore jade cut from the same stone.

"Ask *Xmenoob Ix Chel* how to use the magic stones," Pesh said. "I'll teach you all I know next year."

Another commitment for next year: Pesh had promised Precious-Turtle and the children that she'd return to B'alam Witz, and now Rolana at Alta Altun. Maybe Kedar could get another contract to search for jade in the mountains, beneath the 'X' marked by Foshag in 1955 on the geological map. The legs of Foshag's 'X' crossed above B'alam's Cave.

Next year. Pesh knew she'd visit Alta Altun again.

53

Pesh, Yash, and Pedro returned to Quetzal Centrale late in the afternoon. Pesh used Vanna's telephone to book a flight from Guatemala City to Austin and purchased three tickets, just in case, for Saturday, three days later. The big question was Pedro: he had a birth certificate listing her as his mother but no travel documents. She needed to find Pedro's father. Vanna told her the van was available tomorrow, reminded her that Thursday was a Mayan market day, and walked with her to talk to Andersons' driver, Ignacio.

"*No problema, Señora Pesh,*" Ignacio told her without a quiver of his mustache. "I remember where we went."

The next morning, Pesh and the children piled into the van. Their first stop was the Mayan market, but Maria and Pedro's father weren't there. A Maya who always drank beer with Pedro's father said he hadn't seen him for two moons.

When they returned to the van, Pesh sat in front with Ignacio, Pedro and Yash in the back. Pedro, usually full of cheerful comments, had nothing to say, and Yash wore the stubborn expression that Pesh hadn't seen since Pedro had joined them. They traveled south on Highway 14 without speaking while the radio rocked the car with mariachi songs.

"There's the turn," Pedro said without enthusiasm.

Pesh, Pedro, and Yash got out in front of the wall made of stacked stones. No pickup in the yard. No chickens, either. The house sat empty, shelves bare. No hammocks, no clothes on hooks, as though Pedro's father didn't intend to return.

"Maria might be visiting her mother with her new baby." Pesh asked Pedro, "Do you know where she lives?"

"*No, Señora Pesh.*" Pedro hadn't called her *señora* for weeks. "*¿Mi empleo, terminado?*"

"Of course not," Pesh said. He sounded so formal: my employment, terminated? Yash looked ready to cry.

"*¿Ahora vivo aquí?* Now I live here?" Pedro asked.

"No." Pesh spoke past the lump in her throat. If not here, then where—under a tree? "I cannot leave you here by yourself."

Tears welled up in Pedro's eyes.

"Are you worried about your father?" Pesh put her arms around Pedro and hugged him.

He nodded and settled against her.

"We didn't find your father." Pesh knelt down to look him in the eye. She couldn't leave the boy. Couldn't take him. Couldn't leave him to live on the cruel streets. "We'll look next year."

"Do I go with you?" Pedro said in a small voice.

"*Ko'ox,*" Pesh said. "Now you stay with me."

The children sang with the mariachis all the way back to Quetzal Centrale. Pesh wasn't sure how this would turn out, but she would never abandon Pedro. Would Pedro be caught in a never-never land between Guatemala and the United States?

Two days left. Yash and Pedro spent one last day with Alberto while Pesh did laundry, packed, and cleaned. The children stopped by the bush with the hummingbird's nest, now empty. Yash had left it there undisturbed because the bird might need it. Pedro reached over her head and plucked a bug from a high branch, a colored bug. He let it cling to his T-shirt over his chest.

"Are you going to ask Zia to fry that?" Yash asked.

"No. This is *Maquech* the beetle, my pet," he said. The beetle looked like a piece of jewelry: colored yellow, blue, green, red, and orange, and iridescent and shiny with raised black lumps.

"I want one, too." Yash reached out to touch the bug, about the length of her thumb.

"No, little sister." Pedro pulled away. "*Maquech* is getting used to my heartbeat."

"But I won't hurt him."

"If I find another, I'll give him to you," Pedro said. "*Ko'ox.* Let's visit Alberto."

They raced across the yard.

"*Señorita Jade y Señor Pedro,*" Alberto said, standing in the workshop doorway.

"This is our last day," Yash said, her voice trembling.

"You cannot leave. Your work is unfinished." Alberto set them up to polish jade under the magnolia tree and said he'd be right out to join them.

Yash felt the smoothness of jade, smelled honey from Jesus's polishing machine, and heard the rhythmic bump-bump of the rock tumbler. She didn't want to leave.

Alberto sat next to her, polishing his turtle project.

"You didn't let me try the cutting machine," Pedro said. "I want to learn everything."

"Next time." Alberto turned to face Pedro. "There, on your shirt. Where did you get your little friend?"

"He is *Maquech.*" Pedro stroked the bug with a finger.

"Then I will tell the legend of *Maquech* the Beetle."

"*¡Oh, sí!*" Yash said, and Pedro nodded.

"This is a story about a princess," Alberto said. "She's supposed to marry a prince, but she doesn't want to."

"That happened to my mother," Yash said.

"Then she must really love your father," Alberto said.

As though she heard her name, Pesh joined them, and Alberto invited her to hear his story.

"This is my pet, *Maquech*," Pedro said, pointing to his shirt. "I found him where the hummingbird had her nest."

Pesh admired *Maquech* and waited for Alberto's story.

"Once there is a beautiful princess whose hair is like the wings of a swallow." Alberto flew his hands in front of them. "She is Cuzán the Swallow, the favorite daughter of Great Lord *Dtun-dtun-xcan*. *Dtun-dtun* arranges her marriage to Prince *Ek Chapat*, future lord of the kingdom *Nan Chan*. But one day, when Cuzán visits her father, he is talking to Chalpol, a handsome young man who has flaming red hair and wears a yellow and blue cloak."

"Is this a fairy tale?" Yash asked. "Because they always start with *once upon a time*."

"This is a legend," Alberto said, "about a princess and love. From the moment Cuzán meets Chalpol, their souls are trapped in a bond of fire. They pledge their love under the sacred *ceiba* tree, but when the king finds out, he orders Chalpol put to death."

"Oh, no!" Yash said, leaning forward.

"Cuzán promises she'll never see him again and she'll marry the prince of *Nan Chan*," Alberto continued. "She begs her father not to kill Chalpol, but he doesn't promise.

"That night, alone in her bedroom, the princess walks the path of mystery. A wizard appears and gives her a beetle with red, blue, and yellow spots, saying, *Cuzán, here is your beloved Chalpol. Your father let him live but made me change him into an insect for loving you.*"

"A beetle, like Pedro's?" Yash asked.

"*Sí, Señorita Jade.* Cuzán takes *Maquech* the beetle into her hands and says, *I will never leave you. I will always love you.* Then the best jeweler of the kingdom covers the beetle with precious stones and attaches a gold chain to his tiny foot. Cuzán pins the chain to her dress over her chest, saying, *Maquech, hear my heartbeat. You live here always.*"

Alberto patted his chest and finished, "And that is how the princess Cuzán and her beloved Chalpol, who became *Maquech*, love each other through the passage of all time."

"I will keep him on my shirt, always," Pedro said.

"That would be good if you were a Maya warrior," Alberto said. "*Maquech* would protect you in battle. Are you a Maya warrior?"

Pedro shook his head.

"No? Then you must release him before you leave."

"Could I wear him?" Yash asked. "I'd love him."

"But he belongs here," Alberto said. "This is home. If you were a Maya princess from long ago, you could have worn him, over your heart. A love charm."

"Oh. What if I stuck him in my suitcase?" Yash asked.

"No," Pesh said. "You cannot take him home."

"U.S. Customs checks everything," Alberto said. "It's against the law. They're fussy about bringing in live animals or fresh produce. Even though you can buy a live bejeweled *maquech* beetle on the Internet for $500. Even though they import bananas from Guatemala."

"Five hundred dollars," Pedro said. "*Maquech* is worth as much as a piece of jade."

"Or worth his weight in gold," Alberto said. "To sell the beetle online, they glue rhinestones on his back and give him a six-centimeter leash, a fine gold chain connected to a pin. He walks around on your shirt but he cannot get away."

"*Maquech* would not like that," Pedro said.

"That's cruel," Yash said. "I will let him run around."

"Yash, you cannot take him with you," Pesh said. "There's a big fine, and we're already going to have a challenge getting Pedro through immigration."

Pesh wondered how she would pull that off. What if they sent Pedro back? She'd have to go with him, but her classes at the university started next week.

"You mean he's going home with us?" Yash asked.

"We can't leave Pedro here alone," Pesh said. "He has nowhere to go, nowhere to live."

Pedro smiled.

"Alberto, thank you for being such a good friend for Yash and Pedro," Pesh said. If this were Texas and if Alberto weren't Maya, she would have hugged him. "We have all enjoyed knowing you. If things work out the way I hope, we'll visit you next year."

"I hope that, too," Alberto said. *"¡Hasta luego!"*

54

On their last morning at Quetzal Centrale, Pesh had three airline tickets but no travel papers for Pedro. She checked the children's packing and helped Yash with her braid while Pedro carried out their suitcases.

"It's time to say goodbye," Pesh said. She and the children stood in the shade of the magnolia tree next to the van, waiting for their driver, Ignacio. "We must thank the Andersons for their hospitality."

Vanna and Paul had stepped outside to wish them *bon voyage*.

"I can't thank you enough," Pesh said to Vanna. "Perhaps I'll see you again next year. Kedar is applying for a grant to map mineral deposits."

"You'll stay with us, of course." Vanna hugged Pesh. "You've become part of my family."

"Thanks again for filing the paperwork for Pedro's birth certificate," Pesh said. "There wasn't enough time to arrange a visa, but I bought him a ticket to Austin. I don't know if I can pull it off."

"Good luck," Vanna said. "If they stop you at security, come back here."

"Gracias," Pedro said. "Adiós."

"Goodbye, Mr. Anderson," Yash said. "Thank you."

"You're welcome," Paul said. "Next year, no jaguars in your room."

Paul and the children laughed, and Ignacio loaded the van: suitcases in the back, children in the second seat, Pesh in the front.

Pesh watched Paul and Vanna wave as they drove out the gate on their way to the airport in Guatemala City. She'd miss them—they're like family. *Would Pedro be sent back? He couldn't live with the Andersons. Where could he go?*

At the airport drop zone, Ignacio promised to wait until Pedro was safely aboard.

"You will call me?" he asked, tapping his cell phone.

"As soon as we all have boarding passes," Pesh said.

Dressed in his new school clothes and carrying his new suitcase, Pedro looked more like an American visitor than a Guatemalan peasant.

"Remember, not a word." Pesh instructed Yash not to speak until after they passed through security, a much simpler instruction than telling her what not to say. "Pedro, stay with me and don't talk. If they don't let us board, I'll go back to Quetzal Centrale with you to plan our next move."

"But you said you have to go to the university in a few days," Pedro said.

"You're more important," Pesh answered. "I won't abandon you."

"They don't like Guatemalans in Mexico," Pedro said. "What if the United States doesn't like me either?"

"Then we go to plan B," Pesh said. "If they don't let you enter the United States, I'll send Yash home with her grandfather and bring you back here."

Pedro shrugged. He looked worried but seemed to have accepted the situation.

Pesh checked their bags with no problem, but the boarding passes came next.

"Passports, *por favor*." The woman behind the counter wore a blue airline uniform.

Pesh handed over her passport and Yash's and pretended to fish around in her carry-on. The line built up behind her.

"What's your problem?" a rude man behind her asked.

"I need to process all the travelers," the clerk said. "What about your boy?"

"I can't find his papers." Pesh emptied her carry-on onto the counter, and the man crowded her and banged her leg with his briefcase.

"Pick all that up." The woman's voice had an unpleasant edge, and she pointed to an empty check-in station. "Move over there and let other passengers step forward."

"But I have his birth certificate as proof." Pesh turned sad eyes toward the woman, feigning embarrassment, and took hold of Pedro's arm.

Pedro kept a stiff face and Yash moved closer to him.

"A Guatemalan certificate?" The woman looked back and forth between Pedro's paper and Pesh's American passport.

"*Sí.*" Pesh leaned over the counter and spoke softly. "He was born before I was married. He was with his father. I found him only last week."

"No visa?" The clerk frowned.

"I really must take him. He has no life here." Pesh traded a ten-dollar bill she had palmed for the paperwork.

"I understand," the clerk whispered. "But I don't know how you will get through immigration in the United States."

"I'll find a way, or we'll be back here next week."

"Okay, three boarding passes," the counter employee announced. She called the man next in line.

With their luggage checked, they each had only a shoulder pack for the flight. At the security line, Pesh ushered the children along in front of her, showing only her American passport and the three boarding passes. No one asked about the children, and they cleared security with no problem.

"That should be our gate," Pesh said. "We'll wait there for an hour and a half."

Yash, seated next to Pedro, pulled out her second level Spanish reader, and said, "We're almost to the end."

"Then read to me so I can hear how you're doing," Pesh said.

Yash read the last three pages effortlessly with only an occasional question about an unfamiliar word. When it was his turn, Pedro, whose first language was K'iche Mayan, read as smoothly as a native Spanish speaker and without hesitation.

"Not one mistake!" Pesh said. Had he memorized what Yash had read aloud? "Can you read this page, too?"

"Of course." Pedro grinned and read perfectly again.

"Looks like you're ready for the third book. How'd you learn this so fast?"

"I can read it because I can sound it out," Pedro said, turning in his seat. "But I don't always know what it says until after I hear myself say it."

"You can ask me when you don't know," Pesh said.

After boarding, Pedro had the window seat, Yash in the middle, so they could read a book together. Pesh relaxed and leaned back. Sitting on the aisle, she'd know if they tried to move around.

Pesh closed her eyes. She'd heard about children who rode on the top of freight trains all the way from Guatemala to the United States to escape violence and poverty. On the journey, those children risked death or being beaten or raped—children, younger than Pedro. Life on the streets in Guatemala City was little better. Drug lords captured smart, good-looking boys like Pedro, started them on drugs, and then forced them to sell drugs at elementary schools. She couldn't leave him in Guatemala—alone. She knew what it was like to grow up without parents.

Guatemala: where her grandmother had told her never to go. She thought about her earlier visit to Guatemala, where she had married Five-Owl in a ritual "to join both sides of the river." *Dios bo'otik*, a ritual only: she rubbed her right fist, the one that had bloodied his nose.

She needed to write up her trip notes: a treatise on Mayan jade, its legends, and her search for the source of it. The story of B'alam Ha, the premier jade carving site in the ancient Mayan world: she had pictures and a piece of stone with a jaguar glyph carved onto it, but she'd promised never to give the location. In Xiu's cave, she had found a jade deposit, too far underground for Kedar's instruments to detect it. After many *baktuns*, or perhaps another creation, it would move to the surface in an earthquake and rumble to the valley in a torrential rain—thrown down by *Chaac* the Rain God.

Airborne for Mérida, she shifted in her seat. They had to change planes there but would not leave the secured area. They'd make it as far as Austin. She was an American citizen, and she'd find a way to bring Pedro to his new home. Kedar would be pleased.

The stewardess pushed a beverage cart to their row, handed each of them a bag of tortilla chips and a napkin, and asked what they wanted to drink.

"For me?" Pedro asked.

"Orange juice," Yash said. "He wants one, too."

"They feed us?" Pedro asked. "For free?"

"We might have dinner, too," Yash said.

When the feature film appeared on the tiny screen on the back of the seat ahead, Yash showed Pedro how to use the headset.

"I've never seen a movie before," Pedro said.

After the movie, Pesh heard Yash and Pedro reading "Cinderella" in a Spanish edition of *Grimm's Fairy Tales*. Pedro would have to learn English, but he'd feel comfortable because the schools in Austin had many Spanish-speaking students.

Pesh reached for B'alam and Firebird, both safely under her shirt, and remembered how Xiu had taught her to be *Xmenoob*: *Helping them is not doing what they want, not doing things for them. Teach them to help themselves.* With the combined power of Firebird and B'alam, Pesh no longer feared Cimil. Perhaps he should fear her.

55

Below, somewhere beneath the heavy clouds obscuring the Gulf of Mexico, the southernmost coast of Texas beckoned. Pesh glanced out the window and expected turbulence even before the airline captain put on the "fasten seatbelts" sign.

"We're close to the end of the flight," Pesh said to Yash and Pedro. "Let's visit the restrooms now."

Before the three of them returned, the airliner began to buck. They grabbed seat backs on the way up the aisle to keep their balance and flopped into their seats.

"I am glad for a seatbelt," Pedro said, "because I don't want to fly to the ceiling."

"This is perfectly normal," Pesh said. She'd have to help him learn English and soon—all three of them were speaking Spanish. "You won't be able to see out until just before landing."

"How does the pilot do it, then?" Pedro asked.

"He uses special instruments," Pesh said. "Perhaps Kedar will take you on a trip through clouds."

"Daddy took me up in the clouds once," Yash said. "Is Daddy going to meet us?"

"Not this time, sweetheart. He has to attend a weekend training seminar for pilots." Pesh filled out the family customs form: Nothing to declare.

"Our luggage will be on Carousel 6," Pesh said. "Grandpa Burt will meet us outside the baggage claim area."

"Will Grandma come, too?" Yash asked.

"I don't know. But, before that," Pesh said, "we have to go through customs and passport control. That means we have a huge problem because Pedro has no visa."

Pesh held Yash's arm. "Please remember, say nothing. You too, Pedro. You do not speak!"

Pesh and the children stood in a line for returning United States citizens. At the customs window, she handed her passport and Yash's to the official. He had a square jaw and wore his light brown hair in a crew cut, and the bronze badge on his khaki uniform said Andrew Millhouse, U.S. Customs.

"Where is the boy's passport?" Millhouse frowned.

"Here is his birth certificate," Pesh said. "I am a citizen of the United States. He's my son. He's traveling with me."

"Guatemala," Millhouse said. "He needs a medical clearance before entry."

"He will see a doctor tomorrow." Pesh's stomach cramped. *What if they don't let him in?*

"Sorry. Have to quarantine him. No visa—have to send him home."

"He has no home, except mine," Pesh said. "The rest of his family died of cholera two months ago."

The line was building up.

"No visa, no entry. A rule is a rule."

"That is completely unsatisfactory," Pesh said. "Let me speak to your supervisor. I need a female customs official."

"You will wait here." Millhouse escorted them to a glass-encased room with a door that locked from the outside and gestured to four straight-back chairs facing a long table.

"I am a citizen of the United States," Pesh said. "You can't treat us this way."

Without a word, Millhouse left and locked the door.

"Am I quarantined, like Jaguarcito?" Pedro asked.

"Looks that way." Pesh tensed. *What now? How could they do this to a U.S. citizen?*

"Jaguarcito gets movies," Yash said. "We don't even have TV."

"Grandpa Burt will take us home soon." Pesh hoped that wasn't a lie. She tried to call Burt, but her cell phone was dead.

After what seemed like hours, a gray-haired woman in a U. S. Customs uniform unlocked the door. She squinted through glasses with heavy brown frames and stood over them, judging. Above Pesh's eye-level, her bronze badge labeled her *Mathilde Herold.*

"You are smuggling a Guatemalan refugee into the United States." Her voice was loud and strident.

"No, absolutely not." Pesh stood to face the woman. "I'm returning from a six-month archaeological study grant."

Ms. Herold responded with a glare.

"Maybe you know my husband, Kedar Herold," Pesh said, noting the last name.

"Your passport says you are Chanlajun … Pecks … Yaxuun B'alam." Ms. Herold held their paperwork close to her eyes, but stumbled over the name. "Not Herold."

"That's correct," Pesh said. "I teach Mayan studies at University of Texas. I had a research grant to work in Guatemala."

"The boy." She pointed a claw-like finger at Pedro and inspected his birth certificate. "Why doesn't he have a passport? He appears to be your relative."

"He was born in Guatemala before I was married. His father is not Kedar Herold." Pesh, feigning embarrassment, looked at the floor and lowered her voice. "That's why I wanted to speak to another woman."

"I see the resemblance—he's your son. But why, after nine years, isn't he with his father?"

"His family is gone." Pesh remembered how it was to grow up without parents, even though her grandmother Chiich had loved her. "His half-sister died of cholera two months ago, and his birth father has disappeared."

"Why doesn't he have a visa?"

"There wasn't time." Pesh broke out in a sweat. *Does she have no compassion?* "I must return to the university next week."

Ms. Herold drew in her breath and shook her head. For ten minutes she lectured Pesh on illegal immigrants and terrorists, drug lords and street gangs in Guatemala.

Pesh wore her frozen Mayan face, but her heart raced and her stomach churned. She knew she must remain quiet until Ms. Herold ran down. Pedro and Yash looked frightened.

"Pedro is only nine years old," Pesh said. "He has no place to return to."

"Against regulations." Ms. Herold glared at Pesh, then at Pedro. "You may be prosecuted. They send them back anyway— he's illegal."

Pesh looked down and prayed to Hun Hunahpu, her patron god, for guidance.

"All right," Ms. Herold said, spitting out the words. "I will schedule a court date."

"Thank you. *Dios bo'otik.*" *At least she isn't sending him back.*

"You will pay required fees and penalties." The customs official handed Pesh a sheaf of papers. "You will get a doctor's certificate as soon as possible."

Pesh nodded. "I will do that."

"Here are your travel documents." Ms. Herold puckered her forehead and drew back her thin lips. "Your luggage is on Carousel 6. You are free to go."

"Thank you." *Dios bo'otik!*

"Remember, Pedro must not leave your custody." Ms. Herold strode out without a goodbye, leaving the door open.

"Agreed," Pesh called after her. "Thanks for your understanding."

Carousel 6—Burt is waiting. Pesh checked her cell phone—below 10%. How long has it been? She couldn't call Burt. *Dios bo'otik:* Burt had taken her under his wing. And now she would do that for Pedro.

56

At Austin-Bergstrom International Airport, Pesh and the children
followed the signs to baggage claim. How long had they been
detained? It seemed hours, and she hadn't called Burt because
her cell phone needed charging. She saw him standing on one
foot, then the other, behind Carousel 6. Unclaimed luggage,
including one tied with a piece of red ribbon, still revolved, and
no customs officials hovered there.

Pesh, trailed by Yash and Pedro, ran to hug Burt. "I'm sorry
to make you wait so long. I was unable to call you."

"That's all right," Burt said. "I'm just glad you're home.
All of you."

Yash wrapped herself around Burt's leg while Pedro stood
awkwardly. Looking up, she said, "Grandpa, this is Pedro."

"I heard you were coming," Burt said. "*¡Bienvenido!*"

"*Mucho gusto.*" Pedro smiled.

"Where's Grandma?" Yash asked.

"Waiting for you at home," Burt said. "She loaned us her
handicapped placard so I could park by the door."

"Go get us a luggage cart," Pesh said to the children, pointing to a line of handcarts. "Help me find our suitcases. They're
the ones with red ribbons tied around the handles."

"Come on, Pedro, let's go," Yash said with her usual enthusiasm. They all loaded the cart, and Pedro pushed it through the
automatic doors. After Burt transferred everything to the back of
his Ford station wagon, they all piled in, Pesh in the front.

"Customs took you a long time," Burt said, pulling away from the curb.

"It's a long story," Pesh said. "Pedro has no visa."

"And they let him into the United States? Incredible!"

"Temporarily," Pesh said. "The customs official questioned me—it seemed like hours—but she scheduled a court date."

"Can I talk now?" Yash asked from the back. "You said I couldn't."

"What's that about?" Burt asked.

"Mommy wanted to talk to the customs lady without us interrupting."

"Because Pedro doesn't have a visa." Pesh looked both ways when Burt turned onto Highway 71, only a few miles from home.

"Grandpa." Yash leaned over the seat behind Burt. "Pedro found me when I was kidnapped. He doesn't speak English yet."

"Buckle up, Yash!" Pesh said.

"Then we will speak some Spanish and some English," Burt said.

"*Gracias, Señor* Burt," Pedro said.

"Just call me Burt. You rescued my granddaughter." Burt turned off the highway, only blocks from home. "You're part of my family now."

Two minutes later, Burt clicked the remote to open his garage door.

"*¿La negra caja, es mágica?*" Pedro asked.

"No, not magic. It's an electronic key. You try it."

Pedro grinned and ran the door up and down twice before Burt parked the car.

"Yash, Pesh, I'm so glad to see you!" Isolde, leaning on a walker, greeted them from the kitchen door that opened to the garage. "And you must be Pedro. Come in, come in!"

"*Mucho gusto,*" Pedro said.

"He's glad to meet you," Yash said. "Grandma, why are you holding that thing?"

"I can walk perfectly fine but my balance is bad," Isolde said. "Ever since I was hit on my head. Sometimes I don't remember things."

"I love you, Grandma," Yash said, hugging her. "I thought Yellow Teeth killed you."

"My little *Liebchen*." Isolde smoothed the child's hair. "I love you, too."

"Kedar will be here soon," Burt said. "After his class finishes."

Yash whispered to Pedro, and he said, "I carry in the luggage." Yash and Pedro put the bags beneath the coat rack in the hall.

"Sit down, sit down," Isolde said. "I baked a chocolate cake to celebrate your homecoming."

After they all were seated at the dining room table, Yash asked, "Can I open my suitcase, Grandpa?"

"Now?" Burt asked. "You're not home yet."

"But I brought back something to show Grandma." Yash returned and held out—

"*¡Maquech! Ay Caramba!*" Pedro cried out. "*¡Pesh dice NO!*" The beetle in the palm of Yash's small hand looked like jewelry, shiny and iridescent yellow, blue, green, and red.

"It's beautiful, but what is it?" Isolde asked.

"*Es el insecto*," Pedro said. "*Es Maquech*."

"Well, he's here now." Pesh frowned. "What if they had opened your suitcase?"

"I'm sorry, Mommy," Yash said, handing the beetle to Pedro. "I just wanted my friends to see him."

"We were *so* lucky!" Pesh said. "We could have had a huge fine!"

"I'm sorry, Mommy."

"Well, he's here now. You have to take care of him. What does Maquech eat?"

Pedro said, "*No come durante muchos meses.*"

"Lucky again. Pedro says he doesn't eat for months." Pesh heard someone at the front door.

"It's Daddy!" Yash jumped up and greeted Kedar by wrapping herself around his legs while Pesh hugged him. Pedro stood politely by the table, Maquech on his shirt.

"I'm glad to see you, Pedro," Kedar said, looking at the boy as he entered the dining room.

"I'm glad to see you," Pedro said, and Maquech moved higher on his shirt.

"What's that?" Kedar asked, pointing and taking a seat.

Pedro looked down, and Yash said, "He's my beetle."

"I have never seen a beetle like that one," Kedar said. Then he pulled a small book out of his shirt pocket. "Here, Pedro. I brought you a present."

"*¿Para mi?*" Smiling, Pedro held out his hand. "*Gracias.*"

"It's a phrase book. See, *gracias* in Spanish is *thank you* in English."

Pedro's face lit up. "Thank you, Kedar."

"Now you can talk to me in English," Yash said.

"Well, Princess," Kedar said. "You're home, complete with beetle. I'm glad you didn't bring a jaguar. By the way, Jaguarcito is at the zoo here in Austin."

"Hurray!" Yash danced circles around the room. "We can go see him!"

"What's this about a jaguar?" Burt looked puzzled.

"Pedro rescued a baby jaguar," Pesh said. "I'm sure Yash will tell you all about it."

"You'll have to wait to go to the zoo," Isolde said to Yash. "School starts Wednesday. Did you work on your lessons?"

"No, Grandma. I helped Pedro read Spanish instead."

"He knows no English?" Isolde asked.

"*Un poquito Inglés,*" Pedro said.

"We'll all help you, then," Isolde said.

Yash worked through the phrase book with Pedro, but of course, his conversations were limited to polite greetings, the weather, and what to order in a restaurant. Pedro sat next to her in the third grade class. Pesh had insisted that the school start him there because he could read Spanish, but Yash's teacher, Ms. Williams, didn't like it.

"If you talk to Pedro in my classroom," Ms. Williams said, "I will transfer him to first grade for Mexicans, where he belongs."

"But he's from Guatemala," Yash said. "He can read Spanish and he learns fast."

"You do not talk back to me, young lady." Ms. Williams frowned and twisted her mouth around smeared lipstick. "He doesn't belong here."

"Thank you, Ms. Williams," Pedro said without any accent. Yash looked down and then sat quietly until recess, when, still not speaking, she and Pedro walked to the playground.

"She doesn't like me." Pedro kicked an errant ball back toward the players, then stood near the swings.

"She calls me Mary Yam, like something to eat. She won't call me Yash."

"She'll send me to first grade with the babies." Pedro pushed an empty swing so hard that it wrapped around the standard.

"Don't worry," Yash said. "If she kicks you out, I'm going with you."

Sally Anne and Mary Jane, two of Yash's friends from last year, ran over.

"You've been gone for months." Sally Anne flipped her blond curls. "Where were you?"

"I went to Guatemala with my mother and father," Yash said.

"Aren't you going to introduce us to your friend?" Mary Jane looked Pedro up and down with her blue eyes.

"This is Pedro," Yash said. "He found a jaguar kitten and gave it to the zoo."

"Good morning. I'm glad to meet you," Pedro said.

"You had a jaguar?" Sally Anne asked. "Aren't they really big cats, like tigers?"

"One hundred kilos. Jaguarcito is a baby."

"Didn't he bite you?" Mary Jane asked.

"Jaguarcito likes people," Yash said. "He's at the Capital City Zoo, right here in Austin."

"Why doesn't Ms. Williams like you?" Sally Anne asked Pedro.

"I do not know," he said. "I did not reserve my seat."

Sally Anne and Mary Jane giggled.

"Your English sounds funny, but I like it," Mary Jane said. "Why does she want you to go to the Mexican class?"

"I am a stranger here," Pedro said, another phrase from the book.

"Pedro reads Spanish better than we do," Yash said. "He lives at my house now. I can show you some pictures of Jaguarcito. Can you come over on Saturday?"

"Okay," Mary Jane said. "Will your grandmother bake a chocolate cake?"

"Of course," Yash said. "Bring your brothers, and we'll show you Maquech."

"What's *maquech*?" Sally Anne asked.

"He's a secret," Yash said, smiling at Pedro. "Maquech is my beetle," he said in clear English.

The bell rang, ending recess.

57

Pesh walked into her favorite classroom at the University of Texas. Painted murals of the temple at Chichén Itzá and the Sacred Cenote decorated the walls. Lupe Garcia, her friend and teaching assistant, held today's handouts. All twenty-five chairs were filled and three students stood in the back.

"Hi, Lupe," Pesh said. "The trip to Guatemala was amazing. I'll tell you about it over coffee after class."

"I can hardly wait," Lupe said.

"Good morning, everybody," Pesh said. "We start with Mayan writing this quarter, but after the lecture, I'm happy to talk about anything Mayan."

"This is my name written in Mayan." Pesh projected a PowerPoint slide and addressed a section of Mayan Studies. "I am Chanlajun Pex Yaxuun B'alam. In Mayan, *b'alam* means *jaguar*, and here are two ways to draw the glyphs."

"The Maya wrote in logograms and syllabic signs, similar to Egyptian hieroglyphics. The scribe could draw a jaguar head or put syllables together: a jaguar's paw for *bah*, a symbol for *lah*, three balls underneath for *mah*. So, you could learn to sound out the glyphs, but then what do they mean? It's like sounding out classic Latin and knowing only modern Italian.

"The Mayan glyphs form a complete writing system, developed independently. The Maya were one of only five civilizations to develop true writing, along with the Chinese, Egyptians, Harappans, and Sumerians." Pesh was pleased that all of her students were taking notes.

"They had complete libraries," she continued, "of hand-painted manuscripts, but most were burned in 1562 during the Spanish Inquisition. Burned, like the great library of Alexandria in Egypt. In fact, that huge bonfire at Maní in Yucatán marked the intersection of the ancient Maya with modern history."

With her next slide, Pesh posted a multicolored page of a Mayan manuscript, its script partially obliterated. "That black section is blood."

"Blood?" The class erupted. "Did you say blood?"

"Yes, blood." *That grabbed them!* "This book was the scribe Nachi's lifework, a treatise on astronomy. He refused to give it to the Spaniards, even though the penalty was death. In silent protest, he carried his book to the temple platform above the plaza where the Mayan books burned—there." Pesh pointed to the temple on the classroom mural.

"Precious books, burning!" Pesh paused for effect. "It was more than he could bear. Nachi slashed his own throat. Clutching his book to his chest, he threw himself down the steep steps. Rolling, bumping, splattering blood."

Silent a few seconds for effect, Pesh didn't tell them she'd been there, in a vision.

"His friends hid the book from the Spaniards, and I found it by a lucky accident at B'alam Witz, the ruin where Professor Burt Wallace and I worked." *Lucky indeed: Kedar tripped over the loose stone—without falling to his death.*

"Back to today's lecture. Only three other complete *codices* exist." Pesh stepped back to the computer and showed a color photograph of a page from the *Dresden Codex*. "You can use

Google to see more. In fact, that's your homework today. Next time I'll ask you what a *codex* is. And I'll bring a logogram chart. Lupe and I will help you each to write your name with Mayan symbols."

"But my name is Hungarian," a blond girl seated in the front said. "Will that matter?"

"No, because they used the sounds of syllables," Pesh said. "Besides writing books, the Maya inscribed monument stones for every new ruler and to commemorate every battle. We have learned to read them only recently. The history of Mayan territories goes back 7,000 years, and writing, 2,000 years. The region is hidden by jungle, and perhaps ninety per cent of their artifacts are still underground.

"Mayan secrets, still guarded by the gods of *Xibalba*, the realm of spirits according to legend. Who knows what treasures are still to be unearthed?"

"You went there?" the blond girl asked.

"Yes. Throughout Central America, hundreds of ruins lie hidden by the jungle, plenty of new places to explore. My husband and I hiked over rough terrain for two days and then found evidence of buildings under all that vegetation."

"My husband took this one." Pesh showed Kedar's picture of the stone step from B'alam Ha. "And no, I'm not sure what it says. The Maya often wrote on the front faces of pyramid steps.

"We had arrived at the site of the best jade carving of all the ancient Mayan kingdoms. My little b'alam was carved there." Pesh pulled out her jaguar talisman and walked around showing it.

"We have guests," Lupe said.

Pesh turned and saw Dr. Engelhamm, President of the University, and Dr. Burt Wallace. Often people dropped in to evaluate her performance, but never the president. Her father-in-law, Dr. Burt, was beaming.

"Forgive the interruption, Professor Chanlajun Pesh." Dr. Engelhamm held up an envelope. "This news was too exciting to wait."

Pesh was so surprised she couldn't speak.

"*Profesor* Carlos Léon de la Barra sent a clipping from the Guatemalan newspaper *Prensa Libre,* and your students need to hear this." He opened the envelope, took out a folded letter, smoothed it out, and began to read through glasses perched halfway down his nose.

"*El Museo de La Democracia* announced the return of the Mayan mask stolen last month. This exceptional greenstone mask was part of funerary offerings uncovered in the grave of a nobleman buried in 527 AD. The Mayan artifact was turned in to the police by *Chanlajun Pex Yaxuun B'alam de Taller del Jade Maya en Antigua.*"

He looked at her students and said, "I think your teacher deserves a round of applause."

Dr. Engelhamm, Dr. Burt, Lupe, and all of Pesh's students applauded. Not used to such attention, she felt her face redden.

"Thank you. *Dios bo'otik.*" She couldn't say more.

"In addition, *Profesor* Léon de la Barra suggests that Chanlajun Pesh should return to do more research. Here's my invitation to apply for a grant for next year," he said, handing Pesh an envelope.

"Thank you. *Dios bo'otik.*" *Next year!*

"Well-deserved praise," Dr. Burt said to Pesh. Then he turned and addressed her class. "I see you are studying Mayan glyphs. Professor Chanla Pesh taught me how to write Mayan numbers when she was only eight."

"Dr. Burt came to the Mayan ruin where I lived with my grandmother, and I watched him copy inscriptions from monument stones." Pesh thanked the two visitors and invited them to drop by anytime. Again aware of her class, she glanced at the clock.

"That's enough for today," she said. "Let's see. Homework. Read about the *Dresden Codex* and where the other four complete writing systems were developed. Did I forget anything, Lupe?"

"Only the extra credit," Lupe said. "Report on what Christopher Columbus wrote in his ship's log about Mayan trading ships. Then answer these questions and support your opinions: Could the Maya have obtained jade from China? Could the Maya have learned to write from the Egyptians?"

Glossary: Yucatec Language

Spoken Yucatec is rhythmic and mellifluous. When written, the Mayan language Yucatec uses Spanish phonetics. An apostrophe within a word denotes a glottal stop, a sound made in stopping the breath, such as that in *uh-oh* in English. Phonetic representations below approximate English pronunciation. The letter "x" is "sh" in Mayan.

b'alam (bah-lahm): jaguar

bak'tun (back-toon): calendar term; 144,000 days, approximately four centuries

balche (ball-chey): alcoholic drink fermented from honey

chanlajun (chahn-la-hoon): fourteen

Chicxulub (cheek-shoe-lube): meteor crater off Yucatán

chiich (chee-eech): grandmother

Dios bo'otik (Dee-ohs boh-oh-tick): thanks; the gods pay

Hun Hunahpu (hoon hoon-ah-poo): maize god

kizin (kee-zen): minor devil

ko'ox (koh-osh): let's go

pex (pesh): little one

sacbé (sock-beh): ancient road paved with white plaster

t'uut' (too-oot): parrot

wayob (why-ohb): a person's "spirit animal"

witz (wheats): manmade mountain or hill

Xibalba (shee-ball-bah): the underworld; land of the dead

xi'ik tech utzil: may good go with you; goodbye

Xmenoob (shah-mey-nohb): the most powerful female shaman. She can be X-Pul Ya (she who throws pain) or X-Dzac Ya (she who medicates pain).

Xiu: (shoe) A Mayan name

yaxuun (yash-you-un): cotinga flower or bird

Yax K'uk' Mo (yash-cook-moe): Precious Quetzal Macaw

Grammar point: Maya vs Mayan. Maya can be singular, plural, or an adjective: the Maya king; five Maya; Maya warriors. Mayan refers only to the language spoken by the Maya, but English speakers often use Mayan as an adjective.

CPSIA information can be obtained
at www.ICGtesting.com
Printed in the USA
FSOW02n2014200516
20637FS